NAVY SEAL
CAPTIVE

BY
ELLE JAMES

First Published 2016
First Australian Paperback Edition 2016
ISBN 978 0 263 91901 1

Printed and bound in Spain
by CPI, Barcelona

MILLS
BOON

First Published in Great Britain 2016
By Mills & Boon, an imprint of HarperCollins*Publishers*
1 London Bridge Street, London, SE1 9GF

© 2016 Mary Jernigan

ISBN: 978-0-263-91901-1

46-0416

Our policy is to use papers that are natural, renewable and recyclable products and made from wood grown in sustainable forests. The logging and manufacturing processes conform to the legal environmental regulations of the country of origin.

Printed and bound in Spain

Jenna swayed, bracing her hands on his chest. "You have to stop doing that."

"Why?"

"I barely know you."

"You knew enough about me to find me on the beach and save me from an assassin. I reckon that gives us a pass on convention."

She rested her forehead against his chest. "I didn't come to Cancun to get involved with a man." But, boy, had that backfired on her.

"And I have no business getting involved with you." He gripped her shoulders and set her at arm's length. "As a SEAL, I'm gone more than I'm home. And with an assassin after me, I can't risk you becoming collateral damage."

Elle James, a *New York Times* bestselling author, started writing when her sister challenged her to write a romance novel. She has managed a full-time job and raised three wonderful children, and she and her husband even tried ranching exotic birds (ostriches, emus and rheas). Ask her, and she'll tell you what it's like to go toe-to-toe with an angry three-hundred-and-fifty-pound bird! Elle loves to hear from fans at ellejames@earthlink.net or www.ellejames.com.

This book is dedicated to my sister, Delilah Devlin, who was an officer in the US army. She has inspired me to be the best I can be in my military career and in my journey to publication. She's my mentor, sounding board and critique partner. And she isn't afraid to tell me like it is. I love you, Sis!

Chapter One

"Seriously. I can't believe you talked me into this. And to go straight for the biggest first? Isn't that pushing it?" Sawyer Houston adjusted the web seat and waited his turn on the platform. Perched on the edge of a two-hundred-foot cliff, staring down into the vast jungle, Sawyer balked. Cancún Adventures boasted the longest, most exciting zip line in Mexico, guaranteed to make you scream. Not, in Sawyer's opinion, the most reassuring advertisement.

"It's not like you to turn away from a challenge, Houston," Quentin Lovett ribbed. "You've fast-roped out of helicopters, entered buildings full of terrorists and been shot at by rifles, machine guns and mortars." Quentin snorted. "What's a little ol' zip line gonna hurt?"

"I don't know who set it up, whether the cable is strong enough to withstand my weight or if there's a way to stop me at the other end. Hell, I can't see the other end, and plunging into a tree at the bottom isn't my idea of fun. Besides, how would that look on my tombstone? 'SEAL ends his navy career on vacation, sliding to his death on a poorly rigged zip line.'"

"Step aside." Quentin circled Sawyer. "Let me show you how it's done."

"That's right. Test the line. I'll be sure to send your

mother a letter telling of your bravery in the face of a zip line."

A couple of women stood in front of Quentin. The curvy one in the khaki shorts and white Cancún T-shirt shook her head, her dark red curls bouncing with her nervous movements. "No. I've changed my mind." She backed away from her friend with the short dark hair, running into Quentin.

"Whoa, darlin'." Quentin steadied her, his brows rose and he winked at Sawyer.

"Sorry." Her cheeks bloomed with color, and she hurriedly stepped away from him.

"Jenna, you have to do it," the dark-haired, petite woman said. "It's part of your kick-the-boring therapy."

"Yeah, but I was thinking more along the lines of riding a roller coaster, not speeding through the jungle at Mach ten on a cable probably salvaged from a shipyard by people who might have used office staples to nail it to some tree ready to fall over at any minute."

Sawyer took a breath for Jenna. How one woman could say all that without inhaling was beyond him. But she was kind of cute, and he didn't blame her for her trepidation.

"Hey, I'll go first to test it out," the other woman said.

"No way, Carly. If you die, I'm stranded in the jungle with no one to get me back to the hotel to find my lost luggage."

Sawyer's lips quirked at the redhead's adamant refusal to participate in the death-defying feat of zip-lining. "I'll give you a ride."

Jenna shot him a narrow-eyed glance before turning back to her friend. "Or you'll be leaving me at the mercy of strangers, possibly mass murderers."

The brunette rolled her eyes, then gave Sawyer a considering look. "He's not a mass murderer, and he's really cute. You could do worse. Now, I'm going. I'll see you back at the parking lot." She pulled on the gloves they'd been given and stepped up to the man in charge.

The man in the red Cancún Adventures T-shirt and black cotton shorts stubbed out his cigarette and hooked her belt to the cable. "If you want to slow, grab the cable with your glove. But don't do it too soon, or you will stop in the middle of the cable," he said in heavily accented English.

"Here's to shaking it off and plotting a more adventurous course in your life." The brunette leaned toward the cliff.

Jenna swayed toward her friend. "Carly, don't—" But she was too late. Carly leaped off the cliff and raced toward the jungle at breakneck speed, squealing in delight.

Quentin chuckled. "Damn, she beat me to it." He turned toward Sawyer. "Are you going to let a girl shame you?"

Sawyer crossed his arms over his chest. "There's no shame in preferring to keep my bones intact."

The redhead nodded, her gaze on her friend as she disappeared into the dark green jungle below. "That's what I told Carly." She glanced back at Sawyer. "Don't get me wrong. I'm all for adventure." Jenna bit her lip. "Or, at least, that was the point of this exercise." Turning toward the cliff, she straightened her shoulders. "And, for the record, I'm not boring."

"Didn't say you were. Actually, you're far from it," Sawyer agreed, admiring her curvy figure and the shock of auburn hair that refused to be contained in the ponytail.

Quentin performed a sweeping bow in front of the woman. "Allow me."

"Sure. I'm not in a hurry to plunge to my death." She stepped back, this time bumping into Sawyer.

He wrapped an arm around her, absorbed the impact

of her body and breathed in the flowery scent of her hair. Nope. Not boring at all. With her small body pressed close to his, he forgot all about the zip line and his argument with Quentin.

"Sorry," she mumbled and stepped to his side and out of his embrace, her cheeks flushing a soft pink.

Everywhere she'd touched him still resonated with the warmth of her body. Sawyer's groin tightened.

"Nothing to it." Quentin allowed the attendant to hook his D-ring to the pulley and held on to the cable with his gloved hand. "See you at the bottom, if you have the guts to do it." He winked, lifted his legs and took off, sliding to his doom in the jungle, whooping and hollering as he went.

Jenna drew in a long breath and let it out on a sigh. "I did come to Cancún to start over and be more adventurous."

Sawyer smiled. "You don't have to do the zip line to be adventurous."

"No?" She glanced at him hopefully, her face brightening. Then her brows drew together, and she stiffened. "Yeah, but I don't ever want to be accused of being boring again."

"I take it someone called you boring," Sawyer said.

She lifted her chin. "My ex-fiancé."

"He must have been blind."

"And a cheating bastard." She stepped up to the attendant. "I'm going."

"You want me to go with you?" Sawyer offered.

She shook her head. "No. I'll be fine. If Carly can do it, so can I." Jenna stared at the attendant, biting her lip. "I'm ready."

The attendant gave her the same instructions he'd given to Quentin and Carly.

Jenna closed her eyes and said, "Could you give me a

little push?" Her hands shook on the line hooked to the pulley as she drew in a ragged breath.

The attendant nodded, a smile teasing the corners of his mouth, and gave her a hefty shove. Her small body flew out over the cliff and raced to the bottom. A long, high-pitched scream ripped through the air, fading the farther away she went.

"Damn." Sawyer checked his nylon web belt, which fit snugly around his legs, and stepped up to the attendant. "Guess I'm going, too."

He turned to the man behind him, hoping that one last person would talk him out of taking the plunge.

The tall, muscular man with light brown hair and steely gray eyes stared right through him.

Nope. There'd be no help on that front.

When he stepped up to the edge, the attendant blocked him with his hand. "Wait until the senoriita makes it to the bottom."

The attendant waited a full minute before he snapped Sawyer's link onto the line, repeated the instructions and left Sawyer teetering on the edge of the cliff, praying the cable held and the glove would do its job and slow his descent. In the back of his mind, he hoped that he'd find the woman he'd held in his arms for that brief second to thank her for shaming him into jumping off a cliff when his gut told him he was crazy.

He jumped.

Sawyer fell into the jungle, his speed picking up as he swished past treetops, the wind clearing his head and sharpening his mind. As he dropped below the canopy of trees, he could make out the base and Quentin standing at the bottom.

But he wasn't slowing, and at the pace he was going, he'd crash into the pole at the bottom. How had he let his teammate talk him into sliding down a cable he hadn't personally inspected? If he lived through this, he'd have a word or two with Quentin.

He gripped the line with his gloved hand, slowing a little, enough to give him a slight amount of reassurance he could stop himself before he crashed into the pole at the other end. For the first time since he jumped off the upper platform, he glanced around at the jungle below. When he looked back at his destination, his heart leaped.

The distance closed faster than he expected and before he knew it, he was careening the last fifty feet into the base. Sawyer grabbed the cable with the gloved hand and squeezed. The wind no longer whipped past him, and his descent slowed the closer he came to the bottom. He couldn't remember being that terrified since his first fast-rope experience out of a fully operational helicopter hovering thirty feet from the ground.

Ten feet from his feet touching the ground, the cable jolted in his hand. Sawyer bounced in the harness and then dropped like a ton of bricks to the ground. He tucked and rolled, absorbing the impact, and then sprang to his feet. What the hell had just happened?

The attendant at the bottom yelled something in Spanish and threw himself into the jungle. Quentin followed suit.

Sawyer spun in time to see the cable springing back toward him, detached from the pole at the other end. He dived to the right and ducked behind a tree. The cable whipped through the treetops like an angry snake and finally lay still on the ground.

His heart pounding like a bass drum, Sawyer leaped to his feet and yelled, "Everyone okay?"

Quentin climbed out of the brush, pulling leaves out of his hair. "Holy crap. Did you see that?"

Sawyer's jaw tightened, and he forced himself to take a deep breath. "Saw and felt it."

"If you'd been a couple seconds later on that cable…" Quentin shook his head and clapped Sawyer on the back. "Damn, buddy. I hate it when you're right."

Sawyer brushed the dirt off his hands. "In this case, I wish I hadn't been right."

While the zip-line attendant scrambled to his feet, swearing in Spanish, Sawyer unbuckled the nylon straps from around his legs and let the harness drop. "Next time you want me to slide down a zip line…"

Quentin held up his hands. "Don't worry. There won't be a next time." He felt his pockets and cursed. Then he dived into the brush and came up with his cell phone. "The good news is I got it all on video. The guys are gonna die when they see this."

Sawyer snorted. "I almost died living it."

Quentin shoved the phone into his pocket and turned toward the exit. "I have to admit, I was surprised to see you coming. But even more surprised when the redhead came down first."

Sawyer glanced around and didn't see the woman named Jenna anywhere. "I take it Jenna arrived safely at the bottom."

"She did. She and her pretty friend left, claimed they needed to get back to find a piece of missing luggage. The redhead told me to tell you thanks for the encouragement."

Disappointed he'd missed her, but glad she'd gone before him when the cable was still intact, Sawyer asked, "You didn't happen to catch her full name, did you?"

"She didn't offer a last name." Quentin turned back to Sawyer. "Why? Are you interested?"

Again, Sawyer shrugged. "Just wondered." Hell, yes,

he was interested, but he'd be damned if he let Quentin know. He'd pick at him incessantly.

"I did get her roommate's name, though." Quentin patted his smartphone. "Carly Samuels. We have a date tonight."

Figured. Quentin didn't waste time when it came to women. He was a charmer, and women fell for him all the time. Perhaps the best-looking man on the team with his black hair and ice-blue eyes, he usually had his pick of the ladies.

Quentin had a date and Duff was with his lady friend, Natalie, leaving Sawyer and Montana fending for themselves for dinner and drinks. Which suited Sawyer just fine. Montana was a big, outdoorsy mountain man who didn't say much but was good company. They had a week and a half left of their two weeks in Cancún. Granted, he loved his SEAL teammates like brothers, but he could use a little quality time away from them, preferably in the company of someone of the opposite sex.

As they slid into the rented Jeep, Quentin turned to Sawyer. "You had a few minutes alone with her. Why didn't you get her name and number? We could have gone on a double date."

"We weren't alone. The attendant was there. And who said I wanted to go out with her, anyway?" And he sure as hell wouldn't go on a double date with Quentin. No, if Sawyer had gotten Jenna's number, he'd have taken her out alone. Maybe for a walk along the beach in the moonlight. If she showed even the slightest interest, he might have stolen a kiss. Those pretty pink lips she'd chewed on prior to taking the big leap on the zip line were full and plump. Made for kissing.

"You've got to get out there, be more sociable, network and sell yourself."

Sawyer's fingers tightened on the steering wheel at Quentin's comment. He'd heard the same words from his father's mouth on more than one occasion. Quentin was right. He hadn't dated in a while, and he was getting rusty at socializing with women.

What Quentin and his father never understood was that Sawyer didn't like being in the limelight. Especially in front of all of his father's peers. He'd rather be the best he could be at his job in the navy SEALs, the one place he'd proven he was good enough to make the cut. Besides, wearing the uniform was usually all he needed to find a date when he really wanted one. Too bad he was in civvies here.

"So do you have plans for tonight?" Quentin asked.

"Yeah. I plan on spending the afternoon on the beach. Maybe I'll rent a WaveRunner. Then I'm going to eat seafood and have a few beers with Montana. I don't have to live for excitement like you."

Quentin shook his head. "Since excitement seems to follow us, you might need a little rest and relaxation." He linked his hands behind his neck. "Missions always leave me wired, ready to expend some energy."

"Like winding the springs on a watch?"

"Yeah. Something like that."

"Not me. We've spent the past few months either training or performing back-to-back missions. I could use some downtime to regroup and get my head on straight."

"Well, you do your thing. I'll do mine." Quentin shot a grin his way. "With the adventurous and beautiful Carly."

Sawyer almost opened his mouth and asked Quentin to secure the phone number for Carly's friend Jenna. Then he thought better of it. He didn't need Quentin to find him a woman. If he really wanted to go out with her, he'd find her himself. She had to be somewhere in Cancún. The resort area wasn't that big. He might even run into her on the beach.

His pulse quickened at the thought.

EVEN AFTER THE long drive back to the resort, Jenna Broyles still shook from her experience on the zip line.

"I can't believe you actually did it," Carly said for the tenth time as she got out of the rental car and met Jenna in front of the hood. "I'm so proud of you." She hugged her and stood beaming like a mother bird on her chick's first flight. "So how does it feel to be adventurous?"

Jenna pressed a hand to her belly. "A little nauseating."

Carly laughed. "You'll get over it. Just like you'll get over being stood up at the altar."

That reminder bit into Jenna's newfound adventurous spirit. Though it had been almost two months since she'd stood in the anteroom at the church, wondering where Audra, her maid of honor, was and waiting for her cue to walk down the aisle, it still hurt that her groom hadn't bothered to come to his own wedding. He'd not only failed to appear but also run off with the maid of honor.

Jenna had been adjusting the veil over her hair, wishing her mother could have lived to be there at her wedding, when the text had come through.

Sorry. Can't make the wedding. Changed my mind. Keep the tickets for the honeymoon.

She'd stood dry-eyed, shocked and unable to comprehend what had happened, until her father came through the door to lead her down the aisle. One look at her face and he'd grabbed the phone from her hand.

After a few choice words, he'd hustled her out of the church into the waiting limousine and taken her to the home she'd grown up in, where she could lick her wounds. Carly had done the honors of sending everyone home and canceling the reception and wedding band. She'd joined Jenna and her father at the ranch, ready to take one of the rifles over the mantel to Tyler's lying, cheating heart.

Jenna had heard through the grapevine that Tyler had slept with Jenna's former best friend, Audra, on the night of his bachelor party. He claimed Audra was more fun than his boring bride, and he couldn't go through with the wedding knowing he'd be stuck in a mundane marriage for the rest of his life.

Jenna had planned her wedding for the date her parents had been married in February. But as an accountant, she couldn't plan their honeymoon until after tax season. She'd almost forfeited her tickets until Carly talked her into going. She needed to show Tyler and, more important, herself that she wasn't boring. She knew how to be adventurous.

Of course, she had to take Carly along with her to show her how to do it.

Carly pulled in front of the resort hotel, shifted into Park and got out.

"Aren't you going to park it yourself?" Jenna asked. "I don't mind walking a little."

Carly clucked her tongue. "Don't be so tight. We're only here for ten days. You might as well live a little. Let the valet park it for us." Her friend tilted her head. "Come on. It won't kill you to be a bit extravagant."

"I just don't like spending when I don't need to," Jenna grumbled as she got out of the vehicle and joined Carly on the sidewalk.

Carly handed over the keys to the valet and sauntered into the hotel.

Once inside, Jenna eyed the front desk. "I'm going to ask whether my suitcase has arrived."

"Okay. I'll go on up and be first in the shower. I have a date with Quentin tonight." Carly frowned. "You don't mind, do you?"

Jenna did mind. She didn't enjoy eating alone in a restaurant. But she didn't want to hold Carly back from having fun. "I don't mind at all. I was thinking of splurging, like you said, and ordering room service and soaking in that incredible hot tub."

"Mmm." Carly grinned. "Sounds great. And I'll definitely want to be out of the room when you do it. That's one disadvantage to having the bridal suite. It was meant to be shared with your lover, not your girlfriend." She winked. "You should order champagne and do it right."

"Why? It's not like I'm celebrating."

"Yes, you are." Carly hooked her arm and marched her toward the concierge. "You're celebrating your liberation from marrying the wrong guy." She stopped and faced the concierge. "We'd like to order a lovely bottle of champagne delivered to the bridal suite."

"No, really." Jenna's face heated. "It's not necessary."

The man behind the counter stared from Carly to Jenna and back. "Which is it to be?"

Carly shook her head. "Champagne to the bridal suite within the next twenty minutes." She named a brand that Jenna hoped was on the cheaper end of the wine list. "Thank you." She grabbed Jenna's hand and tugged her toward the elevator. "Come on. You have some hot-tubbing to do."

Jenna dug her feet into the tile floor. "I will, but I need to check on my missing luggage."

Carly let go of her hand and nodded. "That's right. And I was headed for the shower and a date." She saluted. "I'll see you in the suite. I hope your bag came in." Her overwhelmingly cheerful friend spun away and disappeared into the elevator.

Jenna waited at the bellman's stand next to the registration desk. A rush of young people converged on the desk, tying up the bellmen and the clerks. A gentleman stood close to the bellman's stand, tapping his toe impatiently as he checked into the hotel.

Jenna could see everyone was busy and figured it would take time for anyone to free up and help her. Prepared to return later, she spotted her hard-sided gray case between the registration counter and the bellman's desk.

Excited that her suitcase had finally arrived, she scooped it up and headed for the elevator, saving the bellman one more person to deal with. Glad to have the case with her dinner clothes inside it, now she could relax and enjoy the rest of her "honeymoon."

As she stepped into the elevator, she thought of Carly and the man she'd just met at the zip-line excursion. Was her friend brave or foolish to go out with a man she knew nothing about?

Deep down, Jenna wished the man called Sawyer had asked for her number or asked to take her out on a date while in Cancún. She and Carly could have double-dated with the two men.

Perhaps she was being silly, but she'd thought she'd felt a connection with him. The warmth of his body at her back, the security of his arm around her waist.

Was she so desperate to be with a man, she had started reading into things? Hadn't she learned with Tyler that men weren't attracted to women like her? Or at least not for long. She was too boring, afraid to take risks, stuck in her ways.

Jenna tugged the rubber band out of her hair and shook her unruly curls loose. Well, maybe it was time to be more daring. She'd ask Carly to get the number for her date's friend.

In the meantime, Jenna had a date with a bottle of champagne and a hot tub.

Funny thing was…she didn't even like champagne.

No sooner had she entered her room than Carly stepped out of the shower. "I'm done if you want to rinse off," she called out. The door to the bathroom stood wide-open. Carly leaned against the counter, applying makeup, her slim, athletic body wrapped in a towel.

"No, I'll wait for the hot tub," Jenna said and set her case on the floor.

"The champagne beat you here. Help yourself. I already poured a glass." She turned and raised her glass, then drank a sip of the sparkling liquid.

Jenna figured that since it was paid for, she might as well try to enjoy it and poured a glass. She carried it to the huge floor-to-ceiling windows overlooking the ocean. The sun was still up, shining over the water. People crowded the beach, some swimming, others soaking up the sun. Families corralled children, and lovers lay entwined on towels, smooching as if they were the only ones on the beach.

Sighing, Jenna downed a long gulp of the bubbly liquid. This would have been her and Tyler's honeymoon had he gone through with the marriage.

Now, two months after the horrible embarrassment of being jilted at the altar, she was glad she hadn't married Tyler. They might already have been divorced or had the wedding annulled. Jenna would never have been happy with him. They were too different. She wanted a man who could be faithful. He wasn't.

The ping of a cell phone sounded from the bathroom.

"Whoops." Carly raced out of the bathroom, fluffing her short, dark, damp hair. She threw on a powder-blue sundress and strappy stilettoes and grabbed her purse. "Quentin is waiting for me downstairs."

"Isn't it early to go to dinner?" Jenna stared out at the beach.

"He wants to take me driving around first. Then we're going to walk on the beach. After that, we'll do dinner and dancing." She smiled. "He wants to get to know me." Carly hugged Jenna and bussed her cheek. "Don't do anything I wouldn't, and enjoy your hot tub and champagne."

"I will." Jenna sighed as Carly hurried out, the door closing automatically behind her.

As soon as the door closed, Jenna cursed. She'd meant to ask Carly to get the phone number for Quentin's friend.

She teetered on the balls of her feet, tempted to run after her friend, but didn't. For a long moment Jenna stared at that door as if it were a barrier to her self-esteem.

Why was she staying in her room, soaking in a tub, when she could be out, enjoying the sunshine and salty air? Wasn't she there to be adventurous? What better way than to go outside and experience life?

Scrapping the idea of a long soak in the hot tub, she stripped down to her underwear and slung her case up on the bed. She refused to hide in the honeymoon suite when she could be out having fun. With a determined flip of her hair, she flicked the latches. They didn't open. Funny. She hadn't locked them, knowing airport security would want to inspect for illegal or potentially dangerous items. Hell, she hadn't thought to bring the key. And yet somehow, the locks had engaged.

She fished in her purse for her metal file and went to work jimmying the locks one at a time until finally they each sprang open. Jenna straightened triumphantly. One more hurdle overcome. She could do anything when she set her mind to it. "Boring… Ha!"

Jenna flung open the case, ready to pull out her sexy black dress.

For a moment, she stared into the case, her mind slow to realize this wasn't her case at all.

"Oh no." On top was a layer of clothing. Dark trousers, dark, long-sleeved T-shirts, a black ski mask. Things she would expect to see in a case bound for the ski slopes or a really cold climate, not the tropics.

Jenna closed the case and stared down at it, wondering what to do with it. There was no luggage tag on the outside identifying the owner should the case be lost.

Feeling guilty already about forcing the case open, she lifted the lid and glanced inside again. Maybe there was some form of identification buried inside.

Carefully lifting the clothes, she set them aside on the bed. Beneath the clothing was nothing. Strangely, the case still seemed heavy, and it was deeper on the outside than the inside. Was there a false bottom? She ran her hand around the inside of the case, searching for a lever or button to push. Finally she found it, sliding the device to the left. The divider popped up enough that she could slip her fingers beneath it and lift.

Jenna gasped.

Parts of what appeared to be a rifle lay disassembled in a bed of foam, including the stock, butt, scope and bolt. A manila envelope lay on top of the weapon.

Why would a man need to bring his gun to Cancún? Was he part of a marksman team?

Her stomach knotting, Jenna refused to think past this being a competitive marksman's prize rifle. With no other identification to be found, she lifted the envelope, hoping to find the owner's name and cell phone number inside.

Flipping up the prongs on the metal clasp, she opened it and spilled the contents onto the bed.

Photographs, money and a note lay on the comforter.

She examined the wad of cash secured by a rubber band and counted fifty one-hundred-dollar bills. Holy crap. Five thousand dollars. Her knees trembled. Who carried around five thousand dollars in cash?

Jenna picked up the photographs, her eyes widening. The man in the picture had dark hair and dark eyes. He was nice-looking, dressed in dark jeans and a black T-shirt. The material of the shirt stretched over broad, muscular shoulders. Tattoos peeked from beneath the sleeves.

Jenna peered closer, her breath catching in her throat. She recognized the man in the photo as the man she'd met on the zip-line platform not an hour earlier.

Her hand shaking, she unfolded the note. Her pulse slowed and her blood turned cold.

Bring him to the agreed-upon location by 9:00 p.m. Dead or alive.

A lead weight sank to the pit of Jenna's belly. She'd wanted adventure, but not this much. At that moment, she'd settle for being boring Jenna.

Chapter Two

When Sawyer returned to the resort, he went to the bungalow he'd rented for his two-week stay, shed his jeans and pulled on a pair of swim trunks. After sweating in the humidity of the jungle, he could think of nothing he'd rather do than go for a dip in the ocean.

Grabbing a towel, he headed out the door and nearly ran into Montana.

"Hey, Sawyer!" Montana backed up a step. "You look like a man on a mission."

"I am. There's a WaveRunner with my name on it out there somewhere."

Montana chuckled. "I take it the zip-lining wasn't your style."

"Not particularly." Though the woman he'd met was. Jenna. Damn, he could kick himself for not asking for her number. Oh, well. He eyed Montana in his swim trunks, T-shirt and flip-flops. "You heading for the beach?"

"I am. Thought I'd improve on my tan." He grinned. "Girls love a tan, right?"

Sawyer turned on the boardwalk path, heading for the ocean. "No date for tonight?"

Montana shook his head. "No. But then, I wasn't really looking."

"Me, either." He hadn't been looking and hadn't made

an attempt when the opportunity bumped into him. He'd be smart to go ahead and ask Quentin to get her number, or he'd spend the rest of the vacation wishing he'd been quicker to seize the moment. "I'm going to rent a Wave-Runner. Wanna go in half?"

"Sure!" Montana flung his towel over his shoulder. "Been a while since I've ridden one."

"Can't imagine the lakes getting warm enough in Montana for a WaveRunner."

"You'd be surprised. We have long days in the summer. Gives the water a chance to warm up."

"From snowmelt?" Sawyer snorted. "Not as warm as the water gets off Virginia Beach."

"Maybe not that warm, but a little warmer than the water off San Diego."

Sawyer shivered. "BUD/S training gave a whole new meaning to word *miserable*."

"Yeah, but I have no regrets."

"Same here." He'd grown up in a wealthy household. Everything he'd wanted, he could have by just asking. BUD/S training had been a real culture shock and an assault on his body, physically and mentally. But he'd be damned if he failed and went home to hear his father say "I told you so."

Everything Sawyer did was to prove to himself he could do anything he set his mind to. Not because his father could get him the position or smooth his way. He didn't want his father's help. Hell, he didn't want anything to do with his father.

The man had given him anything money could buy, but he hadn't been much of a parent. He'd never played ball with him. Never made one of his parent-teacher conferences at school. When Sawyer crashed his motorcycle and broke his arm, his father was in Paris with his fiancée. He didn't bother to come home and check that Sawyer was all right.

He never once showed up at one of his football games. Hell, he didn't *want* him to play football. He'd said the sport was too hard on a man's body. It wrecked the knees. Not that he cared if his son was injured. His advice was from a practical viewpoint. Why destroy your body when you needed it to get you through to old age?

Being raised in a mansion with formal living areas and white carpets had been stifling to Sawyer. He'd never thought he could be himself. He was always the politician's son. On display in his best clothes. Sawyer felt more at ease near the sea, with sand between his toes and the sun warming his skin, wearing nothing but a swimsuit.

"There." Montana pointed down the beach, where a number of WaveRunners rested on the sand. A small tent stood nearby with a menu of prices listed on a chalkboard.

They wove their way between families playing with their children in the sand and bikini-clad beach babes slathered in oil and baking in the sun. Sawyer didn't slow to stare at the beautiful bodies. He wanted to be racing across the water, crashing through the waves, letting the wind and ocean wash thoughts of his lonely childhood from his mind. He had his SEAL brothers now. They were the best family a man could have. They'd be there for him, no matter what.

Sawyer slapped a wad of bills in the attendant's hand. "We'll take one for an hour."

The man pocketed the cash, instructed them on the use of the equipment and helped push a WaveRunner out to the water's edge.

Sawyer nodded to Montana. "You can go first."

"You sure? This was your idea."

"I can wait. Just don't wreck it before I get a chance

to ride." He twisted his lips into a wry grin. "It's not like riding a horse."

Montana laughed, hitched his shorts as if he were a real cowboy dressed in jeans and cowboy boots, and then swung his leg over the seat as if he was mounting a horse. "It's more like riding a horse than you think. But then, riding a horse can be a lot more difficult for you city slickers."

"Keep it up, Montana, and I'll show you a real rodeo on the water."

"Only thing that'll convince me is if you rope a shark, hog-tie him and bring him in to roast on a spit. Montana-style." Montana gunned the throttle and shot out into the water. He hit a small wave head-on, crashing through the crest to emerge on the other side. "Yee-haw!" he yelled and raced out to sea.

Sawyer sat in the wet sand, adjusting the cell phone in his pocket, glad he'd thought to slip it into a waterproof bag before he'd left the bungalow. He let the water lap over his feet and legs, enjoying the sun on his back, the fresh air and the taste of salt on his lips.

The first few days in Cancún had been a lot more than any of them had bargained for. Looking for relaxation, fun and maybe some female companionship, they'd come to Cancún ready for a much-deserved vacation.

Duff had been the first of the men to find a female companion. And boy, did he know how to pick one. Natalie, a former government secret agent, had come to find her sister, who'd disappeared on a diving excursion.

When Duff offered to help, all four members of SEAL Boat Team 22 who'd come to Cancún were engaged to find and liberate women who'd been kidnapped and readied for auction in a human trafficking ring.

Rest and relaxation. Ha!

Since when did getting shot at count as recreation?

Quentin, Montana and Sawyer could have told Duff where he could go with his plan to help, but that was not what friends did—not what SEAL brothers did. They stuck together and helped each other through good times and bad. And if there were guns and bad guys involved, that was when they did their best work.

Sawyer leaned back in the surf and let the warm, clear ocean water ebb and flow over his skin. Now that they'd retrieved the women and sent most of them to their respective homes, the team could finish their vacation in peace.

Montana hopped across several more waves, shouting like a fool and laughing in the sun. A wave hit him broadside and knocked the big cowboy into the water.

Laughing, Sawyer stood, brushing sand off his shorts.

Montana dragged himself up the back of the craft, mounted the WaveRunner and powered into the shore, pulling up on the sand beside Sawyer. Grinning, he shook the water from his hair. "You're gonna love it."

"Great."

Montana climbed off and stood to the side.

Finally Sawyer had his turn. He and Montana turned the vehicle in the sand to aim it outward.

Sawyer swung his leg over the body of the craft and settled onto the cushioned seat. As he twisted the throttle, a shout sounded behind him.

As soon as Jenna realized who the man in the photographs was, she'd grabbed her cell phone and called Carly.

Her friend didn't answer. Instead, she texted.

What do you need? We're in a convertible. I can't hear over the wind.

Get Quentin to give you the number for his friend.

Carly responded with a smiley face and a note.

His name is Sawyer.

Her heart racing, Jenna paced the floor. Every time she passed the case on the bed, her stomach clenched and she muttered, "Holy crap."

Someone had been paid to deliver Sawyer dead or alive to some undisclosed location. Armed with that information, Jenna couldn't stand by and let the would-be assassin succeed in his mission. She had to warn Sawyer. The sooner the better. The assassin might have more than this rifle at his disposal. And he had a deadline to meet.

Her first thought was to call the police. But no crime had been committed at that point. And hell, what if they thought she was the owner of the weapons? They'd throw her in a Mexican jail to rot. All the reports she'd heard about the Mexican government being owned by the drug cartels didn't give her much faith in their ability to stop this kidnapping or assassination from occurring.

Jenna glanced at the clock on the nightstand. It was already three in the afternoon. That meant six hours until the assassin had to deliver his prize.

Jenna's phone pinged with Carly's text. It contained a phone number, the name of a nearby resort hotel and a message.

Sawyer was planning to go to the beach this afternoon and rent a WaveRunner. You might find him there. Have fun!

"Have fun? Are you kidding me?" With a near-hysterical laugh, Jenna dialed the number and waited, gripping her cell phone so hard, she was afraid she'd break it. On the third ring, a male voice answered.

"Leave a message and I'll get back to you as soon as possible." The voice was the same rich baritone she'd heard on the zip-line platform.

Jenna closed the damning suitcase and shoved it high on a shelf in her closet, hoping that would calm her frazzled nerves. It didn't. She still had to warn Sawyer.

Unwilling to deliver the bad news to him via a recording, she hit the end button and glanced around the room. Still dressed in nothing but her underwear, she yanked the bright pink bikini Carly insisted was adventurous out of her carry-on bag, shed her bra and panties and slipped into the suit. She threw on a short, lacy beach wrap and grabbed her room key.

She'd considered texting Carly about what was in the case but was afraid Carly wouldn't believe her. Or worse, the text message would be intercepted. Nobody could know she had the case. Not until she figured out what to do with it.

First she had to find Sawyer and warn him about the note's contents.

Riding the elevator from the bridal suite to the ground floor was a study in patience. The car stopped several times on the way down to fill with people wearing dinner clothes or beach apparel, depending on where they were headed. They laughed and joked with each other while Jenna bit down on her lip and counted the seconds until they reached the bottom. She wanted to shout and rail at the people slowing her down. Didn't they realize a man's life could be hanging in the balance?

Somewhere in Cancún, possibly on the beach, an assassin could be following Sawyer or aiming at him through a scope similar to the one in the case. One pull of the trigger and Sawyer would be delivered dead.

The elevator hit the ground level and the doors opened, disgorging the numerous passengers.

Dancing in the rear, Jenna tried to get around some of them but was cut off every time. When she found a clear path, she darted through the lobby, making a beeline for the concierge, where she cut in front of an elderly couple and asked where she could find the hotel Carly had given in her text message.

The concierge pointed and told her it was two hotels south along the beach.

Jenna didn't wait for clearer directions but ran out the back door of the hotel, past the pool and the myriad lounge chairs flanking it and out onto the sand. She didn't slow as she raced past the umbrellas and people stretched out, capturing the afternoon sunshine. Eventually she ran along the water's edge, finding better purchase in the wet hard-packed sand. Passing the first resort hotel, she kept her gaze forward, searching the beach in front of her and the water to her left.

God, she hoped he was close to the water, where she could find him easily. If she had to look at each patron on the beach, it could take too much precious time.

As she neared the second resort hotel with its rainbow-colored beach umbrellas, Jenna saw a small tent set up close to the water with a number of WaveRunners parked in the sand.

Barely able to breathe by then, she staggered to a stop in front of the startled attendant.

"Have you—" Jenna wheezed as she leaned against the tent pole and dragged in a deep breath "—rented a Wave-Runner—" she breathed again and finished in a rush "—to a tall, dark-haired man with tattoos on his arms?"

The attendant's brows pulled together. *"Sí."*

"Where is he now?"

The man pointed to the water's edge a hundred yards farther along the beach.

Jenna glanced past the teenagers throwing a Frisbee, the father tossing his child in the air and the girls playing in the surf to a man standing near a WaveRunner and another slinging his leg over the seat.

"Wait!" Jenna cried and took off, running as fast as her legs and lungs could carry her.

Neither man turned at her shout the first time.

"Wait!" she cried as she got closer. This time the man standing beside the WaveRunner looked up. The one on the vehicle revved the engine and started sliding toward the water.

Giving it her all, Jenna lifted her knees and elbows, running faster than she ever had in the fifty-yard dash in high school and pounded across the wet sand, out into the surf. She flung herself onto the back of the watercraft, wrapping her arms around the man with the tattooed arms.

"What the hell?" Sawyer twisted in his seat to stare at his passenger. "Jenna?"

"Go!" she cried. "Go fast! Get as far out as you can."

His gaze sharpened on her face, but he revved the engine. "What's wrong?"

"Just do it. I'll explain when you get away from the shore."

"Are you serious?"

"Yes," she said, holding on tightly as they sped away from the beach and hit a wave full-on. Water splashed up in her face before she could close her mouth. She swallowed some and choked, spitting salt water.

He slowed. "Are you okay?"

"Please, just go out to sea." She clung to his back, her

arms wrapped tightly around his waist. "Your life depends on it."

"Okay." He shook his head but twisted his hand on the throttle, heading out to sea, taking them farther and farther from the beach.

When they were a good quarter of a mile out, he slowed the vehicle to a stop and half turned to face her. "Now, do you mind telling me what the hell just happened?"

Jenna glanced back at the shore. "How far can a bullet travel?"

"What?" Sawyer stared at her as if she'd lost her mind. "Not that I'm not flattered, but what does that have to do with hijacking me and my WaveRunner?"

She wiped the salty water from her face and bit her lip. "You're not going to believe this." Shaking her head, she tried to pull the words together in her mind before blurting them out.

"Believe what?" His scowl deepened. "Woman, you aren't making sense. And if you don't start talking, I'm heading back to shore before we run out of gas or the engine decides to quit. I'm pretty sure we're farther out than the attendant recommended."

Jenna's heart thumped against her chest and her fingers dug into his waist. "Someone is going to try to kill you."

For a long moment he stared down at her. "Is that your prediction? Are you a psychic or something?" His lips curled in a derisive smile. "Lady, I'm a SEAL. I get shot at on every mission."

Jenna shook her head. "How can you believe me when I barely believe what I saw?" She pressed her forehead to his shoulder, grasping for the words. Then she straightened, firming her jaw. "I picked up the wrong suitcase in the lobby of my hotel. When I opened it, I found what I assume were the parts to assemble a sniper's rifle, complete with a scope."

Sawyer snorted. "How do *you* know what a sniper's rifle looks like? Do you even own a gun?"

Her cheeks heated, and anger spiked inside her. "So, I don't own a gun, and I don't know exactly what a sniper's rifle looks like. But it's what was with the rifle that made me assume the owner was a sniper, hit man or assassin."

With a chuckle, Sawyer ran a hand through his dark, wet hair, standing it on end. "Could it be you've been watching or reading too many thrillers lately?"

She smacked her palm against his arm. "Damn it, I'm trying to tell you that I found photographs and a note with the weapon. Your photographs. Pictures of you and a note telling the gun owner to bring you to wherever they were going to meet by nine o'clock tonight. Dead or alive."

This time Sawyer sat still, his gaze pinning hers.

Jenna held steady, lifting her chin.

"How do I know you're not some nutcase desperate for male companionship and will come up with any cockamamie story to get one alone?"

Jenna let go of his waist and scooted back on the seat of the WaveRunner. "Is that what you think?" She slipped even farther back until she teetered on the edge, refusing to touch even one inch of the man's body. "Do you think I'm so desperate I'd chase a man out into the middle of the ocean just to get him alone?" She shook her head. "You know, I could have taken that case to hotel security and let them handle it."

"Why didn't you?"

"It doesn't matter. It's your life on the line. Not mine. If you want to ignore the warning I've given you out of the sincerest desire to save your sorry carcass, you do that. I'll just get myself back to shore, because I'd rather swim

a mile in shark-infested waters than ride back on a Wave-
Runner operated by a man with an ego the size of a whale."
She dived into the water before he could say anything or
reach out and grab her.

Jenna struck out, headed for shore, weighed down by
her beach wrap. She hadn't done much swimming since
she'd been on the high school swim team, and she realized
almost immediately that she didn't have the strength she
once had. But sheer anger should fuel her long enough to
make it back to shore.

She sure as hell wasn't going to ride with an arrogant,
self-centered, stupid man who could be dead by morning
because he thought she was a desperate crackpot.

The WaveRunner engine fired up behind her.

Jenna continued to swim freestyle, trying to remember how to time her breathing and making smooth, steady
strokes, pacing herself so that she wouldn't get too tired
too quickly.

Sawyer pulled up beside her. "Get on."

She ignored him, choosing to breathe rather than waste
her strength arguing.

Damn the man, but he kept pace with her, bobbing beside her on the water craft.

"I'm sorry," Sawyer said. "I shouldn't have called you
a desperate nutcase."

It was a start, but he had a long way to go before she
forgave him for saying all those nasty things to her. Jenna
plowed through the buoyant salt water, one stroke at a time,
refusing to acknowledge the man.

He sped up, pulling ahead of her.

Fine. Go back to shore.

Jenna would make it on her own. She didn't need a man
to rescue her. The men in her life hadn't proven to be very
reliable. Or at least her ex-fiancé hadn't. Sawyer, though

not really a part of her life, wasn't much better. She'd done him a favor. Tried to save his sorry life. And what did she get in return? Grief. To hell with him. He could be shot for all she cared.

A splash ahead made her stop and tread water.

The WaveRunner seat was empty, and Sawyer was nowhere to be seen.

Chapter Three

Jenna's pulse jumped and she spun in a circle, searching for him.

Had the assassin gunned him down?

She looked for the telltale sign of blood mixing with the ocean water but couldn't see any. Dragging in a deep breath, she dived beneath the surface in search of Sawyer's body.

Salt water stung her eyes before she'd swum four feet toward the WaveRunner. Jenna surfaced, blinking.

The water erupted, and Sawyer's face appeared in front of her.

Jenna started to scream, inhaled a gulp of ocean and coughed until tears streamed from her eyes and she sank below the water.

A strong arm wrapped around her middle and dragged her to the surface. "Are you all right?" Sawyer spun her to face him and pushed the sodden hanks of hair from her face.

"I thought you were dead," she said, her voice hoarse from coughing.

He shook his head. "I'm okay. It's you I was worried about. It's too far for you to swim back, and there might be a riptide. I couldn't let you do it."

She drew in a steadying breath and glared at him. "You could have been shot."

"Yeah, well, I wasn't."

"But you could have been." She wiped tears from her eyes, pushed at his chest and swam away from him, using a breaststroke.

"I'm really sorry I didn't take you seriously," Sawyer said, easily keeping pace.

Jenna nodded toward the watercraft, drifting farther and farther away from them. "You better go catch your ride before you lose it, too."

"I'm not going to leave you out here. If I have to let the WaveRunner go, I will." He stuck with her.

Jenna's conscience couldn't let him sacrifice an expensive machine for her. Besides, she was wasting time. The expense was the least of his worries. She stopped swimming and trod water. "Okay. But we need to bring it in at a different location. If you know you have a sniper gunning for you, you can't just present yourself as a target. I would have presumed they'd taught you that in SEAL training."

Sawyer chuckled. "They did. I promise to bring it in to a different location." He didn't make a move. "Are you coming with me?"

She glanced at the shore, admitting to herself, even if not aloud, that it was farther than she really had the strength or stamina to achieve. "Yes."

"Can you make it to the WaveRunner? Or do you want to wait here and let me come back and pick you up?"

"I can swim," she said, refusing to show any weakness to this man.

"Okay, then." He struck out.

Jenna followed, barely able to keep up with his stronger strokes. By the time she reached the WaveRunner, Sawyer had climbed aboard and revved the engine.

When he reached out a hand, she took it.

With very little effort, he pulled her out of the water, and she settled on the machine behind him. Her arms aching, she wrapped them around his waist and held on while he set the watercraft on a path toward the shore, but not toward the resort where he'd entered the water. He aimed toward her resort hotel.

"I'm not sure this is a good idea, either. Apparently the gunman is staying at this hotel."

"Well, where would you have me stop?"

She sighed. "You might as well stop here. You need to see for yourself what I'm talking about. But you can't stand still long. He could be targeting you as we speak."

Sawyer pulled up on the sand and shut off the engine.

"We'd better get inside. It's not safe to be out in the open." Jenna glanced at the sun starting its descent toward the horizon. "There are only a few hours until nine o'clock. If the gunman wants to make his deadline, he'll be coming after you."

Jenna scanned the beach, searching beneath the umbrellas. Then she faced the multistoried hotels, looking for anyone positioned on a balcony, aiming a rifle at Sawyer.

"You'll have to come to my hotel room. I can show you the case, the gun and the note. Hell, you can have them, for that matter. I don't want the Mexican police to catch me in possession of a weapon."

Sawyer frowned. "You say you mistook the case for yours. Where exactly is your case now?"

Jenna shook her head. "It was supposed to arrive by the time I got back from zip-lining. That's why I grabbed the one I found."

"If you mistook the case with the gun for yours—" Sawyer's jaw tightened "—is it possible the gunman took your case instead?"

Jenna nodded. "I suppose it's possible." She grabbed his arm and started toward the hotel. "The main thing right now is to get you out of rifle range." She marched ahead, holding on to his arm until he brought her to an abrupt stop. Jenna faced him. "Do you have a death wish?"

Sawyer shook his head. "Sweetheart, you realize that if this man finds out he has the wrong case, he'll come looking for the right one."

"Yeah. So?"

"Did you leave any identification on or inside your case?"

"Of course. How else was the airline going to know who it belonged to?" Jenna bit her lip, dread filling her belly. She'd been so concerned about warning Sawyer, she hadn't thought about herself.

Sawyer's glance shot left, right and forward as if he now was searching for the gunman. "You could be in as much danger as I'm supposed to be, if that gunman finds out where you're staying."

"Then we'd better get back to my room before he finds his case."

Sawyer shook his head. "I'm not so sure that's a good idea, either. He could already be there."

Jenna's heart slipped to the pit of her belly. "We have to get there. Fast."

"Why?"

"I have a roommate."

"Isn't she the one Quentin is with right now?"

"Yes. But I don't know when she'll be back." Jenna walked with purpose toward the hotel, digging her bare feet into the sand. Should the gunman come looking for his case... Holy hell...

Sawyer kept pace.

Jenna shot a glance toward Sawyer. "Shouldn't you be ducking your head or hiding your face?"

"I'll grab a hat in the hotel's gift shop on the way back to my hotel." He held out his hand. "First let's get that case. Give me your key. I'll check your room."

She dug the key out of her wrap pocket, amazed it hadn't floated out when she'd gone swimming. Slapping it into his palm, she stepped into the elevator.

Sawyer entered behind her, his finger hovering over the keypad. "What floor?"

"The top," she said and cringed. The last thing she wanted to tell Sawyer was that she was staying in the bridal suite. Hell, he'd find out soon enough.

As the elevator rose, Sawyer pulled a cell phone out of a waterproof bag.

"I doubt the police will be of much help," Jenna commented.

"I'm not calling the police. I'm texting my friend I left back on the beach to let him know where I left the Wave-Runner." He finished his text and hit Send.

When the elevator stopped at the top floor, Sawyer held out a hand, stopping Jenna from exiting. "Wait until I clear the hallway."

"My room's at the end." Jenna stood back, holding her finger on the door-open button while Sawyer disappeared down the corridor.

With her breath lodged in her throat, Jenna waited for Sawyer's signal.

It wasn't long before his voice echoed down the hallway. "What the hell?"

SAWYER HAD MADE a sweep of the hallway, checked the stairwell and tried the handles on the doors to the other penthouse suites. Each door had a fancy black placard with gold lettering naming the suite. When he'd come to the end of the corridor, he stopped and took a step backward.

"Seriously? You're staying in the bridal suite?"

Jenna left the safety of the elevator and joined him in front of the door. "It's a long story."

"I'd love to hear it sometime." He slid the key over the lock, and the light blinked green. "Soon." Sawyer opened the door. "In the meantime, stay here."

Again, he went ahead of her, stepping into the spacious living area with floor-to-ceiling windows overlooking the ocean. With the sun angling toward the horizon, the beachgoers had thinned, leaving a few couples walking hand in hand along the shoreline.

He didn't spend much time checking out the scenery. He was more concerned about who else might be occupying the room. Still not convinced he or Jenna had anything to worry about, he made a thorough sweep of the living area, bedroom, closets and bathroom. "All clear," he called out and turned to find Jenna standing in the doorway of the bathroom. "You were supposed to wait."

"Sorry. I can be impatient. It's one of my flaws. Along with being boring." She left the doorway and crossed to the closet.

Sawyer followed. "I can see the impatience, but you don't really believe you're boring, do you?"

Jenna shrugged, her lips pressing into a thin line, her cheeks turning a light shade of pink. "I don't know what to think about myself. I suppose I am boring."

Clenching his fists, Sawyer wished he could punch the person who'd fed Jenna that line of bull. "You're repeating what your ex-fiancé said."

"In so many words." She slid the door back to reveal a gray hard-sided suitcase wedged onto the top shelf. Jenna pointed to it. "That's it. Proof I'm not a desperate female after your gorgeous body to save me from dying alone."

He touched her arm.

She flinched away.

He wished he could take back what he'd said to her. He didn't need to add to her self-esteem issues. She had enough of those already. And as far as he could tell, she had no reason for them. With her long, dark ginger curls and bright green eyes, she was practically perfect, except for the frown denting her forehead. Sawyer wanted to brush his thumb across the lines. "I said I was sorry." He gave her a crooked smile. "You don't let things go, do you?"

"Add that to my list of faults." She backed away and let Sawyer pull the case off the shelf.

He carried it across to the bed and set it down. "I'll add that to your list of positive attributes. If this case holds what you say it does, I'm lucky that you don't give up easily." He flicked the catches, and the case remained locked.

Jenna handed him a metal file. "Use this."

She was not only beautiful, and anything but boring, but also smart and resourceful. He jammed the file into the locks and flipped them open one at a time.

Inside were neatly folded shirts and trousers. As he peered closer, he noticed the inside of the case wasn't as deep as the exterior indicated. He set the clothes to the side and looked again.

With a huff of impatience, Jenna reached around him and ran her finger along the inside. A partition popped up.

As he lifted the divider, his gut clenched. Just as Jenna had said, there were parts that would make a complete sniper's rifle with a military-grade scope, giving the shooter the capability of firing at long distances.

"This is what made me find you." Jenna lifted the envelope and turned it upside down, shaking the contents out onto the bed.

Photographs of Sawyer fanned out on the comforter. Pictures of him walking on the streets of New Orleans when he'd spent a weekend there with his teammates, shots of him outside his apartment near Stennis in Mississippi, and even more of him when he'd last visited his father in DC three months ago. Whoever had been following him had been doing so for some time.

"I don't understand." He shook his head. "Why me?"

"Darlin', if you don't know—" Jenna let out a short, hard laugh "—I can't help you. Have you pissed off someone in your past? Someone who would want revenge?"

He thought back on the missions he'd been a part of. The most recent sanctioned mission had to do with a terrorist training camp in Honduras. Surely the terrorists involved hadn't come all the way to Cancún and singled him out. Why not the rest of his team? He shuffled through the photographs.

Whoever the assassin was, Sawyer was his only target.

Sawyer drew in a deep breath and let it out, then glanced across at Jenna. "My father is a US senator. Not many people know, but this doesn't make sense. The note doesn't make sense."

Jenna read it aloud. "'Bring him to the agreed-upon location by 9:00 p.m. Dead or alive.'" She stared at the paper, her face pale, her eyes wide. "I don't know. Why would someone kill you and then deliver you somewhere?"

"Unless they're trying to make a statement."

Her pretty brow furrowed. "What kind of statement?"

"Perhaps it's a drug cartel or terrorist organization picking off SEALs to show they can." He shoved a hand through his hair. "Whoever it is hired an assassin. He might get paid more if he delivers me alive."

"Or he might just decide to take a lesser payoff because he's dealing with a highly trained SEAL. If he can pick you off at a distance, he has less of a chance of being taken down."

Sawyer's lips quirked. "You're pretty smart." He cupped her cheek and stared into her beautiful green eyes, wanting to do so much more. When he finally looked away, he dropped his hands to his sides. Settling the photos and note into the case, he closed it and let the locks click into place. Then he stared around the room as if for the first time. "Why the bridal suite?"

She turned and walked toward the floor-to-ceiling windows. "It's a dumb story."

"I still want to hear it." He followed and stood behind her, watching her instead of the view. He liked what he saw: petite, yet strong; slim, yet curvy; smart and a bit sassy.

"I was engaged to a man who found my maid of honor more interesting than me." She shrugged. "He texted me on our wedding day that he couldn't go through with the marriage." She turned and waved her hand at the room. "The hotel was nonrefundable, so I came with a friend." She lifted her chin and faced him, her eyes slightly narrowed as if daring him to laugh.

Again, he cupped her face. "His loss, my gain. If you'd come with him, you might not have found the case and come to warn me." He lifted her hand and pressed a kiss to the backs of her knuckles. "Thank you. And for the record, your fiancé was a fool."

"Ex-fiancé," she amended, staring at the hand he kissed. "And I agree. I'm better off without him." She stood as if frozen to the spot, her eyes widening as her tongue swept across pale pink lips.

Sawyer couldn't resist. He bent to brush his mouth

across hers in what he'd intended as a brief sweep. But as soon as his lips connected with hers, he couldn't back away. He slipped his hands around her waist and pulled her close, deepening the kiss.

She rested her palms on his chest. Instead of pushing him away, her fingers curled into him, her nails scraping against his skin.

He skimmed the seam of her lips, and she opened to him.

He caressed her tongue with his, fire burning through his veins, searing a path south to his groin.

Jenna's hands slid up his chest and linked behind his neck, pulling him closer.

The sound of a metal lock clicking brought Sawyer out of the trance Jenna's mouth had him in, and he lifted his head.

"Oh." The woman who'd been with Jenna at the zip line stopped in the middle of the doorway, her eyes rounding. "I'm sorry. I didn't mean to disturb you." She pointed to the closet and hurried across the room. "I'll just be a minute," she said, tiptoeing into the room, grimacing. "Don't mind me. Go back to what you were doing." She grabbed a dress and raced into the bathroom, calling out over her shoulder, "I didn't see anything. Continue kissing."

Jenna stepped away from Sawyer, her cheeks bright red, her eyes averted. She pressed a hand to her lips and stared out the window.

When the bathroom door opened again, her friend smiled. "Don't wait up for me. I might not be back. I'm taking my toothbrush just in case." She rushed to the door, yanked it open and turned with a full grin on her face. "And for the record, Tyler didn't deserve you. And you deserve to have fun. You go, girl!" She pumped her fist and let the door close automatically behind her.

"Don't mind Carly. She has no filter." Jenna chuckled softly. "She'd tell you that herself."

"I get that."

"Should we catch her before she gets on the elevator and warn her about the hit man?" Jenna started for the door.

"No. Text her and tell her you'd like to have the room to yourself. That should keep her from coming back to a potentially dangerous situation."

Jenna texted the message.

Carly texted back with a smiley face.

God, she probably thought Sawyer was staying the night. Jenna's cheeks heated and she couldn't face the man. Instead, she walked back toward the gunman's bag. "What do I do with the case? Should I take it back to the lobby and leave it for its owner?"

"No use making it easy for him to kill me. If he wants me badly enough, he'll have to find another weapon to do the job."

Jenna shivered. "I'd just as soon he didn't do the job at all."

"You and me both."

"In the meantime, what do I do with it?" Jenna waved at the case.

"I'll take it. I know someone who might help." He lifted the suitcase off the bed and headed for the door.

Jenna jumped in front of him. "Wait a minute. Where are you going?"

"Back to my room."

"If he knows you're in Cancún, the assassin will know which room you're in." She touched his arm. "You can't go back there."

"What do you suggest?"

She glanced around the bridal suite. "I figure if he

hasn't already come after me for the case, chances are he doesn't know I have it."

"Then this will have to stay here for now." Sawyer hefted the gun case onto the shelf in the closet and straightened, facing Jenna. "We need to find your case before he does."

"Right." Jenna nodded. "I guess you can stay here until I get back. I hope my case has been delivered from the airport by now."

"Uh-uh." Sawyer shook his head. "You're not going anywhere without me."

Her brows pulled together. "But he'll recognize you as soon as you set foot into the lobby—if he didn't see you coming in the first time."

"Not if I wear a hat and sunglasses." He glanced around the room. "I don't suppose you have a T-shirt that will fit me and a baseball cap or sunglasses." He stared down at his naked chest. "I seem to have come ill-prepared for undercover ops. If not, I'll pick up something in the gift shop."

Jenna's gaze zeroed in on his chest, and as they had so often in the past few minutes, her cheeks flamed. "I might have something," she said and hurried toward the dresser. After riffling through her clothes for a few seconds, she surfaced with an oversize black, white and gold New Orleans Saints football jersey.

Sawyer held it up. "Are you a fan?"

"I am." She lifted her chin. "And damn proud of it. So don't talk bad about my Saints."

He winked and dragged the jersey over his head and shoulders. "I wouldn't dream of it. But isn't the shirt a little big for you?"

"It's perfect to sleep in," she said, her cheeks reddening again. She handed him a pair of mirrored sunglasses and a Saints ball cap. "Ready?"

He slipped the glasses onto his face and the cap on his head and nodded. "Let's go. But me first."

Jenna frowned. "Do you think he might be on the other side of the door?" She stepped in front of him. "Maybe I should go first."

"Lady, you're killing my ego." He smoothed his hand behind her head, grabbed those lush red curls and tugged, tilting her head back. "But you're beautiful when you do it." Sawyer kissed her hard on the lips, set her away from the door and reached for the handle.

Chapter Four

Jenna bunched her fists. If the assassin waited on the other side of the door, it would take only one bullet to kill Sawyer.

"Stand back." With one hand on the door, Sawyer pushed Jenna out of sight. He glanced through the peephole and then stood to the side as he eased open the door. "Stay."

"I'm not a dog," she muttered, her breath catching and holding as Sawyer peered into the hallway and then stepped out. "I'll be right back." He left her in the room, the door automatically closing between them.

Jenna ran to the peephole and peered through. She could see only straight across the hallway to a blank wall. No Sawyer.

She gripped the door handle and remembered Sawyer's order. Instead of opening the door, she made herself count to ten. If Sawyer wasn't back by then, she'd go looking for him.

At nine, a light knock sounded on the door.

Jenna glanced through the peephole and then jerked open the door, flinging herself into Sawyer's arms.

"Hey." He chuckled. "I was only gone three seconds."

"Eight," she said, peeling herself off him, feeling foolish for being so dramatic. "But who's counting?"

"The hallway and the stairwell are clear. Let's go." He took her hand and drew it through his arm, bringing her body close to his.

She liked being against him. Something about Sawyer made her feel protected and safe in this new world of danger and intrigue in which she'd landed. Who would have thought mild-mannered, boring Jenna would end up embroiled in an assassin's plot to murder a navy SEAL?

Well, she'd wanted to break out of her normal routine. This was as far from normal as she could have imagined.

They walked arm in arm down the corridor.

A doorway opened across from the elevator.

Sawyer stepped forward, putting his body in front of hers.

Jenna's heart squeezed hard in her chest. Tyler hadn't done anything to protect her. Not even hold an umbrella over her head in the rain. And hell, she'd never been in a situation where bullets were involved, but she was pretty certain Tyler wouldn't have stepped between her and a potential shooter.

Jenna's knees shook as she peered around Sawyer, praying he wasn't about to be shot.

A young couple dressed in semiformal clothes spilled out of the room, laughing and holding each other like newlyweds. They walked straight across the hallway and hit the button on the elevator to go down.

By the time Jenna and Sawyer reached the elevator, the bell dinged and the door slid open.

Again Jenna had a moment of panic, expecting a gunman to spring from inside, wielding a machine gun, mowing down anything that moved. Her hand tightened on Sawyer's arm.

He covered it with his own. "It's empty," he whispered, leading her in next to the clingy couple.

"Are you the newlyweds from the bridal suite?" the woman asked, practically wearing her man.

Jenna's cheeks heated and she opened her mouth to stammer a denial, but Sawyer beat her to it.

"Yes, we are." He slipped his arm around Jenna's waist and pulled her snugly against his side. "Aren't we, sweetheart?" He bent to kiss her.

Taken off guard, Jenna couldn't think of a response and was saved from having to by the brush of his lips across hers.

"Umm," he said, deepening the kiss.

Jenna's pulse quickened.

"We tried to get the bridal suite, but it was booked when we made our reservations," the woman said. "Not that I'm complaining. They assured us our room had most of the same accoutrements, minus the hot tub for two." She pouted and stared into her new husband's eyes. "We'll have to come back on our one-year anniversary, won't we?"

Her husband winked and bent to nuzzle her neck. "Maybe we'll just stay here forever."

She giggled, and the bell rang announcing their arrival at the lobby level.

The door slid open, and Sawyer tensed against Jenna.

Before Jenna and Sawyer could move, the gushingly happy newlyweds stepped out. "Congrats on your wedding," the bride said, her eyes sparkling, a smile splitting her face. Blissfully unaware of potential danger lurking around every corner.

"Congrats to you," Jenna called out. That was supposed to be her on this trip. Happily married to Tyler, giggling and clinging to him.

Then Jenna realized that would never have been her. She and Tyler had never been openly demonstrative, preferring to kiss in private. Or had that been mostly on Tyler's part?

Jenna frowned.

Sawyer had kissed her in front of the other couple, something Tyler would never have done willingly. Then again, Sawyer had been playing the part of the newlywed who couldn't keep from kissing his bride.

Jenna bet he wouldn't be a prude about open displays of affection with the woman he loved. Which made her think. "By the way, are you married?" she whispered.

Sawyer had taken a step out of the elevator into the lobby. He ground to a stop, and the elevator nearly closed before Jenna could get out.

At the last second, he grabbed her hand and tugged, dragging her through the door and into his arms. He bent to kiss her firmly on the mouth and then trailed a line of kisses up to her earlobe. "I might not be the best boyfriend material," he whispered into her ear.

His warm breath sent shivers of awareness throughout her body.

"But I wouldn't kiss another woman if I were married." He kissed her again on the mouth. "Satisfied?"

Satisfied? Hardly. One kiss didn't seem to be enough with this man. She might never be satisfied. If it had been a different situation, she might demand more kisses to see if she finally grew tired of them.

She couldn't imagine that ever happening.

Sawyer straightened and glanced around behind the relative anonymity of the mirrored sunglasses and ball cap.

Meanwhile, Jenna's body trembled. She feared she might have melted into the floor if Sawyer hadn't been holding her around the waist.

"We should check with the concierge to see if your bag has arrived from the airport," Sawyer said.

"Yes. My bag." Jenna's cheeks burned. Did she sound

that airheaded? The SEAL's kisses made her forget everything, including the fact that a gunman was after him.

An image of the sniper-rifle parts flashed through her mind, bringing her back to reality. Sawyer was in danger. She needed to focus on him and keeping him safe.

"Over here." Jenna led him toward the registration counter. To the side of the long counter was the concierge's desk. Jenna couldn't help but stare at every man they passed and wonder if he was the assassin.

The gray-haired man with the handlebar mustache could be an undercover assassin. Who would suspect an older guy? And the mustache would make it hard to run facial-recognition software on him. He could be a highly experienced assassin with a long list of kills in his lifetime.

The man in the khaki slacks and pale blue polo shirt could be a master at blending in. Was he staring at them? Jenna tried not to stare back, watching him from the corner of her eye until they'd passed him. A shiver of awareness trickled down her back. Was he the one?

Intent on studying the man in the blue polo shirt, Jenna bumped into someone else. "Pardon me," she said and scooted out of the way of a man with light brown hair and gray eyes. He wore jeans and a gray T-shirt and seemed slightly familiar, but not in a distinct way—more as if she'd seen a hundred similar guys before.

Her gaze shifted to the sandy-blond-haired gentleman wearing jeans, a button-up white shirt and cowboy boots. He could have learned to fire expertly on a ranch in west Texas. Jenna's imagination concocted all sorts of scenarios, and she didn't see the woman until she ran into her hard enough to knock her own purse out of her hand.

"I'm so sorry," the woman said. "I can be pretty clumsy." She dropped to her haunches to help Jenna retrieve the contents of her purse.

Jenna bent to gather a pen, a tube of lipstick and her luggage receipts. "No, it was my fault. I should watch where I'm going." When she straightened, she smiled at the woman with the long dark hair pulled back in a neat, stylish ponytail.

She wore a tailored pantsuit in a soft cream color with a pale blue blouse beneath. "Are you sure you're okay?"

"I am." Jenna slipped her purse strap over her shoulder.

"Whew. I didn't want to start my vacation off causing an injury. I hope you enjoy Cancún. I plan on it." She smiled and walked away, stopping at a brochure stand near the excursion planner's table.

Sawyer cupped her elbow and led her toward the concierge's desk.

A man stood behind it, talking on a house phone. When they approached, he ended his call and set the handset on the base. "How can I help you?"

Jenna stepped forward. "My suitcase didn't arrive with me, and the airline assured me it would be sent on as soon as they found it. I don't suppose it's shown up?"

The concierge clicked on a computer keyboard, his head bent, his eyes skimming the screen. Then he glanced up. "We had a delivery over an hour ago, and I believe that's another arriving right now." He nodded toward the door. "Do you have your claim ticket?"

She handed the claim ticket to the concierge and waited while he checked in a room behind him, coming out empty-handed. "It's not in the storage room, but let me check with the bellboy bringing in the latest arrivals' luggage."

Before he finished speaking, a bellboy wheeled in a cart loaded with luggage. On top was a case just like the one back in the bridal suite with a sniper's rifle inside. "That might be the one. The hard-sided gray one with the chrome grip." Jenna pointed to the case.

The bellboy grabbed it from the top and handed it to the concierge, who held the claim ticket up to the strip of paper looped around the handle and smiled. "This is your bag."

Jenna resisted the urge to snatch the case and run. Instead, she smiled and handed the bellboy a tip. "Thank you." With as much dignity as she could muster, she turned toward the elevator and walked, though her feet wanted to fly.

The elevator was already crowded, but several others entered the elevator with her and Sawyer. The man in the cowboy boots and the one with the blue polo shirt stepped into the car right before the doors closed. As more people crowded in, Jenna bumped into someone behind her.

A feminine chuckle sounded. "We have to stop meeting this way."

Jenna turned in the tight space to find the brunette standing against the back of the elevator car.

"We're bound to since we're in the same hotel." The woman held out a hand. "Hi. I'm Becca Smith."

Jenna took her hand. "Jenna Broyles."

Becca eyed Sawyer. Jenna opened her mouth to introduce him, but he beat her to it.

"I'm Mr. Broyles, Jenna's husband." His lips turned up at the corners, causing her heart to flip. "We're still trying to get used to the fact we're married now."

Becca's brows rose. "Oh, newlyweds." She glanced at Jenna's hand. "Show me your ring. I'll bet it's gorgeous."

Heat crawled up Jenna's neck, and she hid her hand behind her back.

Sawyer's arm slipped around her waist and pulled her close. "She had to leave it at the jeweler's. One of the prongs holding in a diamond came loose."

"Yes," Jenna said, relief making her gush a little too

much. "I didn't want to lose a diamond on the trip. I thought it best to have it taken care of while I was gone."

"Good thinking," Becca said. She nodded toward the suitcase. "Only one suitcase between the two of you?"

Jenna laughed. "Hardly. This one was late."

The elevator slid to a stop on the third floor, and the man in the blue polo shirt got off without having spoken a word or glancing in their direction the entire ride up.

One fewer suspect in the car with them didn't make Jenna any more relaxed.

Becca glanced down at the brochures in her hands. "Are you two planning any excursions? I was thinking of deep-sea fishing, parasailing or zip-lining."

"I don't know about the fishing or parasailing," Jenna responded. "But the zip-lining was okay."

Sawyer snorted. "If you don't mind heights and plunging hundreds of feet down a cliff into the dark jungle."

The brunette looked from Jenna to Sawyer and back. "I take it you two went and didn't enjoy it?"

Jenna shrugged. "The anticipation of a violent death was worse than the actual event."

"You have no idea," Sawyer muttered.

The bell dinged and Becca said, "This is my floor. I hope to bump into you again." She edged her way through several others and exited.

The man in the cowboy boots got off on the next floor, stopped and turned back toward the elevator doors as they closed. He stared into the car, his eyes narrowing. Jenna could swear he was looking straight at her.

A shiver shook her frame as the elevator rose. People got out until she and Sawyer were the only two left to ride the rest of the way to the top floor.

Jenna held her comments until they stood outside the bridal suite. "I'm getting twitchy."

Sawyer ran the key card over the reader. The green light flashed on, and he pushed the door open. "What do you mean?" he asked, holding the door for Jenna to enter.

He followed, letting go of the door. It closed, shutting them into the room, away from prying eyes and curious people. Once inside, he pulled off the cap and sunglasses, exposing his gorgeous dark brown eyes and rumpled brown hair.

Off balance because of his mere presence, Jenna put distance between them. "I couldn't read the people in the lobby." She crossed the large living area and ducked into the bedroom.

"What people were you trying to read?" Sawyer followed her, stopping in the doorway, his arms crossed over his chest.

Jenna hefted her suitcase onto the bed and flicked open the clasps. With a sense of relief, she stared down at the beautiful clothes she'd purchased with Carly's help before the trip. For the past year, she'd scrimped and saved for the wedding and the honeymoon. And for what? Her groom ran off with her former best friend. Fortunately, they hadn't combined their bank accounts, or she might have been out all of her savings.

She'd taken half the money they would have used for a down payment on a house and bought a whole new wardrobe, including sexy lingerie, with the intention of having the time of her life…and maybe even a fling while in Cancún…without Tyler.

She glanced from beneath her lashes at the man in the doorway, her imagination running rampant. A fling with Sawyer would far exceed her expectations. He was infinitely more muscular than Tyler, besides being utterly sexy and dangerous. Her heart fluttered, and she had to bring herself back to what was important. The danger that surrounded them.

"What bothered me most about going to the lobby and even riding up in a crowded elevator was the unknown," Jenna said. "The assassin could have been any one of the people in the lobby or elevator. He might appear to be a man on vacation in khaki slacks…"

"Or a guy in a blue polo shirt," Sawyer finished for her.

She nodded. "You were looking, too, weren't you?"

He straightened. "Now that you have your suitcase, you might be in the clear. All the more reason for me to get the gun case out of your possession."

Jenna gnawed on her lower lip. "What are you going to do with it?"

"I know someone who could run fingerprints on it."

"Haven't we handled it too much to lift clean prints?" she asked. What was she saying? She knew nothing about fingerprints and how to collect them.

"Did you pick up the rifle?" Sawyer asked.

"No."

"Neither did I. We might be able to lift prints from the stock or scope."

"Well, let's get it to your guy." She closed her suitcase and started for the closet where she'd stored the gun case.

Sawyer stepped in front of her, his eyes narrowed as if thinking. "I'd have to go back by my bungalow to deliver the case."

Jenna's pulse sped. "You can't." She stopped in front of him. "If the gunman knows you're here in Cancún, he'll know where to look for you. The hotel you checked into. You can't get near the bungalow. That would be giving him an easy target."

Sawyer's lips curled upward, making Jenna's insides quiver. "Unlike being on a WaveRunner jetting out to sea?"

She frowned. "At least I got your attention, as well as getting you out of range of a sniper's rifle."

"Which he didn't have because you pilfered it, mistaking it for your own case."

Jenna sighed and looked up at him. "What if I hadn't mistaken the case? You never would have known someone was after you until it was too late."

He took her hand and drew her closer. "In case I haven't told you already…thanks for saving my life."

Jenna stared down at his hand holding hers. "Anyone would have done it."

"No. Not anyone. You might have taken the case straight to the police."

She glanced up. "I did consider them, but concluded they might not understand the case isn't mine. They might have thrown me in jail rather than help you. You were in more immediate danger, and a visit from the Cancún police would have slowed me down."

Sawyer lifted her hand to his lips. "Thank you again for risking your life to save mine."

Jenna's gaze was captured by Sawyer's, and she fell into his dark brown gaze. "You're wel—"

He covered her mouth with his. His hands dropped to her waist, pulling her hips against his. The hard evidence of his desire pressed against her belly.

Jenna moaned and opened to him.

Sawyer slid his tongue between her teeth and she met him, her tongue twisting and turning in a dance of desire. When at last Sawyer raised his head, Jenna swayed, bracing her hands on his chest. "You have to stop doing that."

"Why?"

"I barely know you."

"You knew enough about me to find me on the beach

and save me from an assassin. I reckon that gives us a pass on convention."

She rested her forehead against his chest. "I didn't come to Cancún to get involved with a man." But, boy, had that backfired on her.

He sighed. "And I have no business getting involved with you." He gripped her shoulders and set her at arm's length. "As a SEAL, I'm gone more than I'm home. And with an assassin after me, I can't risk you becoming collateral damage."

Jenna stared up at him, narrowing her eyes. "What do you mean?"

His jaw tightened. "Since you found your case, we can probably assume the gunman didn't mistake it for his. He can't know you have his gun. You're in the clear."

"So?"

"If you're in the clear, I need to step away so you aren't caught in the cross fire if things go bad. I don't want anyone connecting the dots between us."

What he was saying slowly sank in, and Jenna stepped back, out of his grip. "Does this mean you'll take it from here? I'm not needed anymore?"

He nodded. "That's exactly what I mean. As long as someone is after me, I'm a target. Anyone who gets close to me becomes a target, as well." He walked to the closet and pulled down the case. "Once I leave this hotel, I'll ditch the hat and glasses and resume my existence as Sawyer Houston."

"The walking target." Jenna shook her head. "That's crazy. You should hide. The assassin might have a backup rifle pointed at your bungalow, just waiting for you to return."

"Or he's scrambling to find a new one." Sawyer faced her, the case in his hand. "You don't happen to have a laundry bag or beach bag big enough to disguise the case, do you?"

Jenna stood motionless, her mind racing, her thoughts focused on Sawyer. "I have a beach bag," she said and moved toward her other suitcase with the giant folding beach bag she'd packed to carry her beach towel, hat and sunscreen. It was big enough to carry the small gray suitcase with not much room to spare. As she pulled the beach bag out of her luggage, she faced him. "So, you're just going to walk out of here and not let me help anymore?"

He took the beach bag from her and nodded. "That's right. I couldn't live with myself if something happened to you because of me."

Jenna propped a fist on her hip and squared off with him. "Don't you think that's my choice?"

He shook his head. "Not when it could cost you your life." He stuffed the case into the oversize bag and tied the handles together. "You shouldn't be seen with me, especially if I'm not wearing the disguise."

"I'll take my chances."

"Okay, I don't want you to follow me around."

Her mouth firmed. "I do what I want to do."

"I won't allow it."

"Look. I found the note and the gun. I risked being drowned or shot to bring you that information." She laughed shakily. "I feel like I have a vested interest in keeping you alive."

Once again, his hands came down on her shoulders, his fingers pressing into her skin gently but firmly. "I'm a trained SEAL. I'm used to being shot at. When was the last time someone tried to kill you?"

Her back ramrod straight, she tilted her chin upward. "The last time I drove on I-10 to New Orleans." She touched a hand to his chest. "There are no guarantees in life. For the first time, I've stuck my neck out, and I refuse to bury my head in the sand again."

Sawyer's lips twitched. "Your fiancé was so wrong about you. You know that, don't you?"

Jenna refused to be sidetracked by his sexy grin and the way his eyes shone when he smiled. "You're avoiding the subject."

"You are not a bit boring. Annoyingly protective, but never boring." He bent to touch his forehead to hers. "I'm not taking you with me this time." Sawyer straightened. "But I'll give you my cell phone number in case you run into problems."

She started to open her mouth to argue with him, but he touched a finger to her lips.

"I promise not to go by my bungalow," he continued. "I'll get the case to my guy another way."

Jenna drew in a deep breath and let it out. "I'd rather go with you."

"Sweetheart, I like you, and I like being around you. If we were two people on a regular vacation, I'd rather you came with me, too. But we're not. Please stay here. And remain vigilant in case the gunman figures out what happened to his case."

"Fine," she said. She'd stay long enough for him to leave. Then she'd do whatever she pleased.

Sawyer's eyes narrowed. "My mother always said 'fine' when the situation was anything but fine."

"I'll stay," she said.

He stared at her a moment longer, then nodded. "Where's your cell phone? I want to give you my number and the numbers for my buddies in case something happens to me."

"See? You do need someone with you at all times to keep something from happening to you."

He shook his head and held out his hand. "Your phone?"

She marched to the table where she'd dropped her purse and dug out her cell phone, handing it to him.

He keyed in several numbers and names, then handed it back. "I'll contact you later to let you know I'm alive and I've passed off the case."

"Thanks." She hugged the phone to her chest, her heart heavy at the thought of Sawyer leaving. For the few short hours she'd known him, she'd gotten used to having him around. But she didn't have a real reason to stay with him. She'd done her best to warn him about the threat to his life. It was up to Sawyer to heed the warning and stay alive.

Then why did she feel more alone than ever when he left the bridal suite?

Jenna stared at the closed door, her heart thumping hard against her ribs. Sawyer Houston wasn't her responsibility, but a part of her left with him. Her instincts were screaming at her to go after him. He was in dire danger.

But he was a grown man and a navy SEAL. What could a jilted accountant do to protect him from an assassin?

Chapter Five

As soon as Sawyer left Jenna's suite, he called his wing-man, Dutton Calloway.

"Hey, Sawyer, wanna rent some fishing poles and do some shore fishing this evening?"

"I thought you and Natalie weren't surfacing from your bungalow for the duration of this vacation?"

"That was the general idea. But we were thinking about coming up for air and getting in some fishing."

"Duff, as much as I'd love to do that, I need your help." Sawyer explained what had happened with Jenna and the case containing the rifle and the note. "If someone is truly after me, I need to find out who. I can't walk around in the open without marking myself with a great big bull's-eye."

"Damn, bro." Duff's easygoing attitude of a moment before turned serious. "Where are you now?"

"In the stairwell of Jenna's hotel, two over from ours."

"I'll gather the gang and meet you."

"Where?" Sawyer asked. "I can't stand out in the open."

"Meet ya at the dock. You know which boat."

Sawyer knew the boat Duff mentioned. Natalie's boss had some influence. One of the perks of having him as a boss was the use of a boat belonging to one of his rich friends. They'd used the forty-foot luxury yacht in a res-cue operation to save her.

The boat had gotten them onto the island and…well…it was beautiful and luxurious. What better place to schedule a clandestine meeting?

"Gotcha. See you there in fifteen?" Sawyer paused. "And by gathering the gang, you don't intend to arrive in a group, do you? I don't want the gunman to follow you to me."

"Hey," Duff said. "We're experienced SEALs."

"And we're supposed to be on vacation."

"I know. This is the second unsanctioned operation we've conducted since we've been here."

Sawyer shook his head even though Duff couldn't see him. "Less than a week and we're fighting battles when we should have been sipping mai tais on the beach, served by beautiful waitresses in bright bikinis."

"Yeah. There's something wrong with this picture," Duff agreed. "See ya in fifteen." He ended the call.

Pulling his cap low, Sawyer kept his head tilted down. With the shadows provided by his cap bill and the large mirrored shades, he was nondescript. No one would look twice.

The bottom of the stairwell gave him the option of entering the lobby or exiting the building on the side. He left the building, coming out in a concrete parking lot. The marina was a mile away. He could walk that in fifteen minutes, easy.

Glancing left then right, he hurried away from the resort hotel and out onto the beach. Ideally he would move fast enough that no one could get a bead on him from one of the windows in the high-rise hotels. He needed to get to his own clothing and out of the New Orleans Saints football jersey. If someone recognized him, it would be too easy to follow him in the distinct white jersey with gold-and-black accents.

Thirteen minutes later, he arrived at the marina, having

zigzagged from the beach to the street and finally to the marina. He spotted the Jeep that Montana had rented. He wondered if Quentin would be there with Carly.

He marched on, carrying the big beach bag, trying to look like a tourist preparing to go out on a fancy yacht. When he reached the yacht, he leaped on board and dropped down the stairs into the living quarters.

"About time you got there," Montana announced.

Duff stood beside a smoky-gray quartz table, his arms crossed over his chest. "Quentin took Carly out dancing. He won't be back for a while."

"What gives?" Montana asked.

Sawyer tipped his head toward Montana, and then his gaze slid to Duff.

Duff returned the look, concern drawing his brows together. "We just got here. I haven't filled him in on much."

"Where's Natalie?"

"I left her at the bungalow," Duff said. "She had a conference call with her boss."

"She going back to the Stealth Ops group?" Montana asked.

Duff nodded. "Now that her sister doesn't need her around anymore, she'll report for duty with SOS when she gets back from Cancún next week."

Natalie had told them SOS stood for Stealth Operations Specialists. They were a secret government organization established to take care of anything that needed even more secrecy than the FBI or CIA could provide.

"Thanks for ditching the WaveRunner way down the beach from where we rented it," Montana said. "By the way, who was the babe who jumped on with you?"

"That's why you're here and not at the bungalows." Sawyer pulled the case from the beach bag, laid it on the table and held out his hand. "Got a knife?"

Duff pulled out a slim pocketknife and handed it to Sawyer.

Montana asked, "What's in the case?"

"Trouble," Duff answered for Sawyer.

Sawyer flipped the latches open and lifted the lid, exposing the dark clothing on top.

"I don't get it."

"Give me a sec." Sawyer ran his finger over the spot Jenna had rubbed earlier, and the divider between the top and bottom halves of the suitcase popped upward. When he lifted it all the way, Montana stood.

"What the hell?" He reached for the rifle parts. "You could spend a lot of time in a Mexican jail if they caught you with that kind of equipment." He shot a puzzled glance at Sawyer.

"It's not mine."

"Whose is it? The woman who kidnapped you on the WaveRunner?"

"No. She thought it was her case, took it to her room and discovered the rifle and this." He pulled out the envelope and showed them the photos and the note. "Apparently, someone wants me dead."

Duff grabbed the note, and Montana leaned over his shoulder to read it.

When he finished, Duff shook his head. "But why?"

Sawyer's lips tightened. He suspected the reason had something to do with his father. "If I knew, I might also figure out who could be gunning for me." He paced away from his teammates and back. "All I have are the rifle, the photos and the note." He glanced at Duff. "Has Lance left his bungalow yet?"

Lance had come to Cancún with Natalie to provide SOS technical support in Natalie's mission to find her sister and the other women who'd been abducted. He was a top-notch techno guru with the ability to hack into just about anything.

Duff nodded. "He asked his boss if he could delay his return by two days to catch some of these tropical rays before he returns to his cave in the DC area."

"Do you think he could run a fingerprint check on the rifle?"

"You'll need to provide yours and Jenna's so he can rule them out."

Sawyer frowned. "She didn't handle the rifle, but if he wants to lift prints from the inside of the case and the contents of the envelope... I guess I could go back and get hers."

"You spent part of the day with a woman who hijacked you on a WaveRunner." Duff gave him a hard stare. "Why hesitate now?"

Running a hand through his hair, Sawyer couldn't help but grin. "Actually, she was very nice. Quentin and I met her on the zip-line excursion earlier today."

"Does she have any connection to the woman Quentin took dancing?"

Sawyer nodded. "Roommates and best friends."

Duff tucked the photos and note back into the envelope. "We need to get these to Lance ASAP. The sooner he runs those prints, the better."

"They may come up blank," Montana said. "An experienced assassin wouldn't leave prints on his weapon, would he?"

"You would think he wouldn't leave his case with his gun lying around for a stranger to take, either."

Duff glanced up. "Speaking of which, where *did* Jenna get the case?"

"From the lobby between the concierge and reception desks," Sawyer replied. "Why?"

"It's a pretty modern resort. They probably have a good security system."

Sawyer nodded. "I noticed cameras in the hallways and the stairwells. Stands to reason they'd have them in the lobby."

"I'll ask Lance to hack into their system," Duff said. "He could do that while he's waiting for the match on the latent prints."

"In the meantime, you should be thinking about who you pissed off." Montana grinned. "Maybe it's one of the terrorists we ousted in the Honduras operation."

Sawyer frowned. "If that were the case, why target only me? You'd think whomever was mad about how that went down would go after all of us."

Montana scratched his chin. "That's the case for every one of our missions. It doesn't make sense. Why would anyone pick on only you? What makes you so different?"

Sawyer could think of one thing, but he didn't mention it, because it didn't seem to have any bearing on what was happening in Cancún. Still, he would make a call as soon as he left the boat and his friends.

"For whatever reason they want Sawyer," Duff said, "he can't just walk around in the open. He's tall enough that he would stick out in a crowd. He might as well wear a target on his back. A good assassin with the right tools could easily take him out, even at a distance."

Sawyer's lips twisted. "Thanks, Duff. You're not helping my peace of mind."

"I'm just saying, you can't walk around Cancún without protection." Duff's brows dipped. "At least our assassin has lost his high-powered rifle."

"What you need is a flak jacket. I bet Lance has one in his stash of equipment he brought along with him," Montana offered. He glanced around the boat. "Or we might find one on the boat. It has a better arsenal than we have back on base. Wait here. I'll see if I can find a vest." Montana headed for the back of the boat, where they'd found rifles, handguns and explosives in an arsenal that would make Gunny salivate. Their gunnery sergeant back in Mississippi made it his purpose to obtain the best weapons available on the market for their unit and missions. He'd find everything he could ask for here.

"And I'd hide a flack vest under my loose-fitting Saints jersey?" Sawyer darted a downward glance at the shirt Jenna had loaned him. "I don't think so. We have to find the assassin before he finds me in the crosshairs of whatever weapon he can get his hands on."

Montana shook his head. "The sooner we can get back to Lance with this case, the sooner we can get him started hacking into the resort security system."

"Right." Sawyer glanced around. "I don't suppose Natalie's boss would mind if I camped out here while I'm waiting for an assassin to put a bullet through me."

"I'm sure it would be all right." Duff stared at Sawyer. "How do you want us to go about getting Jenna's fingerprints to compare against those Lance finds on the case and its contents?"

Montana grinned. "I can drop by her room and get them."

Sawyer bristled. "Like hell you will."

"Remember, you can't just waltz in and out of the resorts. You're a wanted man."

"I got out, didn't I?" Sawyer pulled the ball cap over his head and stuck the sunglasses on his nose. "Besides, in Jenna's hotel, I'm her newlywed husband, Mr. Jenna Broyles."

Both Duff and Montana grinned.

"I've heard of love at first sight," Duff drawled, "but marriage at first sight? Isn't that taking it a bit far?"

Sawyer's chest tightened at the thought of being Jenna's

husband for real. He could do worse. She was pretty, spunky and smart. He loved her dark red hair and the way it felt when he sifted his fingers through the silken strands. "Had to come up with a good cover, going up and down the elevator with her. And she's got the bridal suite."

Duff's forehead wrinkled. "Why?"

Sawyer grunted. "Jilted at the altar. She was supposed to be here on her honeymoon, but the bastard didn't know how good he had it."

"Wow. Crappy way to spend your honeymoon," Montana said.

"Yeah. And now, she could be a target if the gunman learns she was the one to find his case."

"You think there's a chance he'll connect her to his missing case?"

"As much of a chance as we have to find him," Duff said, his steady gaze locking with Sawyer's.

"I didn't want to have to go back to Jenna's resort."

"You don't want her to end up collateral damage."

"Exactly." But now that he'd talked himself into going back to the resort and Jenna, he wanted to be there immediately. His belly tightened at the thought of the dangers she might face because of him. "I'm heading back. Let me know what Lance finds."

"Will do." Duff stuck out a hand.

Sawyer took it and shook.

Duff pulled him into a man hug and then let him go. "Later."

"You bet."

With the cap on his head and the shades across on his nose, Sawyer looked like any other tourist who happened to be a New Orleans Saints football fan. He'd have to figure out how to sneak back into his room without being seen to grab a change of clothes. In the meantime, he wanted to get back to Jenna. Now.

Even though they'd found her case before the assassin did, Sawyer didn't have the level of confidence he needed to think Jenna was perfectly safe.

Montana and Duff dropped the case into the beach bag and climbed the steps to exit the boat's hold, leaving Sawyer there alone. Before he went back to Jenna's hotel, he had a call to make.

He touched his smartphone and brought up his emergency contacts, then hit the number at the bottom of the list. The last person he wanted to call when he was in trouble. But this...relationship...was the only striking difference between his teammates and himself that might hold a clue to why he was being targeted.

The line rang three times before someone answered. "Sawyer. Thank goodness, it's you."

The tension in the voice on the other end of the line made Sawyer tighten his hand on the phone. "Senator, have you got anything you want to tell me? Anything I need to know?"

"As a matter of fact, son, I do. Can you make it to DC by morning?"

"No," he said, his tone flat, emotionless. Just like his father's usual demeanor toward him.

"Then I'll come to you," his father said, his voice not nearly as confident and forceful as usual. "There are some things you need to know."

Sawyer ground his teeth together. "Could you start with why I'm being targeted by an assassin?"

AFTER SHE'D CHANGED, Jenna left the bridal suite and descended to the restaurant level. She'd sat alone and picked at a beautifully prepared salad, wasting most of it before she wandered over to the bar, where a reggae band played upbeat music that didn't manage to lift the blue funk settling over Jenna.

In the bar she spotted the man who had been wearing the blue polo shirt earlier that day. Now dressed in a nice pair of black trousers and a white button-up shirt, he sat staring into his glass of beer. When he looked up, his gaze found hers and narrowed.

Although her pulse accelerated, she told herself any good assassin wouldn't so openly glare at her. Still, she questioned her decision to get out and enjoy herself. But now that she was there, she could hardly scurry back to her room. Anyone watching her would know she was nervous. So Jenna found a corner table and sat with her back to the wall. Color her paranoid, but she was damned if someone snuck up on her, especially the guy staring at her full-on.

When he didn't look away, Jenna's ire hitched up. She lifted her chin and glared back at the rude man, giving him every bit of attitude he seemed to be giving her.

Just when she'd had enough staring at the man, he stood and walked across the floor toward her.

Holy hell. Jenna wasn't prepared to die. If he had a gun with a silencer, he could shoot her there in the bar while the band's music drowned out the light thump. She'd seen the movies. Knew just what it sounded like. Heck, he could probably shoot her without pausing and no one would think twice about her slumping over the table—just another drunk tourist.

She ducked her head and pretended she didn't see him approach. From the corner of her eye, she noted every detail of what he was wearing. She searched his hands for a gun and checked for telltale lumps beneath his suit jacket. Was he wearing a shoulder holster with a handgun tucked neatly inside?

Then he was standing right next to her, forcing her to glance upward. "Would you like to dance?"

What she thought he would say and what he did were so divergent, Jenna could only stare and nod, unable to form a coherent thought.

He held out his hand.

As if on autopilot, she placed hers in his and let him draw her to her feet.

"My apologies if I stared at you today," he said as he drew her into his arms and moved to the music. "You remind me of someone."

"Oh, yeah?" Jenna finally found her voice, marveling at how normal she sounded. "Who would that be?"

He didn't answer immediately, swaying to the lilting melody. Then he slowed and stared down into her face, coming slowly to a stop. "My wife."

Jenna stepped backward. "Your wife? Shouldn't you be dancing with her?"

He gave her half a smile. "I would, if she was here. We planned this vacation a year ago." He started to move again, his gaze drifting over Jenna's shoulder as if he didn't see her there at all. "She would have loved it here," he whispered.

Jenna sensed a deep sadness in the man and she asked, "Why didn't she come?"

"She died of breast cancer two months ago."

Her tension bled away in the face of his obvious sorrow, and she scratched him off her list of possible assassins. "I'm so sorry for your loss. My mother died of breast cancer when I was twelve."

"That's tough on a kid. My wife suffered a lot at the end, and it was a relief for her to let go."

"But it wasn't a relief to you," Jenna finished for him.

He gave her a crooked smile and held open his arms. "I

promised you a dance, not a pity party. Let's show these people how to dance to reggae."

In an attempt to cheer the man, Jenna threw herself into mastering the reggae beat. By the time the song ended, she and her dance partner were laughing.

Jenna stuck out her hand. "I'm Jenna Broyles."

"Stan Keeting."

"What was your wife's name?"

"Angela."

"We can dedicate that last dance to Angela."

He smiled. "She would have liked that."

"Thank you for the dance, Stan."

"No." He held her hand a little longer. "Thank you. You made me realize Angela would want me to get on with my life and live it to the fullest."

"I'm glad to hear that." She pulled her hand away and retreated to her table and the watery drink she'd left.

Her gaze snagged on dark-haired Becca, who strode across the barroom floor wearing a silvery dress that hugged every inch of her body and came down to midthigh.

When she spotted Jenna, she crossed to where she sat. "I'm surprised your new husband let you come to the bar alone." She nodded to the empty chair. "Or are you saving this seat for him?"

Jenna's pulse kicked up a notch as she concocted a lie about why she was there without Sawyer. "He was taking a nap. I left a note for him to join me when he woke." She glanced toward the entrance. "I expected to see him by now. I guess he was more exhausted than even he knew." Settling back in her chair, she smiled. "No worries. I'll just finish my drink and join him."

Becca sighed. "You two must be so in love."

Heat rose in Jenna's neck and suffused her cheeks. "It's wonderful." Or at least she thought it would be.

Now that she had some time and distance between her and her ex-fiancé, she realized she'd never really been in love with Tyler. While all of her friends were getting married and having children, she'd fallen in love with the idea of marriage and rushed Tyler into making a commitment neither of them had really been ready for. In effect, he'd done her a favor by jilting her. He'd saved her the heartache and expense of a divorce later.

"I take it he's not the jealous type."

Jenna really didn't know Sawyer well enough to guess. "Why do you ask?"

Becca tipped her head toward Stan, who sat at the bar with a beer in his hand, not drinking, just staring into space. "You two danced well together. I can't say that I've ever danced to reggae."

Jenna smiled. "Stan's a nice man. Maybe he could show you some moves." Her smile slipped. "He lost his wife recently." She glanced down at her drink, suddenly depressed about being alone. She lifted her glass to her lips and sipped. The drink was so watery it no longer had the same appeal as when it was first served.

Jenna had no desire to drink it or to stay in a bar full of strangers. What she really wanted was to see Sawyer again. She pushed away from the table and rose. "It was nice chatting with you, but I think I'll go check on my groom."

Becca nodded and stood, too. "Sleep well."

"You, too." Jenna left the bar, crossed the lobby and punched the button for the elevator. As she waited, she had the distinct feeling someone was watching her. She turned around and stared at the people milling about the lobby. Each one of them was involved in another conversation, with the reception desk, with a companion or on a cell phone. No one was looking her way.

The bell rang, announcing the arrival of the elevator, and the doors slid open.

Jenna stepped in and turned around to press the button for the penthouse floor. When she glanced up, she saw a man in a New Orleans Saints football jersey, a baseball cap and sunglasses enter the lobby and head toward the elevator. Her heart skipped several beats, and a storm of butterflies fluttered inside her belly.

Sawyer.

When he spotted her, he sped up.

About that time, the doors started to slide together.

Jenna scrambled to find the door-open button, and she jammed her finger on it, holding it until Sawyer entered the car. Then she let go and the doors closed.

"I thought you weren't coming around," she said, her voice breathy and unlike her normal confident tone. What was wrong with her? He was just a man. A man with broad shoulders and deep, dark brown eyes she could fall into every time.

He opened his arms. "Even if I didn't have a real reason to come back, I couldn't have stayed away."

Jenna took a step toward him, afraid she'd misread his intention until she was close enough that he gripped her arms and pulled her against him.

"For someone I've only known for today," he said, "I can't seem to get you off my mind."

"Ditto," she mumbled against the New Orleans Saints jersey she'd loaned him. It no longer smelled of her detergent and fabric softener. The shirt held his scent, a hint of rugged, heady, masculine musk and the salty sea air. She inhaled, committing that unique smell to memory.

The elevator car rose to the top floor without another

word being spoken. When the bell rang and the door slid open, Sawyer checked the corridor before letting her step out.

When they arrived at the door to the bridal suite, he held out his hand for her key card, scanned the card and shoved the door open.

Once through, he closed the door behind them and pulled her into his arms, his mouth crashing down on hers, his tongue sweeping in to claim hers.

This was where Jenna had wanted to be all evening. Not eating alone, dancing with a widower or talking to another woman she didn't know or care to know. She'd wanted to be in Sawyer's arms, her heart beating close to his, his mouth melded with hers.

Yes, he was the target of an assassin, and she could be putting herself in the line of fire, but she didn't care as long as Sawyer held her close like this and made love to her all night long. Tomorrow would be soon enough to get to know him better and find whoever was tasked with eliminating her SEAL.

Chapter Six

Sawyer's conversation with his father hadn't yielded enough information to determine who might be after him. The senator insisted he needed to meet with him in person. In the meantime, Sawyer still had an unidentified assassin after him.

All the way back to the resort, Sawyer told himself he would get the fingerprints he needed and leave. Staying with Jenna wasn't an option. Being so near put her at risk. He couldn't let her get hurt because of him.

However, the moment he'd stepped into the lobby of the hotel and saw that flash of auburn hair in the elevator, his heart raced, and he couldn't wait to get her alone. Now that he had her in her suite, he didn't want to leave.

He kissed her, tasting her, feeling her body beneath his fingertips, wanting to get closer, but afraid he'd frighten her by moving too fast.

And there was the matter of being the target of an assassin. He couldn't push that completely out of his mind. After slaking his initial thirst for her, he lifted his head and stared down into her bright green eyes. "You're beautiful, and for some reason, I can't get enough of you."

She chuckled softly, the sound gravelly and sexy as hell. "Funny. I feel the same. And I've never felt that way about anyone before. Especially a virtual stranger."

He cupped the back of her head and pressed a kiss to her forehead, each of her cheekbones and the tip of her nose. "Why is it I don't feel like we're strangers? It's as though I've always known you."

"But you don't know me."

"You're brave and sexy."

"What's my favorite color?" she asked, her eyes closing as he pressed kisses to her eyelids.

"Not important." He brushed her lips with his and skimmed the line of her jaw. "You're gutsy and exciting."

"What do I do for a living?"

"Not important," he repeated. "You have the cutest dimples when you smile, and your eyes twinkle, making them shine so brightly."

She grinned up at him. "Where do I live?"

"In my mind, in my thoughts. In my arms." He tightened his hold, bringing her hips flush up against his. The hard ridge beneath his shorts pressed into her belly. He wanted more. "Your favorite football team is the Saints and you can kiss like nobody's business. What more do I need to know?"

She laughed and rose on her toes to press her lips to his. "You're right. What more do you need to know?" Jenna took his hand and backed toward the bedroom. "Now that you're here, maybe you could stay awhile."

He started to follow her but stopped, his shoulders sagging. "I can't. I came to get your fingerprints. My guy needs to match yours and mine to rule them out before he can run the others on the case through the fingerprint databases."

Jenna nodded, her expression tightening. "Okay. Let's do this." She glanced around the room. "What did you have in mind? I'm fresh out of an ink pad."

"I'll use my cell phone."

Her brows dipped. "Cell phone?"

"Sure. The camera on the phone is sufficient to take a good image of all of your fingers. And it'll take a digital image, which will save my guy time in the transfer." He pulled the waterproof bag out of his back pocket, reminding himself he needed to get fresh clothes soon.

He walked her over to a wall and had her hold each hand up, palm facing the camera, while he took several shots. When he was satisfied the images were sufficiently detailed, he sent the photos to Duff, who would see they made it to Lance.

"That was easier than smudging in ink. And no messy cleanup."

He nodded, staring at her for a long moment, thinking how hard it was going to be leaving her again. "I guess I should go. I only came back to get the prints."

She gave him a small, tight smile. One he hated seeing because again, he sensed her disappointment.

"Where will you go? You can't go back to your bungalow and you can't stay with your friends. That would be the first place the gunman would look."

"I can't stay here," he said.

"Why not?" She tilted her head, her eyes narrowing. "The way I see it, you don't have much of a choice. I have my case, which means the shooter won't know I got his. You're safer here than you are wandering the streets of Cancún in the dark."

He frowned. Maybe he could stay. But did she mean for him to take the couch or join her in the bed? His body tightened, but then he shook his head. "I need fresh clothes."

She shrugged. "I probably have another shirt big enough for you. I brought one to wear over my swimsuit."

"I still need pants."

Jenna smiled. "Can't help you there."

Sawyer shook his head. "I don't want to put you in danger."

"I told you—"

"Yeah, the shooter wouldn't know to look here and it's your choice." He closed the distance between them and cupped the back of her head. "You're making it really hard for me to walk away," he said, his voice roughening.

Jenna slid her hands up his chest and locked them behind his neck. "Then don't."

"I'm not good boyfriend material."

She shook her head and pressed a finger to his lips. "I'm not looking for a boyfriend. I had one. He ran out on me the day of our wedding. Why would I want to do that again?"

He grabbed her hand and removed her finger from his lips. "You're a nice woman. I'd be using you."

Again, she lifted on her toes, this time silencing him with a kiss. "Have you considered I might be using you?"

"Then we'd be even." He kissed her back and pulled her hips against his. "No regrets in the morning?"

"None." A small smile played on her lips. "So, are you staying?"

"For a while."

She shrugged. "Good enough."

"But I want to rinse the sea salt off my skin."

"Help yourself." She waved her hand toward the bathroom and walked away. "We have champagne."

"I'd rather have beer, but champagne will do."

"It'll be waiting when you're through in the shower." She walked toward the living area, pulled the loose cork out of the bottle and poured sparkling liquid into a champagne flute.

Sawyer strode to the bathroom, hoping Jenna would join

him in the shower. She'd invited him to stay in her room, not to make love to her, but if she came into the shower, she'd remove all doubt.

Shucking his swim shorts and the New Orleans Saints shirt, he stepped into a huge shower. What a shame he was the only one inside. Squirting a line of shampoo from the courtesy bottle, he lathered his hair and body, standing in the pulsing spray from the showerhead, getting harder the more he thought about the woman in the room on the other side of the door.

With his life in danger, and hers by default, he had no business thinking of anything but the problem at hand. Instead, his mind went to Jenna's body pressed against his and her lips, velvety soft, yet firm and passionate.

Ducking his head beneath the spray, he reached for the handle to turn the temperature down. Before he could do that, a pair of hands slid around his waist, and soft breasts pressed into his back.

Sawyer groaned.

Jenna's hands stilled. "Was that a good groan or a 'get the heck out of my shower' groan?"

He turned in her arms, the evidence of his desire obvious and prodding her belly. "I was just thinking about you."

Her eyes widened and she lifted her face to accept his kiss.

Sawyer threaded his hands in her hair and tugged, tipping her head so that he could trail kisses down the side of her neck and lower to the swells of her breasts. He scooped her up by the backs of her thighs, wrapping her legs around his waist.

Jenna rested her hands on his shoulders. "You have protection?"

He moaned. "Yes." Setting her back on her feet, he dived out of the shower and grabbed for the waterproof container, yanking it open so fast, his cell phone and wallet flew across the counter.

A giggle behind him only made his fingers move faster. Finally he found what he was looking for in a dark foil packet. Back inside the shower, he ripped open the packet and removed its contents.

She took it from him and slowly rolled it down over his shaft, her fingers circling him, her touch gentle, as she made her way down his length to the base.

Past control, he lifted her, pressing her back against the cool tile wall.

She wrapped her legs around his waist again and lowered herself over him as he thrust upward, gliding into her warm, wet channel, filling her all the way.

Jenna drew in a long, deep breath and held it as he froze, giving her body time to adjust to his length and girth. When she pressed down on his shoulders and eased up, he pulled out to the very tip and thrust back inside.

With Jenna leveraging herself on his shoulders and Sawyer pumping in and out, they settled into a smooth, fast rhythm, the pace increasing until a firestorm of electricity ripped through Sawyer.

Jenna tensed and called out his name. "Sawyer!"

One final thrust and Sawyer spent himself inside her, buried deep, wrapped in her tightness.

When at last he could think again, he lowered her to her feet, grabbed the bar of soap and lathered her entire body, memorizing every curve and dimple, every edge and angle until he had her covered in suds. Then he swung her beneath the spray and rinsed her off.

"My turn." Jenna returned the favor, her fingers skimming over the muscles of his back and shoulders, down his chest and around to the curve of his bottom. When she came back around to his front, he was amazed at how quickly he'd recovered from their first round. "Let's take it into the bedroom."

"Better yet, let's take it into the hot tub." She helped rinse him off, running her hands all over his body, bumping him with a breast, tempting him with the brush of her hips. Finally she reached around him and shut off the water. "Ready?"

"More than you can imagine."

She glanced down and winked. "It doesn't take much of an imagination to see that." Then she was out of the shower and streaking naked across the suite to the hot tub in a secluded alcove on the deck outside.

When he slipped into the water beside her, he commented, "Your ex-fiancé was a complete idiot. But remind me to thank him."

"Thank him?" She moved to straddle his lap. "Why?"

"For leaving you at the altar so that I'd find you alone in Cancún. His loss was my gain." He captured her face in his hands and kissed her long and hard while he slid inside her, taking her for the second time that night.

After soaking in the hot tub for twenty minutes, they dried each other off and fell into the king-size bed, exhausted and satiated.

Jenna fell asleep curled beside him, her cheek resting on his shoulder, her hand lying on his chest.

Hell, he could get used to this. Way too easily. He lay for a long time holding her naked form against his body, for the first time in his life wishing he could be with a woman for more than a night. For a lot more than just a night.

After the upbringing he'd had with absentee parents who rarely spent time in each other's company, Sawyer had never considered himself good boyfriend or husband material. He hadn't had the best examples set for him. How was he supposed to be the man a woman needed?

And Jenna had said she wasn't in the market for a replacement fiancé. Burned once, she was less likely to fall into that trap again.

Still, Sawyer didn't want to let go of her.

He had drifted into a light sleep when his cell phone buzzed on the nightstand beside him. Careful not to wake Jenna, he checked the text message.

Come to the Bungalow. You need to see this video.

The message was from Duff, who was probably standing over Lance's shoulder in the bungalow near Sawyer's. And then came a second text.

Will position Montana for cover.

Sawyer replied, Roger.

Easing out of the bed, he dressed in his shorts and the New Orleans Saints jersey. He bent to press a kiss to Jenna's lips, his body tightening at that touch.

He hated leaving her. If they found something on the security video that could point them in the direction of his would-be assassin, he had to go. The sooner he put an end to the attempt to abduct or kill him, the sooner he could get on with his life.

Pulling the ball cap down low on his forehead, he pocketed the sunglasses but chose not to wear them unless he had to. In the dark, they would limit visibility. He took the back way out of the resort and jogged along the beach to his hotel complex, keeping a watch on all sides. He didn't want someone surprising him by running up behind him. Once he neared the path leading between a stand of palm trees and the bungalows he and his teammates had rented for their vacation, he slowed.

Something in the shadows moved.

Sawyer dived for the sandy soil, rolled and leaped to his feet, ready to rumble.

A low chuckle made him tense.

"You're getting slow, Sawyer." Montana stepped away from the trunk of a palm. "I did a recon of the path. All clear. You can proceed."

Sawyer brushed the sand off his body, shaking his head. "I'm supposed to be on vacation, not an operation."

"You do what you have to do to stay alive, on vacation or not. We kind of like you on the team." Montana clapped a hand on his shoulder and nodded toward the bungalow. "Go. Lance has something he wants you to see."

Sawyer didn't argue. Trusting his teammate to have his six, he went straight to Lance's bungalow and knocked. Within seconds, Duff yanked open the door. "About time. I thought you were coming straight back after you got Jenna's fingerprints."

"I was distracted."

Duff snorted. "Women can be pretty distracting. I tell you, I'd rather be with Natalie than a bunch of guys staring at a video monitor. Let's get this done so we can actually have a shot at a real vacation."

"You're not going to get any arguments out of me." Sawyer stepped behind Lance. "Thanks for taking on this assignment."

Lance shot a look over his shoulder at Sawyer and returned his attention to the screen. "Not only did the boss give me permission, he also assigned me to you until you don't need my services." The man shrugged. "I can't complain too much. I'm in Cancún. Every once in a while, I step outside and actually see the sun and the beach. I might even get a chance to put my feet in the water when we solve this case."

Sawyer patted Lance's shoulder. "We'll try to make it as short and painless an assignment as we can."

"I'm counting on it." He pointed to the screen. "It took some finagling, but I was able to hack into the resort's security system. Based on what you told us about when she took the wrong case, I was able to get several shots of the lobby right around the time Jenna took the case. Now watch."

He pointed to the screen. "This is the lobby. There's Jenna, and she's heading for the concierge."

Sawyer's chest tightened. Seeing her on the screen made him wish he'd brought her with him rather than leave her lying naked in the bed in her suite. Alone. Potentially vulnerable.

"There's the case standing beside the concierge's stand." Lance tapped the screen.

Sawyer could make out the shape and size of the case. But no one stood close enough to indicate who the case belonged to. "Why is this a big deal? You're not showing me anything different than what Jenna told me."

"We started at this point and then backed up." Lance set the video in rewind, backing up slowly enough that they could make out all the people coming and going in the lobby in reverse motion. For several seconds, the case remained static, apparently left long before Jenna had arrived to claim it mistakenly.

Then a figure moved in front of the concierge, and the case disappeared.

"Wait." Sawyer leaned closer. "Run it forward."

"Hold on. We're working on the resort server, and it can be slow." Lance played the video in forward slow motion. A man walked into the lobby, carrying a case. *The* case. He set it down by the concierge, straightened, glanced around and left through a side door.

"Can you get a clear image of his face?" Sawyer asked.

Lance nodded. "Already did. We're running facial-recognition software on him." Lance switched to a different screen, where an image of the man who'd dropped the case was being compared to a database of potential suspects, flipping through one after another so fast Sawyer could barely keep up.

"What about after Jenna picked up the case? Did anyone else go by the concierge's desk looking for a case?"

"There were several people in the minutes following Jenna's arrival and departure on the scene," Lance said. He switched back to the video from the resort, fast-forwarded to Jenna taking the case and then set the footage in slow motion.

A man wearing jeans and a T-shirt strode across the lobby and stopped at the concierge desk. No one manned the desk. The man looked behind the desk, walked around it, shook his head and left.

A woman in a broad-brimmed hat approached the counter. She set her purse on the counter and dug into it for a moment. The concierge never appeared. The woman found what looked like a powder compact, opened it, applied fresh lipstick, returned her compact and lipstick to her purse and then moved on.

"Can you get a clear shot of the woman's face?" Sawyer asked.

Lance shook his head. "No. All I could get was her chin."

A man dragged a large suitcase up to the concierge's desk and tapped his fingers on the wood. When the concierge finally appeared, he took the case, handed the man a ticket and stowed the case in the room behind him.

"I skimmed through the next hour of footage but didn't find anything else unusual," Lance said.

The image of the hotel lobby blinked out, and an error message displayed on the screen.

"Did you just click off?" Sawyer asked, even though he hadn't seen Lance touch the mouse or keyboard when the screen disappeared.

Lance frowned. "No." He tried to bring up the resort's security system again. "I can't seem to get into the system. Let me try another route." Lance's fingers flew across the keyboard. "There. I've hacked into the registration system. Damn." He clicked a few more keys.

"What?" Sawyer leaned closer to the monitor.

Lance's frown deepened. "I'm getting a message that the fire alarm has gone off. The resort employees are to evacuate the main hotel building."

Sawyer straightened, his chest tightening. "Do you suppose whoever is looking for that case could have hacked into the security system and seen the same footage we did?"

Lance nodded. "It's possible. The system was a breeze to get into for even the clumsiest hacker."

Sawyer sprinted for the door.

"Where are you going?" Duff asked.

"If we saw Jenna pick up that case, the assassin could have seen her, as well. I've got to get to her."

"What if the assassin is using this as a way to lure you out?"

"I can't leave Jenna without protection."

Chapter Seven

Jenna was in the middle of a very sensuous dream with Sawyer when an alarm went off, yanking her out of his dream arms and into reality. She sat up and stared bleary-eyed at the empty pillow beside her. The alarm clock blinked a green 3:46 a.m. Jenna patted the alarm to shut it off, but it kept blaring. "Sawyer?" she called out.

When she was met with nothing but the piercing squall of the continuous alarm, she realized it was the fire alarm in the hallway. She leaped out of the bed and ran to the bathroom, just in case Sawyer was there and hadn't heard her call or the fire alarm's scream.

Sawyer wasn't there, and his clothes were gone.

The persistence of the alarm forced Jenna to take action. She pulled a sundress over her naked body, stepped into panties, slipped on a pair of sandals, grabbed her purse and headed for the door—all in a matter of seconds.

"Fire alarm! All guests must evacuate," a voice announced in the hallway.

Jenna yanked open the door.

Before she could take a step out, someone dressed completely in black came at her, hunched over like a linebacker. He plowed into her belly and lifted her off her feet, carrying her back into the room.

She screamed, but the door to her room closed, her cry for help drowned out by the fire alarm.

The man threw her on the bed.

Her heart racing, Jenna rolled over to the other side, dropping her feet to the floor.

The man in black ran around the end of the bed and grabbed for her.

Jenna somersaulted back across the mattress and hooked her hands in the comforter.

When the man launched himself across the bed, she dragged the comforter over his head and twisted it, wrapping him in the fabric. Then she ran for the door and yanked it open.

Footsteps pounded after her.

Unable to slam the door behind her, she ran as fast as she could, pushing through the exit door leading into the stairwell. Running downward, she took two steps at a time, braced her hands on the railing and vaulted at the turn, landing four steps lower.

From the tenth floor, she ran down the ninth, then the eighth. Other guests flowed into the stairwell. She pushed past them and kept running. When she reached the sixth floor, she ran into Becca, who was working her way up the stairs. She stopped in front of Jenna, forcing her to come to a halt.

Jenna shot a glance up the stairs, her heart pounding and her breathing coming in ragged gasps.

Becca gripped her arm. "Jenna? What's wrong?"

"Someone attacked me."

"Where?" Becca looked over Jenna's shoulder. Guests dressed in bathrobes and pajamas marched down the stairs, wide-eyed and worried.

"In my room."

"Let's get you out of here." Becca cast another glance

up the stairs and then turned. She put an arm around Jenna and hurried her down to the ground floor and out the back of the resort near the pool.

People milled around the grounds, clutching each other and staring at the hotel, searching for the smoke expected with a fire.

"I need to report the assault," Jenna said, looking around for the hotel security staff, a Cancún police officer or anyone she could tell about the attack. Still shaking, she wondered if the man was actually walking among them, merging with the frightened guests leaving the building.

When they finally came to a stop near the outdoor bar, Becca gripped Jenna's arms. "Are you all right?"

Jenna rubbed her hands over her arms and shivered. "I think I am."

"What happened?"

"I don't know." She could barely believe she'd gotten away. "I opened the door and someone rammed into me, then threw me on the bed."

"What did he look like?"

Jenna flung out her hands. "I don't know. He was wearing all black and a black ski mask."

"Did he say what he wanted?"

"No, he just tried to grab me and I...I...got away." Her body trembled in the aftermath of her near miss. If she hadn't been able to slip away, what would have happened?

Her breath caught in her throat, and her heart skittered to a stop. The assassin. He had to be looking for his missing weapon.

"Jenna?" Becca's eyes narrowed. "Are you sure he didn't say anything?"

"He didn't say anything." Jenna had to get to Sawyer and warn him that the assassin had found her in his attempt to locate his missing weapon. He'd known who she was and where to find her. "I have to go."

"Where?" Becca asked.

"Jenna!" A deep male voice called out from the far side of the crowd gathered around the pool.

Jenna stood on her toes, trying to see over the throng. A tall man, towering over many of the others, emerged from the darkness. "Jenna!"

"Sawyer?" she cried out and ran toward him.

He held open his arms and engulfed her in his embrace. "Whoa, sweetheart, what happened?" He held her close, brushing the hair from her face.

She pressed her mouth to his ear. "We have to leave here. Now."

"Let's go." He curled her into his arm, shielding her body with his, and moved toward the beach.

"Jenna?" Becca called out.

Jenna stopped, feeling guilty for abandoning her new friend without explanation. "I have to go. Thank you for getting me out of there."

"Where are you going? I'm sure someone probably pulled the fire alarm as a prank, but we can report your attacker to the police when they get here."

"I can't stay. I have to go."

Becca nodded. "I understand. Do be careful." She stared past Jenna to Sawyer. "She's had quite a shock."

"I'll take care of her," he promised.

His words warmed her insides, which still trembled from her encounter.

When they escaped the crowd milling around the pool, Sawyer asked, "What happened?"

She told him about the man in the black clothes and mask. "It had to be the guy after the case. But how did he find me?"

Sawyer didn't answer. Instead, he took her hand. "Can you jog?"

"Yes. I work out at home."

"Then come on. We need to get out of the open." He set off at a fairly easy pace, running along the shore near the waves washing up on the harder-packed sand.

They passed one resort, and as they approached the next, two men stepped out of the shadows of a palm tree.

Jenna dug her feet into the sand and backed away, pulling at Sawyer's hand.

He stopped.

"Sawyer," one man said. "It's me, Montana."

"And Duff," the other man said. "Glad you found her before the gunman did."

Jenna shot a glance up at Sawyer, his face visible in the starlight. "You knew he'd come?"

He nodded. "Just a few minutes ago. It's why I came back. We were able to review the security-camera footage from the lobby and saw when you retrieved the case."

"And who came looking for it?"

"That wasn't as clear." Sawyer led her onto a path connecting pretty little bungalows. "The point is, if we could hack into the security system and see the footage…so could the gunman looking for his case."

Jenna's heart dropped into her belly like a heavy weight, and she swayed. If not for Sawyer's arm around her waist, she might have fallen to her knees.

As the moved down the path, another figure appeared out of the shadows, this one with a more feminine shape.

Duff stepped up to the woman and bent to kiss her lips. "I take it the path is clear?"

"For now." She glanced across at Jenna. "This must be Jenna."

Sawyer nodded, leading Jenna through the other three. "Let's get inside, and then we can do the introductions."

They stopped in front of one of the bungalows, and Sawyer knocked. Montana, the woman and Duff stood close behind them, shielding Sawyer's and Jenna's bodies from any potential threat.

The door opened, and a man waved them in. Once they were all inside, he closed the door and turned to take his seat at a desk.

"Jenna, this is Lance," Sawyer said, pointing to the man who'd opened the door.

"Hey." Lance didn't glance up from the two monitors.

"Are you a SEAL, as well?" Jenna asked.

The man snorted. "Not hardly. I work much harder than they do."

Sawyer nodded to his teammate's girlfriend. "Natalie and Lance are special agents."

"What kind of special agents?" Jenna asked. "FBI, CIA, Interpol?"

Natalie chuckled. "None of the above. We work with a top secret agency. That's all I can tell you."

"Or she has to kill you," Lance quipped.

Jenna stared from Lance back to Natalie.

Natalie glared at Lance. "Don't listen to him. He's just grouchy because he's been here four days and has yet to set foot in the water."

"Yeah. While you guys are having all the fun, I'm stuck in my geek cave, doing all the real work." He touched his mouse, and one of the screens lit up. It displayed a somewhat blurry image of a Hispanic man. From what Jenna could tell, he was standing in the lobby of a hotel.

She peered closer. *Her* hotel.

Lance pointed at the screen on the left. "This is the man who left the case with the concierge."

"Is he the gunman?" Jenna asked.

"We don't think so," Sawyer replied.

Lance chimed in, "We think he left the case for the gunman, who would have picked it up if you hadn't snagged it first." He shot a smile at her. "By the way, great job warning Sawyer."

"Yeah," Montana added. "I got to thinking, went back to the rental company and found something that looked suspiciously like a bullet hole in the rear of the WaveRunner you two sped off on."

Sawyer raised his eyebrows at Montana. "When did you do that?"

"While you were out earlier." Montana's glance shifted to Jenna and back. "I haven't had a chance to tell you."

Her throat constricting, Jenna swallowed hard. "Are you sure it was a bullet hole?"

Montana's lips twisted. "I'm sure. When it got nailed into the back of that WaveRunner? I don't know the answer to that. I wasn't looking for bullet holes when we rented it."

Sawyer's fists clenched, his face hardening. He reached for Jenna's hand and pulled her close. "Damn it, Jenna. You should have turned that case over to the police instead of coming after me."

She leaned into Sawyer's hard body, his strength helping her deal with the fact that she could have taken the bullet if the shooter aimed a little higher or they hadn't gotten out to sea fast enough. "It doesn't matter now."

"It sure as hell does. You were attacked tonight. Whoever is after me has now come after you."

"He might have come looking for you and found me instead."

Sawyer gripped her arms. "He attacked you."

"If you two could pay attention for a moment…" Lance

clicked the mouse and the other screen blinked to life, displaying several images of what appeared to be the same man from the hotel in various other places. "I found these on the CIA's database. This man is one the CIA and DEA have been watching. Jorge Ramirez."

"Why?" Sawyer moved closer, staring hard at the man on the screen, memorizing his features. If Ramirez had anything to do with the attack on Jenna, Sawyer would find him and take him out of everyone's misery.

"He works for Carmelo Devita, the same drug runner who had a hand in the human trafficking case we just busted wide-open."

"But Devita wasn't the orchestrator of that operation," Duff said. "He was only hired help to get the job done."

"Question is, who hired Devita this time, and how do we find him? If we can get to Devita, we can figure out who's gunning for me," Sawyer said.

Natalie tapped her chin and narrowed her eyes. "Our boss has other connections here in the Cancún area."

Sawyer's lips curled up at the corners. "I'm not surprised." He raised his hand to Natalie. "Don't worry. I'm not looking that gift horse in the mouth."

Natalie grinned. "Good, because I don't even know half his contacts. He has them all over the world."

Jenna stared at Natalie. "Is your boss on our side? Or is he also involved in criminal activities?"

Her grin disappeared. "Royce is one of the best human beings you'll ever meet. Whatever he does, he does for the good of the people of our country."

Jenna raised her hands. "Okay. I get it."

Natalie stared at Jenna a moment longer and then relaxed. "Sorry. We just got through a pretty hairy situation with a human trafficking operation. I'm a little punchy."

"Are you two through talking?" Lance asked. "The boss sent us an address where we might be able to find Ramirez."

Sawyer's eyes narrowed, and his hand tightened around Jenna's waist. "Good. I'm going."

"Me, too," Duff added.

"Count me in," Montana said. "And Quentin will want to get involved as well when he wraps up his date." The big SEAL shook his head. "Some guys have all the luck."

"I'm just glad my roommate was out with him when the guy attacked me," Jenna said.

"Speaking of which." Sawyer pulled out his smartphone and keyed some letters. "Just texting Quentin to keep your roommate occupied for the night and not let her go back to the room."

"Good. I wouldn't want her to run into the attacker. She hasn't been clued in on the case, the rifle, the attempt on Sawyer's life or my involvement in any of this." Jenna ran a hand through her hair. "Perhaps I should call her and fill her in on all of this. Quentin can probably take good care of her."

Sawyer glanced down at Jenna. "In the meantime, you can't go back to the suite."

"What a waste. I have the best suite in the entire hotel and I can't even use it." Jenna clapped her hands and rocked back on her heels. "So, what's next? Who are we going after, and what do we hope to gain from them?"

"We need to find Devita," Sawyer said. "And the way to find Devita is to follow Ramirez back to him."

"Are we going to wait for Quentin?" Duff asked.

Sawyer shook his head. "I think the three of us can handle this."

"Four," Jenna interjected.

"Quentin isn't coming with us," Sawyer said.

Jenna squared her shoulders and braced her feet slightly apart, preparing for battle. Then faced Sawyer. "*He's* not, but *I* am." Her heart fluttered. The mild-mannered, boring accountant had stood her ground.

"You're not trained for covert operations."

"Maybe not, but that's not the point." She propped a hand on her hip. "Where will I stay while you gentlemen are off interrogating thugs?"

"You can stay here," Lance offered.

"The gunman thinks I have the case with his rifle. And if he put the bullet in that WaveRunner, by now he knows I might be with Sawyer. He'll be looking for me, and what better place to look than near where Sawyer has a room?" She lifted her chin, daring them to argue.

Sawyer frowned. "You're not going. I'll get you another room."

"Where I'll be by myself, unprotected by you big, strong navy SEALs?" She stared up at him in challenge.

Montana coughed. "She has a point."

Sawyer's jaw hardened. "No, she doesn't. Members of the drug cartels are dangerous. They'd just as soon shoot you as look at you." He glared at Jenna. "You're not going."

She nodded. "Very well. I'll just do one of two things. I'll either go back to my hotel and sit in my room, where I might or might not be attacked again, or perhaps I'll hire a taxi, snoop around and ask my own questions about the cartel. That might get me killed, but I've already become a target anyway."

Duff's lips twitched. "She has a point."

"Damn it!" Sawyer grabbed the ball cap Jenna had loaned him and the mirrored sunglasses. "We're wasting time. Let's go."

"YOU'LL STAY IN the Jeep and keep out of sight while we go in to question Ramirez," Sawyer said, giving her his sternest frown. He still wasn't happy she'd ended up in the backseat of the vehicle with him.

"I want to be there when you question Ramirez."

"No."

"But—"

"We need someone to stay here and guard the car," Duff said. He pulled a nine-millimeter pistol from beneath the front seat. "Know how to use one of these?"

She swallowed, the muscles in her throat convulsing. "Uh. No. Not really."

Sawyer rolled his eyes and then grabbed the weapon from Duff. He pointed to the end of the barrel. "This is the business end of the pistol. Don't point it at anything you don't intend to shoot."

Her brows lowered. "I'm not a complete idiot," she muttered.

"Yeah. Well, I don't plan on being shot accidentally." He glared at Duff and released the magazine from the handle. "And you don't give a loaded weapon to someone who has never fired one before."

Duff grinned. "She's smart. I'm sure she could figure it out."

Sawyer slid the bolt back, cleared the weapon and handed it to Jenna. "If bad guys try to break into the Jeep while you're in here, aim this gun at them."

"Aren't you going to put the bullets back in it?"

"No." He stowed the magazine beneath the seat in front of him. "Just waving the gun will scare them enough to leave you alone."

"Nice of you to decide the best way to protect myself is with an empty weapon," she said, her frown deepening.

"And if I pull the pistol and the other guy has a bigger, badder one with actual bullets...then what?"

"We'll be back before then," he assured her, even though he didn't know how long it would take to find Ramirez and extract the information they needed. All they had was an address. If he was at that location, he might slip out the back before they could get close. If they had to chase him, that would put them even farther away from the Jeep and Jenna.

Sawyer touched Montana's shoulder. "Give her the keys."

"What?" Montana clutched the keys in his fist. "Why?"

"If she needs to get away in a hurry, she'd be better off driving out of the barrio and back to the resorts than going on foot." Sawyer shook his head. "Give her the damn keys."

Jenna's eyes narrowed. "I'm not leaving without you."

Sawyer gripped her shoulders. "You have to do whatever it takes to survive." He gave her a gentle shake. "Do you understand?"

"Yes." She took the keys from Montana. When the men climbed out of the vehicle, she rolled down the window. "Be careful," she whispered.

"Stay out of sight." Sawyer leaned into the Jeep, gripped the back of her head in his palm and kissed her hard on the lips. "Please." Then he left before he decided to stay with her when he had a man to find and question.

Montana had chosen what appeared to be a deserted back alley located two blocks from Ramirez's last known address. Since it was early in the morning, few people were out on the street.

Sawyer took point, followed by Duff and then Montana. They slipped between buildings and cut through alleys, making their way to the address.

"Ramirez's place should be on the next street." Sawyer slowed, eased up to the edge of the alley and peered around the corner of the building. The early-morning sun cast a deep, dark shadow over the alley where he stood, giving him good concealment until he stuck his head out.

People were beginning to stir, waking to a bright, sunshiny morning. With the image of Ramirez firmly in mind, Sawyer pulled his cap low and left the relative safety of the alley. He walked past the wall surrounding the house Royce had indicated was Ramirez's last known residence and ducked around the side.

When he was sure no one was looking, he braced his hands on the top of the adobe wall and pulled himself over, dropping to the hard-packed dirt on the other side. Fortunately, he'd landed on a side of the house with few windows. Crouching low, he eased along the base of the stucco home until he arrived at a window. The scent of grilled beef and tortillas drifted through the open window, making Sawyer's belly grumble, reminding him he hadn't eaten anything since the day before.

He swallowed hard, focusing on what he needed to accomplish. Rising up, he peered over the edge of the windowsill into the kitchen.

A petite Hispanic woman stood at the stove, flipping a tortilla. She called out over her shoulder in Spanish that the food was ready.

A man's voice came from deeper inside the house. From what Sawyer understood, he was telling her to wrap it. He'd take it with him.

The woman filled a tortilla with a scrambled egg and sausage mix, and then folded foil around it. She made two more just like the first and carried them into another room, out of Sawyer's sight.

Sawyer whispered into one of the headsets Lance had outfitted the team with. "I haven't laid eyes on the man of the house, but if it's Ramirez, he's coming out. Be ready."

"Roger," Duff responded. "Spotted an empty building two doors down. We can take him there."

Already on the move, Sawyer crept toward the front of the house, peering into the windows as he went, following the woman's footsteps until they halted and she said something in Spanish that Sawyer couldn't quite catch.

He edged up to the window closest to the front and peered over the ledge into the modest home. The woman handed a woven bag to a man with his back to the window.

Without kissing her or saying another word, he stuffed a pistol under his guayabera, grabbed the handles of the bag and turned toward the door.

Bingo.

The profile of the man matched the one Sawyer had seen in the resort's lobby video. They had their man.

Or rather…they'd located their quarry. They still had to extract him.

Sawyer dropped to his haunches. "It's him."

"Moving in," Montana said.

Ducking beneath the window, Sawyer eased toward the door.

Ramirez exited the house, crossed the small yard and opened the wooden gate.

As soon as the gate swung open, Sawyer rushed forward, silent on his feet, and slipped the gun from beneath Ramirez's shirt.

"Huh?" Ramirez glanced downward.

Sawyer took advantage of Ramirez's surprise by grabbing one of the man's arms and yanking it up the middle of his back. Then he shoved Ramirez out into the street and kicked the gate shut behind him.

The SEALs closed in.

Montana slapped a strip of duct tape over Ramirez's mouth.

With Sawyer still twisting the man's arm up the middle of his back and Duff holding him steady, they maneuvered him into the alley, shuffled to the back of the houses and guided him to the abandoned building. Duff used his knife to break through a lock and pushed the door open.

Once inside, Montana secured Ramirez's wrists by taping them together behind him.

Duff called out, "In here."

Sawyer and Montana shoved Ramirez ahead of them into an office with a table and two rickety wooden chairs.

Sawyer pushed Ramirez into one of the chairs, grabbed the duct tape over Ramirez's mouth and yanked it off with a layer of the man's skin.

Ramirez cried out and cursed in Spanish.

"Where is he?" Sawyer asked.

Their captive squeezed his eyes shut and ran his tongue across his raw lips. When he opened his eyes, his gaze shot daggers at Sawyer. "I should kill you myself," he said in English with a thick accent.

"Where's Devita?"

Ramirez sneered. "No one knows but Devita. You waste your time."

"Then we should just kill you." Sawyer pulled the gun he'd confiscated from Ramirez, cocked it and held it to Ramirez's head.

Montana touched Sawyer's arm. "Let me." He pulled his knife from the scabbard strapped to his calf, the tip razor-sharp. "I've always wanted to do this." He shoved the table in front of Ramirez and sat across from him. "Let me have one of his hands."

Using his knife, Duff sliced through the tape holding Ramirez's wrists together and brought his hands forward. Then he taped one of his wrists to the chair and the other to the tabletop, the fingers splayed out.

Sawyer almost laughed at the maniacal look in Montana's eyes. What Ramirez didn't know was that Montana was an expert with the knife. He'd perfected his skill on hunting trips with his friends in the Crazy Mountains of Montana. When the hunting day was done, they sat around the cabin entertaining each other with knife tricks.

Ramirez stared at the knife in Montana's hand. "What are you going to do?"

"I suggest you remain very still." Montana's hand shot out, and he planted the tip of the knife in the desk between Ramirez's thumb and forefinger.

Ramirez stiffened, his eyes widening.

"Better start talking." In lightning-fast movements, Montana stabbed the knife between Ramirez's fingers, over and over, alternating the pattern, never hitting the man's fingers.

Sawyer leaned close to Ramirez's ear. "When he gets tired, he starts to miss."

Ramirez's eyes grew wider, and sweat beaded on his forehead. "I don't know where Devita is. He sends his people to me."

Montana stabbed the knife so close to one of Ramirez's fingers, he nicked it, drawing blood.

Ramirez cried out. "I do not know!"

Montana went faster.

"Por favor!" Ramirez closed his eyes and sobbed. *"Por favor.* I do not know."

Sawyer touched Montana's shoulder, and the mountain

man slammed the knife into the table one last time, drawing another drop of blood from Ramirez. Then he stood, pulled the knife out of the table and wiped the blood on his pant leg.

Sawyer sat in the chair across from Ramirez. "Tell Devita I'm coming for answers, and he'd better have them. I won't be nearly as neat as my friend with his knife."

"I will tell him, but he will laugh." Ramirez's lip curled. "He has many people. You will not get close to him."

Sawyer stood, his eyes narrowed. Ramirez didn't know anything. He was useless to them. But he might lead them to Devita through his contacts. "Let him go."

Duff yanked the duct tape off the man's wrists, grabbed him by the back of his collar, jerked him to his feet and shoved him out the door, aiming him away from the road where they'd parked the Jeep. "Run."

Ramirez took off running and didn't slow down.

Sawyer turned in the opposite direction. "Let's get back to the Jeep." They'd been gone long enough. He wanted to see Jenna. His instincts were never wrong. They'd saved him in too many operations to count. And right then, they were screaming at him to save Jenna. She was in trouble.

As he sprinted back the way they'd come, he heard the sound of gunfire.

Chapter Eight

Jenna lay on the backseat, peeking out the window every few minutes, counting the seconds until the men returned. Though they'd parked the Jeep in the shade and it was early morning, the outside temperatures were heating up, and so was the interior of the Jeep.

Ten minutes passed and the guys hadn't returned. She stared at her watch as the minutes ticked away like molasses dripping in the wintertime. At the fifteen-minute mark, she bit her lip and dared to look out the window again.

When she popped up, dark eyes stared down at her, and a male voice yelled something in Spanish.

Damn. She's been spotted.

Before she could gather her wits and brandish the gun, three more men appeared, surrounding the Jeep, talking in rapid-fire Spanish. One of them raised a tire iron.

Jenna jerked her hand up and aimed the pistol at the man with the tire iron. "Stop or I'll shoot," she yelled.

The men laughed and pointed at the gun in her hand. They must have somehow known it was empty.

Jenna's heart sank and her pulse spiked as the man with the tire iron raised it high and slammed it into the passenger window, spewing glass all over the inside of the vehicle.

Jenna dived for the floorboard, where Sawyer had dropped the magazine full of bullets. Where was it?

The man poked the tire iron through the window and used it to clean out the jagged edges of the glass.

Covered in pieces of window glass, Jenna searched feverishly for the magazine, her fingers finally closing around the cool metal. She jammed it into the handle of the pistol and rolled to her back as one of the men reached inside and opened the door.

Jenna pointed at the man's leg and pulled the trigger.

The gun went off, jerking back in her hand.

The man in the door screamed, grabbed his leg and toppled backward, crashing to the ground. The other three men backed away, holding their hands in the air.

Jenna eased up on the seat and waved the gun at the man on the ground. "Take him and go," she said, her voice shaking almost as much as her hands.

Two of the men rushed forward, grabbed their friend under the arms and dragged him away.

Jenna didn't lower the gun until the men disappeared around the corner. Then she scrambled across the center console into the driver's seat, fumbled getting the key into the ignition, dropped it and had to fish it off the floor. When she finally had the key in the ignition, she twisted it. The Jeep lurched and died.

What the hell? She stared down at the shift on the floor and almost cried. She'd forgotten the vehicle was a standard shift, and she hadn't driven one since she was a freshman in high school and even then only in a flat, empty parking lot.

She glanced around for the men who'd broken the window. When she ascertained the coast was clear, she laid the gun on the seat and gripped the shift, scraping through her memory for how to drive without an automatic transmission.

Jenna placed both feet onto the pedals on the floor, remembering one was the brake, the other the clutch. With the clutch pressed to the floor, she twisted the key in the ignition, and the vehicle hummed to life.

"Oh, thank God." She shifted the gear into First and eased her foot off the clutch and onto the gas. The Jeep jumped forward, rolling up on the curb and back down, jolting her insides.

If anyone reported the gunshot, it wouldn't be long before the Mexican police arrived. She had to leave with or without Sawyer, Montana and Duff. They were fully capable of finding a ride back to the resort, and Jenna didn't want them to be blamed for her shooting someone. If anyone was going to jail, it would be her.

Still, she didn't want to leave without knowing what had happened. The men could be in serious trouble. They could have run into more of Devita's men than they were prepared to fight off. Perhaps she could drive past Ramirez's house in case they needed a getaway car.

The engine built to a crescendo and Jenna slammed her foot to the clutch, shifted into second gear and popped the clutch loose. The Jeep jerked and trembled, threatened to die, then chugged into second. As she neared the intersection taking her out of the alley, three men skidded around the corner.

Jenna nearly cried with relief.

Sawyer was in the lead.

When she slammed her foot on the brake, the Jeep slid to a halt and the engine died.

Sawyer yanked open the door. "Scoot," he ordered.

Jenna crawled across the console into the passenger seat while Montana and Duff dived into the backseat.

Sawyer had the car in gear and moving before the doors closed.

Sirens wailed, the sound coming through the broken back window.

Without a word, Sawyer zigzagged through the narrow streets, angling away from the resort.

Jenna gripped the armrest, her body shaking, her breathing ragged.

When the sirens faded away, Sawyer turned back, taking the long way around, but eventually returning to the resort. Finally he turned toward Jenna. "Where's the gun?"

Her eyes widened. For a moment she couldn't remember. Then she became aware of the hard lump under her. She fished the nine-millimeter pistol from beneath her and held it out.

Sawyer pressed his hand against the side of the weapon, pointing it toward the front of the vehicle instead of his head. "Remind me to teach you how to use one of these."

"I shot him," she said.

"Who did you shoot?"

She jerked her head toward the broken window. "The man who broke the window. There were four of them, and waving an empty gun didn't impress them one bit." Jenna glared at Sawyer. "I could have been killed."

Sawyer reached out and took her hand. "You're right. I should have left the bullets in it."

Still frowning, she gripped his hand and held on until he had to free himself to shift into a lower gear at a traffic light.

Duff leaned forward. "Did you kill the guy?"

She shook her head. "I don't think so. I shot him in the leg. When his friends dragged him away, he was still conscious and cursing."

Montana chuckled. "I'd take her on my team anytime."

Sawyer shifted gears and pulled through the intersection, taking her hand again. "I'm sorry. Leaving you alone was a bad idea."

Jenna squeezed his hand. "I was the one who insisted on coming along. And besides, I survived." Now that she wasn't shaking, she could think straight. She'd managed to defend herself and survive. But it could have turned out so much worse. Perhaps Sawyer had been right. Maybe she should have stayed behind. "Did you question Ramirez?"

"We did."

"And? Did he tell you where to find Devita?"

Sawyer shook his head. "Not exactly."

Jenna stared at Sawyer's profile as he pulled into the resort parking lot. "What do you mean?"

Duff chuckled. "We planted a tracking device on him."

"Lance should be picking him up," Montana added. "Ideally, he'll take us right to Devita."

"Then why are we going back to the resort?"

Sawyer's lips pressed into a straight line. "To grab the handheld tracker and to drop you off with Lance. Going into Devita's compound will be a lot more dangerous than wading into the dark side of Cancún to catch Ramirez. And despite shooting a guy in the leg at point-blank range, you don't have the combat training or experience."

"But—"

Sawyer pulled to a halt between two other vehicles and faced her. "Jenna, you'll slow us down. Which puts my guys at risk."

Her gut clenched. God, she'd been selfish. Her lack of training and experience could cost the lives of these fine men. "I understand. But remember, the man who hired these people doesn't care whether you're brought in dead or alive."

"I've been in tougher situations." He gave her a gentle

smile. "Situations in which the people I went up against didn't have a choice. Kill me or be killed. At least with these people, I have a fifty-fifty chance." He winked.

She was sure he had been in tougher circumstances. But she hadn't known him then. Now that she did, she felt connected, as if she had a stake in his life. She wanted him around so that she could get to know him better. And if she wasn't careful, she might even fall in love with the SEAL.

Butterflies fluttered in her belly, and her cheeks heated. *Damn.* Now was not the time to fall for anyone. She was fresh from a colossal jilting, and Sawyer had one of the most dangerous jobs in the world.

Unfortunately, she feared it was already too late.

SAWYER WOULD WAIT for only a few minutes. Now that it was broad daylight, he didn't dare walk to the back of the resort where the bungalows were. He'd be a sitting duck for the hired gun waiting to polish him off.

Montana had texted Lance to meet them in the front parking lot. He should be there any moment.

The sandy-haired SOS agent emerged from the side of the hotel building and jogged across the pavement, searching for them, his head craning, swiveling right and left. When he spotted the Jeep between the other two vehicles, he made a beeline for them, carrying a large satchel.

As he reached the Jeep, Sawyer got out and stood in the V of the open driver's door.

No sooner had he left the vehicle than something plinked against the metal door.

"What—" Jenna cried out.

"Get down!" Duff yelled.

Sawyer ducked back into the vehicle.

Duff opened his door and slid to the middle of the seat. "Get in, Lance!"

Lance dived in, landing in a heap across Montana and Duff's laps.

Sawyer didn't wait for the back door to close. He ripped the shift into Reverse and slammed his foot on the accelerator. The Jeep shot out of the parking space and stayed in Reverse until they reached the road. More bullets pelted the exterior, several hit the windshield, blasting through the interior. Then Sawyer twisted the steering wheel around, spinning the vehicle in the road, and sped away from the resort high-rise.

"Do we have what we need?" Sawyer asked.

"If we don't, it's too bad." Lance righted himself and pulled the satchel off his shoulder. "You can't go back to the resort."

Sawyer snorted. "I sure as hell can't take you and Jenna to confront Devita."

"And we need Quentin in on this operation," Duff pointed out. "Anyone seen him lately?"

"After you left this morning, he and Jenna's roommate stopped by to see if they could help with anything. He told me to let you know that he and Carly will be at the marina, checking out all the boats, but ready for anything. All you have to do is say the word."

"Good. We need him now." Sawyer turned the Jeep toward the marina.

Duff called Quentin's cell phone number and barked, "We'll be there in five." When he ended the call, he said, "Quentin's ready."

Sawyer pulled into the marina and parked. His gaze slid over Jenna's chalk-white face. To the men in the back-seat he said, "This works out perfectly. While we follow Ramirez, Lance and the ladies should be fine on the boat."

"I'll have Natalie join them for additional protection."

Duff's lips curled. "She hasn't been too happy about being left out of all the action."

Montana laughed. "I would have thought she got all the action she wanted when she put herself out there to be sold into the sex trade."

Duff's lips thinned. "That was a close call. I truly believe she would have found a way out, even without our help. She's that kind of tough."

"Call her," Sawyer said. "I'd feel better knowing Lance has some help protecting Jenna and her friend."

"I can take care of myself." Jenna held up the nine-millimeter pistol, which wobbled in her hand.

"Hey." Sawyer grabbed for it and shoved the muzzle toward the front of the vehicle. "Watch where you're pointing that thing."

Jenna's cheeks suffused with color, making her even more adorable. Sawyer wanted to end this chase and kiss this woman who'd risked her life to save his.

Duff called Natalie and passed on the information she needed. "She'll be here in less than fifteen minutes. She's coming from the airport, after seeing her sister onto her flight back to the States." Duff shook his head, a grin spreading across his face. "She says she's up for some adventure."

Sawyer glanced at the look on Duff's face, envying him for having found a woman who was his equal, someone with whom he could potentially spend the rest of his life. And he'd found her in a matter of a couple of days in Cancún.

Frowning, Sawyer nodded to the rest. "Let's get to the boat and make a plan. We don't have much time. If Ramirez really doesn't know where to find Devita, we'll need to follow his contact. And that contact will not have a tracking device."

The men piled out of the Jeep.

Sawyer rounded the vehicle to open Jenna's door, but she'd already gotten down.

She touched his arm and stared up into his face. "You don't have to provide protection for me. I'm not the one they're after."

"But you were the one who took the case and you've already been attacked once. The gunman might come back, looking for the case and you."

"I have it hidden back at the resort," Lance said. "It's in the rafters of the bungalow. Unless someone is looking straight at it, they won't find the case."

"Good to know." Sawyer gave Lance half a smile. "That's one less gun aimed at my head." He caught Jenna's hand and led the way along the dock to the slip where the yacht was moored.

Jenna's eyes rounded, and she laughed. "This isn't a boat. It's a yacht. Is it yours?"

Quentin, Montana and Duff all laughed as one.

"We wish," Quentin said. He helped Carly into the boat and entered the glassed-in lounge area, his arm around her, all the way.

Sawyer didn't join in the humor. His father had a yacht he kept moored at the Capital Yacht Club in the DC area. His teammates didn't know that. Hell, only Duff knew Sawyer's father was US Senator Rand Houston, a self-made millionaire who'd clawed his way to a huge fortune in the oil and gas industry.

When Sawyer was growing up, his father never spent more than three days a month at home with his family. Vacations were interrupted or short-lived for the man. When he'd turned to politics, Sawyer had seen even less of his father. But by then, he didn't care. As soon as he'd graduated from college, he joined the navy and applied for the

SEALs, as different and far away from his father's life as he could get.

Of course, his father had been disappointed—no, he'd been livid at his son's choices. He'd planned on Sawyer taking over the business and following in his footsteps.

"What's wrong?" Jenna pulled Sawyer to a halt before following the others into the lounge.

Sawyer frowned. "Besides being the target of a mad gunman? I can't think of a thing. Why do you ask?"

"You frowned when everyone else laughed." She pulled her hand free. "I don't want to be a burden to you or your team. I should probably go. I can always see if Carly and I can catch an early flight home."

Sawyer hated that his thoughts regarding his father had turned his expression sour. He didn't like Jenna feeling as though he didn't want her there. "In the meantime, where would you go? And if the gunman thinks you and I are in any way connected, he might still come after you to get to me."

She ran her tongue across her bottom lip, making Sawyer all kinds of crazy. "I've put you in a bind, haven't I?"

He gripped her arms and stared down into her eyes. "You saved my life. The least I can do is make sure you're not in danger."

She laughed and pushed a strand of her hair behind her ear. "It gets complicated, doesn't it?" The hair refused to stay and fell in her face.

He brushed the lock of hair back, tucking it behind her ear again, his knuckles skimming her jaw as he drew his hand away. He ached with the need to kiss her.

"Okay, I've got him on the screen," Lance said from inside. "Sawyer, you want to see this?"

"Yeah." Sawyer cupped Jenna's cheek. "Whatever you might think, you're not a burden. And I'm really glad you hijacked my WaveRunner." He winked and pulled her into the lounge with him.

Lance had a laptop computer set out on a tabletop with a map of the city of Cancún displayed. In the center, a dot blinked bright green, moving along a boulevard to the east. Lance pointed at the dot. "That's Ramirez. He's still on the move."

"That's good news." Sawyer glanced at his fellow SEALs. "You ready to find Devita?"

"Hell, yeah!" Montana, Quentin and Duff all answered as one.

"You'll need these." Lance dug in his satchel and pulled out a handheld two-way radio, several headsets and a hand-held tracking device. "I can keep tabs on Ramirez from here and give you directions if the handheld device fails you. Find the weapons you need in the arsenal below and get out there before Ramirez stops."

While the men hurried below, Jenna moved to Lance's side. "Why do they have to catch up with Ramirez before he stops?"

"When he stops, most likely he'll be meeting with Devita's contact. We don't have a tracker on the contact, and he's the guy we'll need to lead us to Devita."

Jenna nodded.

Carly stepped beside Jenna. "Why didn't you tell me you were in trouble?"

Jenna snorted softly. "You were otherwise occupied. Besides, I'm not the one in trouble." She tilted her head toward the stairs leading down into the bowels of the yacht. "Sawyer's the one who is in trouble."

"Yeah, but Quentin tells me you found a sniper's rifle in that case you picked up by mistake in the lobby. The sniper could turn on you to collect that case." Carly slipped an arm around Jenna's waist. "Sweetie, when you said you wanted a more adventurous life, I thought zip-lining was pushing the envelope." She laughed. "This is above and beyond proving to your ex that you are nowhere near boring."

Jenna watched the stairs, waiting for the men to reappear. "I think we could all use a little boredom right now." Her heart flipped and fell to the pit of her belly when Quentin climbed the stairs carrying a small machine gun.

Montana followed with a similar weapon and a pistol. Duff was next with a rifle and a pistol.

Finally Sawyer appeared, dressed in jeans, a dark T-shirt and black tennis shoes. He held a rifle and a handgun. "Ready?" he asked the others.

"Let's do this," the men said in unison.

They loaded the larger weapons into a duffel bag and tucked the pistols into the waistbands of their trousers.

Sawyer stopped in front of Jenna. "Please, stay here until we get back."

She nodded, knowing now wasn't the time to argue. They might be about to confront the head of a dangerous drug cartel. Sawyer didn't need any distractions to keep him from his goal. If Devita was at the root of the kidnappings or this assassination attempt, Sawyer needed to know why.

Was Devita acting on his own, expecting to collect some ransom? Or was he being paid to take Sawyer out of commission by someone else?

Jenna wished with all her heart she could go with the men. Not knowing what was happening or if they would even return unharmed would kill her.

Before Sawyer turned to leave, she grabbed for his arm, leaned up on her toes and brushed his mouth in a brief but heartfelt kiss.

His arm came around her, and he crushed her body to

his, deepening the kiss, his mouth firm and insistent. Then he let go and was gone.

Jenna ran outside onto the deck as the SEALs marched across the dock and out to the damaged Jeep in the parking lot. When she could see them no more, she still stood staring at the empty street.

"Sweetie." Carly's arm circled her, and she pulled Jenna close. "You might as well come inside. The fewer people who see you, the less your chance of being discovered here."

Jenna allowed Carly to lead her into the luxurious lounge, where Lance remained glued to the laptop monitor, his hand on the two-way radio, the device held close to his mouth. "Turn left at the next street. It appears to be a shortcut."

Jenna paced, pausing several times to glance at the green blip on the screen.

Ten minutes after the men left, a tall, beautiful blond-haired woman came aboard the yacht.

Lance glanced her way and smiled. "Natalie. Glad you could make it." He tipped his head toward Jenna. "Jenna and Carly are friends of Sawyer and Quentin."

Natalie smiled and held out her hand to shake hands with Jenna and Carly. "Nice to meet you." Then she turned to Lance, her expression all business. "You want to fill me in on what's going on?"

In a few short minutes, Lance told Natalie what was happening with the SEALs.

She frowned. "Do they know what they're up against? Devita is one of the most notorious kingpins of the primary drug cartel in the Cancún area. He probably has an army of bodyguards surrounding him at all times. How in hell do they expect to reach him without getting themselves killed?"

Jenna's chest clenched. She'd had similar thoughts, having read all about Mexico's troubles with cartels running the country. She stepped up to Natalie. "There has to be another way to find out who is after Sawyer."

Natalie's lips firmed, and she glanced at Lance. "How involved is Royce in this investigation?"

"Very. He assigned me to help while he's checking his connections."

"Why Sawyer?"

Lance clicked on the touch pad, bringing up a blank screen. His fingers flew over the keypad and finally brought up an image of Sawyer Houston in his navy uniform, along with all his personal data. He zoomed in on his next of kin and pointed. "That would be my guess."

"What?" Jenna leaned over Lance's shoulder, squinting to see the small print on the monitor.

"His father is Rand Houston."

Jenna straightened. "Rand Houston? As in Senator Rand Houston?"

Natalie let out a low whistle. "A senator's son makes a lot of sense for a kidnapping and ransom. But why kill him?"

Lance shook his head. "Perhaps the good senator has some enemies who are trying to make a point."

"Does Royce know this?"

Lance shook his head. "He hasn't said anything to me about being the son of a senator."

"Wow." Jenna ran a hand through her hair. "I wonder if the senator knows his son is being targeted."

"I don't think Sawyer has contact with his father. From what I can tell, his teammates don't know he's Senator Houston's son. He doesn't advertise the fact that he was born with a silver spoon in his mouth."

Jenna would never have guessed. Sawyer seemed to be

an equal among the members of his team, not better than anyone and willing to put his life on the line for them.

Her heart swelled at that kind of commitment. To have friends willing to do anything for you… What a concept. Unlike her former friend who'd been having an affair with her fiancé behind her back while helping her plan a wedding that would never be.

"Wow," Carly said. "Who'd have thought that when you jumped on the back of a WaveRunner, you'd be saving the life of a senator's son?"

Whether or not he was the son of a rich and highly influential politician didn't matter to Jenna. Who his father was didn't make Sawyer the man he was. Sawyer was who he was because he'd done it on his own. Nobody could buy his way onto one of the navy's elite SEAL teams.

Lance switched back to the tracking screen and lifted the two-way radio. "Where are you now?"

A blast of static was followed by the names of two streets at an intersection.

"You're two blocks from Ramirez and he has stopped. You better hurry if you're going to catch him. You have to be there to follow Devita's contact if he doesn't trust Ramirez."

"On it."

Jenna's heart thumped against her ribs and she held her breath, waiting to hear something. Anything that indicated the men had found the man they were looking for, and that they'd come out of it alive.

The thought of waiting for hours on the boat, not knowing if they lived or died, was unbearable. But where else would she go? At least here with Lance she might hear something sooner. So she stayed put and waited, her pulse pounding in her ears.

Chapter Nine

Sawyer muscled the steering wheel, taking the corners at breakneck speeds, sending the Jeep sliding sideways several times.

His teammates kept their comments to themselves, gripping the handles located above each door. Duff sat shotgun, the handheld tracking device in front of him. Quentin had responsibility for maintaining communications with the two-way radio in the backseat.

Static erupted from the radio, followed by Lance's tinny voice. "Turn left at the next corner."

Jamming his foot to the brake pedal, Sawyer skidded around the next corner, then hit the accelerator and straightened the vehicle.

Duff glanced up and barked, "Kid chasing a dog."

Once again, Sawyer slammed on his brakes, let the kid and dog pass, then hit the gas.

"Ramirez has stopped," Duff said.

"How far?" Sawyer demanded.

Duff glanced at the tracking device. "Two blocks, parallel to our position. Drop me at the next alley. I'll go on foot to spot the vehicle."

"I'll go. Montana, get ready to drive. Headsets on." Sawyer touched the on switch for the headset he had already embedded in his ear. As he came to an alley, he shifted the Jeep into Park, grabbed the tracking device and leaped out of the Jeep.

Montana was out and into the driver's seat before Sawyer entered the alley between run-down buildings and stucco walls.

The display not only indicated where Ramirez was but also gave Sawyer the location of the tracking device Sawyer held in his hand. He was quickly closing the distance between himself and Ramirez.

At the end of the alley, he glanced both ways before crossing a dingy, deserted street and entering another alley between older, derelict buildings covered in faded advertisements and graffiti. As he neared the street where Ramirez had stopped, he slowed and halted at the corner.

Crouching low, he eased forward to peer around the side of the building in the direction Ramirez had stopped.

A dark four-door sedan sat at the side of the street. Alone.

Sawyer studied the vehicle. The darkened windows gave no clue to how many men were inside. The steady blip on the screen reassured him Ramirez was one of them.

"What do you see?" Duff asked, his tone tight.

"One vehicle sitting. Nothing moving."

The squeal of tires on pavement alerted Sawyer. "Got company."

A large black SUV careened around the corner, coming fast.

Sawyer backed into the shadow of the building until the vehicle screeched to a stop behind the sedan.

Four heavily armed thugs climbed out of the SUV, aiming their weapons at the sedan. One shouted in Spanish for the occupants of the vehicle to get out.

Ramirez stepped out of the passenger door, his hands

held high, a pistol dangling from one finger. The driver slid out and straightened slowly, his eyes wide.

Ramirez spoke so fast, Sawyer couldn't make out all the words. He picked out mention of Devita, the word for *woman* and then the words for *son*, *senator* and *Houston*. In the heat of the day, a cold chill settled over his body.

After speaking sharply, the leader of the four men turned away, motioning to his men to follow.

Before they'd taken one step toward the SUV, a shot rang out. Ramirez's guayabera blossomed with a bright red splash of blood, and he fell to the ground.

What the hell?

Sawyer glanced down the street in the direction the bullet had to have come from.

The leader of the group dived for the SUV. His men followed suit. Once inside, he lowered a window, pointing his submachine gun everywhere he looked. When he turned toward the alley where Sawyer stood, his eyes narrowed, and he paused.

Sawyer froze, praying the bright sun in the street made the shadows where he stood dark enough to conceal him.

Ramirez's driver flung himself into his vehicle and burned a layer of rubber off his tires in an attempt to get away as quickly as possible.

"I heard a gunshot. What's happening?" Quentin asked.

Sawyer didn't respond, not willing to move his lips, whisper or even bat an eyelash until the men moved on.

The SUV jerked forward, raced to the end of the street and squealed around the corner.

"I'm all right," Sawyer finally responded. "Devita's contacts came and left. Someone shot Ramirez, but it wasn't Devita's contact. The contact is on the move, heading east."

"On our way," Quentin said. "Meet you one block east

of Ramirez's last position. And for Pete's sake, keep your head down!"

Sawyer remained in the shadows until the SUV sped away and turned left at the end of the street. As soon as the vehicle was out of sight, Sawyer sprang to his feet, backed down the street cut through an alley and arrived as the Jeep slid to a halt.

"Turn right." Sawyer jumped into the backseat and yelled, "Go! Go! Go!"

Before the door closed, Montana yanked the steering wheel to the right and hit the accelerator, shooting the Jeep forward. Sawyer nearly fell out during the turn and then slammed back against the seat, the door shutting automatically with the blast of forward motion. "Left at the end of the street." He leaned forward, peering between the seats at the road ahead.

"What happened back there?" Duff asked.

"Apparently, Ramirez was informing Devita's contact what had transpired. I didn't catch everything they said before the shooting started. *Devita*, *woman* and *Houston* were what I got out of it." He didn't mention he'd heard the words *son of a senator*. Sawyer wanted to check out that angle on his own before he brought it up to his teammates. "Someone fired a shot at Ramirez."

"Who?" Duff asked.

"Not Devita's contact or his men," Sawyer said. "They were just as surprised as I was."

Montana snorted. "Great. I'll bet it was your gunman." He whipped the steering wheel to the left at the corner the SUV had taken a minute before.

Sawyer's heart skipped several beats when he didn't see the SUV. "What the hell?"

"Had to have turned." Montana raced down the street, slowing at every crossroad.

"There!" Duff pointed to the right at one of the narrow streets they passed.

Montana slammed on the brakes, shoved the gear stick into Reverse, backed up, turned and hit the gas.

The SUV was three blocks ahead, turning left on another road, moving fast.

"Don't get too close. We can't spook them," Sawyer warned. "We need to find Devita."

"We won't get to Devita if we lose that SUV," Montana said, flooring the accelerator.

At the corner where the SUV had turned, Montana barely slowed as he entered an area with several large, abandoned warehouse buildings. They couldn't see around the corner until they turned and it was too late.

The SUV stood sideways in the middle of the narrow road, blocking it completely, the four men inside climbing out with their weapons held at the ready.

Montana slammed on the brakes, throwing Sawyer forward. He hit the back of the driver's seat, momentarily stunned. Then he dived for one of the loaded submachine guns on the floor. "Duck!" Sawyer yelled.

All four SEALs ducked in their seats as the cartel thugs opened fire on the Jeep. Bullets peppered the hood and blew through the windshield.

Montana shifted into Reverse and backed out of the street, unable to look behind him.

Sawyer prayed they didn't hit a building before they got out of range of the bullets pelting the front end of the Jeep. One must have hit the radiator, because steam spewed from beneath the hood.

Sawyer hit the button to lower the window. When it was down, he leaned out, pointing the submachine gun at Devita's men, letting loose a stream of bullets. They ran behind the relative safety of the SUV, buying the SEALs enough time for Montana to swerve backward around the corner and out of sight of the cartel thugs.

Montana whipped the Jeep around and sped away.

"What are you doing?" Sawyer turned to look behind him. "We need to follow them."

"This mission is over. They won't lead us to Devita now. If anything, they'd lead us to a bigger ambush than we just experienced," Duff reasoned.

"Besides, the Jeep might not last until we get back to the marina." Montana drove the Jeep full throttle to get them as far away from the SUV and Devita's men. "The water in the radiator is leaking fast. Either the engine will burn up or other damage will bring us to a halt before we get back."

Sawyer and Quentin kept a close eye on their rear in case the men from the SUV came after them. When they were certain they weren't being followed, they settled back in their seats.

"Everyone all right?" Sawyer asked.

"I'm good," Montana responded.

"Good here," Quentin said beside Sawyer.

"Duff?" Sawyer prompted.

For a moment he didn't respond. Finally he said through gritted teeth, "I'll be fine when we can get back and put a plug in the hole I have in my right arm."

Quentin handed Sawyer the radio equipment and leaned forward to check the wound. "The good news is that the bullet went clean through and lodged in the back of your seat." His lips twisted. "Lucky for me. Otherwise it would have hit me in the head. The bad news is, you're bleeding like a stuck pig."

Sawyer laid the radio in his lap and yanked his T-shirt over his head. "Here." He handed the shirt to Quentin, who used it to apply pressure to the wound and stem the flow of blood.

"We should get him to a hospital," Sawyer said.

"Hell, no," Duff muttered. "We'd have the Mexican police all over us in two seconds flat. We can't go to the hospital or the police. Not with a Jeep full of bullets and guns. And if Devita has control of the local government, we'd be playing right into their hands."

"Good point." Quentin grinned. "Guess you'll have to let one of *us* sew you up."

"It sure as hell won't be you," Duff mumbled.

Sawyer lifted the handheld radio to let Lance know they were coming in. "We have one wounded. See what you can find on the yacht that we can use to patch someone up."

WHEN JENNA HEARD the call come through on the radio, she recognized Sawyer's voice immediately and breathed in a deep lungful of air for the first time in the thirty minutes the men had been gone. When he mentioned someone had been injured, her chest pinched tight, and she was right back to being worried. Was it Sawyer? Had he called in and played it off like it was nothing? Or was it one of the teammates he cared so deeply about?

Natalie's lips pressed together as she responded. "Roger." When she turned to face Carly and Jenna, she stared hard at them. "Either of you good at first aid?"

Carly raised her hand. "I'm a nurse."

Natalie let go of a long breath. "Good. I'll get the first-aid kit."

"I'll get towels and cloths to clean the wound." Jenna scrambled down the stairs into the lower level of the yacht. She opened doors, locating what appeared to be a store-room for scuba gear and fishing equipment. A panel in one of the walls jutted out from the others. When she neared it, she realized it was a hidden door to another room. When she stepped inside, she gasped.

From floor to ceiling, the room was filled with weapons of all kinds. This must have been where the men found their machine guns, rifles and pistols. And there were more than any normal yacht owner could possibly use by himself for protection.

Who owned the yacht? And how were the SEALs connected to that owner? From what Jenna had gathered, Lance wasn't a SEAL or in the military. Neither was Natalie, but they knew what the equipment was and how to use it.

Jenna ran her hand over one of the rifles, caressing the long, sleek barrel. It was cool against her fingertips. What was it like to be in a shoot-out? Hell, was it even called a shoot-out? Was this the kind of life Sawyer led on a daily basis? One filled with danger, the possibility of being shot—or worse, coming home in a body bag?

She flinched away from the rifle and pressed her hand against her belly where her stomach knotted. What kind of life was it for the women who loved men who put their lives on the line every day?

If something ever developed between her and Sawyer, could she see herself sitting at home, waiting to hear if he was dead or alive? Then again, people died every day in automobile wrecks. Who was to say she wouldn't be the one to die first?

She left the arsenal and found a linen closet filled with sheets, towels and cloths. With her pulse pounding, Jenna grabbed a couple towels and washcloths, and then shot up the stairs and through the lounge as the four SEALs boarded the yacht. Her gaze went immediately to Sawyer, skimming his body for any sign of injury.

Natalie rushed toward Duff and slipped her hand around his waist, allowing him to drape his arm over her shoulder. "Figures you'd be the one to take a bullet." She shook her head, her lips held in a tight smile that didn't reach her eyes. "You're in luck today. We have a nurse on board."

"Oh, yeah?" He glanced around. "Where?"

"That would be me." Carly carried the first-aid kit to a table and pointed to a chair. "Sit."

"I don't know which is worse, getting shot or taking orders from bossy women." He winked and did as he was told.

Natalie held out her hand. "Knife."

Quentin and Montana pulled their knives out of the scabbards on their hips.

Rolling her eyes, Natalie selected the one closest to her and turned to Duff.

His eyes widened. "It's only a flesh wound."

Quentin backed him up. "The bullet went clean through."

Natalie chuckled. "Relax, I'm only going to cut away the shirt." She shook her head. "What did you think? That I was going to go all Clint Eastwood and dig the bullet out?"

Quentin, Duff and Montana all exchanged sheepish grins.

Natalie snagged the shirtsleeve with the tip of the knife and yanked it up, ripping the sleeve away from his arm and exposing the wound. Still holding the knife, she nodded toward Carly. "Your turn."

Carly eyed the knife and the woman. "You sure you're not going to use that knife on anything else?"

Natalie laughed. "Do I look like that much of a badass?"

Carly and Jenna nodded and answered as one. "Yes."

Duff glanced up at Natalie. "It wasn't just me." And he winked, reaching out to pat her bottom.

"I'll leave Carly to it, then." Natalie handed the knife to Quentin and walked away. "Silly men."

Jenna only half listened to the banter, her gaze following Sawyer as he paced the interior of the lounge. A deep frown creased his forehead, and he kept looking at Duff's injured arm. Finally he spun toward the stairs and descended to the lower level of the yacht.

Jenna hesitated at the top of the stairs before going down.

She located him by the harsh sound of his voice, talking fast and angry.

He'd gone into the storage room with the hidden arsenal, leaving the door slightly ajar.

"Get him on the phone now. Tell him it's an emergency. I don't care if he's with the president himself. Do it!" A few moments of silence stretched by.

Jenna decided to let him know she was there and had just reached for the door to open it wider when Sawyer spoke again.

"What the hell did you do?"

For a moment Jenna thought he was talking to her, but he had his back to her, his phone pressed to his ear, his body rigid.

"Don't even pretend to be ignorant. I'm on my damn vacation with a couple of my teammates in Cancún, and I'm getting shot at. When I chase down some of the drug cartel to find out who's responsible, I overhear them talking about Senator Houston's son. Ringing any bells yet? Did you get on the wrong side of a drug cartel in Mexico? Because if you did, you'd better let me know now. One of my guys took a bullet today. And an innocent woman is now being targeted, as well. If she or any of my men are seriously injured or killed, I swear I'll…"

Jenna's cheeks warmed at his mention of her. Guilt at eavesdropping forced her to take a step backward. She could wait to talk to Sawyer after he'd finished his call. Clearly, he'd gone below to complete the call in private.

She took another step backward, her heel catching on something. Jenna teetered and lost her balance, her arms flailing as she fell over a scuba tank, toppling it and the one beside it, making a loud metal clanging sound.

Sawyer threw open the door and glared down at her. To the person on the other end of the conversation, he said, "Great. Just what I wanted to hear. I'll be in touch once I nail the bastard trying to kill me. And mark my words, I'll get to the bottom of this."

Sawyer hit the end button, reached for her hand and pulled her off the floor and into his arms. "How much of that did you hear?"

Her cheeks burned. "Enough."

He hugged her close, holding her tightly against him, crushing the air out of her lungs. For a long moment he held her this way.

Jenna wrapped her arms around his waist and told herself she didn't need to breathe as badly as Sawyer apparently needed to be held.

When she thought she might have to remind him she needed air, he finally loosened his hold and lifted his head to stare down into her eyes. "Duff took a bullet for me." He ran a hand through his hair, standing it on end. "Hell, any one of us could have been killed today. I asked myself why anyone would target me. I'm just a SEAL." He snorted. "Just goes to prove you can't leave your past behind when your past refuses to go away."

"This has to do with you being the son of Senator Houston." She didn't pose it as a question.

"You knew?"

Jenna shook her head. "Not until a little while ago when Lance pulled you up on a screen and showed us who you really are."

Sawyer frowned. "It's a shame kids can't choose their

parents. I wanted to be known for who I am, not for who my father is. He wasn't even a good father or role model. What I've done, I've earned on my own."

Jenna nodded. "I can't imagine the navy SEALs cutting any candidate slack, no matter who their parents are."

"Damn right. Either you make it on your own or you wash out."

"And you made it on your own," she said softly, glad he was sharing with her. His fierce expression told her he needed to vent more tension.

"But my father's life is still haunting me. Devita's men mentioned the son of a senator. They had to be talking about me. Frankly it's the only explanation for why I've been targeted and no one else has."

Jenna frowned. "I can understand bringing you in alive. The cartel could stand to make a lot of money off your ransom. But to kill you?" Jenna tightened her arms around his waist and leaned her head against his chest. "Why would they kill someone who could be lucrative to them?"

"It's easier to kill someone than to bring him in alive. If they were offered money to kill me, why take the time to kidnap me and hold me for ransom? My father is known for his stance on terrorism. He doesn't negotiate with terrorists. I'm sure he wouldn't even consider paying a ransom for a son he never gave a damn about."

Jenna glanced up at him. "Your father has to love you. Surely he would offer the money they would demand."

Sawyer's jaw tightened. "You don't know my father. He never got to know his only son. He wasn't there for my birth, my first baseball game or my high school graduation. The only times he spoke to me were to point out my faults and tell me how disappointed he was that I chose to enter the navy. And he was even more disapproving of my decision to train to be a SEAL."

Jenna didn't know how to respond to Sawyer's description of his father. Her own had been there for her throughout her life. He'd been there to walk her down the aisle and had been the one to hustle her out of the church so she could avoid the embarrassment of facing all those people who'd come for her wedding. He was the rock in her life, and she loved him dearly.

"Come on." His lips twisted into a frown. "I have to break it to the team that I'm not who they thought I was."

"Don't be so hard on yourself. You're the man they know now."

He kissed the tip of her nose. "Thanks. We really have to get past this mess. You deserve a better time than being stuck fighting a battle you didn't start."

She gave him a lopsided smile. "What would I do with my time in Cancún? There's only so much sun a girl can absorb before she's completely sunburned and stuck inside, bored beyond redemption." Jenna squeezed his hand. "And the thing is, I'm not bored."

"Nor are you boring." Taking her hand in his, he led her up the stairs into the lounge. "Guys, I have something to say."

Duff pushed to his feet, his arm bandaged neatly. "You finally gonna tell everyone who the hell you are?"

Sawyer nodded.

Quentin and Montana looked on expectantly.

"You all might have heard of US Senator Rand Houston."

Montana nodded. "Sure. He's your father."

"Yeah," Quentin said. "But we never held it against you. You can handle an M4A1 like nobody's business."

Sawyer's fingers loosened on Jenna's hand. "You knew?"

Quentin shared a glance with Montana and then Duff.

"Sure. Every man on the team knows. So? What difference does it make?"

Jenna tried hard not to smile. She could feel Sawyer's relief in the way he held her hand. Her heart swelled for the love these men had for each other. What a great team to be a part of.

Sawyer pushed his shoulders back. "What difference it makes is that whoever is after me wants me because I'm the senator's son."

Chapter Ten

In the yacht's vault arsenal, Sawyer dismantled the submachine gun he'd used earlier, to clean it in preparation for the next operation. He found that working with his hands was therapeutic.

After a while, Duff entered with his hand pressed to the bandages on his arm. "You all right, buddy?"

"I'm fine." Sawyer ran a cloth over the barrel.

"I told you it was a flesh wound." Duff picked up the bolt and a soft cotton cloth and began rubbing oil into the metal.

Sawyer snorted. "I can't believe everyone knew who my father was and didn't let on."

Duff shrugged. "Wasn't important."

"Seems pretty important now. While you three should be enjoying a much-deserved vacation, you're getting shot at and chased by killers."

Duff smiled. "A typical day in the lives of us SEALs, wouldn't you say?" He handed the cleaned bolt back to Sawyer.

Sawyer inserted the bolt into the gun, fit the retainer pin and finished reassembling. When he had the weapon complete, he set it on the counter. "None of you should have to deal with my problems."

Duff's eyes narrowed. "Are you saying we aren't good enough to cover your six?"

"No, hell no. You're the best. But this isn't your mission."

"Like hell it's not. If one of us were targeted by a killer, you would have our backs. It's no different."

"But none of you are sons of a senator. Because I am, I bring an unnecessary element of risk to the team."

"And if I were to piss off a terrorist, and that terrorist decided he wanted revenge, you and the rest of the team wouldn't desert me because I was the only one targeted by the terrorist. You'd stand and fight with me." Again Duff shook his head. "You aren't alone in this. No matter what reason this killer has to place you in his crosshairs, you're one of us. We've got your back."

Sawyer faced his friend. This man had been through everything with him. From BUD/S training to multiple missions all over the world in some of the most dangerous, godforsaken situations.

Duff stuck out his hand. "We're in this together. Like it or not."

"Thanks." Sawyer grasped his forearm and pulled him into a quick hug.

"You two wanna join us up here?" Quentin called down the stairs.

Duff turned and led the way out of the arsenal and up to the lounge.

Sawyer followed, his heart swelling with the knowledge he had the best friends in the world. Friends who were the family he'd never had.

Everyone was gathered in the lounge.

Sawyer's gaze sought Jenna's. She returned his glance with a steady one of her own.

He took comfort in knowing she was there and safe.

Jenna and Carly stood on the periphery of the group gathered around Lance at his laptop. Sawyer joined them and leaned over the computer guru's shoulder to stare at the screen.

"My boss tapped into the CIA computers and found some information on Devita." Lance had a report pulled up and was skimming through it, the cursor moving along as he read. "Apparently Devita frequents a certain bar at one of the resort hotels, and he has a weakness for beautiful women."

"What bar?" Sawyer asked.

"It's at the Playa del Sol north of Cancún. He's a regular on Friday nights."

"What's today?" Sawyer asked. So much had happened, he'd lost track.

"Friday," Natalie supplied.

"Then let's go." Sawyer spun toward the door.

"Not so fast," Lance said. "This report says he takes a twenty-man contingent with him each time he goes. They check every man at the door and only allow women to enter unheeded."

"Sounds like you need me to get in," Natalie said.

Duff's brow dipped. "You aren't going in alone."

Jenna stepped forward. "I'll go."

"Me, too." Carly joined her friend. "What do we have to do?"

"All you would have to do is plant a tracking device on Devita," Lance said. "We can pinpoint his location without the ladies having to get any closer to the man."

"No way," Sawyer said.

"Agreed." Duff puffed out his chest. "The man has been known to deal in human trafficking. Three beautiful women might be too tempting a target for him to resist."

"It's a resort hotel," Jenna argued. "Surely they have

some security of their own to keep their guests safe from being kidnapped and sold into slavery. Otherwise, the trip reports would tag them as dangerous."

"Right," Carly added. "You heard Lance. All we have to do is get the tracking device into Devita's pocket. Then we can leave."

Irritated, Sawyer turned his attention back to Lance and the monitor. "Show me the map."

Lance brought up the map of the Yucatán Peninsula and pointed at the red dot that was the location of Playa del Sol.

Sawyer studied the image. "There's only one road in and out of that resort. They could easily set up a roadblock and take you ladies out."

"Then we go in by boat." Natalie pointed at the blue on the map. "It would probably be faster, anyway, and the shoreline provides a lot more room to maneuver should we be chased."

Sawyer glared at Jenna. "You've already done enough for me. I won't have you risking your life again."

She tilted her chin and smiled at him, making him want to grab and kiss her, despite her pigheadedness. "You don't have a choice. But I do. If I want to help, you can't stop me."

Sawyer turned to Natalie. "Don't take her."

Natalie patted Sawyer's cheek. "You can't give orders to us. We aren't in your military, sweetheart."

"Damn it!" Sawyer pounded his fist into his other palm. "Devita is a very dangerous man. Isn't anyone here at all concerned that Devita saw the same video we did and might recognize Jenna?"

Jenna nodded. "There is that possibility. I'll be sure to wear my hair and makeup differently so that I won't be as easily recognizable. Remember, Devita is also just a man who likes beautiful women." Her eyes narrowed. "Or are you saying I'm not beautiful and that I wouldn't have a chance to get close enough to plant a bug on him?"

Quentin laughed out loud. "Oh, Sawyer, your best bet is to walk away from that question. Any way you answer is going to get you in deeper than you already are."

Sawyer opened his mouth, thought about what Quentin said and snapped his mouth shut. He might as well argue with a rock. The women would not be dissuaded.

He took another tack. "Why don't we stage an assault on the bar while Devita is there? We could nab him and take him out without his men knowing."

Natalie shook her head. "He brings twenty men with him."

"We've had worse odds," Montana said.

"That twenty doesn't include the Mexican police and hotel security staff," Carly pointed out.

"Yeah, and why do it if you don't have to?" Jenna insisted.

"We'll be up against even more of his soldiers if we follow him back to his compound."

Natalie waved a hand. "You'd be up against his cartel minions. The Mexican government might be happy if you cleaned up a thorn in their side."

"Undoubtedly," Lance affirmed. "And staging an attack on his compound can be attributed to one of his rivals, whereas staging an attack on a public resort when there are so many other people besides Devita would be far too revealing to the public eye. You could cause an international incident."

Jenna touched Sawyer's arm. "Do you want to risk injuring innocent civilians at the Playa del Sol? What would your commander back home say if he found out, via the international news networks, that you have been conducting black ops?"

Montana chuckled. "She's good."

Cornered, Sawyer couldn't come up with another reasonable argument to deter the women from staging their own covert op. "I don't like it."

"You don't have to." Carly hooked her arm through Jenna's. "We'll be fine. We're just three reasonably attractive women, going for a night on the town at an upscale club. If we happen to attract the attention of a kingpin and drop a bug in his pocket...so be it." She winked at Quentin.

He laughed out loud. "I knew there was something I liked about you. You're not only a nurse but also a spy and a smart mouth? It's a killer combination." He took her hand and drew her into his arms. "I'd rather take you out dancing again than let you go out without me."

"There will be time." She leaned into him and faced the others. "Are we in?"

Outvoted and outmaneuvered, Sawyer was overrun.

"We need to get to our clothes back at the resort," Natalie noted.

"Quentin and I can take you," Duff offered.

"I'll go," Sawyer said.

"No, you need to stay here, out of range of the assassin, whom we have yet to identify."

"I don't give a damn about the assassin." Sawyer moved to follow the women to the door.

Duff stepped in front of him. "Two words. Collateral. Damage."

Sawyer stopped in his tracks, hating that Duff hit the nail on the head. He couldn't protect Jenna when it was his head that was being hunted. Whereas he trusted his own aim, he didn't trust a mercenary to hit him and not the woman standing beside him. "Fine. But let me know when you get there and when you leave."

"Roger." Duff hooked Natalie's elbow and ushered her toward the door. He paused, looking back at the men in the lounge. "Make sure we have what we need in the way of boats and weapons. The girls need us to be nearby in case all hell breaks loose."

"NICE," QUENTIN SAID as he entered before Carly and Jenna to check for intruders. Natalie brought up the rear carrying a gown she'd stopped to collect from her hotel on the way to Jenna's. "But this is the bridal suite." Quentin emerged from the bedroom, his brows raised. "Something you want to tell me?" And he winked.

"Not particularly." Jenna entered the suite and headed straight for the bedroom.

"It's a long story and we don't have time for it." Carly patted Quentin's face as she squeezed past him into the bedroom. "You can wait in the sitting area while we dress." She turned with her hand on the doorknob. "Help yourself to the champagne. Someone might as well enjoy it." Then she shut the door.

Jenna stood in the middle of the bedroom. Though it hadn't been long since she and Carly checked into the hotel, it felt like ages ago, and her entire life had been upended.

For a moment she wondered what would have happened if she'd never picked up that case in the lobby. Or if she'd decided to take a nap instead of going zip-lining with Carly that day. She might never have met Sawyer.

And Sawyer could very well be dead by now.

Jenna shivered.

"Are you going to get dressed?" Carly asked, her head in the closet.

"I was just thinking."

Carly emerged with two dresses. "About what?"

Jenna's lips quirked. "That zip-lining seems a breeze right now."

"Are you afraid of Devita?" Carly laid the dresses on the bed and crossed the room to her. "We don't have to do this."

Jenna shook her head. "I'm not letting Natalie go in there alone."

"I'm fine going in alone," Natalie said.

Jenna shook her head. "You need backup."

"Then stay here, and *I'll* go with her," Carly insisted.

"No way. I didn't bring you to Cancún with me to embroil you in a dangerous operation with drug cartel kingpins and assassination attempts."

"And you didn't come here to get yourself involved." Carly took her hands. "We can tell the guys we're out. That we don't want anything to do with this, and that they can walk away and leave us alone. We'll go back to being two women here on a relaxing vacation."

Jenna laughed out loud. "Do you hear yourself?"

"What?" Carly's brows furrowed.

"There is no going back to that relaxing vacation now. We're in this whether we like it or not." Jenna squeezed her friend's hands. "And the only way out of it is to find out who is after Sawyer and why, so we can nail the bastard and get on with our lives."

Carly's lips curled into a smile. "You like Sawyer, don't you?"

Jenna's cheeks heated. "I guess. I barely know him."

"I've only known Duff since I've been in Cancún," Natalie said, slipping her dress over her head. "And I can't imagine life without him now."

"So, Jenna, have you slept with Sawyer?" Carly asked.

Her face burning, Jenna glanced away.

"You have!" Carly whooped. "Good for you, Jenna.

Tyler didn't deserve you. He didn't take the time to get
to know the strong and incredibly interesting woman you
are."

"You're just saying that because you're my friend."

"No. I'm saying it because it's true." She hugged her and
set her at arm's length. "And you're beautiful."

Jenna raised her hand to her head. "I have crazy hair."

"I'd give my right arm for that curl and color."

"Keep your arm. You might need it tonight." Jenna
hugged her friend and stepped away. "Now, are we going
to plant a bug on Devita or not?" She marched to the bed
and lifted the sexy dress Carly insisted she buy as part of
celebrating her freedom trip to Cancún.

"That's what I'm talking about. You've got more chutz-
pah than any woman I know. Let's do this. I'd have given
my eyeteeth to see you jump on the back of Sawyer's
WaveRunner. That's kickass, if you ask me."

Jenna shrugged. "Anyone would have done the same."

"You're wrong. Most folks would have taken that information straight to the Mexican police," Natalie said. "And
they would have been too late."

Those had been Jenna's exact thoughts. And they were
sobering. The women needed to get the bug on Devita and
find out who had it in for Sawyer.

Fifteen minutes later, Jenna emerged from the bedroom
garbed in a forest-green dress that hugged her body from
her shoulders to her ankles. The neckline dropped almost
down to her belly button in front. The back dipped to the
lowest point in the small of her back without being considered indecent. The overall affect made her feel positively
sexy and shameless.

Because they would be arriving by boat, she knew her
hair would be a disaster if she left it down, so she'd pulled
it up into a chic French twist, anchoring it with enough

bobby pins to hold up against a typhoon-force wind. Carly helped her apply makeup to give her sexy, smoky eyes, emphasizing the deep green of her irises.

Shiny green emeralds sparkled at her throat and ears—a breakup gift to herself. On her feet she wore rhinestone-studded stilettos. She'd have to shed them to get on and off a boat, but to leave the hotel, she'd wear them like a champ, refusing to wobble.

A long, low wolf whistle sounded from near the windows. Quentin's face split in a wide grin. "Wow, Jenna. You look great."

Then Carly emerged wearing a shimmering golden dress that brought out the highlights in her bright cap of dark hair. Her dress emphasized the fullness of her breasts, her narrow waist and the sensuous swell of her hips.

Quentin issued another long, low whistle and held out his hands to Carly. "Wow."

"What?" She winked. "You talked my ear off all day and now you have nothing else to say but 'wow'?"

"You two are more beautiful than words can describe."

Carly tilted her head to the side. "That's better." She turned to Jenna. "Ready?"

Jenna's stomach quivered, on the verge of a full-scale panic attack.

Quentin waved a hand toward the door. "Sawyer called while you two were getting ready. They secured a couple of boats to take us to the Playa del Sol. I checked with Duff. He will pick us up out front. Everything is ready."

Just the mention of Sawyer strengthened Jenna's resolve. "Let's do this." She pushed her shoulders back and marched toward the door.

On the way down in the elevator, the door opened at the eighth floor and Becca Smith stepped in. Her eyes widened and swept Jenna, Natalie and Carly with an appreciative glance. "Wow, you three look amazing."

Jenna smiled. "Thank you. You look pretty great yourself."

Becca wore a long royal blue gown that hugged every curve to perfection, dipped to a deep V in the front and swooped low in the back. "Thank you. Are you going out?"

Jenna nodded.

The elevator stopped again and picked up two couples, all young and talking at once.

When they finally reached the lobby level, the couples piled out. Jenna stepped through after Becca. "Enjoy your evening," she said politely to the woman. Jenna's thoughts moved on to the task ahead.

Darkness had blanketed the Yucatán, the lights of the resort twinkling against the starlit sky. The ride to the marina took twenty minutes, the traffic slow as tourists hurried to make their dinner reservations at the many swanky restaurants and cafés.

Montana met them at the dock and led them to a different slip, where two small jet boats were moored. Sawyer straightened in the bow of one, his gaze going immediately to Jenna, his eyes widening. "Jenna?"

The shock and admiration shining from his eyes made Jenna even more confident in the choice of her dress.

He held out his hand. Instead of accepting it, she slipped out of her stilettoes first, then took his hand and stepped off the dock into the boat. A small wave tipped the craft slightly as she set her foot onto the deck, and she lost her balance.

Sawyer yanked her into his arms, crushing her against his chest, holding her until she was steady on her feet.

Unfortunately, being so close to him made her even

less stable. Her knees wobbled, her pulse pounded and she couldn't quite catch her breath.

"Sweet heaven, you're beautiful," he said against her ear, the warmth of his breath sending shivers across her skin.

"Are you two going to make room for the rest of us?" Carly asked from above.

Jenna reluctantly pushed away from Sawyer, settled on a seat near the rear of the boat and wrapped a scarf around her hair.

Carly joined her and squeezed her knee. "I think he likes you, too."

Jenna didn't respond, her heart still racing and her breaths coming in short, ragged gasps. The man made her crazy with desire, and she was going to a club to seduce another man. She almost laughed out loud at the insanity of the evening ahead.

Quentin would drive the boat with the women, pretending to be the hired boat taxi driver, while the other three SEALs would tag along in the other boat in case they ran into trouble.

If all went as planned, the women would find Devita, plant the bug and leave shortly after. How hard could that be?

Jenna prayed it was as simple as that but suspected it wouldn't go off nearly as smoothly.

The water shimmered like glass, the tide and waves calm, making the ride around to the Playa del Sol smooth and uneventful. Jenna turned in her seat several times, looking for the other boat. Their craft sported the required lights affixed to the front and rear to make them easy to spot on the water. The boat carrying the other SEALs had the lights removed, making them harder to see and even harder to follow.

As they neared the dock at the Playa del Sol, Quentin slowed the boat.

Natalie sighed. "I wish I had my .40 caliber Heckler & Koch strapped to my leg beneath this dress."

"Honey," Carly said, "I don't think you could get anything else under that dress without it being real obvious."

Natalie laughed. "Exactly why we're going in unarmed. Besides, if one of Devita's men found a gun on us, there's no telling what would happen. Tonight we're just three women out for a good time."

"Do you have the tracking chip?" Jenna asked.

Natalie patted her breast. "I have it tucked into a tiny pocket inside the bra of this dress."

"I want the name of your seamstress," Carly said. "Why is it we never have pockets to carry important things?"

"Seriously," Natalie agreed.

Quentin shook his head. "It's a whole new world, taking women into a covert op."

Jenna chuckled nervously, praying she wouldn't unravel before they completed their mission.

Quentin pulled the boat into a slip at the dock, climbed out and helped the women alight.

"Break a leg," he whispered to Jenna as he assisted her onto the dock. Laying on a thick Spanish accent, he pointed to the resort hotel and said, "Follow boardwalk to hotel. I wait here for you."

Swallowing a giggle, Jenna slipped into her heels and trailed behind Carly and Natalie as they made their way along the boardwalk to the lavish hotel on the sand.

She hoped like hell she didn't break a leg, when she might need it to make a quick escape.

At the door, two armed men stopped them and demanded to see identification.

Jenna pulled her passport from the clutch she'd brought

along and showed it to one of the men. He stared at the picture and then her and finally nodded, waving his pistol for her to pass.

One hurdle overcome, they entered the building soon to be occupied by a drug cartel kingpin and his small army of thugs.

Chapter Eleven

"This is a mistake." Sawyer sat behind the steering wheel of the boat, watching from their position a hundred yards from the beach as the ladies crossed the boardwalk to the Playa del Sol.

"Three women at a bar on a Friday night shouldn't raise any red flags with Devita," Montana said.

"Yeah, but they shouldn't have to be there," Duff said. "We should be laying a trap for Devita and capturing him, not letting the women risk their lives to bug the guy."

"Four against twenty," Montana reminded him. "And civilians."

Sawyer's lips pressed together and his jaw tightened as the women disappeared from sight. "I don't like being this far out. Shouldn't we put in and observe from somewhere closer? If they need us, we could be right there."

"That was my plan," Duff nodded toward the beach farther along the strand. "Now that they are in, we can land on the beach and sneak up on the hotel."

"Now you're talking."

"Just remember not to engage unless it's absolutely necessary," Montana reminded them. "If bullets start flying, we put everyone in that building in danger."

"Got it." Sawyer patted the nine-millimeter pistol tucked into the waistband of his jeans as he shifted into

Forward and sent the little boat toward the shore farther along the beach, using the tide to ground the craft. Fortunately the tide was on its way out. They wouldn't have to worry about the craft being carried away if they left it for an hour.

Sawyer stepped out of the boat onto the sand and spoke into his headset. "The eagles have landed."

"The birds are in the cage," Quentin replied, indicating the ladies had entered the hotel.

Sawyer crossed the beach, aiming for the dunes and scrub brush. Moving from bush to bush, he made his way to the trunk of a palm tree at the edge of the hotel property. As they neared the hotel, the men split up. Montana took the corner of the hotel near the beach. Duff took the other corner, away from the beach. Sawyer slipped farther around the front, hoping to track Devita's movements into the hotel.

Two men wearing hotel security guard uniforms stood at the entrance, pistols seated in their holsters at their waists.

"Got a rear exit on this end," Montana reported. "And one security guard at the southwest corner."

"Another guard on the southeast corner," Duff's voice whispered into Sawyer's headset. "Want me to take him out?"

"Not yet. And only if necessary. Remember, we don't want an international incident."

"Gotcha," Montana responded. "Holding until you give the word."

"Same," Duff agreed.

Sawyer hid behind a bougainvillea bush, beneath a plumeria tree, lush with a plethora of blooms, the scent almost overpowering. He could see the circular drive leading to the hotel entrance from his position. So far, he'd seen no sign of Devita or his twenty-man army. For all they knew, the man would choose to skip his Friday-night routine and stay home. In which case it would be a long night waiting for a man who might not show.

Sawyer couldn't get over how amazing Jenna looked in that killer dress. His gut roiled at the thought of her being exposed to animals like Devita and his men. If anything happened, Sawyer and his teammates would get in somehow and get the ladies out, or die trying.

Five large, dark SUVs pulled into the circular drive, and men piled out carrying submachine guns and rifles. Some wore suits and ties. Others wore dark pants, T-shirts and black bandanas over their heads. The suits, carrying the automatic weapons, entered the hotel, blowing past the security guards, who didn't bother to draw their guns. Guests scurried out the front of the hotel, shooting worried glances over their shoulders.

The men dressed in black clothing spread out around the building, taking positions along the sides, standing guard with their automatic weapons at the ready.

Sawyer remained still, a couple of feet away from one of Devita's men.

When two suits came back out of the building, the driver of the middle SUV got out and walked around to the rear of the vehicle. He opened the door and held it while a man Sawyer recognized as Carmelo Devita stepped out, followed by another man—the one who'd been talking to Ramirez when Ramirez was shot in the street.

Sawyer's fists clenched. He didn't dare say a word into the mic, not with Devita's men so close. All he could do now was watch and wait for Devita to leave and take the tracking device with him. Preferably leaving the women behind.

Just knowing the gunman who'd shot Ramirez point-blank was inside with Jenna, Carly and Natalie made Sawyer's insides bunch.

His instincts were telling him this operation was a very bad idea.

JENNA, CARLY AND Natalie wandered through the hotel, following the sound of music from the big-band era.

Once again, they were stopped at the entrance to the bar and asked to show their passports to one guard while the other walked around them, eyeing them from head to toe, probably searching for any bulges in their dresses indicating they were packing guns.

Jenna's pulse galloped as they passed the test and were allowed to enter the barroom.

"Bar or table?" Carly asked, leading the way.

"Bar," Natalie replied. "I could use a drink."

Jenna scanned the room, searching for a man fitting the images of Devita that Lance had shown them on the computer earlier. So far, only a handful of people were scattered around some of the tables. Two older couples were swing dancing to the music the band played. A young couple sat at a table holding hands and drinking frozen concoctions from tall glasses topped with little umbrellas.

Natalie leaned toward Jenna and smiled. "He's not here yet. What's your poison?"

Jenna would have preferred a light beer, but seeing as how they were at an upscale bar, she said, "A mango vodka martini."

Carly gave her preference, and Natalie placed the order.

While they waited for their drinks, Jenna eased onto one of the bar stools, letting the slit in her skirt fall open, exposing much of her long legs, like she'd seen a seductress do in a movie.

God, she was playing way out of her league. How was

she going to convince Devita she was just a woman looking for a good time when she was shaking in her stilettoes?

The bartender set their drinks on the bar and turned to
fill an order for one of the waitresses.

Natalie lifted a tumbler of what appeared to be whiskey
into the air. "To good friends."

Carly lifted her chocolate martini, and all three women
touched the rims of their glasses.

"To friends," Jenna said and drank a healthy swallow
of alcohol, hoping it would calm her nerves without dulling them.

Before she could set her glass on the counter, four men
entered the bar carrying guns and made a sweep of the entire room. Two of them stepped behind the bar and slipped
into the storeroom beyond.

The bartender continued to mix drinks, acting as though
the invasion was nothing out of the ordinary.

When the four men were satisfied, two left. The two
remaining arranged tables and chairs at the back of the
room to seat eight people.

A few minutes later, four guards entered with six men
walking between them. The man in the middle walked
with the air of someone who owned the place. Even in the
dim lighting, Jenna could make out the arrogant features
of Carmelo Devita, kingpin of the local drug cartel.

A shiver rippled down her spine. She turned toward
Carly and Natalie, away from Devita, but watched him
out of the corner of her eye.

"Let the party begin," she muttered beneath her breath
and lifted her glass again to take a sip of the martini.

Natalie nodded, acknowledging she'd seen Devita, as
well.

"So what is it you do, Jenna?" Natalie asked.

"I'm an accountant."

Natalie's lips turned up in a smile. "That's a tough job."

Jenna snorted softly. "I wouldn't say that. Actually, I'd say it's pretty boring."

"I used to have a desk job and worked near the nation's capital."

"What made you change careers?"

Natalie shrugged. "I got into my hobby and made a career out of it."

"What hobby?"

She lowered her voice and gave Jenna a crooked grin. "Marksmanship."

Carly lifted her glass to her lips and smiled. "Too bad we had to come in unarmed," she said, barely moving her mouth. She took a sip and set her glass on the bar.

Sitting sideways on the bar stool, Jenna could see the bartender quickly making a tray of drinks. A pretty, dark-haired, brown-eyed waitress stood at the counter, glancing nervously over her shoulder at the man and his henchmen sitting in the corner.

Finally the bartender nodded, and the waitress lifted the tray of drinks and hurried toward the drug lord.

After setting the drinks on the table, she lifted her empty tray and beat it back to the bar.

Devita lifted a tumbler of something that appeared to be whiskey to his lips and drank the entire glass in one gulp. Carefully setting the tumbler on the table, he scanned the room, his head turning as he observed every person, his gaze lingering on Jenna, Natalie and Carly.

Jenna's chest tightened. She couldn't let fear get the better of her. They were there to tag Devita with a tracking device. She lifted her martini glass and turned toward the dance floor, giving Devita the full impact of the ultralow back of her dress and the leg peeking out to the side of the slit. She drank another sip and set her glass on the bar.

She didn't know if he preferred blondes, brunettes or redheads. They had all three covered. He'd have his choice.

"Look out. Here comes our target," Natalie whispered, her head turned toward the dance floor but observing Devita in her peripheral vision.

"He's got his eye on Jenna," Carly said. "Pass the chip."

Natalie pretended to adjust the low-cut neckline of her dress, all the while slipping her fingers into the hidden pocket. She set the tiny disk on the bar and lifted her tumbler all in one smooth movement.

Out of the corner of her eye, Jenna could see Devita headed toward them, a man on each side, armed and wickedly dangerous.

Her heart thundering in her chest, Jenna reached for her martini, scooping up the disk before wrapping her fingers around the stem of her glass.

She smiled at the couples on the floor. "They're quite good," she remarked, though she couldn't have cared less about how well anyone in the room could dance.

A royal blue dress caught Jenna's attention, and she stared across the floor at Becca Smith sitting alone at a table at the far end of the barroom. What was she doing there alone? Before Jenna could comment, a hand touched her arm.

"Senorita, would you care to dance?" a heavily accented voice asked beside her.

Jenna turned toward Carmelo Devita, drug lord, human trafficker and killer, and shot him the best fake smile she could manage. "Me?" She touched her hand to her chest, the chip tucked beneath her thumb.

He nodded.

She batted her eyes and tried for shy when it was stark terror racing through her. "Oh, I don't know."

"Please," he said. "It would give me great pleasure, *mi armor.*"

Jenna glanced at the other two.

Natalie nodded. "I'll save your seat at the bar. Go. Have fun."

With a smile at the two women, Jenna laid her hand in Devita's and slipped down from the stool. "Thank you. I love to dance."

Devita's hand was warm and slightly damp from perspiration. He took her hand in his and placed the other at the small of her back, the damp, clammy feeling making Jenna want to shake him off and tell him to get lost. Instead, she tolerated his hand on her bare skin and walked out to the dance floor, the chip in the hand Devita wasn't holding. Her mind raced ahead to form a plan to get the disk from her fingers into one of his pockets without being too obvious and alerting him to the fact that he was being bugged.

The band changed music from a swing dance to a slow-moving waltz.

Devita swept her into his arms and whirled her onto the dance floor.

Jenna wasn't expecting a ruthless killer to be so adept at dancing. Careful not to drop the disk, she rested her left hand on his shoulder. This was going to be harder than she'd thought. She had to get her hand down to the pocket at his side to drop the disk into it. Or transfer the disk to her right hand and slip it into his left breast pocket. Since he held her right hand, that wasn't an option. She'd have to manage to slip the disk in when she dropped her hands after the dance.

Completely focused on the mechanics of getting the disk into his pocket, Jenna didn't realize Devita was asking her a question until he repeated it.

"Oh, I'm sorry. I must have been concentrating too hard

on the dance steps." She forced herself to smile up at him.
"What is it you were saying?"

"You are an American?"

"Yes, I am."

"In what state do you live?"

"Louisiana." She blinked and acted the young, ditzy
woman. "Surely you've heard of New Orleans?"

"*Sí*, senorita. I have heard of the city. You are a very
beautiful woman. Not many Mexican senoritas are blessed
with such vibrant hair."

She laughed, the sound breathy and tight. "My mother
had red hair."

"She must be a very beautiful woman to have a daughter such as you."

Her chest squeezed tight. Her mother had once been the
center of her universe. "Sadly, she passed away when I was
a young girl." What would she think about her daughter
playing the role of covert operative?

Devita slowed. "My apologies for mentioning her."

"Oh, it's all right." Jenna forced a smile. "It was a long
time ago."

He swung her away and back into his arms.

If he did it again, Jenna could aim her hand for his waist
instead of his shoulder. Then she could slip the disk into
his pocket and be done with the subterfuge. She, Carly
and Natalie could get up and walk out of the bar without
worrying about being attacked or caught in the act of bugging the boss.

Instead of twirling her outward, Devita pulled her close
against him. Though the man wore an expensive suit, tailor-
made to fit him, and an expensive cologne, his alcohol-laced
breath nearly knocked Jenna over. She fought not to gag and
remained pressed to his chest swaying to the music, when
they should have been waltzing around the room.

"Tell me, pretty lady. What is your name?" he asked, words stirring the loose hairs at the side of her neck, sending cold chills down her spine.

"I'm Jen...nette," she finished quickly, unwilling to use her real name, choosing instead to opt for a form of her name to keep it as close to the truth as possible to cover her faux pas. Damn. She'd almost given the man her real name.

He tipped his head. "Jennette. I am Carmelo." He said it with a flair, his tongue rolling the *r* so easily.

"Nice to meet you." Hell, would he never swing her out and back so that she could drop the disk?

The waltz ended before Devita could swing her out again, and his hands dropped to his sides. With a slight bow, he swept his hand out in the direction of the bar. "It has been a pleasure. I hope to dance with you again."

"Thank you." She let him guide her back to the table, wondering how she would be able to turn or bump into him. Devita walked beside her, his pockets out of reach. There was no way to move her hand closer without making it obvious she was putting her fingers into one.

As they neared the bar, Natalie slipped from the stool. "I'll just make a quick run to the bathroom. Will you watch my seat for me?" she asked. No sooner had she set her feet on the ground than she tripped and banged into Devita, who in turn lurched toward Jenna.

Jenna braced herself for impact, realizing Natalie was setting her up to be crashed into. Her fingers tightened around the disk, afraid she'd drop it if jolted too hard. As Devita stumbled forward, Jenna braced one hand on his chest. The other hand found his pocket and dropped the disk.

One of Devita's men lunged for Natalie, yanking her away from their boss. Another grabbed Devita's arm and helped him upright.

Jenna staggered back, her bottom connecting to the bar stool. She sat down hard. "Oh, my." She pressed her fingertips to her lips. "Are you all right?"

He nodded once, tugging on his suit jacket to straighten it.

Jenna turned to Natalie. "Are you okay?"

"I'm so sorry," she said, reaching out to touch Devita's shoulder. "That was clumsy of me." She glanced at the man who still held her arm in a tight grip. "Thank you for helping me."

Devita's eyes narrowed for a second at Natalie. Then he turned to Jenna, lifted her hand and pressed his lips to the backs of her knuckles. "Until we meet again." He executed an about-face and returned to his table.

His bodyguard released Natalie and followed.

Jenna and Carly both hooked Natalie's arms.

"We'll go with you to the bathroom," Carly said.

"I'm sure I need to powder my nose," Jenna added, ready to make a run for it. "Are you sure you're okay?"

Natalie giggled, a sound so silly coming from an expert marksman. "I must have had too much bourbon." Leaning heavily on Jenna and Carly, she pretended to be a little tipsy and let them help her out of the bar and presumably to the bathroom.

Once they cleared the door to the bar and the men guarding it, Natalie straightened and stepped out, heading for the back of the hotel that led to the boat dock.

Jenna fell in step with Natalie. "Time to go."

Chapter Twelve

Sawyer had been hunkered low in the bougainvillea bush for a good fifteen minutes when he spotted the three truckloads of armed men as they raced toward the hotel.

Devita's guards saw them, too, and rushed forward to meet them before they skidded to a stop in front of the Playa del Sol. Shouts sounded and Devita's men scattered into the darkness, taking up covered positions.

This new development wasn't good. With the women still inside with Devita and what appeared to be a contingent of Devita's rivals on top of them, things were about to go south real fast.

While Devita's men were tied up with approaching trouble, Sawyer saw his chance to fall back and find another way into the building without charging through the front door.

"Rival drug lord rolling up in front of the hotel," Sawyer said into his headset.

"Thought something was funny. The guards at the corners just ran inside an employee entrance," Duff reported.

The sound of gunfire erupted in front of the hotel.

"Can we get inside and find the women?" Sawyer asked.

"We can go in the way the guards did," Duff said.

"Duff and I are going in. Montana, we need you to secure the boat."

"On it," Montana replied.

"Quent?" Sawyer paused.

"Here," Quentin responded. "What's going on?"

"Be ready to bug out ASAP. Devita's rivals decided now would be a good time for gang warfare," Sawyer said. "Duff and I are going in for the ladies." He didn't wait for Quentin's response. Instead, he grabbed the door handle for the back entrance and tugged.

"Needs a key card," Duff noted.

"No, it needs to open." Sawyer pulled the gun from the waistband of his trousers, aimed at the lock and squeezed the trigger.

A single shot blew open the lock, and Sawyer yanked the door open. The corridor was empty. Carrying his nine-millimeter in front of him, his hand on the trigger, Sawyer ran toward the interior of the building, praying Jenna, Carly and Natalie were already on their way out.

Sprinting down the hallway, he slowed as he neared a junction. One of Devita's men barreled around the corner, glancing behind him as he ran.

Sawyer swung his arm, handgun and all, catching the guy in the throat with the barrel of the pistol, crushing his Adam's apple. The man dropped his gun and clutched at his throat, gasping for air.

Sawyer grabbed his arm, shoved him into a one of the conference rooms and dispatched him with a clean sweep of his knife, all in a matter of seconds.

Back in the corridor, he ran toward the end of the hotel where the bar was located, fear for the safety of the women foremost in his mind. The closer he came, the louder the shouts and screams from men and women desperate to get out of the way of the warring factions.

Once again, he came to a junction and slowed. A scream from around the corner made him pick up the pace. As he neared the corner, more sounds of gunfire made his blood run cold. Was he too late to get Jenna out?

"WHICH WAY?" CARLY ASKED.

"I think the bathroom is this way," Natalie said loudly enough the guards behind them could hear.

They headed across the lobby, toward the rear of the hotel.

Before they reached the back doors leading to the board-walk and their boat, the glass doors of the front entrance exploded, shards spraying inward, the sound of gunfire echoing off the high ceilings of the entryway.

"Run!" Natalie yelled and took off for the rear exit.

Jenna lifted her skirt and raced after her.

Men burst through the doors they were aiming for, wielding submachine guns, firing at Devita's men positioned in front of the bar.

Becca Smith appeared in front of Jenna and shouted, "This way!" She grabbed Jenna, Natalie and Carly and shoved them down a hallway, out of the melee of shouting men, screaming women and gunfire.

They ran to the end of the hallway, where another corridor intersected with it.

Carly looked in one direction. "Which way?"

Jenna checked out the other end of the corridor. "There. *Salida.* That means exit." She grabbed Carly's arm and dragged her toward the door. Natalie brought up the rear.

Jenna reached the door first and slammed her body into the lever to open it. The door swung out, and a man dressed all in black brandished a machine gun in their faces and shouted at them in Spanish.

Jenna threw herself to the floor and rolled to the side.

Natalie did the same.

Carly stood frozen.

Becca charged at the frightened woman, hitting her in the backs of the knees, sending her slamming to the hard tiled floor. Then Becca rolled behind a huge potted tree.

The man with the gun shifted his aim downward. Just as he pulled the trigger, he jerked backward, the bullets slamming into the ceiling, nothing but a gurgle coming from his slit throat.

The man fell to the side, and Sawyer waved to the women. "Let's go!"

Jenna, Carly and Natalie scrambled to their feet, kicked off their shoes and ran out the back door of the hotel, following Sawyer to the beach.

The popping sound of gunfire filled the air.

Jenna ran as fast as her bare feet could carry her through the sand, refusing to look behind her, afraid if she slowed, Devita's men would catch up.

Instead of running toward the dock, they ran toward a deserted part of the beach. When Jenna thought her lungs would explode, she spotted the boat Sawyer, Montana and Duff had used to follow them that evening.

Sawyer reached it first and started shoving it toward the water. The tide had gone out, leaving the boat stranded in the wet sand.

Natalie grabbed the side of the boat and helped shove it toward the water.

Carly and Jenna joined Natalie and Sawyer, pushing and shoving the boat toward the sea. It was too heavy and, with the tide so far out, they'd never get it into the water.

About the time Jenna had given up hope, Montana and Duff arrived and threw themselves into pushing the boat out into the surf. A wave rolled in and lifted the hull, giving them just enough help that they could get it out into water deep enough to float.

"Get in!" Sawyer grabbed Jenna and swung her over the side, depositing her in the boat. "Start the motor."

She landed on the floor of the boat, the wind momentarily knocked from her lungs.

Carly flew over the side and landed next to her, upside down, her feet in the air.

Jenna scrambled to her feet, dived for the driver's seat, fumbled for the key and twisted. The motor chugged to life.

Another wave lifted the boat. Duff slipped over the side and landed in the boat, grabbed Natalie's hand and dragged himself aboard. Sawyer and Montana hauled themselves over the side and into the boat.

"Wait." Jenna scanned the beach. "Where's Becca?"

"Who?" Sawyer asked.

"Becca. She helped us get out of the hotel."

"We can't wait," Sawyer said. "Go!"

A barrage of gunfire settled it for Jenna, and she shoved the throttle to the rear. The small boat backed away from the beach. "What about Quentin?"

"He should be out to sea by now. Just go," Sawyer called out. He stepped up behind her, bent over and rested his hand on hers over the steering wheel. Together, they spun the wheel around and shoved the throttle forward, taking the little boat far enough away from Playa del Sol to avoid stray bullets.

Or so they hoped.

"We've got a tail!" Natalie shouted.

They rose and fell in the waves as they pushed past the shore and out into the open water.

Bullets flew past them.

"They'll catch us at this rate," Duff said. "We have more people on board than they do. It's slowing us down."

"Would it help if I jumped?" Carly asked.

"No!" responded everyone on board.

The boat behind them slowly closed the distance between them. Starlight revealed the men aboard wielded automatic weapons.

"Everyone down!" Sawyer yelled, shoving Jenna to the floor. He hunkered low, but high enough to see over the dash to the ocean ahead. He twisted the steering wheel right, then left, zigzagging through the water. Bullets peppered the hull. Some slammed into the windshield, shattering the glass.

Sawyer tossed his gun to Jenna. "Know how to use one of these?" he asked.

She fumbled but caught it. "Not really."

"Then drive this boat."

She slipped in front of Sawyer and took the helm, her hand resting on the throttle, her insides quaking.

"They're coming in range," Sawyer shouted. "On my mark, I want you to shift the throttle all the way back to Neutral." He waited until the trailing boat was almost upon them. "Now!"

Jenna pulled the throttle back, bringing the boat to an abrupt stop in the water.

The craft behind them swerved, barely missing them. All the men aboard the other boat teetered, grabbing for purchase as the boat tipped precariously.

Sawyer, Montana and Natalie all aimed their weapons and fired at the other boat. Duff aimed for the motor and fired all of his bullets into the engine. Smoke billowed from the casing and rose into the night sky, fogging the stars.

Sawyer shifted into Forward and spun the little boat away, putting as much distance between them and Devita's men as possible.

Soon he noticed another boat's lights blinking in the night. "Get ready in case it's Devita," he warned the others.

"I'm out of ammo," Duff said.

"Me, too," Natalie added.

Montana released his magazine and reported, "Five rounds. We better make them count."

"I think I have ten left," Sawyer said, aiming his weapon at the other boat.

"Hey, don't shoot!" Quentin's voice sounded in Sawyer's ear through the headset. "We just barely got out with my skin still intact."

Sawyer drew in a deep breath and let it out. He turned to Jenna. "Want me to take the helm?"

"Yes!" Jenna gladly let Sawyer slide in front of her and she eased out but stood beside him, rocking with the waves, staring at the dark ink of the ocean before them. "Is your life always this insane?"

Sawyer slipped an arm around her waist and pulled her against him. "Sometimes even more so. Stick around. You're likely to find out just how crazy we are, too."

JENNA WAS HAPPY to get back to the marina and the luxurious yacht. Quentin and Montana had gone ahead and were waiting when the rest of the team arrived.

"What the hell happened back there?" Quentin asked.

Duff snorted and dropped onto one of the white leather sofas. "We had a little altercation with some of Devita's men. At least, I think they were Devita's. When their rivals showed up, it was difficult to tell who belonged to which cartel."

"I'm glad we all made it out safely." Natalie eased into Duff's lap and wrapped her arms around his neck.

Jenna envied Duff and Natalie's ease with each other. She was amazed they'd known each other for only about a week. The woman appeared unruffled by all that had happened, while Jenna's head was still spinning from being shot at and nearly killed. She glanced down at her beautiful dress, a little wrinkled and damp from their dash through the hotel and pushing the boat out into the water. She hoped the salt water didn't stain the fabric.

"The question is, did you tag Devita with the tracking device?"

Natalie grinned and stared across the room at Jenna. "Jenna caught his eye. Apparently Devita likes redheads."

Jenna's cheeks heated. "The man definitely likes red hair. And yes, I managed to drop the chip into his pocket thanks to some…uh—" her lips twitched "—fancy footwork by Natalie."

Natalie laughed. "She means I fake-tripped, slamming into Devita, shoving him up against Jenna so she could get her hand into his pocket and drop the bug."

Carly smiled. "They were amazing. And Jenna was as cool as a professional spy, dancing with the man. You should have seen her."

Sawyer stepped up behind Jenna and whispered, "I'd rather have been dancing with you." He rested his hands on her shoulders. "I never should have let you go tonight. It was far too dangerous."

She gave him a sideways glance. "And we did just fine."

"Damn right, you did." Lance sat at his laptop. "Devita is on the move. Ideally he's headed back to his compound. I'd like to get as much information as I can on the layout before you attempt an infiltration into the lion's den. I think I can tap into one of the CIA's satellites. It should be going over this area sometime in the next couple of hours."

"Let us know as soon as you get a clear image. The sooner we get to Devita, the sooner we resolve this nightmare," Sawyer said.

"In the meantime," Duff said, "we should conserve our

energy. We might be infiltrating Devita's compound tonight or tomorrow. Either way, we need sleep."

Natalie slipped off his lap and stood. "I think it's a safe bet to assume it might not be smart for us to return to the resort at this time."

"Even if it was safe, it's getting pretty late." Duff stared around at the people in the room. "This yacht can sleep all of us. I suggest you stake a claim on a room and rest up."

"I'll take the first watch tonight," Montana offered. "Lance might need help going through the images."

"Wake me in four hours," Quentin said. "I'll take the next watch."

"All of my things are back at the hotel," Jenna said. "I could call a cab."

"No, you're not exactly safe," Sawyer said. "We still don't know who the assassin is, but he knows who you are. You can't go back in the middle of the night."

"Each stateroom is equipped with a bathrobe, spare pajamas and toiletries," Quentin said. "And if you don't have everything you need in your room, the steward's cabin has a supply cabinet with everything from shampoo to spare razors."

Jenna shrugged. "Then I guess I'll call it a night." She headed down the stairs to the lower deck.

Footsteps made her turn to see who had followed her down.

Her heart skipped several beats when she realized Sawyer was right behind her.

"You can choose whichever room you like."

She pushed a door open to a stateroom with a full-size bed, the bright white sheets a stark contrast to the wood features stained a deep, rich mahogany. "Which one will you be in?" Jenna held her breath, wondering if he'd think she was coming on to him and half hoping he would. After all that had happened that day and evening, she didn't want to be alone. She wanted Sawyer beside her.

Hands descended on her shoulders and turned her around. "I'll be in the room you choose."

Her heart thumping hard against her ribs, Jenna cocked her brows and tilted her chin. "Is that so?"

Sawyer bent to brush his lips across hers. "Yes. I want to be with you."

Who was she kidding? She wanted to be with him as badly as he wanted to be with her. Jenna reached behind her and shoved the door closed. "This room will do." Rising up on her toes, she pressed her lips to his, wrapped her arms around his neck and pulled him close. She opened her mouth to him, meeting his tongue with hers, thirstily drinking in the essence of the man.

For a long moment, they shared a kiss that rocked Jenna's soul. The need to be closer drove her to drag his T-shirt over his head.

He pushed the straps of her dress over her shoulders and the garment dropped to her waist, exposing her bare breasts.

Jenna let her head drop back, allowing Sawyer to trail kisses down the long line of her throat, and lower, to capture a beaded nipple between his teeth.

A moan rose up her throat and escaped on a gasp as he sucked her breast into his mouth, pulling hard. Then he tongued the nipple, flicking the tip until a tug lower in her belly made her yearn for so much more.

Jenna reached behind her and loosened the zipper on the dress. The green fabric slipped past her hips and pooled at her bare feet. Where her rhinestone stilettoes were, she didn't know, nor did she care. She was naked, standing in front of a man who'd been a complete stranger only days before. Yet she'd never felt closer or more compelled to give herself to a man than she wanted to give herself to Sawyer. She backed away from him until her thighs bumped into the bed. "Make love to me," she whispered.

"No regrets in the morning?"

"The only regret I have now is that I didn't meet you sooner." As he closed the distance between them, her pulse sped and her breathing became more difficult, desire washing over her in a tidal wave of need.

Sawyer caught her face between his hands. "I'm no good at relationships."

Her chest tightened. She wanted more, but she'd take any time she could get from him. "I'm only asking for the night." Jenna ran her hands down his chest to the button on his jeans and flicked it open.

Sawyer kissed her, his hands sliding down her back to cup her bottom. He lifted her, settling her on the edge of the bed, nudging her knees apart with his thigh.

Gently Jenna tugged at his zipper, dragging it down. His shaft sprang free into her hand, and she caressed him, reveling in the smooth hardness.

"Keep that up and I won't be able to control myself."

"Who said I wanted you to?" Her lips curved and she tipped her head back, thrusting her chest forward. "Maybe I want you to lose control."

Sawyer dragged in a deep breath. He stepped back enough to kick off his shoes and shove his jeans down his legs. Stepping out of the denim, he stood in front of her, naked, his body a testament to his dedication to being physically fit, capable of performing the hardest job on the planet.

Jenna scooted back on the bed, making room for the big SEAL.

Sawyer crawled up between her legs and leaned over her. "I don't suppose you thought about protection?"

She shook her head, a chuckle rising up her throat. "No, I really wasn't thinking much at all."

"This place is pretty well equipped. You don't suppose…" Sawyer leaned over her to reach into the nightstand anchored to the floor.

While Sawyer rummaged in the drawer, Jenna ran her hands over the hard planes of his body, loving how solid he was in every way.

"Ha!" He held up an accordion of foil packets and grinned. "I don't know who owns this boat, but he's obviously prepared for everything."

"Let me." Jenna took the accordion, ripped one of the packets free and tore it open.

Sawyer leaned back, giving her access to that hard, thick shaft.

Jenna shivered in anticipation as she rolled the condom over him. Then she lay back on the sheets and guided him to her entrance.

With the tip of his shaft edging into her warm, wet channel, Sawyer paused and kissed the tip of her nose. "What? No foreplay?"

"It's overrated when your body is already on fire." She grabbed his hips and brought him home.

He slid inside her, his thickness filling her, stretching her. Jenna dragged in a deep breath and let it out slowly.

Sawyer leaned close, his lips touching her earlobe. "Are you all right?"

"Yes!" she cried. Then she eased him out and back in. "More than all right."

He laughed. "Just checking." He settled into a steady rhythm, driving in and out, increasing in speed and intensity.

Jenna brought her knees up and dug her heels into the mattress, raising her hips to meet his every thrust.

He rode her hard, and she wanted it even harder as she catapulted over the edge, the explosion of sensations rocketing through her, sending electrical shocks throughout her body.

Sawyer thrust once more, burying himself deep inside, his body rigid, his face tight. He stayed frozen for a long moment, his breath caught and held. Then he released the breath and dropped down on Jenna, rolling her with him to his side.

"You are amazing," he said, kissing her cheek, her eyes and finally her lips.

"I was going to say the same thing." Jenna snuggled into his body, loving that they retained their intimate connection. Her eyelids drifted closed and she yawned. "I could get used to this."

Sawyer's arms tightened.

As Jenna slipped into a deep sleep, she thought she heard Sawyer whisper, "So could I."

Chapter Thirteen

A light tap on the door woke Sawyer. He glanced at the clock on the nightstand. Two in the morning. He'd been asleep for less than two hours, resting comfortably with Jenna in his arms.

Another tap brought him fully alert. He slipped out of the bed, careful not to wake the beauty lying beside him.

He padded naked to the door and opened it.

Duff stood there dressed all in black, his face camouflaged black, as well. "We have intel. The sooner we move on it, the better."

"I'm ready."

Duff grinned, his teeth bright white in his blackened face. "You might want to put some clothes on."

Sawyer closed the door, slipped into his black jeans and grabbed his shoes and shirt. Before he left, he bent and brushed his lips across Jenna's, wishing he could stay and wake with her in his arms.

In the lounge, he shoved his feet into his shoes. "What do you have?" he asked as he dragged his dark T-shirt over his head.

Lance brought up an image on a large monitor housed in a cabinet. "I was able to track Devita to this location." He pointed to a position on the map. "It appears to be a remote, deserted island off the northern tip of the Yucatán

Peninsula. I tapped into the CIA's satellite images. Seems they've been keeping an eye on our man Devita and have this compound tagged. He's got others, but this is the one he went to tonight." Lance touched the mouse, and a satellite image replaced the map. In the image, a sprawling structure could be seen with a wall around the outside and several buildings within.

"From what I could deduce from the pictures and the supporting documentation, the largest structure is Devita's home. If you want to get to him, you have to breach the wall and enter through here—" with the cursor, he pointed to the front "—or here." Lance moved the cursor to the rear of the building. "The windows are too high on the exterior walls. There is a courtyard in the center, but you'd have to get inside the structure to access it, so it will be of no use to you."

Quentin and Montana climbed up the stairs from the lower level, carrying backpacks and submachine guns.

Natalie followed with a couple of helmets and handguns.

"I've got the fireworks." Montana held up a handful of plastic explosives.

"I have the detonators in my backpack," Quentin said. He snagged the packages from Montana. "I'll take those."

Montana tossed a submachine gun at Sawyer and a vest equipped with a body-armor plate. "I can't get over the number of MP5SDs this yacht is equipped with."

"Good. We might need the sound suppression if we want to get to Devita without alerting his entire army." Sawyer slipped the vest over his shoulders and buckled the front. Attached to the vest were several thirty-round magazines for the MP5SD submachine gun.

Natalie had lined the coffee table with the helmets equipped with night-vision goggles. She'd also brought along several P226 handguns. "You might need something a little more personal."

"Are you coming along?" Sawyer asked Natalie.

She shook her head. "I'm staying to help Lance keep the ladies out of trouble."

Sawyer nodded. "Thanks."

"I'd rather go with you, but I don't want to slow you down. You SEALs are better trained at this kind of operation than I am."

Quentin selected one of the handguns. "I want to meet the guy who owns this yacht. He's got great taste in equipment."

"How are we getting to Devita's compound?" Sawyer asked.

"The best way would be to go in by helicopter, but that's one piece of equipment this yacht didn't come equipped with," Montana said.

Duff pointed to the map. "We're going as far as we can up a river by boat. From there, we'll go on foot. It's about a mile from the river to the compound. Shouldn't take more than thirty minutes."

"If the jungle isn't too thick," Quentin added. "And we don't run into any guards along the way."

"When do we leave?" Sawyer asked.

Duff slipped into his vest, slid a P226 into the holster at his hip and grabbed one of the helmets. "Now."

They climbed down from the yacht and loaded into the boat they'd taken to Playa del Sol.

"Would be nice if we had one of our SEAL team's riverboats," Quentin groused.

"We're lucky to have this one," Duff said.

"Okay." Quentin waved at Duff. "I get it. Be grateful for what we have."

Natalie stood on the dock, handing over weapons. "Don't do anything stupid."

Duff was last to get in. He paused as he stood beside Natalie. "I'll be back."

"I'm counting on it. We still have another week of vacation to kill before going back to our real lives. I'd like to spend it with you." She cupped his blackened face. "You look good in makeup." She kissed him, and Duff crushed her to his chest for a brief moment. Then he climbed aboard.

Sawyer's insides tightened. What he wouldn't give to have one last kiss, one last hug from Jenna before he left for a mission he wasn't certain he'd come out of alive. It was better to let her sleep through their departure than to make promises he wasn't sure he could keep. All the more reason not to get too involved with a woman.

He couldn't get over Duff being as optimistic as he was with Natalie. But then, she knew better than anyone the risks of the job. She was a secret agent and ran covert operations that could lead to her own early demise.

Jenna was an accountant. Until she'd run into him, she hadn't known the dangers involved in the life of a navy SEAL.

Quentin untied the line and pushed the small boat out into the channel leaving the Puerto Cancún marina.

They'd follow the coastline north and then cut across the open water, swinging wide of the island. The plan was to land on the northwest side and then go the rest of the way on foot. If they were lucky, they'd get in, obtain the information they wanted from Devita and leave before his men had any idea they'd been attacked.

Duff manned the helm, steering the small craft past the city of Cancún, lit up by street, garden and security lights on the corners of resort hotels and scattered over the campuses. The idea was to give the tourists a sense of safety, no matter how thinly veiled. Despite the beauty of the tall buildings and the highly lit yards and gardens, there was still something decidedly unsettling about the beach resort.

"Been thinking," Quentin said from his seat behind Sawyer.

"That's a dangerous pastime for you, Quent."

Quentin grinned good-naturedly. "I know. But a man does that when he starts to get older."

"What were you on your last birthday? Twenty-nine?" Montana asked.

"Thirty," Quentin responded.

Duff shot a glance in Quentin's direction. "With all that thinking, what conclusions have you come to?"

"It might be time to do something else besides be a navy frogman."

"What?" Sawyer feigned surprise. Quentin had made similar comments over the past year. "I thought you liked your brothers in arms."

Quentin raised a hand as if he was a courtroom witness swearing to tell the truth. "Oh, I do. I'd take a bullet for any one of you."

Duff rubbed his shoulder. "You could have done that earlier and I wouldn't be aching now."

"That's just it." Quentin stared out at the ocean, illuminated by starlight. "Our bodies will eventually be too battered to do this job properly. We have to make way for the younger SEALs to make their mark."

Montana puffed up his chest. "I don't know about you, but this body is in prime shape."

"Until you take a bullet or shrapnel once too often. Traumatic brain injury, torn ligaments, hearing loss. You name it. It could happen to you in training or in the field.

What then? Have you made any plans for your transition out of the military, into civilian life?"

Duff scratched his chin. "I could always go to work for SOS with Natalie."

Sawyer frowned at his friend. "Have you really been thinking about giving up the SEALs?"

Duff shrugged. "It's crossed my mind lately."

"Anything to do with one sexy, kick-ass blonde?" Quentin asked.

With a nod, Duff answered, "Some. It's hard to have a relationship when the parts of the whole aren't in the same state, much less the same country."

"You barely know Natalie," Montana observed.

Duff's lips curled. "I know enough. And I'd like to get to know her even better."

An image flashed through Sawyer's mind of Jenna sleeping peacefully back in the stateroom aboard the yacht. He'd like to get to know her better, too, but part of him held back, wondering why he should bother. She was an accountant. That kept her in one place. He was a SEAL who could be called to duty at a moment's notice. A relationship between them was doomed to fail.

Hadn't his father taught him that? His mother divorced his father because she didn't like being alone more than they were together. As a child, Sawyer saw more of his nanny than he did either of his parents. What little time his father was home, he spent glued to his desk, shuffling papers or talking to someone on the phone. "Relationships are hard when you're never together."

"My point exactly." Duff tipped his head toward the bow. "We're coming up on the island. Gear up. We're going in."

Sawyer plunked his helmet on his head and secured the strap, pushing all other thoughts to the back of his mind.

They had a mission to accomplish, and he couldn't be distracted by something he could never have.

JENNA WOKE TO the sound of a small engine revving beside the little porthole of the stateroom. She sat up with a start and looked to the empty pillow next to her.

The engine revved again and settled into a rumbling hum, slowly fading.

She knelt in the bed and pushed aside the curtain to see a small motorboat pulling away from the yacht with four dark shadows of men hunkered low in the seats.

Sawyer was gone.

Throwing aside the sheet, she climbed out of the bed and rummaged through the drawers, finding a men's extra-large soft blue T-shirt and a pair of men's swim shorts with a drawstring. She slipped into the shorts, pulled the drawstring tight and knotted the T-shirt at her waist to keep it from dragging around her knees. Then she started up the stairs to the lounge area.

Before she reached the top, the yacht's engines fired up, and the vessel shimmied. Jenna stopped halfway up the stairs and held on to the railing. They were moving.

She sprinted to the top and strode into the lounge, where Natalie hovered around the computer monitor. The image displayed was a map of the Yucatán Peninsula with two blinking dots. One was moving across the blue patch of ocean. The other was on a small island off the northern tip of the peninsula.

Jenna pointed to the moving dot. "Is that the guys?"

Natalie nodded. "They should be there in approximately thirty minutes."

"And we're going, too?" she asked.

"We're going part of the way." Natalie stared at the

monitor, her brows puckered. "We won't be involved in the actual event."

"Are we moving?" Carly staggered up the stairs, yawning.

"Yes," Jenna said, staring out the window as they drifted by the lights of Puerto Cancún.

Carly yawned again and stretched. She wore a men's pajama top and nothing else. Dropping her arms to her sides, she stared around the lounge. "Where are the guys?"

"Going after Devita." Jenna returned to the monitor and watched for a while, her stomach knotted, her insides jumpy. "I feel so useless. Isn't there anything we can do to help them?"

Natalie shook her head. "They have to get in and out on their own. They will have the ability to contact us on the two-way radio, but there isn't much we can do from the yacht."

"If they get in a tight spot, could we get close enough to the island to extract them?" Carly asked.

"It would be risky, and they'd have to meet us in the water. The only dock on the island will be heavily guarded. We do, however, have a small dinghy, if we need to go get them." Natalie tapped her fingers on the desk.

"Are they terribly outnumbered?" Jenna questioned, her voice weak, fear for Sawyer making her shiver in the air-conditioned lounge.

"We can only guess." Natalie continued to stare at the blinking dot on the monitor. She appeared as worried as Jenna felt.

"Are you and Duff serious?" Jenna asked. "You don't have to tell me, if you don't want to."

Natalie shot a glance her way and then returned her attention to the monitor. "I just met the man less than a week ago."

Jenna smiled. "Do you believe in love at first sight?"

"Not really. But I believe Duff and I have a connection that neither of us can ignore." She gave Jenna a weak smile. "I don't know where it will go or how long it will last."

"But you're willing to give it a shot?"

Natalie's smile widened. "Yeah. I guess I am. He's an amazingly strong but sensitive man. He's a trained killer, but he's the gentlest soul I've ever encountered. He gets me." She shook her head, staring at the monitor again. "I think I could fall in love with him." She glanced at Jenna, her eyes shining bright, the truth written in the happiness on her face. "If I haven't already."

Jenna's heart tightened. How did someone fall in love in a matter of days, maybe only hours? Was it possible? Did love at first sight exist?

She remembered Sawyer standing behind her on the zip-line platform. His laughing eyes and concern over plummeting to his death on a thin cable had melted her heart from the very first moment her gaze met his. Love at first sight? Maybe not, but admiration and attraction... you bet your life.

Now he was on his way to infiltrate Devita's secret compound. If he didn't come back...

Jenna's heart skipped several beats and raced on to catch up. Having known Sawyer for so short a time, she couldn't believe herself to be in love with the man. But lust and desire had been off the charts and incredible.

For a woman who had thought no man other than Tyler would capture her attention and maybe even her heart, Jenna had been so very wrong. Sawyer was more man than Tyler had ever dreamed of being. Jenna felt a little sorry for her former maid of honor being stuck with the coward.

Nah. They deserved each other for the crappy way

they'd treated her. Jenna gave their relationship three months before they split up.

Tyler might even try to come back to her.

Jenna snorted softly. Never in a million years would she take him back. Not after having Sawyer in her life and in her bed.

Too wound up to go back to sleep and frankly too scared to leave the lounge, Jenna curled up on one of the white leather sofas and waited. When they got closer, she might consider guarding the decks and searching the water for the small motorboat and the man she'd come to admire. A man she could easily fall in love with.

God, she was a fool! From a man who didn't love her to another man who refused to get that involved, she sure knew how to pick them and make her life miserable.

Chapter Fourteen

They'd come ashore unnoticed, sliding the small motorboat up onto the sand near a small outcropping of brush.

Fully equipped with observation equipment, guns and ammo, they could make this mission happen.

Sawyer lay in the brush, eyeing the compound fence through his night-vision goggles. So far he hadn't spotted any green heat signatures indicating warm bodies and guards.

"If we're going, we'd better do it now. There are only a couple more hours until morning. I don't want to be here when the sun comes up," Duff said into his headset.

"Agreed," Sawyer responded. "Let's do this." He took off running.

Duff did, as well. When they reached the eight-foot wall, Duff cupped his hand. Sawyer stepped into it and launched himself over the top.

He landed in the soft, sandy soil on the other side and flattened himself to the earth, staring through his goggles, looking for any sign of movement or heat. So far nothing.

"Clear," he whispered into his headset to the others.

A second later, Duff flew over the top of the wall and landed beside Sawyer.

Montana was next, but he stopped at the top of the wall

and reached back to haul Quentin over. They landed on the ground making no sound at all.

The main building was fifty feet to the south. Nothing moved in the dead of the night except the guards standing watch at the entrance to the house and on the corners of the buildings.

The team split. Montana took the north corner while Quentin, Sawyer and Duff headed for the south corner and the rear entrance.

Sawyer sprinted ahead and caught the corner guard unaware, dispatching him with his knife. The man went down.

Duff and Quentin dragged him into the brush.

Sawyer found a back entrance locked, as he'd expected. He pulled his P226 handgun, fixed a silencer on it and blew a hole through the lock. The door swung open into a laundry room. None of the machines were running and the lights were out, but a light shone through from under the door leading into the house.

Sawyer shifted his night-vision goggles up on his helmet and eased the door open into a hallway with doors leading off each side.

Montana and Duff entered the laundry room behind him.

"Quent?" Sawyer whispered into his microphone.

"Checking all corners and setting charges." The explosives would help create a diversion should they need it.

Sawyer moved down the hallway to a door half-open. The lingering scent of food drifted through. Easing the door fully open, he noted the kitchen with a single light burning over the sink. It was empty and shut down for the night.

Closing the door, Sawyer continued down the hallway and came into a large dining room with a long formal table and a dozen chairs situated around the solid wood surface. The dining room opened into a foyer with a sweeping staircase leading to the upper level of the mansion.

A guard leaned against the wall to the right of the front entrance, his chin touching his chest, his eyes closed.

Sawyer crept up to the man and took him out with a quick slash across his throat. Easing him to the floor, Sawyer nodded to Montana and Duff. They split up, ducking through every door on the lower level, checking for any other guards or people who might be around and cause them trouble. Sawyer started up the stairs, crouching low and hugging the railing. As he reached the top, he noted another guard sitting on the floor in front of a broad wooden doorway. His head was resting against the door frame and his weapon lay across his lap. The man was sound asleep.

As Sawyer neared him, he jerked in his sleep, his head banging against the wooden door. He blinked and stared up at Sawyer. His eyes widened and his mouth opened. Before he could shout, Sawyer dispatched him and dragged him away from the door. This had to be Devita's room.

Montana and Duff arrived on the landing as Sawyer turned the knob.

"Uh, we might have a problem here," Quentin said into Sawyer's headset.

Sawyer paused before pushing the door in.

"Clarify," Montana whispered, farther back from the door than Sawyer.

"I hear an engine overhead," Quentin said. "I think it's a drone."

Sawyer's pulse leaped. What the hell was a drone doing flying over Devita's place?

Sawyer eased the door open and rushed into the room.

A huge mahogany bed with a canopy along the top took up the majority of one wall. Sawyer had crossed the room before the man in the bed knew what was happening. He grabbed Devita and yanked him out of the bed, pressing a knife to his throat.

The woman who'd been asleep beside him squealed and gathered the sheet up over her naked body. She rattled off words in Spanish, sobbing at the same time.

"Tell me who you hired to kidnap or kill Senator Houston's son and I'll let you live."

"No comprendo," he said, his head tipped back to avoid the blade.

"He does not speak *Inglés*," said the sobbing woman. She spoke to Devita in Spanish.

Devita gave a tight shake of his head and responded.

The woman said, "He does not know what you are talking about."

"Then why did he have Ramirez deliver a case with weapons and instructions to the hotel if he wasn't the one who hired the assassin?"

Again, the woman translated what Sawyer said. When Devita spoke, he sneered.

The woman bit her lip and hesitated.

Devita barked an order at her and she jumped.

"He was paid a lot of American dollars to deliver the case unopened. Had he known a senator's son was in Cancún, he would have kidnapped him himself and demanded money for his release."

Sawyer's gut knotted and anger ripped through him. This effort to discover his tormentor could not be a failure. "Who was supposed to get the case?"

Before Devita could respond, an explosion shook the mansion. Walls cracked and debris shook loose from the ceiling.

"Get out now!" Quentin shouted into the headset. "That drone I told you about just launched a rocket."

Montana zip-tied Devita's wrists and ankles. "What about the woman?"

"Bind her. Make it quick."

The woman struggled, but was no match for Montana. He had her zip-tied in seconds.

Sawyer jerked his head toward the door. "Go!"

Duff and Montana raced for the bedroom door. Sawyer brought up the rear. Weapons at the ready, the SEALs ran down the staircase and made it all the way through the dining room when the front door burst open and Devita's men crowded through, heading for the staircase.

Sawyer's team had rounded the corner and was headed down the long hallway when another explosion ripped through the center of the house. They were thrown to the floor, but the walls held. Sawyer scrambled to his feet, helped Montana and Duff up and hustled them out the back door, debris and a dust following them through.

They rounded the side of the mansion, headed for the point where they'd breached the wall. Quentin waited in the shadows with his hand cupped.

Montana went over the wall first, followed by Duff. Sawyer went next, stopping on top to grab Quentin's hand and haul him up.

Quentin dropped to the ground on the other side. As Sawyer started to slide off the top, something slammed into his shoulder.

He toppled to the ground, hitting hard.

Duff and Montana grabbed his arms and helped him to his feet.

"You're bleeding," Duff said. He pulled his hand away. It was covered in blood.

"Flesh wound," Sawyer said through gritted teeth. "Get out of here!"

As they ran for the beach where they'd left the small

boat, Montana spoke into the two-way radio. "Took hits from a drone. Sawyer wounded. Getting out. Need backup."

JENNA HEARD THE crackle of the radio and ran across the lounge to Natalie, who held one of the other two-way radios.

"Roger," Lance's disembodied voice responded from his position up top at the helm of the yacht. "Coming in to rendezvous. Got you on the tracker."

Natalie shoved the two-way radio at Jenna. "Hold this. If the drone is targeting the guys, we need to be ready."

She ran for the stairs to the deck below. In less than two minutes, she was back carrying a gun and a box of shells.

"Either of you ever fire a shotgun?" she asked.

Carly nodded. "I have on my uncle's farm."

"It's been a long time, but I used to go duck hunting with my dad in the bayous of Mississippi," Jenna said.

"You're hired. Load up and get out on deck." Natalie handed the weapon and the box of ammunition to Jenna. She glanced at Carly. "Come with me."

The two women ran down the stairs.

Jenna fumbled with the shotgun, trying to remember everything her father taught her about handling one. After several seconds studying the gun, she managed to load the shells. Then she ran out on deck.

"They're a half of a mile off the bow," Lance called out from the helm. "Watch the sky for a drone, and for God's sake, don't shoot our guys."

Her heart pounding, Jenna ran to the front of the yacht, the shotgun heavy in her hands. But, damn it, she'd do whatever it took to protect the men escaping Devita's island. She hooked the two-way radio to the waistband of her shorts and lifted the shotgun to her shoulder, like her father had taught her, settling it into the soft pocket of her shoulder.

A few minutes later, Carly and Natalie joined her, each carrying a weapon. Carly held another shotgun. Natalie carried a rifle with an infrared scope and a submachine gun.

The yacht powered through the water, racing to meet the men.

"We should see them in the next five minutes," Lance called out. "Watch for them."

The stars shone down on the water, the sun a couple of hours from rising. Jenna strained to see any movement on the water other than the gentle swells.

"There!" Lance shouted from above. "Eleven o'clock, two hundred yards. Closing fast."

Jenna scanned the rippling waves. A boat appeared out of the darkness, speeding toward them. Her heart leaped for joy.

"Watch for the drone," Natalie ordered.

Jenna shifted her focus to the sky over the boat carrying Sawyer and his teammates. She couldn't see anything flying over them.

"There's another boat coming in fast!" Lance yelled. "Be ready to provide cover."

The boat carrying the SEALs was within a football field of the yacht when another boat came at them from the starboard side, nearly crashing into them. Shots were fired from the driver of the attacking boat.

Jenna aimed her shotgun at the attacking boat. It was still too far out for her to hit anything. She raised the gun, aimed at the attacker and fired.

At the same time, the attacking boat turned sharply. The hull of the boat rose out of the water and blocked the bullet. The driver swung around behind the SEALs' boat, taking fire from the SEALs but coming at them relentlessly. Gunning the throttle, the attacker raised the bow of the boat high, running fast at the SEAL team's boat, again the hull of the boat between the driver and the bullets being fired at him.

"Damn!" Lance called out. "There's another boat."

Sawyer's boat turned sharply away from the yacht.

"What are they doing?" Jenna asked.

"Taking the firefight away from us," Natalie said through tight lips.

"But we can help." Jenna watched as the boat carrying Sawyer spun away and the men on board fired on the attacking boat.

"They don't see the other boat," Carly said.

"What's he doing?" Jenna watched as the third boat, a long, sleek cigarette jet boat, raced for the attacking boat, throttle wide-open. The driver of the boat that had been attacking the SEALs apparently hadn't noticed the new boat headed straight for him until too late.

Jenna bit her lip and flinched as the cigarette boat crashed into the attacking boat. The two vessels exploded, sending a fireball of flame into the sky. "Oh, my God, the driver did that on purpose."

The SEAL team circled back to the wreckage.

Lance slowed the yacht and edged toward them, finally bringing the bigger boat to a stop.

Jenna ran to the edge of the yacht and leaned over the side, staring down into the water. She counted the men in the SEALs' boat. Four. "Thank God," she whispered.

"Help!" A shout rose up from the water near the wrecked speedboats.

Lance maneuvered the yacht around the smoldering wreck and stopped the vessel. A figure in a bulky life jacket raised a hand in the air. "Help!"

Jenna was surprised. The voice was feminine. She hurried to grab the life preserver and line and tossed it over the side to the woman below.

The woman swam toward the life preserver and hooked her arm through it.

Holding on to the line, Jenna walked to the back of the yacht, pulling the woman along the side. Carly helped haul her toward the ladder. Once she reached the ladder, the woman climbed aboard.

Jenna gasped. In the exterior deck lights, she recognized the woman. "Becca?"

"Hey, Jenna. Thanks for helping me out." Becca unbuckled the life jacket and let it drop to the deck. A dark wetsuit encased her trim body, accentuating her curves. She pushed her hair out of her face and looked back at the water below. "Did you find the driver of the other boat?"

"There!" Lance pointed to a body floating among the splintered debris. He leaned from the door of the helm enclosure and shouted down to the SEALs. "Can you get to him?"

"We'll do what we can. We're taking on water pretty fast, and Sawyer's leaking blood like a sieve," Quentin called out.

Jenna's breath caught and she leaned over the side of the rail, trying to see for herself. Carly rushed up beside her and shone a flashlight down on the boat below.

"I'm fine," Sawyer said. "Just a flesh wound."

Duff eased the boat into the shards of fiberglass. The SEALs grabbed the man out of the water and hauled him onto the boat.

The next second, all hell broke loose, and the men were shouting. Steel glinted in the flashlight's beam.

"He's got a knife!" Montana yelled too late to stop the man they'd hauled aboard from sinking it into Sawyer.

Jenna screamed and was halfway over the rail when Carly dragged her back onto the deck.

Montana, Quentin and Duff tackled the man and dragged him away from Sawyer.

Sawyer clutched the knife protruding from his belly. "Okay, this might not be a flesh wound," he said. When he moved to pull the knife from his gut, three SEALs shouted at once, "Don't move it!"

Jenna couldn't breathe, her heart lodged in her throat and tears rolled down her cheeks. She stood frozen to the deck, staring down at the man who'd touched her like no other. And he might at that moment be dying.

Duff left the attacker to Montana and Quentin and knelt at Sawyer's side.

Lance dropped down from the helm. "Let's get the sling over the side and haul him onto the deck." Natalie and Becca sprang into action, swinging a miniature boom around to the side of the yacht and dropping the cable equipped with a sling to the boat below.

"I'll get the first-aid kit." Carly ran into the lounge and returned a few seconds later with the kit they'd used to patch Duff's injury not so long ago.

Duff helped Sawyer into the sling and gave a thumbs-up.

Lance flipped a switch and the cable tightened, slowly raising Sawyer into the air. When he was high enough, they swung the arm of the boom over the deck and eased Sawyer down onto the surface.

Jenna dropped to her knees beside him and stared in horror at the knife buried in his belly. For a moment, panic threatened to overwhelm her. "When I said I didn't want to live a boring life, I didn't mean for you to go to all the trouble of making it exciting, just for me." She forced a laugh that sounded more like a sob.

Carly moved in, shoving Jenna aside. "We need to stabilize the knife until we can get him to a hospital."

Natalie brought towels and the first-aid kit.

Jenna gave Carly room to work, but stayed at Sawyer's side.

Sawyer reached up with a bloody hand and brushed his knuckle across her cheek. "This ain't nothing, sweetheart."

She snorted. "Yeah, I bet all the SEALs say that." She'd seen the movies. They didn't end well.

"I'll be okay." He tipped his head to the side. "I'm more worried about getting blood on the deck from the wound in my shoulder."

Pushing aside the panic, Jenna held out her hand. "Got a pair of scissors in that kit, Carly?"

Carly opened the first-aid kit and handed Jenna a pair of scissors. "We need to focus on stopping the bleeding."

Jenna cut away the fabric of his T-shirt and pushed it aside to stare down at the ripped corner of Sawyer's shoulder. The coppery scent of blood filled the air. Forcing back her gag reflex, she went to work, focusing on stopping the flow of blood from Sawyer's shoulder by applying a pressure bandage to the front and one to the back where a bullet had entered. She was careful not to interfere with what Carly was doing to stabilize the protruding knife.

As Jenna worked over Sawyer, the rest of Sawyer's team climbed aboard the yacht, dragging with them the man who'd stabbed Sawyer.

Chapter Fifteen

Jenna placed her body between Sawyer and the man who'd tried to kill him, even though the attacker didn't look as if he had anything left in him for a repeat performance. He bled from several wounds, his face pale and his lips a deepening shade of bluish-purple. Montana and Quentin laid him on the deck, far enough away from Sawyer that the man couldn't do him any harm.

"Who are you?" Duff asked the man.

"What's it matter?" the man responded, his voice raspy. He coughed weakly. "I'll be dead soon."

"Why were you trying to kill us?"

"Doesn't matter."

Becca joined the SEALs huddled around the man on the deck. "His name is Trey Danner. Former FBI. Since being fired from that job, he's gone rogue and has been hiring out to the highest bidder."

"Doing what?" Jenna asked. "Killing people?"

Becca nodded. "He's a mercenary."

Danner shrugged, the movement making him wince and then cough. Blood trickled from the corner of his mouth. "It pays better than flipping burgers."

Duff stepped forward, his fists clenched. "Bastard."

Lance nodded. "He's the guy we saw in the video of

the lobby. The one who came to the concierge desk after Jenna took the case."

"I ran into him in the resort lobby," Jenna shivered. "So he was supposed to receive the case with the sniper rifle."

Danner closed his eyes. "Don't know what you're talking about." He coughed and lay still.

"Who hired you?" Duff dropped to a knee beside the injured man.

"Dead men don't tell secrets…" Danner whispered, his words barely understandable.

Duff reached for the man's shoulders and shook him. "Who the hell hired you to kill Sawyer?"

Montana laid a hand on Duff's shoulder. "Let's get him fixed up, and then we can interrogate him."

Duff released his hold and stood.

Quentin pressed two fingers to the base of Danner's throat. "I don't think there will be any fixin'. This guy's dead."

Lance hurried up the steps into the helm. Before long he had turned the vessel toward Cancún, radioing ahead for an ambulance to meet them at the dock.

While Carly kept pressure on the belly wound around the knife, Jenna held Sawyer's hand in hers, praying he'd stay alive long enough to get to medical help.

Sawyer looked up at her, his eyes glazed, his face pale. "I swear I'll be okay." His voice faded and his eyelids drooped closed.

Jenna glanced up to see Natalie, Montana, Duff and Quentin surrounding Becca.

Duff tilted his head toward Natalie, his eyes narrow. "You'd better question her. I'm not in the mood to be nice."

Natalie's lips curved briefly as she faced Becca. Her expression sobered and she stared at the woman, all trace of humor gone. "Why are you here and why did you know so much about Danner?"

Becca straightened, throwing back her shoulders. "I've been following Danner."

"Why?" Quentin shot at her.

"He killed someone I cared about," Becca said, her voice strong, her chin tilting.

"Who?"

She took a deep breath, her eyes glazing. "My father."

"And what makes you qualified to chase mercenaries?" Natalie asked.

Becca's lips quirked. "Same thing that makes you qualified to go after him."

Lance called down from above. "Natalie, Royce said not to shoot Becca. She's one of us."

Becca smiled. "You've been away for two years." She stuck out her hand to Natalie. "Welcome back to SOS."

Natalie took the hand, her brows furrowed. "You must have come on board after I left."

"That's right," Becca said. "I've heard a lot about you."

Sawyer's eyes blinked open, and he stared up at Jenna. "Did I hear that right? She's an agent?"

Jenna touched his face. "You heard right. Apparently she works with the same agency as Lance and Natalie."

Becca's smile faded. "The difference is, I have a stake in the outcome of this case."

"Revenge?" Duff slipped an arm around Natalie's waist.

"No." Becca crossed her arms. "Justice. I refuse to let the man who killed my father get away with murder."

"Well, you got what you came for," Quentin said.

Becca shook her head. "Almost. But not quite. You heard Danner. Someone hired him to kill Sawyer and Devita. I'll bet whoever hired him to kill those two was also responsible for killing my father."

"The question is, what is the connection between your father, Devita and Sawyer?" Duff asked.

Jenna gripped Sawyer's hand. "The note said to bring Sawyer Houston to a certain location, dead or alive."

"Which leads me to think they were going to use him to lure his father to Cancún."

"And since they didn't care if he was dead or alive, they probably weren't after Sawyer for a ransom."

"I'm still here," Sawyer said. "Not dead."

Jenna chuckled. "Stay with us. We'll figure this out."

Sawyer squeezed Jenna's hand and turned his head toward Natalie, Becca and the others. "My father's on his way to Cancún, despite my request that he not come."

Becca drew in a deep breath and let it out. "Whoever hired Trey could have more than one mercenary working for him. When Senator Houston arrives, he could be the next target."

Sawyer tried to sit up but fell back, wincing. "Got to get to him first."

Jenna laid a hand on his shoulder. "You'll be in the hospital. You're not going anywhere."

"But we can meet him," Duff said. "And equip him with some body armor before he heads to the hospital to visit his son."

Becca shook her head. "The man's a moving target. The man who killed my father and Devita is ruthless. He probably wants the senator to suffer and will kill his son first. Then he'll stop at nothing to kill the senator."

Jenna's mind raced ahead, her thoughts processing all the pieces. "Then we have to kill Sawyer and let the man who wants the senator dead have the senator killed."

Sawyer frowned up at her. "I thought you liked me."

Jenna smiled down at him. "Don't you see? Whoever

wants the senator to suffer won't kill him until he watches his son die."

"My father doesn't give a damn about whether I live or die," Sawyer said softly. "But I kind of like living, if you don't mind."

"So we fake your death, which brings your father to the hospital. When he leaves the hospital, we assassinate him."

"I can go along with a fake death—ideally it'll only be fake." Sawyer's frown deepened. "But though I don't get along with my father, I don't want him to die."

"Yeah, neither do we." Becca tapped her chin. "But until we find out who is behind all these killings, your father needs to fake his death and go into some kind of witness protection program. Otherwise, he'll continue to be a target of this madman."

"Royce can set up the witness protection program," Natalie said.

Becca nodded. "He's done it before. And it might be better if he does. I have a feeling the man behind these assassination attempts is or was someone in a government agency."

"Why?" Jenna asked.

"My father was a member of the CIA working with the DEA on a drug-trafficking case involving Devita."

"How does Sawyer's father fit into this?" Duff asked.

Becca's brows drew together. "I'm not sure, but my father mentioned having meetings with Senator Houston on several occasions."

Sawyer's fingers tightened around Jenna's. "My father was on the Subcommittee for Terrorism, Drug Trafficking and International Operations." He spoke with his eyes closed, his grip weakening. "Now, if you'll excuse me, I think I'll sleep."

His hand went limp in Jenna's. She leaned forward,

touched her fingers to the base of his neck and held her breath. The weak but steady thump of his pulse gave her only a brief feeling of relief. If they didn't get him to a hospital soon, he'd bleed out.

The lights of Puerto Cancún made the sky glow as the yacht turned into the port's channel.

"We need to prepare for boarding." Natalie nodded to the men. "Gather anything and everything to do with weapons and ammunition and stash it in the safe room below."

Montana, Duff and Quentin sprang into action. Carly, Natalie and Becca followed. Before they pulled into the slip at the marina, every weapon and all the ammo and casings had been policed and stored in the hidden room on the lower level. The men had scrubbed their faces clean of the camouflage paint and brought a damp cloth for Jenna to clean the paint off Sawyer's face.

Strobe lights on emergency vehicles blinked on the road beside the marina.

As the yacht pulled in, Mexican police swarmed the decks, followed by emergency medical technicians carrying a stretcher.

Careful not to jostle the knife in Sawyer's belly, they loaded him onto the stretcher, started an IV and affixed an oxygen mask to his face.

"I'm going with him," Jenna insisted.

"Are you a relative?" one of the technicians asked in heavily accented English.

"I'm his fiancée," she lied. She didn't want to let Sawyer out of her sight. There might be other hired mercenaries wandering around Cancún. She refused to let them have a clear shot at Sawyer.

"We'll be right behind you," Duff reassured her. "We won't let anything happen to him."

Before Jenna could climb into the back of the ambulance with Sawyer, Natalie touched her arm. "We'll get my boss to contact Sawyer's father before he lands in Cancún and set the plan in motion."

Jenna nodded. "Thank you. Let me know if I can help in any way. Otherwise I'll be at Sawyer's bedside."

Natalie stared at her for a long moment. "You already know what has to happen."

"I do," Jenna said.

Natalie, Becca, Carly and Lance would stay behind and answer questions about Trey's death, claiming he was the victim of a terrible boat wreck, which was the truth.

"I'll be outside the room to provide protection," Duff said. "Sawyer's like a brother to me."

"And me," Montana added.

"And me," Quentin agreed.

Jenna climbed into the back of the ambulance and smiled at the SEALs. "He's lucky to have you."

"Damn right he is." Duff winked and jogged to the battered Jeep in the parking lot. Quentin and Montana hurried after him.

Jenna hoped they remembered to fill the radiator with water before they started the engine on the bullet-riddled rental car.

She sat as far forward and out of the way as possible so that the medical technician had access to work on Sawyer, if needed. She was comforted whenever she caught glimpses of the Jeep following them to the hospital.

Sawyer didn't awaken.

When they reached the hospital, he was taken directly into surgery.

Duff, Montana and Quentin joined Jenna in the waiting room.

The scent of disinfectant brought back memories of

being in the hospital with her mother as she lay dying of cancer. The last time she had held her mother's hand, Jenna had been twelve.

Her throat constricted and her fists clenched. Sawyer would not die. He couldn't. Though they'd only just met and spent two nights making love, their chemistry was off the charts. Jenna knew Sawyer was special, compassionate and the kind of guy who would never leave a woman standing alone at the altar. He was a man of his word, a man of integrity and grit.

Her father would approve of Sawyer and welcome him into the family, if anything came of their relationship.

She brushed a tear from her eye, shaking her head at how far ahead of herself she was getting. Sawyer had to make it through the operation first. Then, if he was interested, she hoped they could go on a real date. Maybe relax on the beautiful beaches of Cancún without being shot at or stabbed.

If he didn't want to continue seeing her, she'd understand. But damn. She hoped he would consider it.

"Are you all right?" Duff asked.

Jenna stared up at the big SEAL. His jaw was tight. "I'm okay. Just worried about Sawyer."

Duff nodded. "He's been through worse and come out all right."

She smiled. "I believe it."

"Natalie just texted. Her boss was able to get through to Senator Houston. He landed fifteen minutes ago. Natalie is going to meet him at the airport and prepare him."

Jenna drew in a deep breath and let it out slowly. "And so it begins."

Neither Sawyer nor his father was out of the woods yet. Though mercenary Trey Danner was dead, they couldn't be certain others wouldn't come along and try to kill the Houstons.

Finally a man in scrubs entered the waiting room, pulling a surgical mask from his face. "Senor Houston is fine. The shoulder wound will heal nicely, no serious damage to his muscles or bones. The knife missed all major organs. However, he lost a considerable amount of blood. We wish to monitor him overnight."

A nurse led them to a private hospital room, where Sawyer lay against the crisp white sheets, an IV attached to his arm, monitors checking his pulse and heartbeat. Though his face was pale, he appeared to be resting easy.

"He should come out of the anesthesia soon," the nurse said.

After Sawyer's teammates had a chance to see their buddy, they left Jenna alone with him. She sat in the chair beside his bed, holding his hand. The sun had come up two hours ago, but the activities that had occurred over the past couple of days weighed heavily on Jenna's eyelids. Eventually she leaned her head against the mattress and slipped into a deep sleep.

LIGHT EDGED BETWEEN Sawyer's eyelids, forcing him awake. Though he tried to open his eyes, he struggled to perform the simple action. His limbs felt heavy and his belly hurt, as if someone had stabbed a knife in his gut.

Knife. Attack.

Sawyer jerked awake, his eyes flew open and he tried to sit up. Pain forced him to reconsider, and he lay back against the sheet.

Something soft and silky brushed against his arm. When he glanced down, his heart swelled.

Jenna, the woman who'd risked her life to save him by jumping onto the back of a WaveRunner, was asleep with her head lying on the mattress of the hospital bed, her hand next to his.

This woman had done more for him than any stranger ever would. Boring she was not. *Caring, passionate, brave* and *beautiful* described her. Sawyer believed he knew her better in the short time he'd known her than her ex-fiancé had. Hell, the man probably never tried to get to know her properly. When he got out of the hospital and no one was gunning for him, he'd take Jenna on a real date, treating her to dinner, dancing and the romance she deserved.

He smoothed a hand over her auburn hair, wishing she would wake and let him see her bright green eyes. But she was so peaceful and getting some much-needed sleep after the events of the night before.

Jenna stirred and lifted her head, those green eyes shining up at him sleepily. "You're awake."

He chuckled and winced. "I am. How long have I been out?"

She glanced around the room, shaking her head. "I have no idea."

"Before everything starts getting crazy, I wanted to say thank-you."

Her brows crinkled and her lips twisted. "For what?"

"For being the brave, beautiful and exciting woman you are." He brushed a strand of silken hair back behind her ear. "And for saving my life."

She shook her head. "You almost died last night."

"But I didn't. And you saved my life in more ways one."

"What do you mean?" she asked, smoothing her hand over the sheet, her lashes dropped to mask her expression.

Sawyer lifted her chin with one finger, forcing her to look at him. "You reminded me there is more to life than work and I don't have to be a cold bastard like my father."

"Never cold," she said, her fingers linking with his.

"You have a big heart, Sawyer. Your teammates would vouch for that."

"And you?"

She tilted her head. "My instincts say you have a big squishy heart, but I have a problem trusting my instincts. I'd really like to get to know you better. Spend some time with you. But that's completely up to you. You might not even like me."

He snorted. "Not a chance. I think I could really come to love you."

Jenna's eyes widened.

The *L* word coming out of Sawyer's mouth was almost as shocking to him as it was to Jenna, based on her expression. "Wow, did I really say that?"

She nodded. "You did. And you can't take something like that back."

He cupped her cheek. "I don't want to. As I see it, I have almost a week left of vacation and you just got here. I don't suppose you'd want to go out with a man who has stitches in his belly and probably can't dance for a few weeks?"

She smiled. "I'd love to go sit by the swimming pool and soak up some sun with you. Maybe even read a book."

"You've got a date, darlin'." He tried to sit up again, the pain stabbing him in the belly forcing him to lie back. "I'd kiss you, but it seems sitting up isn't in the cards for me yet."

"Allow me." Jenna stood and leaned over the bed, brushing her lips across his.

"Mmm. That's good. But this is better." Sawyer cupped the back of her head and brought her down for a deep, soul-defining kiss that shook him to the core. When he loosened his hold on her, she swayed, her eyes glazed and her lips swollen.

"That was good," she whispered. "I hope they let you out of the hospital soon."

"Me, too." He tugged on her hand. "In the meantime, I bet there's room for both of us on this bed."

A knock on the door kept him from scooting over.

Duff leaned in. "It's time for Operation Phoenix." He stepped through the door and let it close behind him.

Sawyer frowned.

Duff glanced from Sawyer to Jenna. "Jenna didn't tell you?"

Sawyer stared at her. "Tell me what?"

"Your father landed in Cancún a little while ago. He's on his way to the hospital to see you."

Sawyer pushed himself up in the bed, grimacing to fight the pain of pulled stitches. "Damn, that hurts." Once upright, he tried to swing his legs over the side. "You have to stop him. There could be a killer out there waiting to take him out."

Duff nodded. "Yeah. We're banking on it."

"What?" Sawyer stared at his friend. Had Duff lost his mind?

"You don't remember the conversation?" Jenna's mouth twisted into a wry grin. "You were pretty much out of it. Your father needs to die long enough to let Natalie's team of special agents figure out who is behind the death of Becca's father, Devita and all of the attempts on your life, including the cut cable on the zip-line adventure."

Duff nodded. "They're going to get him to go into something like witness protection until they can nail the bastard."

"Sawyer, you really should lie down," Jenna said.

Now that he was up, the thought of lying back in the bed sounded equally as painful as sitting up. "I'm okay."

"You're bleeding through your bandages." Jenna glanced at Duff. "Help me get him to lie down."

Duff hurried to the other side of the bed. "Let us do the work for you. Jenna's right. You have to let the wounds heal." Between Jenna and Duff, they lowered him to the mattress.

Sawyer groaned. "I hate being so damn helpless."

Jenna stared down at the red stain on his belly and bit her lip. "I should call the nurse back in to have her check the damage you've done."

"I'm fine," Sawyer said. "I want to hear how you plan to get my father killed without actually hurting him."

"If the assassin doesn't try to take him out on his way in, *you* have to pretend to die while he's here so the assassin will attempt a hit on his life on the way out." Duff raised his hands. "What? You don't like the plan?"

"What if the killer succeeds?"

"Your father will be outfitted with armor plates."

"What about his head?" Sawyer asked. "If the assassin is worth anything, he could aim for the head. Did you give my father a helmet?"

Duff grinned. "No, but we gave him a Kevlar fedora."

Sawyer shook his head. "A what?"

Duff's grin widened. "Natalie's boss has some amazing connections."

"I still don't like the idea of my father coming here. I don't know why he's here. He never came to anything when I was growing up. Hell, he didn't come to my graduation from BUD/S training."

"Maybe he's finally coming around," Duff said.

Jenna tightened her hold on his hand. "I'm going to run to the restroom and grab a cup of coffee, if I can find a cafeteria."

"I'll stay with him until you get back."

"I don't need a damn babysitter," Sawyer groused.

"No, but you're in no condition to fight off an attack."

"Danner's dead."

"You want to bank your life that there's not another man waiting to do the job Danner couldn't?" Duff asked.

Jenna headed for the door. "I'll let you two duke this one out. I'll be back as soon as possible."

The door closed behind her, leaving Duff and Sawyer alone.

"She's feisty," Duff said.

Sawyer's gaze remained on the door Jenna had disappeared through. "Yes. She is." His lips curled upward. "I like that about her."

Duff stared at Sawyer. "Look at the two of us."

"What?" Sawyer frowned up at his friend.

"You and me. Confirmed bachelors, determined to stay that way. 'A SEAL has no right to drag a female into his life.'" Duff chuckled. "Remember saying that?"

Sawyer thought about it. "Yeah. I do remember saying that. And it's still true."

"What if the woman is fully aware of your profession? Haven't you ever thought it might be up to the woman to make that decision?"

Sawyer chewed on Duff's words. "I guess."

Duff raised his hands, palms up. "We should let them make that choice rather than making it for them."

"Seems kind of selfish to want someone and not be there for them." He tapped the mattress with his fingers. "Like how my father made the choice to marry and have children, then more or less abandoned us to his career."

"How many times do I have to tell you that you're not your father?" Duff paced toward the window, performed an about-face and paced back. "You deserve to be happy. And if the female you care about loves you enough to take you, career and all, she deserves the chance to make that decision for herself."

Sawyer stared at his friend, his eyes narrowing. "Are you trying to convince me or yourself?"

"You, brother." Duff walked to the window again and shot a glance over his shoulder. "I'm already convinced."

"You found the perfect woman for you."

"And you haven't?"

Sawyer's gaze remained on the closed door. "Maybe."

"Then give her and yourself a chance. You said it yourself. She's feisty." Duff turned to stare out the window. "She'll need to be to put up with you."

"Jerk."

Duff didn't respond. His body tensed and he leaned toward the glass. "If I'm not mistaken, your father is in the parking lot and headed for the front entrance."

Sawyer tried to sit up again, but the pain in his abdomen was too much. "What's happening?"

"Well, he's wearing the fedora, and judging from the bulky way he looks in his suit, he's decked out in the armor plating."

"What's going on?" Sawyer demanded.

"Nothing so far."

Sawyer didn't like this. "Get me up. I want to see what's going on."

"No way. You're bleeding— Holy hell!" Duff said. "He's down!"

Again, Sawyer forced himself to a sitting position, the stitches ripping his skin. Warm blood trickled, filled the white bandages and dripped down his belly. When he slipped out of the bed and tried to stand, he almost passed out.

"What the hell are you doing?" Duff was at his side in

an instant, lifting him up and settling him in the bed. "I'm going to get a nurse in here."

"Don't. I'd rather you went to my father and helped him. Armored plates don't cover the entire body."

Duff shot a glance toward the window. "You gotta promise me you won't do something stupid while I'm gone, like trying to join me."

"I'll stay here. But I need to know you're looking out for my father."

"On it." Duff ran for the door and turned at the last second. "SEAL's honor."

Sawyer held up a hand. "SEAL's honor."

Duff left, and the door swung closed behind him.

Unable to sit still while his father could be in trouble, Sawyer swung his legs out of the bed. This time he held on when he got out and waited for his head to clear. He must have lost a lot of blood. He felt as weak as a newborn. But somehow he made it to the window and stared down at the gathering crowd around his father. He could make out Montana, Quentin, Natalie, Lance and Becca. Even Carly was down there, helping make sure the killer believed Senator Houston was dead.

Duff joined them and helped the hospital staff lift Sawyer's father onto a gurney and wheel him into the hospital.

So intent on the drama unfolding on the ground below his window, Sawyer didn't hear the door open. He didn't hear the footsteps crossing the floor until too late.

Something grabbed his head and slammed it into the window with such force, pain shot through his skull and he dropped to the ground, the fog of unconsciousness completely enveloping him.

Chapter Sixteen

Jenna had made use of the facilities, found a café and ordered two cups of coffee. She was backing into the swinging door of Sawyer's room when she heard a loud bang on the other side.

Thinking Sawyer might have fallen out of the bed, she shoved through quickly, her gaze going to the empty bed. Then she saw the man dressed in scrubs crouched by the window with a pillow in his hand, pressing it hard over Sawyer's face.

Jenna flung the cups of hot coffee at the man and charged at him, hitting him like a linebacker tackling a quarterback. Her impact was enough force to knock him into the window glass.

He staggered, righted himself and spun to face her.

Jenna backed away and did the only other thing she could think of—she screamed bloody murder and dived across the bed, landing on the other side.

The man rounded the bed and came at her, his hands reaching for her neck.

Jenna grabbed the lamp off the nightstand and swung it hard.

The attacker knocked the lamp from her hands and it crashed into the wall.

The attacker's hands wrapped around her throat and squeezed.

Kicking and flailing with all her strength, Jenna couldn't get the man to let go. Her throat ached, she couldn't breathe and darkness crept in around the edges of her vision. All she could think of was that she couldn't let this guy kill her. If he did, there'd be no one stop him from killing Sawyer, if he hadn't already.

With renewed resolve, she jerked her knee up, connecting with the man's groin. He loosened his hold. Jenna knocked his arms away. She dropped to the ground, rolled out of reach and stood on the other side of the bed. With the little bit of strength she had left, she shoved the bed with all her might, slamming it against the man and pinning him against the wall.

Then Sawyer was standing beside her, leaning his weight into the bed with her, his face pale but his jaw set.

Trapped at the waist, the man couldn't free his legs. He reached into the waistband of his scrubs and pulled out a handgun.

A large, shiny bedpan sailed across the room and caught the gun as the man pulled the trigger. His arm jerked back.

Jenna's heart stopped. Nothing had hit her, which led her to believe Sawyer had been hit. When she looked over at him, her heart started beating again. He was still upright. The only blood visible soaked his bandages where he'd ripped his stitches loose.

Duff charged into the room and yanked the man out from between the wall and the bed, jerked his arm up behind his back and slammed his face into the wall.

Montana arrived and offered a zip tie to secure the man's wrists behind his back. "Nice to see you have things under control. While you take care of our assassin, I'll check on things downstairs."

Jenna slipped an arm around Sawyer's waist and let him lean on her.

"My father?" Sawyer asked.

Natalie entered the room as Duff left, and went to Sawyer, wrapping her arms around his neck. "Sawyer, I'm so very sorry."

"What?" Sawyer gripped her arms. "What happened?"

Jenna's heart pinched in her chest. Though she knew this was all a sham, she was amazed at how real Natalie and Sawyer made it feel.

"Your father—" Natalie paused, swallowed hard and continued "—was shot dead at the front entrance of the hospital." Then she hugged him again and whispered something into his ear. She stepped back. "They've taken him to the morgue in the basement. His body will be prepared for shipment back to the States."

Sawyer stared at her for a long time before saying, "I want to see him."

"You shouldn't be up and about," Jenna said. "You're bleeding."

"I'll let the doc sew me up again, but I want to see my father one last time."

A nurse entered with two Mexican policemen.

The policemen took the attacker out of the room.

Duff left and returned with a wheelchair. He and Jenna eased Sawyer into it. Then Duff rolled him out of the room and down the hallway to the elevator. Jenna walked beside the chair and held Sawyer's hand. She had to let go as they entered the elevator car.

The trip to the basement didn't take long. When they arrived, an orderly led them into an embalming room, where a body lay on a gurney, covered in a sheet and surrounded by Lance, Quentin, Montana, Carly and Becca.

Natalie spoke to the orderly in halting Spanish, and he left.

As soon as the door closed behind the orderly, Senator Houston flung back the sheet and sat up on the gurney. "I thought you'd never get rid of that orderly." He rubbed his chest. "I have to admit, I didn't expect it to hurt that much. But I'm damn glad I had the armor plating." He directed his attention to Sawyer, his brow furrowing into deep lines. "Son, are you okay?"

Sawyer frowned. "Why did you come?"

The frown eased from the senator's brow. "I got a message that you would be killed if I didn't come to Cancún immediately." He stared at Sawyer. "I came."

Sawyer's jaw tightened.

Jenna could feel the tension between the two men. She laid a hand on Sawyer's shoulder, wanting to take away the physical as well as the emotional pain. But she remained silent.

Sawyer reached up and covered her hand with his as he spoke to his father. "You realize now that you're dead, you have to stay dead until we figure out who is trying to kill you."

His father nodded. "I spoke with Royce Fontaine, head of Stealth Operations Specialists. I understand what has to happen."

"And you're going to walk away from your office for however long it takes?"

"For good, if I have to." Rand Houston shoved a hand through his hair. "On the flight down from DC, I had time to reflect on my life, yours and what's important. It took me thirty years to come to the conclusion that your life is more important to me than my work in the senate."

Sawyer snorted. "A little late, don't you think?"

His father nodded. "Yeah. But not too late for you. Now

that I'm playing dead, whoever wanted to hurt me by hurting you ideally will stop trying. That's what counts. Look, son, I don't expect you to forgive me for being a lousy father. I just want you to live a full life and be happy. If being a SEAL makes you happy, I think that's great. I might not have told you this, but the proudest day of my life was the day you graduated BUD/S training. I couldn't be there because we had a hostage crisis in Libya going on at the time." The senator shook his head. "I know. It was always something. I'm glad you're going to be okay, and I hope when this is all over, we can meet for coffee and start over." He held out his hand to his son.

For a long moment, Sawyer stared at it. Finally he took the hand and shook it. "I'll take you up on that cup of coffee as long as I get to choose the place. I can't stand that fancy coffee."

Senator Houston grinned. "You're on."

Natalie's cell phone buzzed. She listened and then lifted her head. "Senator Houston, your ambulance has arrived to take you to the plane."

He nodded and looked around the room as if for the first time. "I guess I'm off to a new life and a new identity. Who knows? Maybe I'll like it enough that I won't want to go back to the Capitol." He lay back on the gurney. Natalie covered him with the sheet, and they rolled him out of the morgue, into the waiting ambulance.

Quentin and Montana rode in the back of the ambulance with the senator. Carly opted to go with Quentin.

Once his father was on his way to the airport, Sawyer let Duff push his wheelchair back to the elevator and help him to his room and the bed.

"If you're all right, I think I'll head to the hotel with Natalie and Becca. I'd like to get a shower and shave. I'll be back later."

Sawyer waved at his friend. "Go. I seriously doubt I'll be attacked again. If I am, I have my bodyguard to keep me safe." He smiled at Jenna.

A warm feeling spread through her, but it was immediately cooled when the nurse and doctor entered the room.

They spent the next ten minutes suturing the torn stitches. They gave him a bag of ice for the knot on his head from being slammed into the window and apologized for the lapse in hospital security that allowed a madman to attack him.

All the while the nurse and doctor worked with Sawyer, Jenna hung back. Now that Sawyer was on the mend and out of danger of being shot or stabbed, he no longer needed her.

Jenna wondered if she should go back to her room and get on with her vacation.

The door closed behind the doctor and nurse, leaving her alone with Sawyer.

"Hey," Sawyer said. "Why are you way over there, when I'm way over here?"

Jenna shrugged. "I was thinking I should go, now that you don't need me anymore."

"What are you talking about?" He lay back against the pillows. "You're my bodyguard. All you need is a couple of cups of coffee and a hospital bed to neutralize any threat."

Jenna crossed to him and let him take her hand. She liked the way it looked so small in his bigger hand. "I figured you might not want a boring accountant holding you back."

He caught her chin in his palm and forced her to look at him. "You are not boring. Hell, you're the most exciting woman I've ever had the honor to be saved by." He laced his fingers with hers and brought them to his lips. "A wise old SEAL told me I should give myself and my girl a chance to find happiness. Now, since I don't have a girl, or at least don't have one yet, I was hoping, if you can stand to be around a guy who is all cut up and might bleed on you while making love, you might consider going on a date with me?"

Her heart swelled and threatened to burst from her chest. "I'd love to."

"Good. As soon as I'm out of this hospital, you're on. But while I'm stuck here, I swear this bed will fit two." He patted the mattress beside him. "I won't ask for anything but your warm body next to mine, and I'll even let you sleep, because—" he yawned "—I think they gave me a really good painkiller."

Jenna crawled up beside him, careful not to jolt him. Then she lay in the curve of his arm, snuggling beside a pretty amazing SEAL.

"Mmm. Now, that's more like it," Sawyer murmured. "I could fall in love with a woman like you. Feisty and never boring."

* * * * *

"You're going to tell me the whole story," Sophia said.

He'd never been a fan of her using his general's tone, but if any situation required it, this was the one.

"I am," Frank replied, with both hands on the steering wheel once more. "You're not going to like it."

"I already don't like it, Frank."

"The man following you was one of the top snipers in the Afghanistan military. One word from his boss and your life is over."

She sucked in a breath. "Why?" Who would make her a target?

"That's one detail. I swear to you, as soon as I'm sure we're out of harm's way, I'll tell you everything."

"Harm's way or not, you'll tell me everything tonight." He wasn't the only one who could issue orders.

With a short nod, he rolled his broad shoulders.

She remembered the feel of those shoulders under her hands after a tough day at work when she'd help him work out the kinks...or late at night in the heat of passion.

Oh, how she wanted to trust him, to be sure she could trust him.

It scared her, more than being run off the road, just how much she wanted to believe in Frank Leone again.

HEAVY ARTILLERY HUSBAND

BY
DEBRA WEBB & REGAN BLACK

First Published in Great Britain 2016
By Mills & Boon, an imprint of HarperCollins*Publishers*
1 London Bridge Street, London, SE1 9GF

© 2016 Debra Webb

ISBN: 978-0-263-91901-1

46-0416

Our policy is to use papers that are natural, renewable and recyclable products and made from wood grown in sustainable forests. The logging and manufacturing processes conform to the legal environmental regulations of the country of origin.

Printed and bound in Spain
by CPI, Barcelona

Debra Webb, born in Alabama, wrote her first story at age nine and her first romance at thirteen. It wasn't until she spent three years working for the military behind the Iron Curtain—and a five-year stint with NASA—that she realized her true calling. Since then the *USA TODAY* bestselling author has penned more than one hundred novels, including her internationally bestselling Colby Agency series.

Regan Black, a *USA TODAY* bestselling author, writes award-winning, action-packed novels featuring kick-butt heroines and the sexy heroes who fall in love with them. Raised in the Midwest and California, she and her family, along with their adopted greyhound, two arrogant cats and a quirky finch, reside in the South Carolina Lowcountry, where the rich blend of legend, romance and history fuels her imagination.

Chapter One

Chicago, Illinois
Monday, April 18, 6:45 p.m.

Sophia Leone sat back as the waiter delivered wide shallow bowls filled with the best pasta in the Windy City. From the first warm embrace upon her arrival, her friend Victoria Colby-Camp and her husband, Lucas Camp, had carefully kept the conversation on light-hearted topics.

It couldn't stay that way. All three of them recognized there were serious matters to address. As the founder of the Colby Agency, Victoria never let her mind stray too far from business, especially not when she sensed a friend in trouble.

Was she in trouble? Sophia couldn't decide. She was still processing everything that had happened over the past few days.

She resisted the urge to run her fingers over the fading goose egg on her scalp. Hidden by her hair just above her ear, it was the only remnant of the shocking fight in her kitchen. Though it had been a terrible ordeal, the real culprit was in custody and the people who mattered most were safe. Coming to Chicago gave her a chance to escape and some space to decide how she wanted to move forward.

While this visit to Chicago needed to shift into business, tonight was for pleasure. She wanted time to relax and catch up with her friends. She hadn't realized just how pervasive that undercurrent of tension in her life had been during the months when her daughter, Frankie, refused to speak with her. Now it was marvelous to share how happily Frankie and her fiancé, Aidan, a former Colby Agency investigator, were coming along with their wedding plans. With countless questions and decisions remaining, the two most important details were finalized. They'd set a date for September and Aidan's family would be in attendance.

"I'm still not sure we've forgiven you for stealing Aidan away," Lucas teased when the waiter walked away. "Victoria had to get creative when she recruited him."

"He was ready to try this side of the pond." Victoria shot her husband an amused glance. "I might've implied that when the river turned green on St. Patrick's Day, Chicago would feel like Ireland."

Watching the banter between the pair made Sophia's heart twist painfully. It reminded her so much of the wonderful days when she'd felt that camaraderie and partnership with her own husband. Brigadier General Franklin Leone had been dead almost a year now and she still couldn't quite accept it.

She took a bite of her meal and worked hard to enjoy the fresh flavors of tender pasta and crisp vegetables. She would not let a wave of loneliness ruin the evening. Doing her best to keep up her end of the conversation, she shared more about her future son-in-law. "Aidan is mesmerized with the Seattle area. He hasn't seen much beyond the sights downtown, but when they dropped me at the airport this morning, he and Frankie were planning a visit to Tillicum Village this weekend. It's a traditional native tribal experience."

"I remember making that trip ages ago," Lucas said. "They'll have a fantastic time."

"You know, I think he might be considering it for the rehearsal dinner." Sophia smiled with anticipation. "It would be quite memorable if it works out."

Victoria's eyes sparkled. "Their wedding will be memorable, regardless. I know we're both looking forward to attending."

"And Frankie can't wait to have you both join us," Sophia replied. With so much to celebrate, it was silly of her to dwell on who *wouldn't* be there. She took another bite of her pasta, washed it down with a sip of excellent wine and struggled again to forgive her husband for missing this incredible milestone in their daughter's life.

Victoria leaned forward and lowered her voice. "If everything is perfect and wonderful, why are you only poking at your dinner?"

Sophia lifted her gaze and met the concern shining in her friend's eyes. Victoria was as sharp as any of the private investigators she kept on her staff. While all three of them knew this dinner was meant to be comforting, neither she nor Victoria had ever been good at beating around the proverbial bush.

Sophia smiled. "I just can't say thank you enough." Without Victoria, she and her daughter might never have been reconciled.

Victoria set her fork aside and reached for her glass of wine. "You've said thank you more than enough already—none of which was necessary. I'm happy for you and Frankie, even if it cost me a top investigator."

Why had Sophia come all this way if she wasn't going to be honest about her other concerns? This wasn't something to discuss over a phone or a video chat later. She wanted to see their immediate reactions when she asked her questions. Sophia tried to muster some courage. Shy and uncertain weren't typical for her. She was accustomed to boldly heading exactly where she needed to go in a conversation or in business.

"Aidan is remarkable," Sophia said with a tight smile. "You should see them together." Here she went again, dancing around the more pertinent issue. *Get to the point!*

"We'll see them at the wedding." Victoria's smile didn't quite ease the curiosity in her eyes. "But I'm sure that's not why you've come all this way, Sophia."

"Should I excuse myself?" Lucas asked.

"Of course not," Sophia replied immediately. Whatever she told Victoria would find its way to Lucas anyway. She didn't begrudge them that. It had been the same in her own marriage. Until those last two years anyway, when his overseas operations put more than geography obstacles between her and her husband.

Why couldn't she just get the words out? It wasn't as if Victoria wouldn't understand her predicament. By now her friend had probably guessed why she'd made the trip. "You know I still have questions about Frank."

Both Lucas and Victoria nodded, though neither offered any comment.

Her husband had been found guilty of treason during his last deployment. Before he could be transferred to prison, he'd killed himself, leaving Frankie and Sophia to deal with the fallout. When she closed her eyes at night, the memory of watching that closed-circuit monitor fill with the image of his pale, lifeless face haunted her. Sophia suspected he had carried terrible secrets to his grave. Secrets that might not even have answers.

Though Frankie believed her father was innocent of the treason charge and was certain he'd been murdered, there had never been a scrap of evidence to support her theory. It was only one facet of the complex situation that had wedged them apart.

While Sophia had accepted she'd always be curious about her husband's last days, it was her internal battle that had brought her to Chicago. During her career as a military analyst, she'd taken information and made concise assessments. Now she wondered if her ability to read people and situations had failed her.

"Not just Frank." Sophia shook her head. "It's Paul, too." In the wake of Frank's suicide, she'd needed to act quickly to protect her future and Frankie's, as well. Paul Sterling, an old friend, had helped her launch Leo Solutions, the security company she and her husband had envisioned to keep them busy after his retirement. Mere days ago she'd found out Paul had betrayed her in favor of his own interests.

How had she allowed two men to fool her so completely?

"Every way I look at what's happened," Sophia went on, "the common denominator is my judgment or lack thereof." She picked up her fork, stabbing a stem of roasted asparagus and dragging it through the light cream sauce. "Forget I said anything." She glanced from Victoria to Lucas. "I don't really know what I need, or even what I want to do next. Please, let's talk about something else."

"All right," Victoria said. "Have you found your dress for the wedding?"

"I have something in mind." Sophia felt her smile bloom. It happened whenever she toyed with ideas for the upcoming wedding. While the final choices would be up to Frankie and Aidan, she loved window-shopping and perusing magazines and online sites for creative ideas to present to the bride and groom. "It's all happened so quickly, I've only been shopping online so far. Frankie hasn't had any time to decide on colors or venues, though she made me promise not to wear something that fades into the decor. I thought I might shop a bit while I'm here."

"We should go together," Victoria said with an eager smile. "The mother of the bride should dazzle, but not quite as much as the bride herself. Has Frankie given any thought to her dress?"

"Not particularly. You know she wasn't the type of little girl who played wedding day dress up like so many of her friends." Sophia curled her fingers around the hemmed edge of the napkin in her lap, assaulted by memories of happier times. "I don't want to jinx it, but I'm hoping she'll choose to have my wedding gown altered and restyled to make it hers."

"Oh, that would be beautiful." Victoria blinked rapidly. "You're all right with the idea?"

"I suggested it." Sophia forgot to take the bite of pasta she'd gathered onto her fork. "She loves the traditional, understated lines of my wedding dress and it's a way for her to include her father." Sophia felt bittersweet tears at the back of her throat. She would not cry another tear for Frank or his memory. "She wants to honor the start of our family as she starts her own."

"Sounds as though your daughter's a thoughtful and compassionate young woman," Lucas said.

Sophia could have hugged him. It was the perfect assessment and a lovely way to put it. "Thank you. I think so, too."

Her gaze dropped to her plate as her mind drifted back to that idyllic time when the future was a bright, hope-filled horizon. The Leone family had faced the world together as a team. She'd weathered the highs and lows with her husband during his military career. Just when they were on the cusp of the next stage—ready to enjoy their empty nest and launch a new venture—life had fallen to pieces. Countless times over the past year, she'd fought off the urge to scream and wave her fist at that deceptive horizon. *Life is not always fair, Sophia.*

"Frankie still believes he was innocent, doesn't she?" Lucas asked.

Sophia nodded, her heart heavy. "Her faith in him is relentless and even stronger now since Paul revealed his true colors."

"She's Frank's daughter through and through," Victoria observed. "I saw it the moment she walked into my office. She has his stride, his chin and all of his tenacity."

"Among other things," Sophia admitted. There were moments, such as this one, when the sadness at the scope of her loss flattened her. She tossed her napkin over the remainder of her dinner and swallowed back another wave of unanswerable questions. Her fingers locked in her lap and she squeezed until her knuckles protested.

Victoria leaned forward, her voice low. "Keeping your worries bottled up isn't helping you move forward."

"If you'd rather discuss what's troubling you elsewhere, we can wrap this up," Lucas offered.

"That's kind of you both, but not necessary. I'm overthinking things." Sophia tried to believe that explanation as she unclenched her hands, automatically rubbing the place where her wedding rings had been. She'd taken them off the day after the funeral, when any reminder of her ties to her disgraced husband would impede the launch of Leo Solutions. As a family, they'd been so close. As a couple, they'd focused their plans on giving Frankie a solid foundation. How had it suddenly crumbled?

"Frankie wasn't the only one to dig into Frank's case. I've been discreet," Sophia confessed. "I haven't found anything helpful or conclusive yet. It would be nice to confirm my suspicions about his guilt or innocence. Frankie views him with a daughter's hero worship. I won't take that away from her."

"Of course not," Victoria agreed.

"After the things Paul said and did last week, it made me wonder about Frank all over again." Sophia recognized that Victoria knew more than her fair share about pain and betrayal. She understood how betrayal often led a person to ignore some details and put more weight on other points, which blurred the facts into something closer to fiction. "Maybe Frankie's right and we should try harder to clear her dad's name."

"Say the word and I'll have one of our investigators start digging into it."

Sophia appreciated Victoria's offer. It came as no surprise, and professional assistance was one more reason to be here in person. She should say yes and let Victoria handle it while she went back to help Frankie with wedding plans. Would the answers change anything? Her husband was dead, a convicted traitor—it wasn't a simple matter at all. The problem was still too sensitive, too fresh even a year after the verdict.

Now that the offer was on the table, she wasn't sure an investigation was the right way to go. "Maybe we should investigate." As the words left her mouth, everything felt all wrong. "Or maybe not." Exasperated with herself, she tried to laugh. "What do I know?"

Her throat tight with frustration, she raised her glass and finished off her wine. Her hotel was just down the street and she didn't have to worry about driving. The bold flavors of the wine melted on her tongue but didn't give her any insight or steady her nerves. Didn't she *want* the answers? Wouldn't that help her sleep at night?

Assuming Victoria's investigators could find the truth, knowing the facts wouldn't actually change anything. Frankie would still be short one outstanding father. As Sophia had reviewed Frank's last few years, even amid all the chaos and inevitable suspicion, she'd never doubted his love or devotion to their daughter.

"Why don't we launch the investigation? You can call it off at any time," Lucas said.

No, it was better not to start at all. "Perhaps," Sophia replied at last, "his secrets, good or bad, are better left buried."

"Even if he was murdered?"

"I know what Frankie believes and I can't blame her. Suicide doesn't fit the Frank Leone we knew and loved." Sophia carried the burden of that heartache in the locked muscles across her shoulders. "I didn't tell her or anyone else how he changed, how he pulled away from me at the end. I'm not sure she ever needs to know about those final months."

Though they hadn't been aware back then that it would be the end. Sophia had thought there would be time for him to come around and be himself once more. She'd talked about it with a therapist, focused on shoring up her weaknesses, never expecting Frank to break.

"You have excellent instincts, Sophia. What do *you* know?" Victoria prompted.

"Certainly my husband had enemies capable of staging a suicide." Though she'd searched, none of his obvious adversaries had been in the area at the time of his death. "Even if by some miracle of detective work we could pinpoint a culprit now, bringing that person to justice would likely be impossible."

"That's a fair point." Lucas nodded sagely. "And it would create a distraction and turmoil when you and Frankie should be focused on happier events."

"Yes," Sophia agreed. "That's exactly the issue. I don't want to do anything that would cast a cloud over her wedding day. She and I might have unanswered, even unanswerable questions, but we're finally at a point where we both feel as though we have strong family ties again." She leaned back as the waiter removed dishes and poured more wine. When he was gone, she admitted, "Part of my hesitation is that I don't want to be proven right, either."

Lucas's brow furrowed. "What do you mean?"

"If the verdict was correct, if Frank did commit treason, I don't want to confirm that and destroy Frankie's fond memories. Whatever happened in his final assignment, he did everything right as a dad."

"We understand completely," Victoria said. "If you change your mind at any time, the offer is there for you."

"Thank you for listening and letting me ramble on about it."

"If you want my professional assessment, I'll say your instincts haven't been compromised in the slightest," Victoria declared in her trademark steely tone. "Paul took advantage while you were distracted by grief, that's all. Whatever Frank didn't tell you about his career or his personal problems, he loved you and Frankie above all else. He must have been protecting you."

"He loved Frankie." During those last two years, Sophia had lost her faith that her husband loved her with equal devotion. He'd grown distant and secretive. She'd tried and failed to chalk it up to his protective nature.

Victoria consulted her watch. "One more minute for self-pity and then I'm ordering an outrageous dessert for all of us to share."

Lucas pretended to protest, shifting his chair close enough to drape an arm across the back of Victoria's.

They looked utterly content as a couple, as a team. Sophia had had that once, for nearly the entirety of her thirty-year marriage. However, that period of her life had ended, and she needed to focus on the good times, to let the uncertainty go.

"I don't need even one more minute." Sophia reached into her purse for her cell phone. "Let me show you some pictures of far more important things."

She brought up a slide show and together the three of them admired the options Frankie would eventually sort out, from bouquets and centerpieces to tuxedo tails and cake flavors. "We've already decided to surprise Aidan with an old family recipe for the groom's cake."

"This will be a dream day for all of you," Victoria said with a wistful smile. "You must be so excited."

"We're going to have so much fun with the planning. Both of them are huge assets to Leo Solutions. I have so much to look forward to." Catching herself gushing, she paused for a breath. "I thought I'd lost that relationship with her forever. You returned it to me, Victoria. You and Aidan." There weren't enough thank-yous to adequately express her joy that her daughter was healthy, happy and thriving again. It truly was time to stop dwelling on the past and let go of the questions that would never have answers.

Sophia insisted on paying for dinner, managing to win a lighthearted argument with Lucas over the check. As they parted ways at the restaurant door, a shopping date scheduled for tomorrow, she chose to walk rather than accept Victoria's offer for a ride to the hotel. The crisp spring breeze drifting off the lake caught at her hair, boosting her mood as she headed down the street.

Moments after Victoria's car pulled away, she regretted her decision. Without the distraction of conversation, she felt eyes on her immediately. A chill raised the hair at the back of her neck and she called on her years of self-discipline not to show any recognition to her observer. She knew she would be safe enough as long as she was surrounded by other pedestrians.

Though she hadn't made a secret of her travel plans to Chicago, she couldn't imagine who would bother watching her. Mind over matter, she thought as she put one foot in front of the other, shoulders back, head high, refusing to let her discomfort show.

The tactic had served her well as a general's wife, an analyst and a mother. Opponents large and small had cowered in the face of her poise and determination. Let whoever was out there watch. Let them see Sophia Leone hadn't changed a bit as a widow or under the pressure of the events that followed.

Poised or not, she felt a wave of relief wash over her when she entered the hotel lobby, interrupting that intense, uncomfortable scrutiny. She crossed to the front desk with a smile on her face. She might as well extend her reservation for an additional night. One day of shopping with Victoria might not be enough.

"Ah, Ms. Leone, of course. And you have a message."

"I do?" Sophia was surprised. Frankie would have called her cell.

The man behind the desk passed her a small envelope embossed with the hotel logo. Sophia noted the precise block lettering of her name on the outside. Memories whispered through her, making her shiver. Frank had preferred that style over his nearly illegible cursive handwriting. They'd often joked that he had the penmanship of a doctor. How rude of someone to try to irritate her by mimicking his habit. She caught herself in the middle of the overreaction. Printed lettering wasn't a personal attack or automatic insult. She chalked up her edginess to having been watched so closely on her brief walk. Moving down the hall toward the elevators, she opened the envelope and pulled out the note.

She quickly read it through. She grabbed at the nearest wall for support as her knees buckled. *You and Frankie are in danger. Meet me at Parkhurst by nine. Prepare to run.*

It wasn't signed, but the writing, the location told

her it had to be from Frank. That was impossible. He was dead.

Parkhurst, the US Army Reserve Center just off the old Route 66. She and Frank had been there once for a dining out, early in his career. They'd just learned she was pregnant. She remembered avoiding the wine but not the curious speculation of the other wives. She pressed a hand to her mouth to smother the whimper building in her throat. This wasn't happening. Couldn't be. She needed to get to her room. Needed to return to the desk and get a description of who had delivered the message.

Her stomach tightened while she read the note again more slowly. The meaning didn't register at all as her fingertip followed the bold swipe of the pen strokes making up each letter and word. Her body sighed with memories of those happier times.

With an effort, she straightened her spine, tucked away the nostalgia and pulled herself together. Whoever had created this note had forged Frank's handwriting perfectly. Sophia swallowed and forced herself to take a deep, calming breath. Frank wasn't the only person in the world to write this way. He wasn't the only person who would choose a remote location for a discreet meeting. At the edge of the nature preserve surrounding the facility, there would be plenty of privacy at night.

She walked back to the front desk, hoping she didn't look as pale as she felt. When the clerk smiled, she held up the note. "Can you tell me who left this and when?"

The young man on duty shook his head. "It was here when I came on an hour ago. Jenny only told me it was urgent, according to the man who left it."

"Man?"

The desk clerk nodded.

She pressed her lips together as potential images and thoughts collided like bumper cars in her head. "Could I access your security footage?"

"Um, no? That kind of thing would have to be approved by our—"

"It's okay," she said, cutting his protest short. What were the odds the person who'd written the missive had had the audacity to deliver it? Zero to none. She tapped the note against her palm. "Thank you for your time."

Shoulders back, she aimed for the elevator once more. Frank was *dead*. She'd seen him in that morgue. Dead men didn't send notes inviting their widowed wives to meetings, advising them to run. Someone was attempting to put her off balance. She hitched her shoulders at the thought of being watched during her walk from the restaurant. Someone wanted to frighten her and lure her from the safety of the hotel.

Defiant, she reached out and punched the call button for the elevator. When the car arrived, she shoved the note into her purse, ignoring it. She would not be influenced by the emotions of her past. It would be foolish to dash out to a relatively deserted area alone. She knew better than to take that sort of risk.

When she reached her room, she found another note on the floor just inside the doorway. Someone had slipped it under the door. No name on the envelope this time. She tore it open and tears sprang to her eyes as she skimmed it. The message was the same handwriting as the note left at the desk, but the first word stole her breath.

Dolcezza.

Stunned, she went limp and slid to the floor, the wall

her only support. Her gaze was locked on the precious endearment Frank had used from their first date through every phone call and letter when they were apart. She pressed her lips together, holding back the wail of frustration and pain swelling in her throat.

So he'd called her sweetheart in Italian. Any number of people might know that detail about their lives. This did not mean Frank had miraculously returned from the dead. Whoever was orchestrating this was pushing all the right buttons, prodding her to make a predictable response. *Melodramatic and cruel*, she thought, checking her watch. If she left now, she'd just get to Parkhurst in time. Options ran through her mind. Victoria could help her sort out who had delivered the message. She could certainly find someone to ride with her or shadow her to the meeting.

But what if it *was* Frank?

What was she thinking? Her husband was dead, his body buried in Seattle. She thought suddenly about the closed casket. *What if...?*

No. Her husband had been an incredible man and she'd loved him from that first moment through all the ups and downs of marriage and career to the farewell she hadn't known would be their last. She'd stood by him against the treason charges despite her doubts.

She glanced at the note, heard his voice whispering "*dolcezza*" at her ear when she read it again. Absolutely not. Remarkable he might've been, but not even Frank could come back from the dead. Shoving the second note into her purse with the first, she dragged herself from the floor and went to the bathroom to freshen up.

When she came out, the notes taunted her. Her maternal instinct kicked into high gear. While she might ignore a veiled threat against herself, she couldn't leave Frankie's safety to chance. Her daughter had worked tirelessly to triumph over a devastating physical injury and subsequent emotional turmoil. She wouldn't let any vicious stunt ruin things now.

Determination beating urgently in her veins, Sophia packed her overnight bag. She considered changing clothes, but only switched from her heels to her flats. Her lightweight black sweater and slacks were easy to move in and the closest things to camouflage in her wardrobe. Whoever was waiting for her at Parkhurst, she had to go.

Nothing and no one would prevent her from keeping Frankie safe and her future secure.

Chapter Two

Sophia sent her daughter a quick text message while she waited for the valet to bring her rental car from the hotel parking garage. She breathed a sigh of relief at the quick, normal reply. She was sure this meeting was bogus and equally sure she couldn't let it slide. Though she might be heading into the unknown alone, she intended to leave a trail of bread crumbs in case things went wrong. A lesson she'd learned from her husband—anticipate the best while creating a strategy to fend off the worst.

When the car arrived, she loaded her suitcase into the backseat and kept her purse up front. She left her cell phone on and synced it to the car's system. When the navigation software had a route ready for her, she pulled away from the hotel.

Frank wouldn't be there—couldn't possibly be there—but she had yet to come up with a plausible reason why anyone would impersonate him to get her attention.

Darkness fell as she made her way along historic Route 66 and headlights winked on under the purpling sky in her rearview mirror. Having memorized the brief note, she let the cadence of the words play through her mind over and over. Rubbing a pressure point on her earlobe, she blinked back a sudden rush of tears.

She'd thought the well had run dry months ago. Those early days after Frank killed himself had been wave after wave of sobbing, until she thought she'd never breathe properly again. Throughout their marriage she'd been alone frequently, always with the confident knowledge that she'd see him again. While their daughter bitterly accused her of moving on too quickly in establishing the security business, the harsh, lonely truth of how much she missed Frank had thankfully been buried under a mountain of new career distractions.

A car rushed up behind her and passed her in a blur. She glanced down, confirming she was driving the speed limit, and forgot the other car as it surged into the distance. She had more important things to consider. Who would be waiting for her at Parkhurst and why? How would she handle the encounter?

Maybe she should *call* Frankie and put her on alert. *You could be in danger* wasn't suitable for a text message. Sophia checked the clock. She could pull over and snap a picture of the notes with her phone and still arrive on time for the meeting.

That sort of move would only send her daughter and, by extension, the upper management of Leo Solutions into a tailspin of worry for Frankie and Sophia. Better to send an update when she had some facts about the situation rather than encourage useless conjecture that might stir up more trouble. Maintaining a good reputation within the industry of security services meant mitigating bad press.

The computerized voice of the navigation system announced the approaching exit number and instructions, and Sophia stayed in the right lane for the exit. As the voice related the next direction and turn, she continued around the curve of the ramp, merging onto the frontage road. She glanced ahead, noting the absolute darkness surrounding her destination. The Reserve Center would be long closed and the protected forest wouldn't be lit, either. Whoever had brought her here would have to speak to her through the car window. She had no intention of getting out and making herself an easier target.

A screech and scream of tires against the pavement brought her attention back to the road immediately. A car in front of her squealed to an abrupt stop. She checked her mirrors, her options limited by the traffic in the other lane, and jerked the wheel. She swerved right onto the rough shoulder so she wouldn't plow into the car. At nearly fifty miles per hour, her tires growled over the rumble strip cut into the pavement. She missed the stopped car by mere inches and braked hard, desperate to stop safely on the shoulder and catch her breath.

The driver in the stopped car suddenly gunned the engine and swerved to the shoulder, pushing his fender into her car. What the hell?

She couldn't see the driver through the tinted windows, but there was no way he hadn't seen her car. Dumbfounded, she swore again as she urged her car forward to escape. It didn't work. She braked, hoping he'd drive by. No such luck. Metal scraped and she was caught, helpless, as the other car forced hers off the road and down into the tree-lined ditch.

As her car slid down the slope, the other driver left her. Sophia struggled to get her car level and back up to the safety of the roadway. With the car off balance, the rear end fishtailed as her tires lost traction in the longer grass. She tried turning one way, then the other, only to find a loose bit of terrain that sent her car sliding farther into a ditch she hadn't seen. The seat belt grabbed at her, holding her tight until the car finally slid to a stop.

Thankfully the air bag didn't deploy. The navigation system warned she was going the wrong way. With shaking hands she silenced the automated voice grating out route corrections. Her headlights were swallowed by the ditch while the lights of other vehicles cut through the darkness on the highway above.

She twisted in the seat, looking for any sign of the other car. Apparently, it was long gone. Furious, she unfastened her seat belt and leaned over to scoop up her phone and purse from the passenger-side floorboard.

Suddenly the passenger door opened and the bright beam of a flashlight made her wince and shy away. "Hurry, Sophie." A hand stretched out to her from the other side of that glaring light.

The voice… *Impossible. Sophie?* Only Frank had ever gotten away with calling her Sophie.

She froze, too startled to move or reply. Maybe she'd hit her head. Maybe she'd been killed and didn't realize it yet.

"Move it!" The sharp command left no room for debate. "We have to get out of here right now."

The urgency in his voice seemed at odds with what must be a hallucination. If, somewhere deep in her subconscious, she hoped for help from her dead husband, wouldn't he be as calm as he'd been through every stress during their life together?

"Snap out of it." He tugged on her free hand. "Or they'll kill us both."

She couldn't see his face, though his touch felt familiar. "You're already dead," she whispered.

"Not anymore," he said, his tone gentling.

First the notes, now this…

What was going on? A terrible hoax was the only explanation. Who would do such a thing? "Go away." She resisted the warmth in his voice. The sense of awareness was a figment of her imagination. "Go away!" Panic swelled inside, expanding outward until she thought her skin would shred from the pressure. "Leave me alone!"

Engines roared closer and faded away, cars of all sizes going on about their business as if reality hadn't spun her world out of control. She snatched up her purse and reached to open her door.

It was jammed. Of course it was jammed; the other car had damaged the driver's side of her car.

"This way. Now!" The man who couldn't be her husband swore as she continued to fight with the door that wouldn't budge.

"That's enough." The flashlight went out. He grabbed her arm and dragged her across the seats and out of the car.

The crush of his fingers burned her skin with undeniable familiarity. She told herself to fight him, told herself she was delusional, and still her body refused to resist.

When her feet hit the ground, she wobbled a bit, whether a result of the shock, the panic or the uneven ground, she couldn't be sure. Probably all of the above. Her determined rescuer steadied her body with his, and in the shadows she recognized the shape and scent of the man who'd been her partner in life for three decades. Impossible…

"Frank?" In the darkness it was hard to tell. Maybe her vision had been compromised along with her common sense. "How?"

"I'll explain everything in a minute. Can you walk?"

"Of course." Offended, she took a step as he did, then stopped short. "My suitcase!" Her computer was in there; she wouldn't leave it behind. "It's in the back."

"At least you came prepared to run." He sounded relieved as he returned to pull her suitcase out of the backseat. "Tell me you didn't check out of the hotel."

She hadn't, though she refused to volunteer anything. "I don't owe *you* any explanations."

"True enough."

She struggled to keep up with his longer stride even in her flats. *Just like old times*, she thought. At just over six foot he was eight inches taller than her, and those inches seemed to all be in his legs. Where were they going? Away from her car…back the way she'd come, she realized. The headlights of a car in the distance allowed her to make out a vehicle waiting in the ditch a few yards away. Black. SUV.

He opened the passenger-side door for her, the way he'd done at every opportunity since their first date. Her stomach churned as her heart floated on a silly, girlish burst of hope. Could this really be Frank, alive and apparently well? She squashed the fluttery sensations. If it was, her husband owed her a great many answers. "Where are you taking me?"

"Does it matter as long as you survive?"

"It might," she replied. "I can take care of myself, you know."

"One of the many things I love about you."

Though he'd surely meant it as a comfort, his use of the present tense deflated her hopes and sent them crashing in an unwelcome thud in her chest. It couldn't be true. If he still loved her, why had he let her suffer thinking he was dead? "The rental agreement is in the car," she remembered, too late.

The SUV bumped and lurched along the ditch until he found enough of a rut to get them back up to the road. "Sophie, they know you were driving the car. You were run off the road because they were following your movements. They've *targeted* you."

She studied what she could see of his hard profile, finally registering his all-black attire. In the dark sweater, cargo pants and matte jump boots, he'd dressed for an operation rather than a reunion. She suppressed the chill of concern about what he'd gotten himself tangled up in. "Who is 'they'?"

"It's a long story."

"Then start talking." How could this be happening?

"As soon as we're safely out of here. The story I have to tell you is too important to be interrupted."

"Convenient." She crossed her arms. "You invite me to a conversation and then you won't talk."

"It's better if you hear *none* of it rather than only some of it," he insisted. "Keep an eye out for anyone on our tail."

"Fine." She wanted to ignore him and the outrageous situation, but she couldn't afford such a childish indulgence. "At least tell me how you faked your death."

"Soon, I promise."

Anger surged through her, fueled by the adrenaline

of sliding off the road into increasingly impossible circumstances. "Tell me now or take me back to the hotel."

"If I take you back to the hotel, they'll kill you tonight," he claimed. "And Frankie tomorrow."

That got her attention and put her focus back on point. She pulled her cell phone out of her purse, her fingers brushing, in the process, the notes he'd written. Goose bumps surged up and down her arms. "I'm calling Victoria. She'll send someone to pick us up."

He shook his head. "No. Turn it off. Please," he added, softening the order to a request. "There's no such thing as safe if they can track you."

She'd deactivated the GPS signal, but he didn't need to know that. Until she could trust him, she wouldn't give him any more advantages. Let him worry that she could turn on her phone at any time and get help immediately. "Give me a good reason to trust anything coming out of your mouth."

"I'm your husband," he stated. "You've always been my top priority."

She laughed. "I might believe such a statement if you were still officially *alive*." Headlights flashed in the side mirror, and her heart rate kicked up. She hoped it was just a speeder and not more trouble.

"Then how about this?" He spared her a quick glance. "I'm the only living person who understands what we're up against."

The "we're" stood out to her, a beacon slicing through the fog of his words. Reluctantly, she cooperated, turning off her phone and dropping it into her purse again.

"You're angry." He checked his mirrors. "You should

be. And I'm more sorry than any words can accurately convey."

"That sounds like a cop-out." She ignored the little voice in her head that wanted to give him the benefit of the doubt. Faking a suicide fell into the category of drastic measures. Frank wasn't the sort to take such a step without good cause. She fisted her hands in her lap, her fingernails digging into her palms. If she left her hands loose, she would no doubt reach out to him just to see if he was real.

"At the time, it was necessary," he said as if he knew what she was thinking. "I knew you'd be okay, better off without me dragging you down."

What did that mean? She heard the bitterness underscoring his words. If she was so much better off, why storm back into her life? Why were she and Frankie in danger? "Being a widow hasn't been peaches and cream, Frank." Her emotions leaped wildly with every heartbeat, unable to settle between joy that he was alive and outrage that he'd chosen a fake death rather than trust her with his secrets. How dare he!

"Yeah, well, being dead isn't all it's cracked up to be, either."

"You've put Frankie and me through terrible heartache. She needed you." *I needed you.* She kept the admission to herself, unwilling to let him have that much of her again. Not before she understood how this had happened.

"You both need me right now." He sighed and in the light of oncoming headlights she caught the tic in his jaw.

"Arrogant as ever." She couldn't resist baiting him. That supreme confidence had been simultaneously one of his most attractive and most frustrating traits when they were young and eager to get out and conquer the world. *Together.* So much for that philosophy serving as the cornerstone of their marriage and family.

False or not, death had parted them, and he'd left her alone to find her own way through the consequences of his mistakes. "You know I can keep a secret," she said, hating the tremor in her voice. "You had no right to keep the truth from me."

"I know." He stretched a hand toward her as he used to do on road trips. "I'm so sorry, *dolcezza*."

She didn't take that hand, though refusing it cost her. She wanted to touch him so badly. "You're going to tell me the whole story." He'd never been a fan of her using an inflection that carried the same gravity and certainty of his general's tone of command, but if any situation required it, this was the one.

"I am," he replied, with both hands on the steering wheel once more. "You're not going to like it."

"I already don't like it, Frank."

He'd saved her life tonight. In theory, anyway. For all she knew, he'd hired the driver to run her off the road so he could look like a hero. She gave herself a mental shake. Regardless of circumstances, she couldn't believe he would willfully risk her safety under any circumstances.

"Give me one thing," she said. "One detail to go on, or I will call Victoria and Frankie and tell them you've kidnapped me."

He muttered an oath, knowing she would follow through. Between the Colby Agency and Leo Solutions, Frank wouldn't have anywhere to hide if they knew he was alive.

"The man following you was one of the top snipers in the Afghanistan military. One word from his boss and your life is over."

She sucked in a breath. "Why?" Who would make her a target?

"That's one detail. I swear to you, as soon as I'm sure we're out of harm's way, I'll tell you everything."

"Harm's way or not, you'll tell me everything tonight." He wasn't the only one who could issue orders.

With a short nod, he rolled his broad shoulders, shifting in the seat as he followed the signs toward Chicago Midway International Airport.

She remembered the feel of those shoulders under her hands after a tough day at work when she'd help him work out the kinks…or late at night in the heat of passion. Oh, how she wanted to trust him, to be sure she could trust him. It scared her—more than being run off the road—just how much she wanted to believe in Frank Leone again.

Chapter Three

When Frank was convinced they hadn't been followed, he decided on a mid-priced hotel near the airport. If they didn't take cash, he had a credit card that matched his false ID. Although Sophia probably wouldn't have complained about the dirt-cheap place where he'd been staying, he didn't want to risk taking her there. If the enemy was this close, anything could happen.

Besides, he couldn't imagine the woman he loved so dearly, with her timeless sense of style, in that flea-bitten decor. The discussion ahead of him would be difficult enough without any guilt over the accommodations. He was distracted plenty by her amazing body. He'd missed her so much. She deserved the best life could offer. Whether she wanted to accept protection from him right now or not, he had to make sure she stayed safe.

Knowing his wife, he suspected their marriage was beyond salvaging. He'd never win back her trust—not in the ways that mattered most. Over three decades ago he'd marveled that the smartest, prettiest girl in the world had fallen in love with him and stuck by him through an army career that carried them around the globe. There had never been any real secrets between them until those last two years. This entire mess rested on his shoulders. *All of it was his fault.*

No avoiding the hard reality of truth. He could offer explanations and apologies—and he would—even knowing it wouldn't make any difference in the long run. He'd started this journey with the best of intentions and it had backfired completely. His mistakes had already cost him the love of his life; he'd never forgive himself if his mistakes got her and their daughter hurt or killed.

Two years ago, she'd sensed the distance he had created to shelter her. Worse, he'd sensed her doubts. That unexpected result had hurt him the most. The wariness he'd seen in her eyes during their last visit, after the guilty verdict had been announced, had plagued him through every lonely day since he'd disappeared.

He parked at the back of the building and came around to open her door, taking her suitcase as she exited the SUV. Finally, he indulged himself with an up-close study of her. Sophia created a fashion statement in any circumstance. Her black sweater and perfectly tailored slacks graced her curves. The long necklace she wore shimmered against the black and he noticed she'd changed from the heels she'd worn to dinner to sleek flats. His arms ached to gather her into a hug, to hold her close and never let go. Without the heels, the top of her head would tuck perfectly under his chin. Despite the memories of how comforting that embrace would be, he managed to keep his distance.

When they were safe behind the locked door of the rented room, he breathed a little easier. If they were lucky, they would survive the night and he could get her on a plane to the tropics tomorrow. He wanted her far away from the inevitable conflict on the horizon.

He dropped her suitcase on the bed, ignoring that potential minefield, while she strolled on by and pulled a chair away from the table. He heard her fidgeting a bit, settling in while she waited for him to explain himself. He didn't have to look to know she had her right leg crossed over her left, her hands linked in her lap.

Where to begin? He studied his hands, not quite ready to face her. "Do you want a drink?"

"No, thank you."

Her voice was cool, aloof, and he could feel her big brown eyes studying him. He sighed. It shouldn't be this hard to talk to his *wife*. On some level he believed she might understand. Too bad that level was smothered by guilt.

"Just get on with it," she urged in the unflappable tone that had guided professional and family meetings with equal efficiency. "I want the truth. The whole truth." She shook her head, the one visible concession to her anger and frustration. "Some sort of reasonable explanation for what you've done to us."

He closed his eyes a moment, pushing a hand through hair that felt too long since he'd abandoned the shorter army regulation cut. "I doubt much of what I'm about to say will sound reasonable."

The silence stretched between them like a high wire over the Grand Canyon, and he was walking without a net. There'd been no training or experience to prepare him for this crisis. "I did what I believed was necessary to protect you and Frankie." He'd allowed his professional life to destroy his family. No excuses would suffice and none of the words in his mind felt adequate to the task. On a deep breath, he perched on the side of the bed closer to her chair. "It started before we moved to Washington," he began, watching the awareness come into her lovely eyes. "Keeping you out of it was essential."

"Because you planned to become a traitor?"

"Never." He winced. "Though I knew it was possible my actions would look that way."

She caught her full lower lip between her teeth. "Your daughter never believed you were capable of treason," she said. "Unfortunately, by that time, I didn't share her confidence."

He deserved that for how poorly he'd handled the situation. "I wanted to explain, to reassure you." The risks had been too great. Any out-of-character reaction from Sophia would have tipped off the criminals the army had been trying to root out. "You couldn't have helped me. I looked at it from every angle. If I'd told you anything at all, if you'd reacted too much or not enough, if you'd changed your analysis or assessment, it would've gotten all three of us killed."

"What happened?" She hurled the words at him. "Names and dates, Frank." She leaned forward, pinned him with those wary eyes. "Give me a clear and accurate picture. Did you know Frankie believed I willfully helped convict you?"

"No!" He pushed to his feet, striding as far from her as the room allowed. He hadn't understood why his daughter had wound up working in Savannah when Sophia launched the new business in Seattle, but he couldn't risk getting close enough to either of them to find out. "How could she believe such a thing?"

"You can ask her yourself. Now keep talking," she

said. "Hold back now and I'll walk right out that door and in my heart you'll stay dead forever."

Sophia didn't make idle threats. If she walked out of this room without the details, without his protection, she'd be dead within the week. Frankie, too. "It's too dangerous. Please, believe that if nothing else."

She drummed her fingertips impatiently on her knee.

He crossed the room again, forcing himself to sit down at the table. He could slow down and do this right. "First, I'm not a traitor." He stopped right there as the emotion choked him. He didn't know quite how to beg her forgiveness, to uproot the terrible seeds of doubts he'd planted. "The Army Criminal Investigations Command approached me just over two years ago." Though he knew all deals were off, his voice cracked on exposing her to the black stain that had ended his career. "Before that last deployment. Equipment had gone missing. Locals claimed army personnel were helping move drug shipments. High-value targets disappeared without a trace. While that sounds logical with the honeycomb of hideouts in Afghanistan, no rumors or sightings were getting out. CID asked me to go undercover and appear amenable to cooperating with one particular drug lord. I did what was required of me, as always."

She gasped, her eyes wide and sad. "The CID didn't back you up?"

"That was *before* the treason charge." He knew she was thinking about the lives lost on that last busted mission. "Cooperating with the drug lord was a test to earn the trust of the criminals CID wanted to net. What I didn't realize at the time was that by passing that test I put you and Frankie in danger." He hitched his shoulders against the impossible burden. "Smoothing the way for that drug shipment earned me a rare invitation to Hell-fire, an elite circle of retired military personnel that CID had been trying to dismantle for more than five years."

She stared at him in disbelief. "They named them-selves after a missile?"

He nodded. "They're cocky. Considering what they've gotten away with and how they've managed to line their pockets, they've earned the moniker. As a general will-ing to cross the line for personal gain, I was a shoo-in. Once I was in, my real goal was to identify the Hellfire leadership and gather evidence against them."

"Which meant working with them in the short-term," she said quietly.

"Yes." He swallowed the lump of guilt in his throat. Good men had died for bad reasons that day. Under-cover or not, he'd been ready to serve time as a pen-ance. "And it eventually led to the treason charge." He cracked his knuckles. "There was a bank account in the Caymans that would've made you blush." His stilted laughter didn't hold any humor. "Doing bad things for the right reasons is no excuse. I should've found an-other way."

The CID special agent running his part of the opera-tion assured him there hadn't been another way, but he would carry those terrible memories forever. On his feet again, Frank paced to the door and back, his mind lost in that cursed patch of dirt and the acrid scents of burn-ing fuel and explosives roiling through the desert air.

With both hands fisting helplessly at his sides, he forced himself to tell her the rest. "We figured out after that fiasco, I wasn't the only CID recruit. An-other team was tracking the drug shipment. Somehow

Hellfire learned the shipment would be seized and used the opportunity to blame it on me."

"Moving illegal drugs is a crime, yes. That doesn't explain the treason charge."

He rubbed one thumb hard into the palm of his other hand. "Hellfire scrubbed the op rather than risk exposure. As Hellfire's newest member, I took the rap for the whole deal, letting the real traitors get away clean, their drug money gushing again like crude oil from a new well less than a week later."

"Frank, if what you say is true, it wasn't your fault."

Of course it was. He looked down to find she'd moved too close, her hands holding his. He wasn't worthy of her sympathy. Reluctantly, he shifted out of her reach. "The treason charge was manufactured just to ruin me, in case I was inclined to flip on Hellfire."

"I didn't want to believe you'd sold information about troop movements and weapons in Kabul, but who else could have leaked those facts?"

Only another general and his cronies, Frank kept to himself. As an analyst, she would've assessed and reported on the intel provided. That was the trouble. With Hellfire railroading him and manipulating the intel, the only possible verdict was guilty.

"I had to do something. Behind bars, I'd never get to the bottom of this, if they even let me live. My CID contact, Special Agent J.D. Torres, came to see me after the verdict and we devised a plan to fake my death. Once I escaped, I knew enough to keep gathering evidence against them without worrying that they'd go after my family."

"And yet here we are, almost a year later." She sank back into the chair.

"Yes." His worst nightmare coming true in full color and in real time. "Based on what I learned during my brief time within Hellfire, I've been piecing parts of the puzzle together. I've learned how the drugs come into the country and I know the top three players in the group. I even managed to stop a drug shipment last month."

"That's progress, I guess. What did Torres have to say?"

He recognized that look. She was shifting gears, playing devil's advocate. He was about to preempt that move. "Torres was the only person who knew about me. I reached out to him to turn in my latest report and let him know where I stashed Hellfire's drugs for the CID to clean up. He didn't respond. I discovered he died in a single-car wreck last month. He'd gone missing more than forty-eight hours before police found the car torched, just off his normal route to and from work. Taking that shipment managed to get another man killed and put you and Frankie in the crosshairs."

"How can they possibly know you were responsible?"

"Process of elimination," he replied. "I'm the only one who understands how the money and drugs move through their sick, private retirement fund. I can't be sure when they learned I'm alive. They must have tortured Torres to discover how we stayed in contact."

"They threatened Frankie and me to draw you out?" She closed her eyes, her fingers sliding the pendant of her necklace along the chain. "How did they tell you?"

"It was a private message on a social media account. They sent me a picture of you, then followed that with the kill order." When she let loose a string of Italian curses for Hellfire, he couldn't have agreed more. "I can't quit now. If I don't stop them, who knows how many more people will get hurt or die while they get richer?"

Her gaze was distant, thoughtful, as she resumed her place at the very edge of her chair. "I felt someone watching me in Chicago."

"Yes," he said with a nod. "I've been shadowing the man they put on you since you arrived this morning. I had to move fast before the sniper could set up the shot."

"So you pulled me out of harm's way."

"It almost worked perfectly." His heart had stopped when they'd forced her off the road. "I'm not sure why they ran you off the road, unless they wanted your death to look like an accident."

"What about Frankie?"

The edge of panic in her voice slid as deep as a blade between his ribs. "I'm hoping this fiancé of hers can watch her back, but the sooner I wrap this up, the better for everyone." Once he eliminated Hellfire and knew his girls were safe, he could think about what to do with the rest of his lonely life.

Sophia nodded, her face pinched as she laced her fingers together in her lap. There had been a time when they'd faced bad news hand in hand. He never should have kept any of this from her. "Is he a good man?"

She lifted her gaze to meet his, blinking as she tried to put his question into the proper context. "Aidan? He's the best. Did you know he was a Colby investigator?"

"Yes. I did a background search on him." While Frank respected Victoria Colby-Camp and her agency, this was his baby girl's life on the line. "I sent him a death threat today."

"You did *what*?"

"Well, I sent it to him, but it was aimed specifically at Frankie," he clarified, realizing too late he'd only made things worse. "I wanted them on alert. I couldn't blurt out what was really going on. I needed them to react quickly, not ask questions."

"Oh, Lord." Her expressive eyes rolled to the ceiling. "Here I was, trying to figure out how to clue her in that you're alive and that we might need her help."

"We can't do that. We can't tell her anything." Panic snapped and clawed at his heart. "The more she knows about me, the more danger she's in."

Sophia's sound of frustration mimicked an unhappy grizzly bear. "If I don't kill you before this is over, she will. Trust me on that."

"I deserve it," he said through another wave of anguish. "But if I don't stop them—"

She held up a hand. "I can fill in the blank." She massaged the lobes of her ears around her earrings. "The treason charge," she began. "Did you knowingly send that team in Kabul to their deaths?"

That she could even think it of him stopped his heart more effectively than the drug he'd used to fake his death. Still, in light of everything, it was a fair question. "I did not." It had been such a sharp edge he'd been walking and he thought he'd done everything possible to make sure only he would or could be injured. A tactic that left him with no allies when the plan backfired. He'd been too new, hadn't known the real players within Hellfire or the full measure of their greed.

Now he did, and he needed to give his wife and daughter the best protection. "I know you don't owe me anything, *dolcezza*. Not your understanding and certainly not your forgiveness."

"Be quiet. I'm thinking of our next step."

"Our?" he echoed, staring at her. "No way."

"You need me," she countered.

He did need her. Desperately. When this was over, maybe they could talk about just how badly he needed her. Assuming he lived through the fight Hellfire would present. "What I need most is to know you're tucked away safely out of Hellfire's reach."

"Is there such a place?"

He didn't say yes fast enough.

"Then we'll do this together," she declared. She stood, the ghost of a smile tipping her lush mouth.

"Absolutely not," he said. He wanted to keep her as far from the chaos as possible. He'd often fantasized about a reunion when the coast was clear. Coming home to Sophia had always been the best part of fulfilling his military responsibilities. Someday this mess with Hellfire would be behind them and, if she gave him a chance, he'd never leave her again.

"Look where you've wound up working alone!" She switched to Italian, indulging in a fiery rant that called into question his intelligence and sanity. "I have contacts and resources. You need my help."

"You think the two of us can do what the CID couldn't?"

"Yes." Her eyes glittered, daring him to contradict her. "As a team," she said pointedly. "We *were* unstoppable. They have regulations and systems. We have a dead man with good intel and a reputable woman with excellent connections."

He knew that look. In full protective mode, she wouldn't back down, even if it was for her own good. He reconsidered his strategy. "Since we're in Chicago," he said, "why don't we ask if you can work your connections from Victoria's offices?" The Colby Agency could keep Sophia safe while he went after Hellfire personally.

"Just me?" she asked too sweetly.

Naturally she saw straight through him. "Standard protocol," he said, defending the suggestion. "You in the office, me in the field."

She tossed her head. "I will *not* let you out of my sight. Our daughter would never forgive me if something happened to you…*again*."

"She already thinks I'm dead. I refuse to take the chance of making her an orphan for real. I don't want her to know anything until this is done."

She pinned him with a wicked glare. "Were you this melodramatic during official briefings?"

"The lives of my wife and daughter weren't on the line in my official briefings," he said, thoroughly exasperated with her insurmountable stubborn streak. "Haven't you been listening to me?" He'd spent more than twenty years commanding troops, so how was it he had so much trouble with this one woman?

"I have been listening very closely. The only real point you've made is that you need my help."

He scrubbed at the back of his neck. How could he have believed she would listen to reason? He needed help, yes, and he'd count her an excellent ally—from the safety of an office surrounded by armed experts. Putting her in the line of fire was taking an unforgivable chance. Not to mention how keeping her close would be torture. Already her familiar lily-and-sandalwood fragrance seeped into his system, giving him more comfort than he deserved. "You can help me—from a safe distance."

"Frank, be reasonable. You need someone at your back."

"Victoria would agree with me," he countered. As arguments went, it was too weak and they both knew it.

Her gaze sharpened. Her keen mind was working through his protests to the crux of the problem. "You're holding back a significant factor here. Who is it, Frank? Who's at the top of Hellfire?"

Furious at himself more than anyone at how he'd been fooled and used, he studied the pattern in the carpeting. He met her gaze, at last. "Kelly Halloran is the top man."

The blood drained from her face, turning her vibrant golden skin to ash. "Sit down," he said, moving to catch her. She slumped to the edge of the couch, her shoulders hunching as if she could physically block the news. He understood her reaction.

"Why?" she whispered. She sucked in a breath, eased away from him and tried again. "We've known him forever. We know his children. His wife and I were once close friends." She rubbed her hand over her heart. "They were at our wedding. They brought me flowers when Frankie was born. Our kids played together. He held me when I learned you were…dead."

All the more reason Frank wanted to see that bastard go down. The few inches of space her retreat created left an icy chill on his skin. "This isn't a quick, fly-by-night operation. It's been developing for a long time. So far I haven't figured out what pushed Halloran over the edge."

She bit her lip. "You believe he'd willfully hurt our daughter?"

Frank nodded. "The man he is today? Yes. He'd give that order." He waited for it to dawn on Sophia that their old friend had issued her death order earlier today.

"Oh." She pressed a hand to her stomach. "I could be sick."

He'd felt the same way. "Please don't ask me to make it easier on him by letting you come with me. This is guaranteed to turn ugly, fast."

"It's already ugly," she said, her voice tight. "Kelly Halloran ordered my execution to scare you into silence," she mused. "The bastard." When she met his gaze, her eyes were clear, her determination shining. "You can't expect me to sit back and watch him run you in circles."

"If that's your idea of encouragement, I don't need any more," he said.

She spread her palms across her knees. "Talk me through everything you have so far and then I'll decide if I can best help from a safe distance or right beside you."

"Now you're in charge?" He wanted to leap on the idea of having an ally, of having her beside him again. If only they weren't going up against a man who knew them both all too well.

"One of us should be." Standing, she crossed the room to her suitcase, pulling out her laptop. "Come on. Catch me up." She rolled her hand, urging him to fill her in while she plugged in the computer.

He marveled at her resilience. He always had. They'd said "for better or worse" on their wedding day and lived it every day since. Until he'd shut her out. She made a good point. So far, going solo had only netted him one easily replaced shipment of drugs. Hardly enough to snare Halloran or put an end to a system as established as Hellfire.

"All right," he said at last. "But I won't be convinced that you should be doing any fieldwork."

Her mouth curved in a smirk. "You will be."

Somehow he was afraid she could be right.

Chapter Four

Breathing in slow and deep, Sophia didn't sit down again until she was sure her stomach wouldn't embarrass her. "Kelly Halloran," she said. Her anger with Frank shifted abruptly to a new target. It was hard to picture one of their oldest and dearest friends orchestrating such an elaborate criminal network, complete with a sniper aiming at her head. "When we find him, I want the first shot."

"I won't let you kill him," Frank countered. "His sorry life isn't worth spending a single day of yours in prison."

She turned at the wariness in his voice. "I didn't mean with a gun. I don't want to kill him. I want to scratch his eyes out, maybe break a rib or two or blow out his knee." Her body hummed with the need to do violence. "He threatened to kill our daughter." The idea of it shocked her almost as much as Frank standing here alive and well. "When I'm done with him, I want him to rot in a dark, slimy little hole for the rest of his days."

Frank gave a low whistle. "Guess I'm lucky you haven't torn me apart."

"The night is still young." She sent him a glance full

of warning. "If I were you, I wouldn't bring up your grand scheme to tuck me safely away again."

"Duly noted."

"Good. Keep talking and let's see what we can come up with."

She logged on to the internet via the hotel connection and created a new online persona for tonight's research. Assuming Halloran had technical experts with credentials equivalent to those of his renowned assassin, she didn't want to tip them off too soon. Behind her she heard Frank resume his pacing.

Hearing those footfalls made her smile. Pacing hadn't been his habit until after Frankie was born. He'd spent many nights walking up and down the hallways to help her sleep when she was a baby. All these years later, his body went through the soothing motions automatically. She doubted he even noticed.

"We can't go directly at Halloran," he said. "I've tried. That's why I went after the drugs."

She sat back on her heels, nearly afraid to ask. "What do you know about him?"

"His current address is a place outside Phoenix, one of those golf communities tucked behind an elaborate gate and rent-a-cop security."

She brought up an overview image of the area, waiting for him to continue.

"He's insulated," Frank said. "I've been thinking if we could pin down one of the others, someone close to the top, we could force them to roll over on Halloran."

She thought through that approach and dismissed it. "We can see about that if we can find a chink in Hellfire's armor." She pursed her lips. "You said the money goes through a bank in the Caymans. Have you tried following that trail? If we put that kind of information into the right hands, it could make a difference."

"Unless Halloran believes any information leaks come from his own men, he'll know it's me and he'll move to kill Frankie. Is there any way you can urge her to take a vacation?"

Sophia shook her head. "Not without a good explanation. With Paul in prison and me out of the office, she and Aidan need to be present and visible at Leo Solutions."

Frank grumbled his displeasure. Hiding and waiting only gave their enemy more power.

"Tell me about your Cayman account."

"The money isn't there," he said. "They redistributed the cash after I was ousted."

"Do you remember any details?"

He gave her the bank, account number and online log-in information. Within a few minutes, she had the full account history, though the current balance was zero. "They made regular deposits," she observed, noting the dates in a new document for further research later. "I know it's been a long time, but do these deposit dates correspond to any actions that you're aware of?"

He pulled up a chair and they talked through what he remembered about that time, matching what he'd seen overseas with what she was seeing in the bank history. She wasn't sure it would be enough, even if she could get it into the right hands.

"Well, they certainly wouldn't have made deposits only to your account on those days. Gotta love the precision and habits of military men." She made a few more notes as she went along. There were other people— friends in the intelligence and media communities—she could approach if necessary. "Based on these numbers, I can see why Halloran's crew has been so loyal. Getting one of them to roll on him will be a long shot."

"I'm trying to find the right pressure point," Frank said. He laced his fingers behind his head and stretched his neck. Another rush of need to touch and soothe him startled her. It had always been so easy to reach out and offer him comfort and support.

It didn't feel right to hold all that in. It didn't feel right to approach him, either. She tamped down the uncertainty. This wasn't her first uncomfortable classified meeting. Her feelings could wait until they'd accomplished the current "mission."

And then what? She had no idea.

"Do you know if he's threatened the families of the others in the group?" She couldn't quite reconcile the friendly Kelly Halloran she remembered with this uncaring criminal. She hadn't missed Frank's refusal to give her the other names of those involved. "Money can't be the only hold he has over them."

"Money can be a big incentive. Any secrets or crimes they committed are long buried."

"Mmm-hmm." She kicked off her shoes, getting comfortable. She was tempted to launch an immediate search into Halloran and stopped herself just in time. The resources at Leo Solutions would make this easier, but she wasn't ready to log in and risk leaving such an obvious trail for Halloran. By now he knew his attack on her had missed and he'd be waiting for some reaction.

"From what you've said, we can't beat them by just interfering with their pipeline. Manipulating the money could work. If we can find a way to tie up their cash—"

"I'm not letting you do anything remotely criminal," he said, scowling at her.

"But it's okay for you to steal drugs and who knows what else?"

He shrugged a shoulder, his blue gaze sliding back to the laptop monitor. "I'm officially dead," he pointed out. "My real name and reputation can't get any worse."

She wanted to shake him. He couldn't have just given up on everything, could he? The best possible outcome here was to restore his name and reputation so he could reclaim his life as a husband and father, as a friend and partner. Already, she could see Frankie's delighted face when she learned her father was alive, healthy and not a convicted traitor.

But could he be her husband again? Sophia's throat attempted to close. Could she be his wife? So much hurt stood between them.

"We could notify the authorities about the next incoming shipment," she said.

Frank's scowl deepened and he covered his eyes. "Based on the schedule, there should be a shipment coming into Seattle in a few days. Which is another reason I think he's targeted you and Frankie. He can't take the chance I'd ask you for help." He leaned forward and tapped his fingers together. "He knows I'm alive and that I know his system."

"And he knows you have his drugs."

"He's behaving as if that's irrelevant," Frank said, clearly troubled by the fact. "He removes the only person who can vouch for me. Then he sits on you and Frankie, issues a kill order, knowing I'll show up."

"Which you did." Thank heaven. She forced her thoughts away from what might have happened if Frank hadn't been so diligent. It took more effort to keep from reaching for her phone to call and check on her daughter.

"His hired gun didn't work very hard to kill either of us." Frank stood up and resumed his pacing. "It's the strangest game of cat and mouse I've ever played and the stakes are too high."

She agreed completely. "You said you've identified the top players. Let's start at the bottom and work our way up."

"Divide and conquer?" He faced her, his dark eyebrows knitting over those clever blue eyes.

"It's a valid strategy for a reason." She smiled, aiming it at the screen rather than her husband. "There has to be a weak link within Hellfire. Start talking," she said, ignoring the clock in the corner of her monitor. They couldn't stay here indefinitely and, based on the signs of tension radiating from Frank, he was at the end of his rope. Though he might not be ready to admit it, he needed her—or someone—to help him put an end to this nightmare.

Frank turned the chair around and straddled it, bracing his arms along the top rail. "I backed up my handwritten notes to a cloud server."

She brought up the website and he gave her the username and password as if they were random, but her fingers stuttered in recognition. He'd used the day and date of her first miscarriage for those fields. No one even knew about that except the two of them. She hadn't been far enough along to share the news yet.

She told herself to say something and couldn't find sufficient words. If a single shred of doubt had existed inside her that this man was her husband, it was gone now.

"I've been tracking movements and making connections for months," he said as if she hadn't noticed. "If this was my pet project, Darren Lowry would worry me most. He was on Halloran's staff for a few years."

"Go on," she encouraged as she opened another tab and typed the name into her search engine. As Frank gave her the details he knew about Lowry's background, Sophia's determination firmed.

This would be so much easier with the assets at the office, but she couldn't think about that yet. Much as Halloran had pulled Frank out of hiding, she wanted to draw any confrontation away from Seattle and their daughter.

"Is this the same Lowry, retired four years ago? This report has a Darren Lowry under investigation for sexual misconduct in Iraq on his second tour." She leaned to the side to give Frank a better look at the pictures she'd brought up on the screen.

"Same guy," Frank confirmed. "Maybe the charges were fabricated against him, too."

Sophia's lip curled and her mouth went dry as she read through the report. She kept digging, using Frank's information and online sources. She found a current address and the press release when Lowry had been hired by a defense contractor based in Washington, DC, after retiring from the army.

"Could I have some water please?" She didn't want Frank nearby when she logged in to an administrative email account for a law firm website in DC. Leo Solutions had handled the security for one of her oldest friends when he transitioned to private practice after fulfilling his military commitment in the army's Judge Advocate General's Corps. She wasn't doing anything particularly illegal, though Frank wouldn't be happy. Assuming her friend was in town and Frank cooperated, she could follow up tonight's discreet inquiry in person tomorrow.

She accepted the glass of water from Frank and chose her next words carefully. "I have a friend in DC who can give us some guidance about how to exploit that old complaint against Lowry," she said, tracing the rim of the water glass. "I'm thinking we cast an ugly spotlight on the skeletons in his closet and make the old fogies of Hellfire sweat a little. It's a fair response to what happened near Parkhurst today."

He sat down across from her, his intense gaze holding hers. "You want Halloran to know we can get to his people, too."

"Exactly."

She struggled to keep her mind on point while her eyes devoured the face that had meant so much to her for more than half of her life. She remembered how those laugh lines had added character to his face, year after year. Anger, raw and cold, surged through her veins. If Halloran hadn't upped the stakes, would Frank have kept tabs on her at all? Would he have watched her grow old from a distance, without ever allowing her to know he was out there?

Something that resembled dismay flickered across his face. "You're angry."

Of course he could read her changing expressions. He'd always been too good at that. "It comes in waves," she admitted. She dismissed it with a flick of her fingers. Throwing a tantrum wouldn't help either of them. If they successfully dismantled Hellfire, she could be mad at Frank personally for the rest of her life. "Lowry first," she said through gritted teeth.

He bobbed his chin slowly as if uncertain about agreeing with her. "What do you hope to get out of your contact in DC?"

"I won't know for sure until I get there," she hedged while she opened more searches, this time exploring the contractor who had hired Lowry.

"You mean you don't intend to tell me."

"Can you blame me?" She tucked her hands under her legs, squashing the urge to throw something at him. "After what you've described, we need more intel to involve the authorities and take down Halloran the right way. I want him to rot in prison, not slip through the system to lounge about on a sunny island beach."

"I want him to rot, too," Frank said.

She knew that tone. "Not six feet under," she said briskly. "If I can't kill him, neither can you. The bastard isn't worth either of us spending any time in jail." However things worked out between them personally, she wanted to be clear on that point.

She fumed when he sat there silently studying his hands. "That was your plan?"

He opened his mouth, but she cut off his reply. "It would be fine if you killed him because you were already dead and out of our lives?" she demanded. Furious, she clamped her lips together before she said something too terrible to retract. "I must question your logic," she managed.

"If Halloran is dead, he can't give an order to hurt you or Frankie."

"Funny. You were dead and that hurt us plenty."

He reeled back as if she'd slapped him. She would

not regret it. The harsh words needed to be said. "We're going to DC, Frank."

"It's a huge risk."

"Do you know how determined Frankie was to clear your name? Do you have any idea?" She didn't wait for a reply. "You saved me tonight and I'm grateful, but I won't sit back and let you disappear again. I won't take on Hellfire in half measures that leave you hanging in some legal limbo. We're going to DC so I can discuss this with a friend I trust."

FRANK TRIED TO ignore the sting of her trusting someone else more than she trusted him, even though her instincts were spot-on. He didn't ask her for the name of her friend. She wouldn't tell him anyway. Shouldn't, in fact. Sophia's connections ran deep thanks to her analysis work with the CIA and others in the alphabet soup of DC. It pissed him off the way Halloran had managed to twist Sophia's analyses against him during the treason trial.

"I believe my friend can help us," she said, her anger having ebbed once more.

He admired her ability to ride through the emotions. He wasn't having nearly the same success. If he got too close, he wanted to take her in his arms and be closer. If he shared a little, he wanted to tell her everything. "In what way?"

She pressed her fingers to her temples and dropped her gaze. "At this point it's only an educated guess. Can't you extend me a little faith and leeway for a day or two?"

"Of course."

Her confidence didn't surprise him. It had been one

of her most attractive traits. At the moment her confidence gave his a boost. He refused to be the thundercloud rumbling with doom and gloom in the distance, threatening to rain on every hopeful step forward. He didn't have to tell her he'd make a plan for the worst-case scenario while she was seeking help. She knew him well enough to expect him to come up with a contingency.

"I'll book the flight," he said, pulling out his cell phone and calling the airline he'd used most frequently with his bogus identification. "Wait." He disconnected the call before a reservations agent picked up. "You can't go as you."

"I don't have much choice," she said. "We don't have the time for an alternate identification to be made."

"Victoria knows people. She could help, couldn't she?"

Sophia sighed. "You know the best work takes time. Do you really want to sit here and wait for Halloran to make the next move?"

"No." None of their limited options appealed to him. "We'll drive out. We can leave early—"

"And waste half a day? How does that work in our favor? If Frankie is in danger, we need to move quickly to trap Halloran."

His stomach tightened again. Halloran would stop at nothing to protect his retirement cash cow. Another man's family wasn't nearly as valuable as an endless flow of money and power.

It had been tough enough for Frank to live without his girls when he thought he was keeping them safe. If the distance were permanent, if by some twist of fate he had to go on breathing, knowing his mistakes meant their lives had been cut short...

"Frank?" Sophia's voice brought him back from that bleak abyss he'd been staring into. "Talk to me."

He rolled his shoulders. "They ran you off the road. I'm sure they know I rescued you." He wouldn't sleep at all tonight, waiting for one of Halloran's thugs to track the rental car and break down the door.

"Look around, Frank. You created a safe place. They haven't found us yet."

Yet. The word echoed through his head. Every way he looked at it, Halloran had the advantage.

"We have to take the chance," she said. "You're obviously worried. What can they really do between now and morning?"

Considering Halloran's established organization, Frank could think of several bad examples, none of which he wanted to outline for her in any great detail.

"Our best choice is not to circle the wagons. He'd expect that of me," she said. "He knows how devoted I am—we are—to Frankie. He has to be confused. I didn't run back to my hotel, contact Victoria or call Frankie. All things I should've done if I encountered trouble in Chicago."

"All of which points like a neon arrow to my involvement in your rescue."

"Yes. They probably watched you pull me out of there somehow. More important, where would two capable parents run if their daughter was in danger?"

"To her."

She nodded. "Instead, picture his reaction when he learns I went to DC. He'll flip out with the possibilities."

It was a solid approach. So far all he'd been able to do was observe and keep some drugs off the streets. Nothing he'd done seemed to get under Halloran's skin. The man was too confident in his system. "And if we rattle him, you're hoping he makes a mistake."

"The sooner the better for us."

She was right. They had to keep Halloran on edge. Words of gratitude backed up in his throat. Knowing she wasn't doing it for him but for Frankie didn't matter. His wife was back in his life and, for the moment, they were a team.

"All right." He picked up his phone. "Let's book the first flight out."

When they both had confirmation emails about the flight, they discussed tomorrow's plan. He couldn't go with her wherever she was headed. There were too many people who might recognize him. He agreed to stay back and make sure she wasn't followed.

Using tourist maps she pulled up on her screen, they chose rendezvous points and times, and then she closed the computer and tucked it back into her suitcase. Retrieving her cosmetic case and whatever she used for pajamas now, she headed for the bathroom.

While she was busy, he stripped off his sweater and removed his boots and socks. A few minutes later, he heard the bathroom door open and the flick of the light switch. He kept his focus on perfecting the arrangement of an extra pillow and blanket on the small couch, afraid to look her way. The last thing he needed was a refresher course on how alluring she was at bedtime.

Whenever he was deployed or traveling, those first nights apart from her had always been the worst. He missed the scent of lilies clinging to her skin after she applied her favorite lotion. Longed for the feel of her bare feet caressing his calf as she snuggled into his embrace. He couldn't say he'd taken her for granted; the frequent times apart prevented that. No, he'd simply assumed coming home to her was always an option.

"I'd planned to take the couch," she said, rooted in place between the bathroom and the bed.

He turned, pulled by a force he couldn't fight. From the moment he'd dragged her out of the car, he felt a craving to soak her in, as though he could somehow carry a bit of her with him through the foreseeable loneliness ahead. His mouth watered at the sight of her in one of his old T-shirts, her preferred sleepwear. It wasn't a ploy or some balm to his ego. She'd traveled to Chicago solely to see a friend and she'd packed *that* shirt. Did that have any significance? Should he assume she missed him, too, or was it just a comfort factor? He couldn't stop his eyes from roaming over her from head to toe—her hair down and the hem of the shirt skimming high on her toned thighs. She kept trying to push it lower.

"Take the bed." He gave her a smile, though he thought his jaw would crack from the effort. "I'll be fine over here."

"That's silly. You need more room."

His skin tingled from his scalp to the soles of his feet as she gazed at him. What was he supposed to make of that look? "Don't worry about it. You know I've slept well in far worse."

She came to the corner of the bed and stopped, a worried frown pulling at her eyebrows. "You won't be able to stretch out at all."

"Just take the bed," he said through gritted teeth. Unless she was offering to share. Was that it? It would take a better man than him to turn her down if she was.

She slid between the sheets, putting as much of the

bed between them as possible. A clear enough message to keep his distance.

He turned out the last light before he stripped off his undershirt and pants. The gear in the pockets rattled as he set the items within easy reach if trouble found them.

"You know, I should thank Halloran." Her voice drifted across the dark room.

It seemed like a damned poor thing to be thankful for. He stared at the ceiling, creased with a blade of light from the parking lot bleeding through the top of the curtains. "I don't want to ask."

"Without him I might never have seen you again."

Could it be possible that she had missed him as much as he'd missed her? She'd turned their retirement dream into a profitable reality so quickly. And that damned snake Paul Sterling had moved in on her with equal speed. "Without him, we wouldn't be in this mess to begin with," Frank pointed out.

"True."

He was sure she'd drifted off, leaving him with his thoughts and regrets, when she spoke up again. "After… all that happened," she said, "would you ever have come home to me if my life hadn't been in danger?"

He could hardly stand being in this room, so close and still so far removed from her. "I've been searching for a way home to you ever since." He stifled a groan as the truth slipped out. A lie that would guarantee some detachment would've been the smarter move. He'd hurt her so badly it was a miracle she hadn't had him drawn and quartered yet.

He heard the mattress shift and he imagined she'd rolled to her side. He remembered the way she curled her hands around her pillow, her face relaxed and her knees pulled up a little, one foot free of the bedding, serving as a thermostat. Countless mornings in their marriage he'd pressed a kiss to her cheek and left her in just that pose. Every morning since going undercover, he'd regretted his decision to push her away in favor of the job. Now he'd dragged her into an unsanctioned investigation that could wind up destroying both of them.

On the books it appeared as though he'd put his duty to country ahead of his family. Not unexpected for a career officer even though it wasn't spelled out in those exact words in the official oath of service. He'd made an unbearable choice with his family in mind, though they would heartily disagree. No matter the cost, men like Halloran couldn't be allowed to run roughshod over the world. Soldiers and civilians had died for the wrong reasons, thanks to Halloran and his Hellfire group, and Frank meant to right that wrong.

Early on, Frank had been so damned confident no price was too high to bring Halloran to justice. Long before the empty casket had been lowered into the ground, he'd realized his error.

Solitude had been his greatest enemy. He hadn't taken Sophia for granted in their marriage, not as a person or partner. No, but he'd drastically underestimated the strength he gained merely knowing she was on his side, available to talk or listen as needed.

Her breathing evened out and he didn't have the heart to wake her. It was too late to thank her for standing by him during the trial anyway.

The only thing he knew to do was keep pushing forward, as a team, despite the undercurrents of hurt between them. If he could bear the distraction, which was the risk of working with her, they might just re-duce Hellfire to ashes.

Chapter Five

Tuesday, April 19, 8:25 a.m.

The flight was nearly into its descent before Frank relaxed. All night he'd slept with one eye open, expecting an attack on the hotel. At the airport, he kept looking over his shoulder, even past the security checkpoint, certain one of Halloran's goons would make a grab for Sophia. Unless he was completely off his game, they were heading to DC without any Hellfire eyes on them. He wasn't sure what to think, so he tried to be grateful for the momentary reprieve.

Still, with no trouble in Chicago, spies were likely waiting for them in DC. It couldn't be helped—Sophia had to travel as herself right now. They could only move as quickly as possible and leave a trail for Halloran to get worried about. With his ball cap pulled low over his face, Frank had pretended to sleep while keeping an eye on her dark hair several rows ahead of him.

Their arrival in Dulles and the rental car pickup all went without a hitch. This much going smoothly made him wary. Hellfire was dialed in tight on Frank now that they knew he was alive, and things would only accelerate when they realized Sophia was helping him.

Following the plan he and Sophia had devised last night, he parked the car in a public garage and she took the metro to her meeting. He fell back once he was sure no one was tailing her. It bothered him to let her go alone, even knowing she could take care of herself on the busier subways. Returning to keep an eye on their primary rendezvous point, he was happy things were clear so far.

Sophia had not volunteered details about meeting her contact, only that she'd send regular text messages and catch up with Frank in front of the Smithsonian Castle at two o'clock. They'd argued the point, last night and again on the way to the airport, until he was forced to concede. As she'd told him repeatedly, he was officially dead and she'd be walking into places where he might be recognized. If the authorities caught Frank too soon, Halloran would have a better chance of skipping the country unscathed.

Still, letting her out of his sight went against everything inside him. His instincts clamored to shelter and protect his wife and daughter, though he knew being obvious about it would push her too hard at this point. A few hours in her company after so much time apart made this necessary absence unbearably worse. He had no idea what he'd do when this was over and Halloran was in custody, no longer a threat to Frank or his family.

Frank wanted his life back; he wanted his wife and daughter.

With a few hours to kill, he ambled between museums and played the part of tourist as memories of Leone family vacations rolled through his mind. He was strolling along, desperate to sink his teeth into some action, when he noticed the man tailing him.

A chill slid down his spine at the thought of Halloran pegging his last clean fake ID, until he remembered how easily Hellfire could track Sophia. Maybe she was right that he'd been at this alone for too long. Frank's pulse leaped at the potential to get some information from the enemy. The challenge was staying calm, letting the man believe Frank hadn't noticed him.

As a career army officer, he hadn't had much training in espionage or spy tactics. Working his way up to general, he'd learned how to assess, observe and stand out. He'd learned to manage his immediate support staff as well as the many units under his command. Blending in, disappearing and operating alone had required practice after his initial escape from prison as a corpse.

The man dogging his heels didn't look familiar. White male, average height and build, medium brown hair, nondescript jacket and jeans. At the current distance, it was impossible to pin down an age range to anything more specific than "over twenty-five."

Frank led the younger man trailing him away from the rendezvous point just in case Sophia returned early. He walked near groups of tourists and then separately, giving him room to make a move. Picking up his pace, he aimed for the metro station and hurried down the stairs, stepping aside to wait for the tail to catch up.

As the younger man hurried by Frank's position, the profile didn't reveal anything helpful about his identity or his affiliation. It had to be one of Halloran's spies. No one else had reason to be this persistent. Frank fell in behind him, keeping out of sight.

A train arrived and people jockeyed for position. Frank stepped up behind the younger man and shoved the knuckles of his fist into his back. "Looking for me?"

Caught, his shoulders slumped. "You're getting better at this, Leone."

"As if I care about your opinion." Up close, he realized the spy was even younger than he'd guessed at first. Probably a recent washout from one of the elite military teams, searching for a way to clear the chip off his shoulder.

Frank struggled against his first instinct to listen and advise. Although he and Sophia had only one child, he'd counseled many young people through the years, urging them to explore one path or another to suit their skills. This wasn't that kind of meeting.

"You should." The kid tried to look over his shoulder.

"To the right," he said, urging the kid closer to the nearest trash can. "Unload any weapons."

"If they'd sent me to kill you," the kid said, dropping a knife and a handgun into the trash can, "you'd be dead already."

Frank ignored him, pulling a cell phone out of the kid's rear pocket while he was distracted. The warning sounded for final boarding and he gave the kid another shove. "Get on the train."

"I knew you weren't armed," the kid challenged.

"If you know me at all," Frank retorted, "you know I don't need to be."

With a terse nod, the kid obediently surged forward, joining the last stragglers to board the train.

"Who sent you?" Frank asked when they were seated and the train was under way. Part of him hoped it was a federal agency rather than a criminal operation.

"You already know the answer." The kid shook his head. "If you'd recommit, I wouldn't be your enemy. You'd have support, a way out. Face it, you need it."

Frank glared at him.

"No one wants to hurt your family. Cooperate and the danger goes away."

"Cooperate how?" Frank asked, willing to play along for a few minutes. He could just imagine what hellish task Halloran had dreamed up for him to prove his renewed loyalty to Hellfire. "The last time I cooperated, your boss hung me out to dry."

"Ease up," the kid said. "No one was going to leave you in prison. You should've been patient. A man's word is his bond."

Neither Halloran's "word" nor Hellfire's promises had been worth the air wasted to explain them. "Right." Frank calculated the upcoming stops and how long he could keep this kid talking until he had to get back to Sophia. "My wife and daughter were no threat. Your boss started this when he targeted them. You can tell him I'll finish it."

"Hey, you're pissed. I get it." The kid flared his hands wide, then stuck them in his pockets. "Easy to lose the faith considering that nasty treason charge." He kept his voice pitched low. "You keep our secrets and this will still work out according to the original agreement."

The agreement had a small fortune flowing into an offshore bank account in Frank's name and a solitary slice of a private beach in the Caribbean. The same bogus agreement that had left his family believing he committed suicide rather than face justice as a traitor. "I can't ever be me again," he muttered only loud enough for the kid to hear. "No matter what I choose."

"Just so we're clear. Are you threatening Hellfire?"

"No more than they're threatening me," Frank replied.

"That's not the kind of response that makes the top brass happy. Check your account," the kid said. "A good-faith payment is already there."

"Top brass" implied the kid was working directly for one of the top three retired generals who'd started Hellfire. Maybe Frank could use this—whatever it was—rendezvous to his advantage. He wanted new intel, some solid detail he and Sophia could exploit quickly. He pulled out his cell phone and checked the account. Sure enough, he was wealthy again. Disgust burned in his gut. Halloran had stolen everything from him. Frank's sole purpose now was to take him down, wrapping it up quickly so Frankie and Sophia could live in peace.

The train intercom announced the next stop and people shifted around them, preparing to exit. Frank used the shuffling to lift the kid's wallet. If he could get something helpful out of this kid—something other than an illegal windfall he didn't want—maybe this little detour would prove worthwhile.

Why wasn't the kid asking about Sophia or the missing drug shipment? The question had a new flood of apprehension rushing through Frank.

"I don't know what they have on you," he said quietly, testing the reaction, "but I can help if you come to your senses before the next stop."

The kid snorted. "You can't do a damn thing for me if you're against them." His lip curled like that of a mean dog sizing up his next attack. "I don't want anything from an outsider anyway."

"Is that so?"

"Look, old man, you've got one more chance to be smart."

The "old man" crack was the last straw. Despite being past his prime, Frank had at least one more good fight left in him. He pretended to consider it while he searched for the most expedient route to the finish line.

"Call the shooters off my family," Frank demanded, holding out the kid's cell phone.

The kid shook his head, kept his hands in his pockets. "I don't have that authority."

"Then you're no good to me." Frank tucked the phone away. With a quick move, he slid his hand up the kid's arm and pressed on a nerve that turned his arm limp.

"What the hell? Wait, you can't—"

"Just did, son." Frank stood as the train slowed for the next stop. "I've got your wallet, too. If you're smart, you'll hurry to the nearest FBI office and trade information for witness protection before Hellfire learns you've turned on them."

"No." The blood drained from his face, his eyes wide and wild. "You can't do that. Engle would never believe I'd turn."

Frank shrugged. "Belief and trust are fragile things. Good luck." He moved through the doors as the warning sounded, glancing back to see the kid fumbling to get his other arm working.

Engle, Frank thought, mentally tucking the new name away, along with every other word the kid had said. Between the two of them, he was sure he and Sophia would find the connections. He started searching through the kid's phone, knowing it could be a morass of fake IDs and cover stories. Time would tell. If they were lucky, Engle would prove to be a loose link in Hellfire's chain of command.

He glanced at the clock on the display and winced. He had a lot of ground to cover to make the rendezvous point in time. If she thought he'd ditched her—again—there would be hell to pay.

Tuesday, April 19, 2:10 p.m.

SOPHIA WANDERED ON past the Smithsonian Castle when she didn't see Frank in the vicinity. Frank should be waiting right here, per the plan. She told herself he hadn't left her, that he *would* be here. Wouldn't he?

Or would her husband, in some ill-conceived notion of protecting her, run away again?

She tried to divert the immediate reaction and the negative spiral of her thoughts with what she'd learned in the chat with her old friend Eddie Chandler. It didn't work. Very little from that meeting gave her hope they could successfully expose Halloran's greedy scheme. It would take some creativity and more than a little good luck.

She couldn't give up. Unless they stopped Hellfire, her husband would be forced to live in hiding indefinitely, an outcome she refused to accept. She checked her watch, circled through a nearby garden and turned back. Where was he?

If he had left her, she'd track him down and wring his neck. Though she could hardly be considered abandoned in Washington, DC, even without her resources and connections, that wasn't the point. They'd agreed to move forward together. If he reneged on his word…

No. A cold fear curled into a fist in her belly. He hadn't reneged. She couldn't believe it. If he'd wanted to leave her out of this mess, he would've found a way to leave her in Chicago. Although it was as clear as the sky above that he hated involving her in this crisis, they'd tossed out any other option. He needed someone helping him unravel Hellfire. He needed her.

She checked the time again, considering the more

likely scenarios, each of them increasingly unpleasant as they flashed through her mind. He'd been tailed and led the tail away from her. He'd been recognized and arrested by federal authorities. He'd been killed by Halloran's prize sniper. Her stomach pitched at the ghastly image, putting an end to her terrible thoughts.

If a sniper had struck Frank out here in the Mall, the police and emergency crews would be crawling all over the place by now. Even his arrest would've drawn a media presence.

So, if not killed by a sniper or picked up by police, Frank should be here. The obvious conclusion was he'd spotted someone tailing him. She should move to the alternative rendezvous point, closer to the parking garage. He was probably there, worrying and waiting for her to show up.

He wouldn't leave her. After last night, she was sure he realized he couldn't defeat Hellfire alone. Frank needed her. As much as she needed him, a small voice in her head pointed out with a vicious snarl. It startled her to have that voice reach out and lash at her. She thought she'd left that near-panic intensity locked away in the early days of their marriage.

When they were young, his career path as a military leader had seemed courageous and bold, almost glamorous. His confidence and conviction of purpose had inspired her. Then the reality of life as an officer's wife had surprised her. He'd gone off on one task or another and the urge to cling had been a sharp contrast to her independent nature. Over time, they'd become a stand-out team in his professional life, as well as their family life.

It was the soothing of other wives suffering with similar anxiety that often left her breathless and weepy. For years she had managed the problem alone, only sharing her secret with a therapist. To support her husband, she had to present a strong example. The same fortitude had held true and served her well in her career as an analyst.

She resented being tossed back to that near-panicked place where she didn't feel complete without Frank at her side. Her lungs constricted and she demanded more of herself. She couldn't give in to these detrimental reactions or this frantic *need* to see him whole and hale.

When she'd identified his body, believing herself a widow, she'd been calm. Not happy, not relieved, but calm. She had been devastated that he was gone—that he hadn't trusted her with whatever had been happening those last months of his life. But he had taken any decision or worry away from her. She had accepted that reality and tried to get on with her life. No more questions about whether or not he was okay, no more wondering if he would return, just a numb finality. Knowing he was alive and being unable to tell anyone presented the strangest paradox. Part of her wanted to celebrate, while an equally strong part of her wanted to shake him.

What would he do if she walked right on past their meeting point? Her knees trembled at the thought and she hurried toward the nearest open bench. As the owner of a security company, she employed the cream of the bodyguard crop. Frank had warned her of a threat. A logical woman would assign a protective detail. Surely with all the friends she had in this city, she could evade Halloran until her detail arrived.

Where would that leave Frank? Damn it. She couldn't leave him to cope with Halloran's schemes alone. If she left him hanging, Frankie would never forgive her. She'd never forgive herself. No matter that his decisions had hurt her so deeply, she couldn't do the same to him.

She glanced around once more, confirming she was alone, before pulling out her phone. No word from Frank. Refusing to give in to the panic, she sent a text message to Victoria canceling their shopping date. Then she sent another to Frankie explaining away the trip to DC as a business lead. Both women responded quickly, giving her a moment's peace. The next incoming message, filled with links to bridal websites, brought a smile to her face.

Sophia was drafting another message to Aidan, a not-so-veiled warning, when she looked up and recognized Frank's rapid, ground-eating stride. He looked well and he hadn't tried to shut her out after all.

Relief propelled her from the bench in a rush. She didn't care if they made a scene as she wrapped her arms around him and pressed up on her toes for a kiss. Looking startled, he seemed to need a second to catch up. When he did, the kiss ignited as they rediscovered sweet, familiar contact. The heat of his wide hands seeped through the soft fabric of her knit dress, chasing away the earlier chill of anxiety.

"I'm still mad at you," she said when they paused long enough to breathe. "And you're late."

"I can tell."

The sexy grin on his face disappeared and he turned, keeping one hand locked around hers as they headed back to the parking garage. The rigid set of his shoulders and the lines bracketing his mouth were evidence enough that something unfortunate had happened while she was talking with her friend.

"How was your meeting?" he asked.

She glanced up at him. "There's good news and bad news. What happened to you?"

"I had an impromptu meeting." He seemed to scan and evaluate the people around them for any threat.

"Care to elaborate?" She was doing her best to keep up with his longer legs, but walking with Frank when he was in a rush always turned into a cardio workout.

"Not here."

She'd never seen him in such a paranoid state. Though he'd always been observant and aware, this hypervigilant attitude was new and clearly a by-product of the situation. It seemed cruel, on this gorgeous spring day, to be plagued by such dark circumstances.

"What happened, Frank?" she asked when they reached the privacy of the rental car.

"I saw a man tailing me. I led him away from you and took care of it."

Took care of it? She choked.

"Relax." His voice was tight, stern. "When did you start believing I'm a cold-blooded—"

"Stop." She couldn't let him finish. "I do *not* believe that. Who tailed you?"

"One of Hellfire's young guns."

"Was he sent to kill you?" Fear tightened around her chest.

"No." Frank sighed, seeming to calm down as he drove toward the Beltway. "He was nothing but a messenger. He mentioned the 'top brass' had filled my account with a comeback incentive. He also gave up a name I hadn't heard before—Engle. I think Hellfire might let each leader hire his own help. The kid made it sound as though he was working directly for this Engle person, though he understood it was a bigger operation."

"Okay." She pulled out her phone and started a basic search. "What else did he tell you?"

"He couldn't call off the pending hit on you or Frankie, though he implied everything would be fine if I started cooperating again."

"He didn't ask about the missing drugs?"

Frank shook his head. "That bugged me, too." He changed lanes, then reached into his jacket pocket. He set a cell phone and wallet in the cup holders between the seats. "I took those off the kid. Told him to turn himself in before I made it look like he flipped on Hellfire. That cut right through his bravado, even as he told me Engle wouldn't believe it."

She checked the ID in the wallet and did a cursory search of the cell phone. "We need to pull what we can from this immediately. Before he can wipe any data remotely."

"You can do that from here?"

She nodded, thinking Aidan would make short work of her request. "My assistant can pass it on to our internal security team."

"No." He checked his mirrors and changed lanes again. "I don't want to give Halloran any reason to move on Frankie or the company."

"Frank, we need them." When would he accept that? "The company we dreamed of is founded on discretion." Her mind leaped into overdrive as she scrolled through the young man's text message history. "If these contact numbers track to real accounts, this is a gold mine," she murmured, sending screenshots to her phone. "We have to verify right away."

"What about the friend you just met with or the Colby Agency? Can't either of them handle this?"

"I promise Frankie and Leo Solutions won't be tied to any of it. She's actually oblivious of any trouble. I just got a text with links to a site full of bouquet ideas."

"Wedding bouquets?"

"Yes. She's so excited—"

He silenced her with a stony look. "You've been texting her from a phone we know Halloran can track?"

She pressed her lips together, breathing slowly through her nose, reminding herself he had many valid reasons to be paranoid. "My GPS is deactivated," she said carefully. "You and I both know they're tracking me through other means. I'd no more put our daughter in danger than you would." She paused when her voice started to shake with renewed anger. "Why don't you take a minute, Frank, and decide once and for all? Either you trust me to help you wipe out Hellfire or you don't."

While she waited for his response, she used her phone to take pictures of the contents of the wallet. In addition to the driver's license and two credit cards, there was an employee badge from a company whose name she didn't recognize. These she sent to her friend Eddie here in DC.

"Do what you have to do," Frank muttered after what felt more like an hour than a minute. "I trust you."

"Thank you."

Sophia sent all the new information to her assistant, asking her to walk the information directly to Aidan. When the information was confirmed to have been received by her assistant, she turned off the young man's cell phone and tossed it and the wallet into her purse.

"Engle doesn't ring any bells for you?" Sophia asked

as Frank started another loop around the city. "Where are we going?"

"I don't know yet," he admitted, adjusting his ball cap. "Tell me what you learned this morning." He turned a bit and one eyebrow lifted over his sunglasses. "Better yet, tell me who you met with."

"An old friend," she replied. As tightly wound as Frank was, the truth would only prove problematic.

"Come on, Sophia. I have a right to know. Was it an old CIA pal?"

Her temper flashed. She wanted to deny his right to everything, but he'd just promised to trust her and she couldn't give him reason not to now. "As far as anyone else is concerned, I met with a lawyer."

"Eddie Chandler?" His grip on the steering wheel tightened and his nostrils flared.

She leaned across the console. "You can't still be jealous. It's been over thirty years." There had been only one man in her past who had eroded Frank's confidence—her college boyfriend and first fiancé. She'd called off the engagement, met Frank within a year of her graduation and never looked back, yet something about that old relationship had always put Frank on edge and filled him with senseless worry.

She drilled her finger into his arm. "I married *you.*" They had far bigger problems than his lingering jealousy.

"I knew it." Frank's eyebrows snapped together over his sunglasses. "Did he start in with that old crap about how you'd be better off without me?"

"That was always a joke. He got married ages ago, remember?"

Frank only grunted.

"And he can't warn me away from you, because I'm still a *widow* per public opinion."

"Knowing how my career imploded, he must have given you some variation of 'I told you so.'"

"Aside from a sincere expression of sympathy for my loss, your name didn't come up." She rubbed the base of her left ring finger, suddenly missing her wedding rings. "I walked in with one purpose—intel on Darren Lowry."

"Right." Frank muttered a nearly inaudible oath. "What did you tell him?"

"I let him assume my inquiry had something to do with Leo Solutions business. He remembered the complaint in Iraq. Naturally, we couldn't go through the official records, but Eddie knew of more than one complaint."

"Doesn't sound like much progress."

Sophia didn't correct her grumpy husband right away. Primarily what she'd wanted, what Eddie had provided, was a clean computer to do more research in the hopes of finding something they could use against Lowry. "I found his civilian résumé, and since I still have access to the archives within the CIA, I took some time and made notes of professional intersections between Lowry and Halloran. I was looking for the catalyst."

"Sophie." Frank groaned. "Might as well send up a flare."

She understood and forgave his dismay. He'd been in the thick of Hellfire longer, his life had been wrecked, and he'd been the whipping boy for Halloran's crimes. And he had no idea what she could do with a computer these days.

"We needed the information. The more we know,

the more options we have." She barreled on when he started to disagree. "You warned me not to go at Halloran directly. I didn't. Unless this is far bigger than either of us can imagine, no one will even be aware of my search." To his credit, Frank gestured for her to go on.

"You have his current address and you know Lowry works at the Pentagon as a defense contractor. I learned his current project is developing new, longer-lasting batteries for special forces units."

"How the hell did you and Eddie discover that?"

Sophia eyed Frank and decided to ignore his jealousy and to treat him as she would a moody, frustrated client. "Lowry and Halloran crossed paths plenty in their early careers. I couldn't identify a particular catalyst, though it's possible Halloran buried a few harassment complaints to get Lowry to go along with his plans."

"I doubt any threats were needed," Frank said. "Lowry is the sort who always keeps an eye open for the chance to make an easy buck. Half the time he sounded more like a shady stockbroker than an army officer."

That was precisely the information she needed from Frank to help them pry open Hellfire. "Is he the money-man?" She couldn't imagine Halloran would be that foolish. "Why put a greedy personality type in charge of the money?"

Frank snorted. "Skills and deniability? Greed doesn't often come with self-control."

"From what you've said, the crew has been greedy and successful in it for a long time." How could they use that?

"You didn't run across anyone named Engle in your research?"

"No." She decided not to pull out the papers she'd printed for further analysis. That would give Frank only more cause for concern. "Then again, I wasn't looking for it."

"You can't go back to Eddie's office," Frank said quickly. "We need to keep moving."

She understood the risks of staying in one place long enough for Halloran to catch them, but there had to be a way to take a swipe at Lowry before they left. "Lowry is in town. We could stay close for a day or two, pick apart his life and find something to wave like a red flag in front of the press. Or we could tip off a reporter with a completely bogus story and hope it starts a chain reaction."

"You tell me what you want," Frank said, sounding surprisingly relaxed.

They definitely couldn't keep driving around the Beltway. "I want a hotel with decent internet access and a few hours to see if I can find the right buttons to push. I'm thinking we can combine what we know and pin an information leak on the guy who tailed you today."

"Then we'll do that," said Frank. "There are plenty of options near Reagan National Airport and we can scoot out of town right away."

The sooner the better, she thought. Eddie had suggested a reporter for Sophia to contact if they wanted the media to start prodding Halloran's operation. It was time to get aggressive. Frank had been going at this quietly and under the radar for a while, but he had backup now, whether he wanted it or not. What she had in mind would keep Halloran's mind off Frankie.

Thinking of her daughter reminded her about the

bridal links. She clicked on them, did a fast cruise through the pictures and sent Frankie a reply.

"Did you think of something else?" Frank asked.

"Not yet. I was responding to Frankie's links."

Her husband paled visibly.

"Do you need to pull over? I can drive if you can't handle the idea of your baby getting married," she offered.

"I trust you." Frank seemed to have trouble swallowing. "I just—" He shook his head and clutched the wheel as a car cut him off.

Sophia stiffened, braced for another attack. None came, though she couldn't quite relax. Part of the problem was the tautness in every line of Frank's posture. "What is it?" She glanced around, twisting in her seat as she tried to identify the threat.

"Nothing." He wasn't convincing. "It's the idea of Halloran getting a hold of Frankie. I believe you," he said quickly. "I *do*." He scrubbed at his jaw. "I just can't shake that image."

"Aidan won't let anything happen to her. I believe he'd be enough even if she wasn't surrounded by bodyguards."

"Yeah." Frank followed the signs for the airport.

"I think our daughter has skills we could use here, but I won't involve her in this unless we agree. I promise we're only trading wedding ideas by text message. It's what we do now." It still gave her a happy maternal thrill, but she was dealing with a dad who felt left out. Changing the subject, she asked, "What else did you learn from the guy who tailed you?"

Frank sighed. "He said Halloran hadn't intended to leave me in prison to serve out the treason charge."

"You're kidding."

"Not a bit. I guess Hellfire would've broken me out. Or that could've been the nice way of saying they would've killed me before I cracked."

He shifted restlessly in the seat until he had his jacket off. The dark T-shirt emphasized his toned chest and arms, making her want to sigh.

"I made a lame offer to help him break free of Hellfire and he basically laughed in my face. Said if I was against Hellfire I was dead and he didn't want an outsider's help."

"Do you think they've brainwashed him?" That would put a new spin on the situation.

"No. I think he's a dark ops wannabe hungry for a bigger slice of the pie."

She didn't want to accept that Frank might be right about Hellfire being impossible to break. Every suit of armor had a weak spot. She just needed a bit of time to really take a look at Halloran's. She wouldn't accept failure here if for no other reason than to make sure Frankie and her father were reunited. "Where are we going?" she asked when he bypassed the airport and headed south.

"Alexandria. I changed my mind. I'd rather make the damned spies work for it if they want to retaliate. It's one of two rooms I booked earlier, just in case."

She recognized that tone. He'd dug in his heels and would be nearly impossible to budge. "Lowry has a meeting at the Pentagon tomorrow."

"How do you know that? Oh, never mind." Frank rubbed his forehead. "You and Eddie planning to crash the meeting?"

She ignored that jab. "Alexandria is close enough."

"For what?"

"Well, if I can find something strong enough to use against him in the next few hours, I thought we might enjoy ringside seats for the media circus." She was thinking in particular of what Aidan could dig up. "His travel records for the past two years shouldn't be too hard to find and could give us some insight if we match them with dates and deposits. It's unlikely to be conclusive, but who knows what will break this case open?"

He didn't respond for a time and she chalked up his silence to traffic congestion and was lost in her own thoughts as they continued on to Alexandria.

"You and Eddie *are* planning something." His voice sounded weary with emotion.

"Yes." No sense denying it. She laced her fingers in her lap, determined to remain calm. "We're planning to clear your name and see the right people brought to justice."

He dropped the argument, though the resistance was evident in the muscle twitching in his jaw.

"Halloran and his cronies owe you and all the people his crimes have affected," she continued. "I want bad publicity and disgrace to be part of his restitution."

"Because you were disgraced by me."

"The treason verdict and subsequent suicide weren't career highlights," she replied carefully. "It required a cautious walk over a bed of eggshells and nails to get Leo Solutions up and running. The company was the key to my future and Frankie's, too."

"I know. Now you and the company are tied to this

mess. I should've insisted you go home to Frankie, surround yourself with bodyguards and sit this out."

"Once I knew you were alive, that was never going to happen. I'm not proud of the admission, but no one believed in you more than your daughter. I lost faith in you."

"You were right to lose faith in me. I don't want to hurt her any more than I already have. If something happens to you…" His voice trailed off.

She understood everything he couldn't quite articulate. "Although it might not be easy, we have to stick this out—together—for Frankie."

"She'll hate me for the lies and all the rest of it."

"I think you're underestimating her." Had he forgotten they'd raised their little girl to be a tough and determined woman who knew how to think for herself? "She'll forgive you in an instant."

His mouth twisted into a frown. "Next you'll want me to get on a video call and apologize to her."

"That's your business." She'd intended to say more but went mute as he pulled into a hotel where they'd stayed after a holiday party when they were newlyweds. "Frank, you didn't?"

"I didn't use my real name. Though it's tough to see the point in hiding. Halloran's spies will pick us up soon enough."

"Then why invite trouble to a place where we have such fond memories?" If this was an attempt to rekindle something, she didn't know how to feel about that. She thought of the kiss earlier. That had been her fault. Clearly the sizzling attraction between them hadn't completely faded. Still, after everything he'd had to do to survive and the choices she'd made as a widow, there was a new awkwardness she couldn't quite navigate.

"It's a hotel, Sophia. They had an opening and I booked it."

She didn't believe that for a minute.

Chapter Six

Frank watched Sophia carefully, searching for any insight to what was going on behind those stunning eyes. Maybe this had been a bad idea, indulging in an opportunity to revisit the fond memories of a holiday nearly thirty years past, but he was only human.

Once they were in the room, Sophia was all business. She wasted no time setting up her computer and starting in on her research. Frank didn't much care how they got Lowry, as long as they did something to show Halloran they weren't going to stop.

While Sophia picked apart Lowry's life, Frank went back through his notes, trying to connect the Engle name to the Hellfire puzzle. The more he thought about it, the more he felt he should know that name. He just couldn't place it.

Taking a break, he stood up and stretched his legs, gazing around the luxurious room, wondering how his wife could be so unaffected by the memories assaulting him. She'd kissed him senseless earlier. Had it been for show, or was he a fool to think he'd felt a remnant of their old passion in her kiss? He understood the concept of her relegating him to the past in order to move forward. Broad concepts be damned, they were back together. They were in the same room for another night. Did she feel anything at all for him?

"Yes!" she cried, giving him a start. "Come take a look." She waved him over. "I've got the travel records." She gave him a sly look. "And I found some rather suggestive exchanges on his contractor email account."

He skimmed the highlighted passages long enough to realize the woman being propositioned wasn't amused by the idea. "What an idiot."

"For which we shall be grateful," she said. "He doesn't need or care about the job. It's little more than a cover."

Frank whistled at the implications. "Show me." He followed along as she explained the business travel records. "Whoa." Frank flipped open his notebook and they compared dates. "That lines up almost perfectly with the shipments I've tracked."

Her smile brightened the whole room. Her laptop keys clicked in rapid-fire succession. "I'm drafting an email to the CID now."

"Anonymous source?"

"Yes. It won't take much work to verify the facts we're providing. I'll copy Eddie, too."

She was so proud of herself. Hell, he was proud right along with her. He'd been working for months to find an angle and hadn't made this much progress. Striding to the window, he peeked through the edge of the curtain. They'd been here for over two hours and he was sure Halloran had to have someone on them by now.

Frank systematically picked apart everything within his view from the window. He'd chosen this hotel and asked for a room on this side for the view of the Potomac, the memories of better days and the stronger defense options. The way this end of the block was laid out, the hotel was hemmed in by the river and a park. It gave Frank a modified box-canyon trap that would allow him to escape safely with Sophia should they need to get away quickly.

"Did you hear me?"

Her question cut through his search for any menace lurking outside. Trying to relax, he smiled as he turned back to her. "I was thinking about other details."

Her dark brown gaze zeroed in on him. "You're expecting company?"

The intensity, her ability to see through any smoke screen was nearly more than he could bear. He shouldn't burden her with these overwhelming feelings right now. Survival first, and the rest would fall into place if it was meant to be or, rather, if she'd have him.

"No," he replied. "We're fine. What were you saying?" He caught the smirk on Sophia's face. He knew that look. "What did you do?"

That smirk turned into a wide, lovely smile. "At Eddie's office today, I took advantage of a computer that couldn't be traced and put a few things in motion while we did our research."

It made him wonder if the beatific smile was for him or her old friend. Didn't matter. Survival came first right now. "Not entrapment?"

"No. We agreed *neither* of us would break the law." Her emphasis served as a reminder to him, as well. He got the message loud and clear. "Although it's not entrapment, since we're not actually representing any branch of law enforcement."

"You know what I mean."

She grinned, unrepentant. "I sent copies of the sexual

harassment article we found last night to the CEO of the defense contractor, a reporter Eddie recommended, as well as to a well-known feminist group. One of them is bound to follow up and make life difficult for him. Add in the travel records to places a little off the contractor's itinerary and I think we can call it a good day's work."

He closed his eyes and shook his head. Assuming she was right, that would stir the pot for sure.

"What? It's public record. I thought you'd be happy. If we're lucky, he'll be under some kind of investigation by tomorrow morning."

"Investigation is a lofty goal," Frank said, amused by her high hopes. He wouldn't be unhappy if it happened that fast.

She flicked her fingers, dismissing his cynicism. "He'll be in the news, that's the point."

"Halloran will be mad as hell." He turned back to the window, thankful one of them was making progress. It wasn't a bad system, him guarding her while she systematically dismantled the people he identified. It wasn't a real life, but it felt good to be working as a team again.

He heard the desk chair squeak as she stood. Although the carpet muffled the sound of her footsteps, he felt her crossing the room to stand at his shoulder. Lilies and spices teased his nose.

"Were we followed?"

"I can't be sure yet. With his assets, it's more than likely Halloran will track us down by nightfall." He felt the heat of her body all along his side as she leaned close to peer over his shoulder while dusk fell outside.

"Because we were together when you rented the car?"

"In his shoes, I'd track airport security cameras for your arrival, then follow along until you met up with me. It's the easiest way to catch us," he said, deciding it was better to be honest about everything.

"If he has the access, that's the right approach."

He glanced down at her, struck as he always was by how beautiful she was. In his opinion the crinkles of laugh lines at her eyes and the deeper lines in her forehead only made her lovelier. The face he'd fallen in love with, with more experience. Everything about her called to him, body, mind and soul. How had he screwed up their lives so badly?

Dropping the curtain, he turned fully, leaning against the windowsill to be closer to eye level. How many things he needed to say and couldn't. Not until he had a right to say them again. How badly he wanted to claim every benefit as her husband. Making a move right now would be disastrous. In the long run, moving too soon would be more disastrous than being framed for treason and forced to leave his family behind. If he confessed everything, asked forgiveness, and she walked away, he'd be broken beyond repair.

She cocked her head, studying him. "Should we go out on the town and party or hit the road and put hundreds of miles between where he thinks we are and where we're going?"

"No. We'll spend the night right here, within the safety of these walls." He wasn't sure he was talking about the case anymore.

"Frank." She folded her arms and rocked back on her heels.

"We'll keep at the research," he said, defending his decision. "We need to figure out who Engle is."

"Okay." She continued to stare him down.

"Would it make you feel better if I said it was too soon to be bait?" When her lips quirked to the side in amusement, he was tempted to steal a kiss as he'd done so often in the past.

"That helps a little." She sighed as she reached for the clip holding her hair up off her neck. "Research, it is. We're giving Lowry something to chew on, but it would be nice to take a swipe at the head honcho himself."

He was mesmerized with the way the sable locks spilled to her shoulders as she massaged her scalp, then piled it all back up again. He cleared his throat. "If Halloran's not playing golf in Arizona, he's doing something with the product or the profit. It's definitely too soon to go after him directly."

She rocked her head gently from side to side, stretching her neck, then frowned as a new thought hit her. "When was the last time you saw him in person?"

"Three months ago," he replied. "I watched him play a round of golf on an ocean-view course in Norfolk, Virginia."

Frank returned to his study of the area outside the hotel. Watching for Halloran's spies was far easier than watching her for signs that she might want to renew their relationship. She probably didn't want to waste any more romantic energy on him after what he'd put her through.

At least he'd booked a room with two beds tonight. No need for a debate as to who would sleep where this time around.

"It's a starting point," Sophia said quietly, not wanting to interfere with the quiet Frank seemed to need.

At the table, she toed off her shoes and drew up her legs, sitting cross-legged on the chair, the skirt of her dress pulled over her knees. She was suddenly cold and weary from one adrenaline rush after another for the better part of the past twenty-four hours. It didn't help that sleep had been sketchy at best last night.

It was difficult to focus on her search for Kelly Halloran when she kept staring at her husband as if she were sixteen again and hopelessly daydreaming about the hunky quarterback of the high school football team. She closed her laptop and picked up her phone, finishing that text she'd started for Aidan. Odds were low Hellfire specifically was on the radar in Europe even though drug trafficking and money laundering were global problems.

Restless, she checked her email, finally pinpointing the real trouble when her stomach rumbled. "We need to eat." She trusted Frank's instincts about lying low tonight. "Why don't I order room service?"

"Go ahead." He walked away from the window and stuffed his hands into his pockets. "I'm not hungry."

She'd heard that before and learned the hard way. Frank would forget about food while his mind worked on a problem; then he'd be famished at the first whiff of a savory scent. Regardless of his appetite, he needed to fuel up. She ordered with great care, being sure to bring in enough food and avoiding anything reminiscent of their stay here nearly thirty years ago. That had been champagne and a decadent snack after a fun night of holiday schmoozing with friends. It felt as though all those years flashed by in a blink. One minute they'd exchanged vows as newlyweds and the next they were moving their only child out of college.

She'd realized months ago that part of her would always love Frank. No matter how their marriage had ended, the lies before and after, it was clear her heart had never stopped loving him. While it would be nice to revisit the good times with her best friend, she kept her thoughts to herself. She wouldn't risk the heartache for either of them by cruising down memory lane only to wind up at the abrupt, unexpected ending when he faked his death.

Room service knocked on the door just as she started to ask Frank where he'd spent those first nights out of prison. With Torres, probably. What about after that? She wanted to know if he'd been grieving the loss as much as she and Frankie had.

She yanked her thoughts away from that crumbling edge of insanity. It wasn't her business. It didn't even matter. He was alive and they would all deal with the effects of that in good time. Frankie should know her dad was alive and well, but Sophia couldn't begin to explain it all by text. As confident as she was about their daughter's reaction to the news, she had to respect Frank's reluctance.

Truly, they both had too much to deal with already.

When Frank was out of sight, she opened the door. After the food was set up and the waiter gone, Frank emerged and they sat down to thick, hot roast beef and turkey sandwiches, a bowl of mixed salad greens and crispy homemade potato chips served with a tangy barbecue sauce for dipping.

He devoured the food as if he hadn't eaten in a week. Sophia managed to hide her smile behind her sandwich. Watching him demolish bite after bite, pausing occasionally for a long drink of iced tea, seemed to make the years and stress fall away. She felt warm all over remembering some of their more memorable meals. Cooking had always been a fun adventure for both of them.

"You know what surprised me the most about playing dead?" Frank twirled a chip in the bowl of tangy sauce between them.

Sophia set aside her fork, still loaded with a bite of salad, as a wave of uncertainty rolled through her belly. She wasn't sure she wanted to do this. Not when the food had been so comforting a moment earlier. "What's that?"

"How much I missed that little iron table set."

Her jaw dropped. He couldn't be serious. Did he know she had it on her front porch now? "You gave me all kinds of grief when I bought it."

"It was clunky and heavy." He popped another chip into his mouth. "I was thinking of the freight when we had to relocate."

"You were thinking of your back," she said, teasing him as he teased her. "I never made you move it once we decided where it would be in each place."

"And I'm thankful for that," he said with a wistful smile.

Her breath caught and her heart twisted a little in her chest, as if it was possible to dodge the sharp blades of pain for what they'd both lost. "We shared a lot over that table." They'd picked it up when Frankie was about three and it had served them well in every home after.

"Even when I was deployed or traveling, I missed that table."

"You never said a word about it."

His ears were turning pink, an outward signal that the

admission embarrassed him. "We all take for granted things that we shouldn't."

Was that some vague reference to her? She bit back the question. Dumb to think it, dumber to ask. "True." She couldn't understand when he'd thought anything was too silly or small to share with her. For twenty-eight years they'd been as close as two people could be. Then he'd pulled away until that little gap was insurmountable.

"We shared a lot over that table," she said. "Coffee on Sunday mornings was the best."

"I was partial to the late evenings after Frankie had gone to bed," he said, a twinkle in his dark blue eyes.

Those had been wonderful evenings, with beer or wine, stargazing or people-watching while they held hands. When the little table set had been in a more private area, she'd often been convinced to sit in his lap and make out under the stars.

Was this her estranged husband's way of hitting on her? She found it more appealing than she should. "Those were good times, too," she admitted, pleased her voice was steady. Those nights bore a striking resemblance to this one: alone, sharing food and conversation across a small table. If he invited her to sit in his lap, she'd have a fight on her hands to remember how to say no. Her body temperature seemed to climb at the very idea, heating her cheeks so he'd know exactly where her thoughts had traveled.

"Assuming your email campaign keeps Lowry busy, we need to think about Engle, Farrell and the next step," he said, leaning back in his chair.

The abrupt change of topic and the shift in his body language as he returned to business gave her a chill. It was as though he'd flipped a switch and all that intimacy had been in her imagination. "Farrell?" She picked up a chip. "Is he the third anchorman for Hellfire?"

Frank nodded.

"Why do I know that name?" She was excellent with names and yet she couldn't put a face with it at all. Probably because the face she was most concerned with was sitting right across the table, scowling fiercely. "Don't leave me hanging." She gestured for him to hurry up with the story.

"Jack Farrell is a retired colonel. He was career military police and honored as a hero when he shot a terrorist who managed to open fire on a forward operating base in Afghanistan a few years back."

Frank didn't have to say another word. She pressed her fingers to her lips as the scene, the reports, all of it surged through her mind with the force of a flash flood. "You don't think it was a terrorist."

He shook his head. "Not in light of what we know now. I think that attack was related to the early days of Halloran's effort to take his piece of the drug trade."

"Good grief. If only we could prove it," she mused, knowing they couldn't. "Halloran's assembled quite a team."

"Yes." Frank leaned back in the chair, his eyes on the ceiling. "Speaking of names to know, I sifted through the old reports and my notes looking for Engle while you were putting the finishing touches on ruining Lowry's reputation. I'm coming up empty."

Her cell phone chimed and she held up a finger. "Hold that thought." She read the message from her assistant, an update on the data they had pulled from the cell phone Frank confiscated earlier. "Pay dirt," she said.

"Tell me. We need good news."

She read the message and related the pertinent details. "My assistant identified the logo on that employee badge along with phone numbers in his text message history. They match up with an import-export brokerage."

She clicked the link in the email to go to the company website. "Oh! Look at this." She hopped out of her chair to kneel at his side so they could look at the small screen together. "I found Engle. He's listed as the operating manager at World Crossing, Incorporated."

Frank squinted at the phone screen. "Stateside offices in Norfolk and Seattle. The man doesn't lack for courage." He took the phone and swiped through the pictures. "Check the logo on the truck." He opened his notebook and showed her. "That's the freight carrier they use with every incoming shipment."

"I can use this." She bounded to her feet and retrieved her laptop.

"I've been an idiot," Frank said. "I should've known he would control every aspect."

Sophia sent an email to the reporter Eddie recommended, complete with the screenshots from the kid's phone. "I hope he took your advice," she murmured as she hit Send. "When this breaks, it will send Hellfire scrambling. If they don't believe him…"

"He made his choices," Frank said, his voice cold. "The more I think about Farrell, the happier I am that we'll have a head start." His gaze drifted toward the window. "Such as it is."

"They can't move on us tonight." She shrugged at

his quizzical glance. "One look out that window and I knew why you'd booked this room. They'd have to scale the wall to get in."

"Or use the main door in the lobby."

"Please. I heard the false name you gave at registration." She wasn't going to fuel his worry. "Halloran's spies might find the car, but they won't figure out the room number before we check out."

He gave her the look she'd laughed at through the years. The twist of his mouth and crinkle at his eye that said he knew she was right but she'd never get him to say the words. Afraid of the happy little skip in her pulse, she returned to the task of digging into the lives of the men who'd founded this dangerous operation and turned their lives upside down.

Frank pushed the room service cart out to the hallway and stretched out on one of the beds, reading glasses perched on his nose as he studied his notebook.

It reminded her they had only days until a new shipment arrived in Seattle. If only Frank would agree, she could put a team on the ports. They needed a smaller target than "the waterfront." And she knew he was right to fear for Frankie's safety if Halloran or anyone else spotted a Leo Solutions team. Although her guys were good, it wasn't worth the risk. Yet.

"Huh. The only thing current on Jack Farrell is a PO box in Arizona." She tried a few more searches with no luck.

"Don't forget the bank account in the Caymans," Frank quipped. He sat up and lowered his reading glasses. "Wait. Phoenix?"

"No. Vail, Arizona. South of Tucson." She used the

internet to pull up a local map. When Frankie was led to believe the worst about Sophia, the trail had taken her through a nearby area. She didn't care for the direction her thoughts were taking.

Following the hunch, she found another, unpleasant connection. "Paul Sterling went to college with Farrell, both political science majors," she told Frank. "And Farrell and Halloran attended the war college in the same year. It might be worth asking Paul about Farrell."

Frank's blue eyes were as cold as ice chips.

"For the record, asking Paul for help isn't my first choice," she stated.

"Visiting a prison isn't mine." Frank tapped his glasses against his thigh, his mouth twitching. "How'd you manage to get Sterling behind bars so fast?"

"You don't know what happened?"

He shook his head.

She didn't want to revisit all the details. "He fooled me, let's leave it at that. While he was in custody in Seattle, I reached out to an old friend inside the Department of Justice. Leo Solutions has a modest government contract arrangement. It wasn't much, but I was thankful they got him transferred to the federal prison in Maryland while he awaits trial."

"I don't think he'll want to cooperate with you after that."

"Us. If we do this, we do it together."

Frank sat up. "You're kidding. I can't walk into a prison, Sophie. Even if I wasn't recognized immediately, Paul would make a scene out of spite. He always hated me because I had you."

"The two of you were always competitive." When she

thought she'd been widowed and needed help, Paul had been there for the business and, after a time, on a more personal level. Thinking of him, of how he'd deceived her so thoroughly, left her wanting a shower.

Frank stretched out again. "All the more reason not to trust anything he might tell us."

She held her tongue. Frank knew as well as she did they couldn't allow any part of Halloran's organization to escape justice. They had to nail all the top players or Frank would never have his life back. "We can't let Farrell off the hook because we can't find him. What we need is something to hand to a prosecutor. Paul could give us that kind of lead."

Frank shook his head and went back to his notebook.

The prison was a short drive and couldn't possibly be on Halloran's radar. There was a regional airport close by where they could park the car and further hide their trail. It would become a pointless exercise if Frank got detained in the process.

She could ask him to wait with the car, but she couldn't bear it, not after her near panic attack in DC. "If I can guarantee you won't be detained, will you think about it?"

"It's a bad idea."

"I know that." Exasperated, she went over and sat on the edge of the bed, leaving as much space as possible between them. "I know there are better ideas. Do we really have the time for any of them? Your fake ID will work." He was shaking his head already. "I need you with me," she blurted. "I mean it, Frank. I'm not letting you out of my sight. My heart can't take the worry." She felt her heart pounding now, terrified if he left her sight that he'd be gone again. "I—I had anxiety attacks when we were younger. Wh-when—" she gulped "—when you were gone. In the beginning. Today when I thought you were gone…"

"Dolcezza," he whispered, reaching for her.

She dodged his hand, scrambling off the bed. If he touched her now, she wouldn't be able to resist him. Sex would only make things worse, blurring the lines and insinuating obligations she didn't want to push on him. If they could clear his name, maybe they had a shot at rediscovering their dreams as a couple, as a family. "I worked past those fears. I managed." She sucked in another breath. "Just not now." She rested her hand over her heart, willing it to slow down. "Come with me. Please."

"Of course."

Relief so profound she swayed with the force of it had her dashing for the bathroom. She splashed water on her face. She was grateful for not crying, though her face was a splotchy mess anyway. Her life was a mess.

Going to the prison to speak with Paul was a long shot. Even if he cooperated and shared what he knew about Farrell, spending a minute in his presence would be difficult enough. If he chose to be a jerk… Oh, it didn't bear thinking about.

She hadn't jumped into bed with Paul immediately following Frank's graveside service, yet trying to explain to her very alive husband that, after a time, she had done exactly that was not a pleasant prospect. She had been entirely fooled by Paul. And Frank.

At last her temper surfaced, saving her from a night of hiding in the bathroom wallowing in what-ifs and what-might-have-beens. She returned to the room and picked up her laptop, ready to review the best way to and from the prison, and how to keep Frank safe in the process. There were still plenty of people who owed her favors and she was ready to cash them in so her daughter could see her dad and they could all decide what came next.

Frank's strong hands landed on her shoulders, radiating warmth. Was she imagining any forgiveness in his touch? Did she want or need that forgiveness? She let him massage the muscles at her neck and shoulders, still aching after the recent attack.

"I've pulled myself together," she said.

"You always do."

"Paul helped me get Leo Solutions off the ground when I needed to move fast," she explained, latching on to the one point she didn't regret. By all accounts, she'd been a widow, personally and professionally. She never would have been able to establish Leo Solutions so efficiently or make the company relevant so quickly without Paul's help. He'd done that much right. Mostly. The bastard.

"To separate yourself from my problems?"

"Yes." She stated the fact calmly, her eyes locked on her monitor. "If the situation were reversed, I would've expected you to do the same thing. It was a future we had planned. A legacy we would leave for our daughter."

He came around to sit across from her, and something deep in his blue eyes contradicted her assessment. His scent surrounded her, and her muscles were loose and warm from his hands. "Frankie was injured, her navy career over." The memory of their daughter in that hospital room surrounded by the equipment and dire prognosis still haunted her. "She was too stubborn to accept any physical limits, then too angry with me for what she assumed was my blithely moving on without you."

She'd gone through all that alone. Frank had been overseas or in custody, unable to help.

"You both succeeded, despite all of it," he said.

Her temper crackled to life again. "Do you think I'm looking for your approval here?"

"No." He held his ground, typical Frank. "But you have it."

She stifled the hateful words that wanted to pour out and burn him as effectively as acid. He hadn't been a traitor, and, knowing that, she couldn't keep blaming him for what was done. They had to find their way forward from here. She had to help him extricate himself from Halloran's schemes.

For Frankie, if no one else. Her daughter needed her father and it was clear to Sophia that the opposite was equally true. Despite the pain his choices had caused, she couldn't let this opportunity to salvage the father-daughter relationship slip away. She hugged her arms around her waist. Frankie had been right all along; her belief had never faltered. Sophia couldn't say the same thing. Even now, understanding his impossible choices, she couldn't quite get past the residual frustration—with herself for giving up on him and with him for heaping sorrow on Frankie's life at the worst possible time.

"Sophie." He lifted the laptop away and cradled her hand, stroking gently along the bones of her wrist, to her elbow and then down to each finger.

Soothing and comforting. Her hand and arm melted at the familiar comfort and her heart followed suit. Here was what she'd been missing, what she'd longed for. Every deployment or career task that kept them apart, they'd had this to come home to: the steady, nurturing support they'd consistently found in each other.

She had considered herself an independent person for the entirety of their marriage. Sharing the burdens and joys of life didn't lessen any part of her or him as individuals. The camaraderie, the acceptance and easy affection, she hadn't known how much she depended on those intangible traits until they had been ripped from her life.

He murmured her name, his gaze full of such raw compassion she knew his thoughts mirrored her own. Slowly, he tipped up her chin. Slower still, giving her plenty of time and space to turn away, he lowered his mouth until his lips brushed softly across hers.

She welcomed his kiss, let it sink into her being. The immediate flash of heat and passion was as reassuring and familiar as everything else about him. This kiss was loaded with more tenderness, more patience than the one she'd planted on him in DC. She raked her fingers through his hair, angling her mouth for deeper access to all that she craved from him.

On a soft sigh, her lips parted. She relished the hot velvet stroke of his tongue over hers. His taste ignited her body in ways she hadn't let herself remember for the sole purpose of preserving her sanity. His palms smoothed over her shoulders, down her back and over the curve of her hips. Fingers flexed and teased, playing her body as though they'd never been parted.

Every reunion had been this way. Sweet and hot, they fell on each other with the pent-up longing distance had created. Her fingers knew the curve of his jaw, the small scar at his hairline. She knew just where to kiss his throat and make him shiver with anticipation.

Her hips flexed into him automatically, and the feel of his erection sent goose bumps racing over her skin. Her body was more than willing to make up for lost time. He could have her. She knew the pleasure she'd enjoy taking him deep inside.

For too long, she'd believed this depth of yearning and fulfillment was out of her reach. She'd spent so many terrible nights regretting every moment they hadn't seized because they'd been so sure they had plenty of time.

On a surge of need she pressed up on her toes and fused her mouth to his. Her husband, the love of her life and her soul mate, was right where he belonged at last. People didn't get second chances as precious as this one. She wouldn't squander it.

He boosted her up and she wound her arms and legs around him, troubles burned away by this glorious contact. The scruff on his jaw rasped against the fragile skin just under her ear as he murmured those delicious Italian endearments between nips of his teeth and soft kisses.

Somewhere in the back of her mind, she heard her daughter's false irritation imploring them to get a room. The memory was as effective as a bucket of ice.

"Stop." She bent her head, keeping her lips out of his reach. "It's not so simple." It took more effort than she expected to put her feet on the floor and remain steady.

"Not simple at all," he agreed, his arms still banded around her, holding her close to the marvelous heat and strength of his body.

She forced her palms flat against his chest, pushing just hard enough to back away. She inhaled, drawing in the first deep breath of air not entirely infused with his masculine scent.

Better. And a thousand times worse. "Guess we've still got it," she remarked, wishing it wasn't true. This powerful attraction complicated everything.

"Feels that way."

"For everyone's sake we, um, should…" She licked her lips, tasting him. "Uh, we should stick to the matter of clearing your name."

"Sophia?"

She looked away. "Don't try to get around me with those eyes and that tone. I can't pretend the past year didn't happen, Frank."

"I don't blame you for *any* of your choices."

She wished she could say the same. She shouldn't blame him—he'd been caught in a precarious dilemma—yet she did. Being disappointed in him when he'd been in such a dilemma added guilt to the rest of the churning mix in her gut. Holding her arm out as if it might be enough of a deterrent, she kept herself just beyond his reach.

"I appreciate that." She wasn't sure she deserved his understanding. Grabbing her toiletry bag, she headed for the bathroom, pausing in the doorway. The words scraped her throat raw as she pushed them out. "But I blame you for yours."

There, she'd said it. Now they both knew how awful she was.

His nostrils flared on a sharp inhale and his gaze shuttered as she closed the door between them.

Chapter Seven

At the regional airport, Frank parked the rental car in the hourly lot. He didn't expect the meeting with Paul to take long. They'd stowed their luggage in a locker near the restrooms and now were waiting for a cab to take them to the prison in Cumberland.

With little to occupy his mind, he congratulated himself on surviving another long night with his wife well out of his reach. Her breakdown, admitting she'd suffered so much anxiety over him in the early years, nearly crushed him. He admired her even more for overcoming it and, given a chance, he'd hold her close—as if a hug now would soothe away her old troubles.

The idea of holding her brought him right back to the spectacular kiss that had put his world to rights again despite stopping far short of his body's ultimate goal. He understood why Sophia had pulled away and couldn't resent her for it. He'd broken the most essential promise—to always be there for her.

He'd abused her trust. She wasn't sure she could count on him anymore. As messed up as things were with Halloran's operation, Frank maintained a fair confidence that they could bring that man and his cronies to justice. But the trust issue, the gaping canyon between husband and wife—that he wasn't so sure could be resolved.

"Breaking news." Sophia nudged him with her elbow and raised her chin at the television mounted in the corner of the tiny coffee shop.

In slacks and a classic sweater set in a pale rose color that put a glow in her golden skin, she looked overdressed for a trip to a prison. Having spent some time on the wrong side of the bars, he knew he was overdressed, as well. He'd chosen khakis and a polo shirt, hoping the guards would believe his impersonation of a lawyer taking a break between the front nine and back nine.

"Hey." She bumped him again. "You're not paying attention."

This time when he glanced at the television, he read the ticker. The overhead shot of the Pentagon on this sunny spring day was layered with a professional head shot of Lowry. When the live feed returned, it was a view of Lowry being led out of the building in handcuffs toward a black government-issue sedan.

"Nice work," he murmured, though no one was around to hear him. Lowry in official custody would definitely get a rise out of Halloran. Frank was more eager for the next confrontation than he should be. He wanted the leader of Hellfire to understand, to absolutely *fear*, what Frank and Sophia planned to dish out. Justice, yes, along with enough pain to qualify as vengeance.

"It may not hold him long, but it should get a reaction. The intel from the phone gave my earlier claims more juice," she said. She held up her hand for a celebratory fist bump.

Preferring a kiss, he understood the line she'd drawn. "We're dealing with some cool heads," he reminded her. Halloran hadn't created his network and cash cow by jumping at every little provocation. Then again, the provocation Sophia had created wasn't so little.

"We're also dealing with egos and profit margins," she returned. "I doubt Lowry will roll on his boss. We just need to cast doubts."

"Regardless, this distraction buys us time to question Paul and move before they can catch up with us."

Beside him, she nodded and crossed her legs. "Anyone here of concern to you?" she asked.

"Not so far."

"Good."

"You seem nervous." He wanted her to share the cause of her antsy behavior. More, he wanted her to trust him to help her fix it.

"I expected them to follow us."

"They'll catch up soon enough," he said. "Are you spoiling for a fight?"

"I suppose," she admitted. "It would be nice to have a clear target for all my frustration."

"Your frustration or your company?"

"The company resources there would give us an advantage." She checked her watch, then the window. "I thought cabdrivers stuck close to airports."

"If we tap the company, we put people we love in the cross fire."

She rolled her lips between her teeth and then gave him a wide, false smile. "We'll table the topic for now. Let's review the interview strategy."

They'd done that for most of the two-hour drive. "We don't have to quiz Sterling at all." He couldn't decide if he wanted her to take him up on that offer or not. A small part of him wanted to gloat that Sophia was with him, again. Except he wasn't sure he'd get to keep her this time. "With Lowry in custody, I'm sure Farrell will show up."

"Do you know where?" She waited expectantly, but he didn't have an answer. "Unless we use other resources, we need the inside line on Farrell that Paul may be able to give us."

The implication was clear enough. Leo Solutions could run everything, if only Frank would agree. He wouldn't take the chance with Frankie's safety. It bothered him enough what Sophia had run through her assistant and that his girls were texting about wedding plans.

"You know, I could always talk to him alone."

"No," she replied a little too quickly. "If we're both there, he can't play either one of us."

"Okay." She was right, though he wondered how long it had taken her to come up with the argument. What he knew about Afghanistan and what Sophia had pieced together afterward would be a system of checks and balances if Paul tried to lie.

"There's our ride," he said as a yellow cab came into view. With his hand at the small of her back, he escorted her outside and into the waiting vehicle.

Sophia slid across the crackled leather seat of the old cab and gave the driver the address of the prison. She took a snapshot of the cabdriver's license on his dash and then entered a text message.

Frank raised an eyebrow in query.

"A precaution," she replied quietly. "My assistant knows I'm on a research trip for a client."

He nodded, unable to come up with a response that wouldn't reveal the turmoil inside him.

They didn't speak to each other or the driver. The vehicle hadn't been upgraded with a screen between the front and back seats, and there wasn't much worth discussing in front of a stranger.

The reached their destination too soon. The driver could've taken all day and the trip would still have been too short for Frank. When they arrived, he got out and held the door for her before giving the cabdriver a hundred dollars in cash to wait for them. When it was time to go, he wanted to get out fast.

If walking into a prison on nothing more than her word that he wouldn't have to stay indefinitely didn't prove how much he trusted her, he wasn't sure what would.

"I know this can't be easy," she said, linking her hand with his.

"I'm fine," he lied through gritted teeth. He couldn't let her know just how much he wanted to run. It wasn't about seeing the bastard who'd taken advantage of her in Frank's absence. He'd had time to process that she'd run to Sterling for help after the verdict and funeral. It was about being trapped and never being able to be with her and their daughter the way he wanted.

Her steps slowed as they neared the gate. "Frank?"

Behind the shelter of his sunglasses, he studied her with unveiled love until his face felt normal again. "A half hour is worth it for a decent lead on hard intel."

Surely his fake ID and the myriad favors people owed Sophia would protect them that long.

Sophia felt terrible for asking Frank to take this chance, but she couldn't risk leaving him back at the hotel area waiting somewhere between here and there. Not to mention, she couldn't face Paul alone. The tendons and muscles of Frank's hand were wound tight, and when she slipped her finger to his wrist, she felt his pulse pounding. He was doing a good job at being stoic and supportive, letting none of the stress show.

She'd cleared the visit early this morning and as they passed through security, the guard told them Paul was waiting. Good. She wanted in and out of here as quickly as possible.

As much as she tried to ignore the awkwardness, it dogged her as she and Frank walked down the faded, industrial-green hallway to a conference room. She was about to stand with her husband and interview a lover who'd betrayed her. If there had been a stranger situation in her past, she couldn't recall it right now.

Her heart hammered in her ears and she tried to imagine the best possible outcome. Though Paul might try to expose Frank's true identity, he wouldn't once he learned about the proverbial ace she had up her sleeve. Still, the potential for such a confrontation put an electric current in the air. The mocking expression she'd come to hate slid over Paul's face the second he spotted them. She raised her chin, entering the room first, daring him to try something. After the havoc he'd created for her and the company in Seattle, he owed her a conversation.

The metal chairs scraped loudly against the concrete floor as Frank pulled out hers, then his own. Paul's handcuffs rattled as he shifted in his seat. "What a pleasant surprise for me this morning."

"We're here for one thing." Sophia wouldn't waste any time on false pleasantries.

Paul's mean gaze darted between her and Frank. "Does that go for the dead guy, too?"

She glanced down and noticed Frank's hand curling into a fist on his thigh. She didn't blame him. Given the chance, she'd happily deck Paul, as well. "You went to college with Jack Farrell. Tell me about him."

Paul's eyebrows climbed his forehead. "Farrell." His eyes slid to Frank again. "Huh. If I knew anything, why would I tell you?"

Sophia cleared her throat, drawing Paul's attention. "You told me you didn't have anything to do with Frank's career troubles, that you only took advantage after the fact."

He gave her a lecherous sneer. "You didn't have any complaints at the time."

Frank shifted in a blink and the table was suddenly pressed against Paul's chest. "What did they offer you to get close to her?"

It seemed she and Frank had independently reached a similar conclusion overnight after discovering the import-export office in Seattle. As a friend, Farrell could have used Paul to be sure Sophia and Frankie weren't uncovering anything that would expose Hellfire.

"She came to me," Paul grumbled.

"Enough," Sophia said quickly. She pulled the table back to neutral territory. "I've been going through the company records. Seems you knocked some sense into me last week."

"What?" Frank asked, his voice low and deadly.

She silenced him with a touch of her knee to his. "Water under the bridge." She focused on Paul again.

"I came to you for help, yes. When did Farrell come to you?"

"He wanted a cybersecurity program. We needed clients." He shrugged. "Later they tossed me a bonus to keep an eye on you and your girl. Money wasn't the best prize." His gaze dropped to her breasts and climbed slowly back to her face.

Her blood curdled at the vulgar look on his face. How had she been so oblivious of his real motives? "Tell me about Farrell and the program he asked for."

"Why? It's not as though you'll make my life any better."

"I bet she can make it worse," Frank threatened. "Or I can."

"You think a dead man scares me?"

"Hey!" Sophia rapped her knuckles on the table. Time to lay out all the cards. "I've been digging, Paul." Money was the man's only priority and she'd found his stash. "That makes *me* the real threat here." Since his arrest, she'd changed his passwords and her tech team had rooted out all his backdoor access to Leo Solutions. One call and Paul would find the money he was counting on using after his time served had been donated to the charity of her choice. She waited, holding his gaze as his skin blanched. "Are we on the same page now?"

Paul nodded solemnly, fear in his eyes for the first time.

"I'm determined to set the record straight," Sophia said. "I can see that you get lumped in with the rest of them, or I can tell the prosecutors that your connection to General Leone's downfall was peripheral. You have fifteen minutes to convince me the latter is our best interest."

With a heavy sigh, Paul shared everything he knew about his college pal. From Farrell's upbringing to the current business interests Paul was aware of.

"Where is he now?" Sophia asked, making notes.

"Last I heard he splits his time between his place south of Tucson and a desk in some accounts receivable department," Paul replied.

"Tucson," she echoed. Paul had planted documents in a safe-deposit box in a bank near Tucson, using the find to manipulate Frankie.

"There's a reason I used that bank." His mouth curved into an ugly smile, confirming he'd read her mind. "Image is everything, isn't it? Especially when the culprit is right under your nose."

Her teeth clenched. "Be clear," she insisted. Frank's future was riding on this.

"World Bridge Shipping, maybe?" Paul's brow wrinkled in thought. "Something like that. I know there's more than one office in the States," he added. "Farrell doesn't do anything for the money. Doesn't need it. He's got a warped thing for power and respect." Paul shook his head. "If you want him, try Arizona." He flattened one hand over the other and leaned forward. "I gave you all you need. I expect you to do the same."

She nodded. Paul was all about the money. The man had her tense from her scalp to the soles of her feet. As much as she hated this meeting, it gave them a fresh lead angle to pursue. She wouldn't rest until the right man—or men—was behind bars for the crimes he'd pinned on her husband.

"Thank you for your time," she said, sliding out of the seat.

Neither man moved, locked in a silent battle of wills.

"Don't you dare make a scene," she said, not certain which man worried her more.

"It was a pleasure seeing you again," Frank said, his chair scraping obnoxiously against the floor. "I look forward to the next time."

Only a deaf woman would've missed the threat in those words.

"Can't wait," Paul muttered before calling for the guard.

Though Paul had been her ally through the years, she knew she'd never speak to him directly again. It startled her how what appeared to be the smallest decisions could have such lasting, enormous impact. Frank had withdrawn from her to attend to an honorable task, willing to endure erroneous accusations for the betterment of his country. Paul had been attentive, heedless of her feelings while he deceived her day in and day out.

Sophia wasn't sure Victoria had been right about her judgment after all.

When the last heavy door rolled back and the sunshine blasted them, Frank swore. "We're stranded."

Startled, she searched the parking area as if she could will the cab to reappear. Thank goodness they'd left their belongings in a locker at the airport. "His dispatcher must have called him back."

"Not likely," Frank mused, donning his sunglasses. "This stinks of trouble."

She pulled out her phone and called the cab company. No answer. "Considering what we paid the driver to stay, it must have cost them a pretty sum to get him to leave."

"Not much comfort in that." He planted his hands on his hips, his mouth set in a stern line.

His eyes hidden, she couldn't see his gaze roaming over the area, but she knew he was searching for the inevitable ambush.

"Get back inside," he said, pushing her behind him. "I've got a bad feeling."

"What?" How was she supposed to manage that? It wasn't a restaurant or a salon—it was a federal prison. "I'm not going anywhere without you."

"By now Paul's telling them who I really am. You need to distance yourself."

She heard the unspoken *again*. "No." Had he forgotten how stubborn she was? "Paul will keep his mouth shut."

He pushed up his sunglasses, and his eyes were blazing. "What do you have on him?"

She gave him her sweetest smile. "About seventeen million dollars."

Either Frank didn't believe that would be enough incentive or he didn't care. "We've been set up, Sophie," he said, covering his eyes again. "Inside is your best chance."

Behind her own sunglasses, she studied the front gate, the towers and the cleared terrain outside the tall fences topped with barbed wire. She and Frank wouldn't be able to outrun an ambush. "A rock and a hard place," she murmured. They needed a car.

"Go on. They'll let you in."

She ignored him. Arguing wouldn't solve their dilemma. "The private ride apps won't do us any more good than the cab at this point. Too rural."

"There's no cover." His voice was little more than a growl as he started to walk.

Sophia followed. She had an overhead image of the

area on her phone. "There's a farm three miles down the road," she said. "If we can get there, we can—"

"They'll pick us off long before either of us can get there," he said. He stopped pacing in front of the warden's vehicle parked at the front of the lot and urged her to join him. "Let's see how determined they are."

The grit in his voice gave her a boost of confidence. "What do you mean?"

"I'm waiting right here." He sat down on the curb, his hands resting on one knee, his other leg stretched out long. "They'll get impatient and make a move or we'll find another ride out of here."

"It is a nice day to sit outside," she said, playing along. At least he wasn't implying they steal a car from in front of a prison. "All we're missing is a picnic."

He tilted his head up to her, his lips curved in a genuine smile. If she didn't know better, she'd say he looked happy.

"I've missed that," he said.

"What?"

"Your wit," he replied. "Your unflappable nature."

"Both are essential survival skills in our worlds."

"I agree." He scanned the parking lot once more.

"You're using the reflection in the windshields to check behind us, aren't you?"

"Surprising what skills you pick up when you're on the run."

She sat down beside him and tried to call the cab company again. "How can they just not answer?"

Frank shrugged. "Halloran plays a ruthless game."

"And you?"

"I've learned to play that way when there's no other choice."

She left that comment alone, sending a quick text to

Leo Solutions. Frankie or Aidan would figure it out if something happened to her. She had yet to explain anything other than that she was running down leads for an old friend. Frankie would flip out, temper blazing, if she discovered her dad was alive and avoiding her.

"What are you thinking?" she asked after a few more minutes of silence.

"Time is on our side. Coming directly at us would cause them more problems than it solves. Walking to the farmhouse is iffy, gives the advantage back to them. Between the two of us I'm sure we can convince one of the deliverymen to give us a lift out of here."

"Putting that driver in jeopardy."

"Face it, Sophia—anyone near us right now is in jeopardy. That doesn't make us the bad guys."

True. She just didn't want to see anyone else get hurt.

"Do you believe Sterling?"

"Yes." She pulled up the regional airport, checking departures. "Do you think we'll get lucky and pin down Farrell in Tucson?"

"Until Halloran shows his lousy face, it's our best option." Frank stood up at the sound of an approaching engine. "Well, well," he said. "Look who has a conscience."

Sophia noticed the number on the top of the yellow taxicab pulling into the lot. "It's the same car." She squinted but couldn't identify the driver through the glare on the windshield. "Is it the same driver?"

"Can't tell yet. Stay alert," he warned, walking out from between parked cars. "Could be a setup."

The cab came to a stop and the driver, the same man who'd brought them to the prison, stepped out. "I went to fill up the tank. Hope you haven't been waiting long."

"Thought you might've changed your mind about the fare," Frank said, opening the closest rear door for Sophia.

"No, sir. My apologies for any confusion."

"Back to the airport," Frank responded. He laced his fingers with hers, their joined hands resting on his thigh, his smile a hard counterpoint to the gentle touch.

She understood the unspoken message that he now considered the cabdriver an enemy until proved an ally. Hopefully he could still read her well enough to know she agreed.

They'd barely made the main road when she heard the growl of a burly engine speeding up behind them. Frank twisted in the seat, his eyebrows dropping into a ferocious scowl at the car closing in on the rear bumper of the cab.

"Get down," Frank said, urging her to the floorboards behind the driver's seat. "I guess they're convinced you could make Paul talk."

"They aren't wrong," she pointed out.

Frank leaned across the back of the front seat. "Any weapons?" he asked.

"No, sir."

Frank swore and her stomach clutched. They'd left Frank's weapons behind in the luggage. Assuming Halloran's men were armed and their intent was to stop her and Frank permanently, they were sitting ducks.

The car behind them slammed into the back of the cab. The impact knocked the cab forward with a hard jerk and tossed Sophia into the hard frame of the driver's seat.

"Floor it," Frank ordered.

When the driver obeyed, Sophia put him in the ally column and said a prayer all three of them would survive.

The cab took another hit, this time closer to the right rear quarter panel. They were being pushed into the oncoming traffic lane and the driver eased off the gas.

"I'll pull over," the driver said.

"Do that and we're all dead," Frank snapped. "These people don't leave witnesses."

"Do you?" the driver asked.

Sophia lurched upright from her sheltered position. "Yes! Get us back to the airport in one piece and I'll make sure you can buy a new cab."

"You can do that?"

Under her feet she felt the cab accelerating again. "Yes!" she answered. "I can make sure you have money to put your kids through college or whatever you need."

The driver's eyes lit up and the heavy cab sped up a little more. "You are good people. College money is too much, but you are good people."

Sophia sent another text to her assistant, giving her instructions to track down the driver's family, just in case something happened. She intended to keep her promise.

Frank swore. "What are you doing?"

She couldn't answer as the other car sideswiped them, attempting to knock them off the road.

"Gun!" Frank pushed her back to the floorboards. "Brakes," he yelled at the driver.

Glass from the window showered down on her and the cab's tires squealed against the pavement. The car rocked on its chassis at the sudden stop. She heard Frank scramble into the front seat.

"Move over!" Frank commanded the driver.

"What are you doing?" she asked, daring to sit up.

"He overshot us." Frank put the car in Drive and

muscled the heavy car into a U-turn. He wasn't escaping, he was going on the offensive.

She was thrown back as Frank took control of the cab and floored it. Wind whistled through the broken window and she held her breath as he charged toward the attacking car.

She knew this wouldn't be the end of it. If they made it to the airport, if they survived the next leg in this convoluted journey, Halloran would just keep coming. They had to force his hand and dismantle Hellfire completely.

She pitched discretion out the window and sent Aidan a request to put a plainclothes bodyguard on the cabbie and his family until further notice. Frank wouldn't be happy she'd directly involved the company, but she'd soothe his ruffled feathers later. If they survived.

The engine labored and she and the driver were tossed around like rag dolls as Frank plowed into the path of the attacking car. It was a dreadful game of chicken and she knew Frank wouldn't be the first to blink. Bullets skittered off the hood and windshield, but the attacking driver veered at the last second.

Anticipating the move, Frank pulled hard on the wheel, managing to clip the front fender and send the other car spinning away. Frank stomped on the brakes, executed a three-point turn in record time and accelerated into the attacking car again.

Startled, she screamed, expecting an air bag to erupt from the steering wheel, belatedly remembering the cab was too old for those safety advancements.

As Frank backed away from the wrecked car and sped down the road toward the airport, she stared at the wreckage behind them until they rounded a curve.

The adrenaline spike plagued her. Her body couldn't

be sure if she should be relieved or furious. Although she was grateful Frank's quick thinking and actions had saved them all, he'd put himself at risk in the process. He could've been killed.

It was a stupid thing to focus on now that they were safe. But safe was only temporary. Halloran was trailing them too easily and the greedy bastard held every advantage. She wouldn't let him win, wouldn't let him rob her daughter of a father all over again.

A renewed sense of purpose washed over Sophia, dulling the anger. She would do whatever it took to defeat Hellfire and Halloran. Frankie needed her father, and Sophia was determined to make that reunion happen.

Chapter Eight

Frank's concern grew exponentially with every hour. Sophia wasn't talking to him and he couldn't get a read on what was going on in that brilliant head of hers. She'd been friendly with the cabdriver, even sending him on his way with some cash and a business card, but she continued to give Frank the cold shoulder. She hadn't let him take her hand, hadn't allowed him the briefest moment to hold her close and assure himself she was in one piece.

He'd pulled their belongings from the locker while she'd scrambled for transportation. The fastest way out of the area was a short drive to Columbus, Ohio, so they retrieved the rental car and hit the road. While he kept an eye out for any pursuit, Sophia took care of the details with a charter flight service that expedited air travel for Leo Solutions. Despite his reservations, she was proving her point time and again that they needed what her company could offer.

"I've got a plane scheduled to get us from Columbus to Arizona," she said, breathing a sigh of relief.

"By now Halloran has people moving to intercept us no matter what we do."

"So we brave it out and keep pressing. It's worked so far."

He wasn't willing to trust in that kind of luck anymore today. "You ordered protection for the cabbie and his family, didn't you?"

Her chin came up and he stifled a smile at her marvelous defiant streak. "I did. He took care of us and we'll take care of him."

"I'm not disagreeing."

She stared straight ahead. "You don't have to worry that Frankie knows anything. I'm keeping your secret. No one at the company has any idea what I'm really up to."

He studied her. "You mean it."

"Of course I do."

"You're inviting a Hellfire attack."

That got a rise out of her. "That's inevitable. You know as well as I do we need to draw them out and distract them."

"What's really bugging you?" he asked after a few more minutes of silence.

She said his name, then stopped short, her teeth sinking into her full lower lip.

He wanted to pull over and soothe that small bite with a kiss. The need to taste her, breathe her in, was overwhelming. He wanted to run away with her, so far and so fast not even Halloran could find them.

Running away wouldn't fix anything. He'd still be officially dead, his wife would still be miserable and Frankie would be at Halloran's mercy.

"Turn off your phone."

"I've told you they can't track it."

"Do it anyway," he pleaded.

She powered it off and dropped it into her purse. "Why?"

"I want your full attention." Now that he had it, he forced the words out. "I'm sorry I scared you."

She snorted. "At the prison? I wasn't scared."

He spared her a long glance. "I was," he admitted.

"Okay, in the moment, yes, I was scared." She folded her arms over her chest. "Now I'm just angry. With you," she added as if he might miss the point.

"Want to give me a little more than that?" They had an hour left, plus the flight to Arizona. Better to get back on an even footing before Halloran's men caught up with them again.

"You took an impossible risk. You have to stop *doing* that."

He didn't know how else to protect her. "But—"

"We were a team once." She covered her face with her hands and let out a weary groan. Her hands in her lap again, she continued, her words aimed at the roof of the car. "It's as if you've forgotten I can hold my own. You aren't working alone. When Halloran's in custody— and he will be soon, by God—if you don't want to be a team anymore, that's okay with me."

His heart stuttered in his chest. Life without her had been unbearable, and not solely as a result of the pressures of working undercover.

"Frank, you're a father," she continued. "Grown or not, your daughter needs you. Stop behaving as if you're expendable."

This time he didn't interrupt the silence as it grew and swelled and filled the car to bursting.

Tucson, 6:45 p.m.

IT WAS NEARLY sunset when they stopped for the night at a roadside motel south of Tucson. Though they'd been able to clean up, change clothes and rest up on the private plane, they were both exhausted. Offices everywhere were closed, putting any direct search for Farrell on hold until morning.

After parking the rented SUV by the stairs, he peered through the windshield at their room. "Maybe I should sit out here and keep watch." It was agony spending so much time with her and not being able to connect on that intimate, passionate level they'd shared for so many years.

"And let them divide and conquer?" She shook her head, her glossy hair brushing her shoulders. "No way."

They towed the luggage up the stairs and settled into what was becoming a vexing routine. She set to work with her laptop and he brooded over his notes, adding in the new discoveries, looking for any weak spot or leverage.

His gaze and thoughts were drawn to her as unerringly as moths to flame. When he'd proposed, they had been madly in love, and with each year together it surprised him how they could grow apart and together and find themselves deeper in love.

Until he'd single-handedly wrecked everything, trashing her trust and faith in him. Somehow he had to make it right. Eliminating Hellfire would only be half the battle. He needed to make things right with his family, as well.

He had opened his mouth to unload everything

building up inside him when she stood, her hands wrapped around her middle. "Are you okay?" he asked.

She closed the laptop, drumming her fingers on the lid. "I need a coffee or a soda or something."

He checked the change in his pockets. "I'll get it." Any excuse for a break from the cramped room and the feminine scent he remembered too well.

SOPHIA WATCHED HIM GO, fighting the sense that she was being unreasonable with him. Frank had buried himself in this mess for the right reasons. He wasn't her real enemy. No, that was Halloran and Farrell and Lowry and Engle and the rest of the convoluted Hellfire network.

It frustrated her how connected Halloran was, how close they were at every turn. Thinking of the cab and the airport and everything else just kept adding up to one conclusion. Frank would obviously step in front of any stray bullet—or the equivalent—to save her.

While it was honorable and part of his nature, she couldn't abide any result that kept him from reuniting with Frankie. He seemed determined to prevent her from protecting him. They'd never worked that way. From the first moment they met, she'd appreciated the way he accepted her strengths and empowered her. She scolded herself again, rubbing another chill from her arms.

He'd let her talk with Eddie alone. He'd fought off one of Halloran's spies without her. They were finally making progress together. Being frustrated with the circumstances was no reason to make their task of dismantling Hellfire more difficult through a lack of communication.

It was past time to extend an olive branch. She'd always treasured the way they talked through everything.

It hadn't escaped her notice that Frank avoided any mention of a future. Not that she could blame him. He'd been through so much with the nightmare of being abandoned by CID and the demands of chasing down Halloran.

She thought of the terrace on this level overlooking the pool. They'd passed it on the way to their room. It might be nice to enjoy the night air as they'd often done when Frankie was younger and chat about something other than their problems.

Grabbing a room key and slipping into her flats, she headed for the vending machines, expecting to bump into Frank returning to the room. Immediately she knew something was wrong. Everything was too quiet. She glanced over the rail, breathing a sigh of relief that the rental car was still parked in the designated space below. At least he hadn't left her.

Though the dry evening air was cool against her skin, the chill she felt had nothing to do with weather. The vending machines were on the other side of the building, and even in this aging establishment it couldn't possibly have taken so long for him to find one stocked with a soda.

Just ahead, the bright light from the vending area spilled out over the concrete walkway. A large, lumpy shadow blotted out the light for a moment, then it retreated. Sophia caught the squeak of a rubber-soled shoe, a thud and a low grunt. She froze in place, two doors down from the vending machines that connected the parking lot side with the pool and courtyard side of the motel. Holding her breath, she caught the unmistakable swish and snap of a switchblade knife.

"Thelma?" she called out at the top of her lungs. "Which room are we in?" With any luck, no one by that name would be in a nearby room. In the answering silence, she hurried around the corner and into the vending area and skidded to a stop.

"One word and he's done." A younger man with sandy-brown hair and cold eyes held a knife to Frank's throat.

Sophia clapped a hand over her mouth, stifling the scream and the pleas that wanted to pour forth. She could hardly believe her eyes. Not only had they been found, but Halloran's oldest son had overpowered her husband with a knife. She shot Frank a bewildered look.

He gave her a look that urged her to play it cool.

"You're coming with me," the young man said. "Both of you."

Frank's gaze told a different story. He was playing along until a better opportunity to escape arose.

No point wasting time. "Mike Halloran," she said in her best maternal command, planting her hands on her hips as she stared down the son of Hellfire's leader. "What do you think you're doing?"

"Mrs. Leone." He shuffled his feet much as he'd done as a lanky preteen caught in a silly prank. "Yeah. Sorry. It's not as bad as it looks. This is just business."

Was it her imagination or had he eased the knife back? "What kind of business requires you to attack an old family friend?"

"Dad wants to talk, that's all. General Leone hasn't been cooperating."

"Whether or not that's true, your mother would be appalled by this behavior. How is she?"

"Great." Mike relaxed further, leaving more than an inch between that gleaming blade and the skin of

Frank's throat. "She spends most of her time in Saint Croix now."

Hopefully oblivious of her husband's treachery. "That's nice. She always loved the coast." Sophia took another step forward. "You realize no one talks business or anything else with a knife at their throat. Put it down."

Mike seemed to be debating how to carry out his orders. "Will you come along quietly?"

Of course not. "Certainly," she said. "Where are you taking us?"

"Back to my place until Dad can get here. He just wants to clear up this misunderstanding."

She bit back the sarcastic retort, refusing to look directly at Frank again as she nodded at Halloran's son.

"It coulda been just the general," Mike said. "But now that you've seen me…"

"I understand." She smiled. "We'll both come along. Put the knife away."

When Mike retracted the knife, Frank landed an elbow strike to his midriff, knocking the air from his lungs. The knife clattered to the tile and skittered toward Sophia. She scooped it up and pushed it deep into the back pocket of her jeans.

"Call the police!" Frank barked the order as he pushed Mike facedown.

"My phone's in the room." She looked around for anything they could use to tie up the younger man. "What do you want to do?"

Mike squirmed and Frank dropped to one knee, putting all his weight between the younger man's shoulder blades. "I say let his dad deal with him."

"Is that wise?"

"No," Mike said on a creaky exhale. "No. Let me go and I won't say anything. I'll tell him I couldn't find you."

Frank looked at her. "Do you believe him?"

"Not a bit," she replied. What she could see of Mike's face twisted and she shouted a warning half a second too late.

Frank, tossed off balance, fell backward and Mike, showing an aptitude for thug work, came at her.

"Get out of here!" Frank said, diving for Mike's legs.

The younger man tripped, regaining his balance with an agility she envied. Being older, and female, she had different options and skills to call upon, not the least of which was experience.

After Frank's trial and Frankie's recovery, she'd been brushing up on her self-defense skills. As a bonus, the increased activity had put her in prime shape for Frankie's wedding day. Now she was all the more thankful Aidan had joined Leo Solutions. Her future son-in-law was proving to be an excellent coach, willing to create fitness programs for anyone at the company, no matter their level or job description.

She let Mike close in, feinting and spinning out of his reach. Blocking his attack, she put a higher value on patience than her opponent did. She systematically moved the fight closer to the railing and the stairwell, places where her smaller size gave her a better advantage.

Mike countered with fast moves meant to confuse and intimidate. She managed to avoid the worst of it, but an evasive move left her with her back open to an attack.

She saw Frank's eyes go wide, his face a mask of panic. He had no way to help her. With Frank calling her name, aiming threats at Mike, she dropped to her knees and the young man went hurtling over the railing into the night.

A splash sounded as he hit the pool. Voices rose, cries of alarm and calls for help.

She peeked over the side, hoping to see Mike swimming to the edge, only to have Frank drag her back. "Phone cameras," he explained. "We have to go."

They ran for the motel room and gathered their belongings, making the rental car before anyone detained them.

"I can't believe Halloran had his son come after us," Sophia said as Frank searched for a safer place to spend the night.

"I'm not surprised," Frank said. "He was banking on the idea that I wouldn't hurt a kid the same age as my daughter."

"Unbelievable." Sophia stared out at the glowing lights as Frank merged with traffic on the interstate, aiming north. "I guess we're pushing the right buttons."

"I guess you are."

She reached out a hand to stop him. "*We* are."

"Right." His smile didn't reach his eyes. With little traffic, Frank reached the airport in less than half an hour. Per his habit, he drove a circuit of the airport hotels before choosing one and parking under the awning.

When they were settled into the new room, she tried again to make him understand he wasn't alone. In this or anything else. "We're in this together, Frank."

"Much as I wish we weren't," he muttered. "The kid nearly hurt you."

"And he didn't you? He had a knife at your throat!" She reined in her temper. "I knew what I was doing."

"Sophia…" He sighed. "I'm trying to keep you out of danger."

"But that isn't realistic. Either we take risks and gather enough material for CID to work with or we get creative and take even bigger risks."

He slumped into a chair and raked his hair off his face. "Agreed."

She walked over and started rubbing at the knots in his shoulders. Although it wasn't the quiet fresh-air conversation she'd intended, it was still reminiscent of other pleasant moments they'd shared. "When Halloran and Hellfire are done, we should go home and get on with our lives." Frank's muscles tensed under her hands and she plowed on. "We had one cake tasting already. And Frankie plans to use Aunt Josie's recipe for a groom's cake."

Frank muttered something she took as approval.

She smiled to herself. "We'll need to choose a caterer soon. I think Frankie wants me to go along for those appointments, to cast a deciding vote in case of any ties regarding the menu." She kept working out the kinks in his shoulders and chattering about Frankie and Aidan, willing Frank to want to be a part of their future as a family.

"Sophie, hush."

"It's adrenaline," she said in a lame attempt to defend herself.

"It is," he agreed. "Because I made a mess of things. I should've found a way to do this without you."

"You couldn't have."

"I know."

The regret in his voice tore at her. "Tell me something." She spoke to the top of his head, grateful he couldn't see the tears welling in her eyes. "Will you stay?" Her voice cracked on the query. Annoyed with the needs tangling in her chest, she tried again. "Will you stick around for Frankie? She'll believe me if I tell her you survived, but she'd rather hear she was right all along directly from you."

Frank came out of the chair and caught her hands, bringing them to his lips for a brief kiss. *"Dolcezza."* He kissed her hands again. "I promise to do what's best for all of you. I can't promise that will be staying around."

She opened her mouth to argue. To *insist* he come back into their lives. Knowing her too well, he tugged her close, silencing her with a claiming, searing kiss. She couldn't muster any energy to resist. All these months without him, to have him back, she just wanted to wallow in the scent, taste and touch of him. Her hands came up to frame his face and the kiss, rife with need and desire, sizzled through her bloodstream, only more powerful for the memories and familiarity of their long past.

She sighed, her breasts heavy and aching as she melted against his hard, muscled chest. Deep inside, she wanted to pretend this was just one more "normal" homecoming. Preferably the way the last homecoming should've been.

Her hands yanked at his shirt, eagerly seeking his warm skin. She trailed her fingers over the terrain she knew so well.

Holding her close, he turned her and lowered her to the bed, his body covering hers, gently pinning her to the soft mattress. Delicious. Her mind blanked out their troubles when he set his lips to her throat. His thigh wedged between hers, and his erection dug into her hip. She rocked her pelvis, needing him.

The sense of belonging overpowered her. Frank was her everything, always had been. Except he wasn't promising her a future anymore. If Halloran had his way, there wouldn't be any future for the Leone family.

She savored one more kiss, sipping from his lips as tears stung her eyes. She couldn't do this, couldn't leave herself open to a repeat of the crushing loss she'd suffered when she thought he'd died. One last time, her body pleaded, but one last time would leave her devastated.

"Stop," she whispered against his lips. "Stop," she repeated when he raised his head to look into her eyes. She blinked quickly, unable to keep a tear from spilling over her lashes.

Frank brushed that tear away. "Are you sure?"

Her lips caught between her teeth, she bobbed her chin. At last she found her voice. "I can't do this." She felt awful, though she hadn't meant to lead him on. As much as her body wanted him, her heart *needed* him.

She simply couldn't invite that much pain into her life again. Not without some assurance that he wanted to rediscover and reclaim the relationship they'd lost.

Chapter Nine

Thursday, April 21, 7:05 a.m.

She'd rejected him. No amount of reviewing the facts changed that. On the motel room floor, Frank had tossed and turned all night wondering where he'd gone wrong.

Sophia had leaped from that bed as though it were on fire, when he'd been burning up inside to be with her. After fighting off Halloran's boy, Frank had needed to hold her, to assure himself she was okay—they were okay. He wanted to see and feel for certain the kid hadn't managed to hurt her.

She'd apparently needed and wanted something else. How had he misread the situation so completely?

He hadn't actually misread her, he decided as he reviewed last night once more. She'd been right there with him from that kiss up to the point he'd jerked his shirt over his head and fallen on her like a man starved for affection. Which he was.

After faking the suicide, he'd hidden for a while, courtesy of Torres. When the smoke had cleared, he'd poked at the fringes of Hellfire, piecing details together as best he could. He'd stayed far away from the temptation of Sophia in Seattle and Frankie in Savannah.

Knowing he was to blame for his wife and daughter drifting apart motivated him to dismantle Hellfire sooner rather than later. Being aggressive had already gotten Torres killed. He couldn't allow his impatience to kill Sophia or Frankie.

The hardest months of his life had been pretending he didn't exist. Harder than infantry school in the summer. Tougher than winter training exercises in Korea. Too much solitude was bad for the soul, he'd decided early on. Yet the only person with whom he could maintain contact was dead now. Because of Frank's mistakes.

He prepped a second cup of the bitter in-room coffee, needing the caffeine jolt after another sleepless night. He'd been running on fumes since Torres's murder. What he wouldn't give for a restful night with his wife in his arms, her body soft and pliant, his every breath scented with the fragrance of her hair.

She'd always welcomed him home with a kiss, refreshing his soul. Just the way she'd done last night. Why had she pulled away from the connection both of them clearly wanted?

Had it been the visit with Paul Sterling? He hadn't said anything, but he could hardly begrudge her for moving on. She'd thought he was dead. He knew the moment the treason charge had been aimed at him that she would have to distance herself or go down with him.

His biggest regret was the timing. He'd been incarcerated when their daughter needed him most. Hearing about her injuries secondhand had been awful. He'd almost told Torres to go to hell with the undercover plan, that he'd take his chances and expose Hellfire before the evidence had been gathered.

A lot of good that had done. Frankie had healed, but

he was still far from restoring his life or ensuring the ongoing safety of his family.

Halloran would definitely up the ante. It was only a matter of when and how. A man who would use his own son was capable of anything. Frank debated the wisdom of walking into the nearest federal authority and laying out the whole story. Except they believed he was the bad guy and he didn't have anything conclusive to prove otherwise. Yet.

He knew Sophia was sending tidbits of information to the reporter, to Eddie and probably to Leo Solutions as well, dribbling out details that would keep Halloran on edge. They needed to think bigger.

He glanced to the closed bathroom door blocking his view of his wife. She'd been eager to dangle herself like bait when they were in Alexandria. He could see that it might take something that tempting to draw Halloran into the open. Would Frank have the courage to let her do it if and when they needed that kind of ploy?

When she emerged, a silk tank tucked into faded jeans that hugged her gorgeous legs, he scalded his tongue on a gulp of the bitter coffee. He ignored the sting, eager to get busy and stay that way until the case was over. Today they would see if they could find anything incriminating in or around Fort Huachuca, Farrell's last duty station. When she bent to retrieve her bag, his attention zeroed in on her backside. He was definitely glad they were getting out of this room. The sooner the better.

Once they were on the interstate, Sophia said, "I asked my assistant to pull anything on his banking records or credit card activity. Paul said Farrell didn't care about money, only power and respect. That's harder to track."

"I've never seen Farrell accept a delivery. If he's been riding a desk in an office, I would've missed him easily."

"With today's technology, he can probably do desk work anywhere in the world," Sophia said. "But we'll figure it out."

There was a piece he was missing. Frank's mind wandered, lulled by the sound of the tires on the asphalt. His brain sifted through memories and wound them up with daydreams. Why the hell had he thrown it all away?

He remembered how Frankie had come down the stairs, all dressed up and ready for her kindergarten graduation ceremony. He and Sophia had been near bursting with pride. His daughter had leaped from the next to last riser into his arms and giggled as he spun her in a big circle.

"Frank." A familiar touch gave his shoulder a shake. "Frank?"

"Huh?" He blinked away the haze of the memory, focusing first on the road and then on the worried face of the woman who wouldn't have him anymore. Damn it all. "What is it?"

"Trouble." The single word was loaded with urgency.

Adrenaline shot through his blood, clearing the last of the cobwebs. He checked his mirrors and came up empty. "Where?"

"Here." She turned up the volume and held her cell phone so he could hear the video report on her phone.

A breaking news story named Frank as the prime suspect in the murder of Army CID Special Agent J.D.

Torres. "Ruthless," he said with grudging admiration. The report didn't hold anything back, including a reward for any information that led to his arrest. "They'll name you as an accomplice soon."

"Probably by the end of the day." She pushed her phone into her purse as if it were infected with a vile disease. "At least we know we've become more than an irritation." She swore quietly. "I wanted to drive through the post and get a feel for the area, but it's too risky now."

"What about the bank?"

"After that news report?" She shook her head. "I really don't want to take a chance that your face shows up on any security feed."

"We can't give up now," he said. He refused to hide while she handled this alone. "Whatever Halloran does, however we choose to respond, we can't leave any member of Hellfire free to keep up the operation."

"I'm not giving up," she muttered. "I'm thinking."

"Think out loud, please." No way he'd make another assumption about what either of them wanted.

"Paul said he used that bank for a reason."

"A wink and a nod for a friend of Farrell?"

"That's my thought," she said. "The man is always scheming. I found out last night it's a privately owned bank, under the shelter of a corporate name."

"You didn't say anything."

"You were sleeping," she countered.

Doubtful, though he must have slept a little if he hadn't heard her working. "Did he trap you into opening Leo Solutions with him?"

She wrinkled her nose. "No. Just as he leaned on

the friendship with Farrell, I leaned on the friendship with him."

Frank reached over and took her hand. "You were thinking of Frankie. I do understand."

Her mouth tipped up at one corner in a wry smile. "I think I'm starting to." Her breath caught. "Oh, dear God. I have to get word to Frankie."

Frank's gut clenched. "You need to convince her to lie low and stay away from reporters or anyone else asking questions."

Sophia fished her phone. "That won't be easy." Her fingers flew across the keypad. When she finished, she turned to Frank once more. "I'm thinking Halloran has something big planned."

"Meaning?" he prodded.

"With your face plastered all over the media, he thinks you'll be out of his hair."

"It does slow us down." When she didn't respond, he kept on driving, sticking with the plan until one of them came up with an alternative.

She mumbled a colorful oath in Italian. "We can't risk doing *anything* public here," she said. "They know we're in the area. With Lowry snagged, the contacts, text history and World Crossing employee badge, it's an easy guess we're here looking for something to tie up Farrell. One security camera and we're caught. Why else release that story that you're wanted for murder?"

"Which leaves us with no options?" He couldn't believe it, knew her mind was already racing ahead. In the army he'd been known for his superb strategic skills, but few people understood Sophia was his match.

"Turning you in would surprise him and it would

backfire. Halloran would have you killed—for real—at the first opportunity."

Frank suppressed the shudder that shot through him at her words. If he died, who would protect Sophia and Frankie from Halloran's vindictive streak?

"Turn around. We can't go anywhere near Fort Huachuca."

He scanned the road for a place to turn around. "Where to?"

"We need another cheap motel with internet access so I can test another lead."

"What lead?" he asked as he took the next exit, only to swing back and head north, toward Tucson.

"It's something Paul said. The bank, Farrell riding a desk, the import-export and the CID. I can almost make the connections line up."

He was glad one of them could. Maybe he was too tired, but he wasn't following her train of thought. For Sophie it would only be a matter of time before things turned crystal clear. That small confidence was all it took to bring hope flaring anew in his chest. Sophia had been among the brightest military analysts in the CIA. Before his career ended hers by default.

"I should've brought you in on this from the beginning," he confessed.

"You did what you had to do," she replied, retrieving her phone from the depths of her purse again. "Head straight through the city."

"I thought you wanted to avoid security cameras."

"I do," she said. "More important, I want to be where they don't expect us to be." She put a finger to her lips as she raised her phone to her ear.

Listening to her side of the phone call, it baffled

him when she asked to speak with someone. He didn't recognize the name at all.

"He'll take the call," she said. "This is Sophia Leone, General Leone's *widow*."

Oh, hell. Frank goosed the accelerator, joining the faster flow of traffic on the interstate. That was her determined voice, and a determined Sophia was unstoppable.

He really should've brought her into this at the beginning. All the reasons he'd kept her out of it seemed weak now.

Hindsight is always twenty-twenty, he thought. He'd reminded his soldiers of that countless times through his career. It was important to look back only long enough to learn from successes and mistakes. Then it was time to move forward.

He slid her one more glance, hoping like hell he could convince Sophia to move forward with him through the rest of his days.

Chapter Ten

Sophia ignored the ridiculous canned music assaulting her ear while she waited for Bradley Roth, the reporter who'd broken the Torres murder suspect story, to pick up. She knew he'd take the call and, if he didn't, she knew who to call next.

Beside her, she sensed the shift in Frank. He was exhausted but amused. And more than a little relieved they weren't going near an army post anytime soon. If her hunch played out, they might get away with lying low for another day or two, giving Halloran enough rope to hang himself.

As Frank navigated the traffic, she watched, half of her braced for another ambush. Based on the article she'd seen, if they'd continued to the fort, they'd have been caught for sure.

The story had gone national, making it too late to give the news to Frankie gently. Thank God, Aidan was with her. He would get her through this and keep her safe.

"Bradley Roth," the reporter said, picking up the call at last. "Who's this?"

"Sophia Leone," she said, keeping her tone all business. "I saw the report pinning the Torres murder on my dead husband."

"Yes, ma'am. Do you have anything to add?"

She gave the reporter points for audacity and courage. "I suppose a retraction is out of the question?"

"My source is solid, Mrs. Leone."

"Your source must be thrilled to have someone take him at face value," she replied. "He's wrong."

"My source," Roth began, deftly avoiding any gender confirmation, "is above reproach. Unlike your husband."

"I'm not sure how often you've dealt with widows, Mr. Roth. We can be sensitive."

"Then let's cut to the chase so we don't prolong your distress."

"General Leone—"

"Former General Leone," Roth corrected.

She sighed loudly for effect. "The treason charge was fabricated. My husband was neither traitor nor killer."

Frank's hands clenched the steering wheel. She wanted to reach out to him. If only that sweet contact wouldn't leech the steel out of her voice. She needed every drop of it right now.

"Without any corroboration or proof from you, I can only assume your sensitive nature has you ignoring the facts and public record of his trial, the verdict and the new evidence recently discovered in the Torres case," Roth said.

She wanted to laugh as he used her turn of phrase against her. "Mr. Roth, you're being used. My family doesn't appreciate your sensationalized account that my husband is somehow alive and committing crimes. You can be sure I'll take decisive action against you and your employer."

"It's a free country and a free press, Mrs. Leone."

"Thanks in part to my husband and the troops he led," she said pointedly.

"Your own statement seals his guilt regarding the treason charge." Roth's initial curiosity about her was giving way to impatience.

"Ah, thank you for confirming your source," she said smoothly. "I'll let my assistant know what to do with your request when you call for an interview in a few days."

"Beg pardon?"

"Yes." She let the smile show in her voice. "I believe you will."

"Wait!"

She hesitated, let him think she'd disconnected. "Yes?"

"If you're so sure about the inaccuracy of my report, give me something to track down."

"Why should I help you do your job?"

"I'll print a retraction," Roth offered. "My influence can help shift the media tide in the general's favor."

"That's quite a claim." Her gaze lingered on her husband's white-knuckled hands. The traffic wasn't bad enough to warrant the reaction, so she assumed he didn't care for the game she was playing. Too bad. She couldn't let Halloran's gambit go unanswered. With everyone looking for Frank Leone, disgraced general turned killer, they were nearing time for a full frontal assault, and she wanted to be sure they were ready offensively and defensively.

"Although I'm sure you don't carry the clearance to see my original statement, I can assure you I did not testify against my husband." She paused when her voice started to shake. "You need to take a closer look at your source and his connections. I can assure you retired General Halloran has been abusing his authority for many years. In fact, I intend to prove he's smuggling drugs and laundering money through a privately held bank south of Tucson."

"Can you back that up?" Roth asked in a reverent whisper.

"I can," she said. "If you refrain from spreading more lies about my husband, I'll keep you in the loop as the evidence comes to light."

Beside her Frank gave a low whistle. She prayed Roth didn't hear it. "Do we have a deal?"

"Absolutely."

"I'll be in touch." Sophia ended the call, her hands trembling.

"What was that?" Frank asked through gritted teeth.

"An effective counterpunch," she stated.

"Is that a new synonym for *stupid*?"

"You're welcome." She sent another quick text message to Frankie and then turned off her phone. "We need to get to a motel."

"So you can manufacture evidence for another reporter?"

She refused to dignify that with a response. "A motel," she repeated. "Something out-of-the-way, cash only."

"I know how it's done," he said, his voice grim. "I've been living off the radar for months."

She clamped her lips shut while she counted to ten. Then fifty. Not enough. Tears stung her eyes and she blinked them away.

She'd cried many nights, confused and hurt, when he turned distant before the last official army move to Washington. She'd cried, appalled and frustrated, when the treason charges were announced. When the verdict came down, she'd barely had time to absorb the news before they'd called her to identify the body.

"J.D. Torres was in the lab coat, wasn't he?"

"What?" Frank didn't spare her a glance as Tucson whizzed by the windows.

"When I identified your body," she clarified. "That wasn't a doctor. It was Torres in the lab coat."

Frank's sigh was plenty of confirmation. "Yes."

She sank into the memories, reviewing those strange, fractured days when she'd been pulled in so many directions. "Frankie was injured the same day you were charged with treason."

"I remember. The treason charge took me by surprise. I knew going undercover opened up the potential for things to get ugly, but I had no idea of Halloran's true reach."

The words dripped like ice water down her back. She shivered as horrible theories zipped around in her head. Tucson was fading into the distance before she found her voice. "Do you think…" She couldn't finish the thought. She started over. "Do you think," she repeated, her voice stronger this time, "Halloran arranged the attack on Frankie's convoy?"

"No." The one-syllable response was razor sharp and full of conviction.

A relieved breath shuddered in and out of her lungs. Her heart rate, stuttering a moment ago, settled back into a steady rhythm.

When they were several miles north of Tucson, the sunbaked desert stretching out on both sides of the highway broken only by a march of power lines and occasional, scrubby trees, Frank pulled to the shoulder and slammed the car into Park.

"What are you doing?" They needed to keep moving if they had any chance of outmaneuvering Halloran before the new shipment arrived.

Frank tossed his sunglasses onto the dash and scrubbed at his face.

"What's wrong?"

He wouldn't look at her. Instead, he pushed open the door and got out. He stalked a few paces ahead, turned and came back toward the SUV again.

She sat there, watching him as the minutes ticked by, wondering what the hell was going through his mind. She reached over and turned the key, cutting the engine. Pocketing the key, she got out of the SUV and leaned against the passenger door.

"What are you doing?" she demanded when he was only a few paces away.

"Bringing you in was wrong. Selfish. I can't put you through any more of this godforsaken chaos."

Weren't they ever going to get past this? "What I do and don't do isn't up to you," she snapped. "You lost the right to have an opinion about my activities when you took the easy way out."

"Easy?" He ran his fist along the scruff shading his jaw. "You thought that escape was easy?"

She folded her arms, waiting for him to say something worth a reply. She caught his eyes following the neckline of her silk tank. Her nipples peaked, responding to his gaze as though he'd touched her. Despite her best intentions, she couldn't seem to keep her raging desire for him in check.

"Looking at the facts, it seems as if it was easier to fake your death than share the truth with your wife."

"Sophie." He reached for her.

She twisted away. "Don't you touch me." She was so weak around him, despite her anger and resentment for the choices he'd made. Choices that spelled the end of their family. Last night proved how easy it would be to slide into the comfort of old habits. To love and share each other as they'd always done, shutting out the world's troubles. "Thirty years of life and marriage and teamwork, and you just tossed me out."

"You know that's not what happened. I was protecting you."

"How would I know that? It was bad before Hellfire, Frank." She poked a finger into his chest. Saw the truth in his eyes. "You know it. Our relationship was going south before we moved to Washington." She clenched her teeth, determined to see this through. This wasn't the place to rehash the past, recent or otherwise. "Get back in that car and let's finish this."

"After what you just did, it's suicide to go to Seattle."

She did a double take, then heard herself cackling at his choice of words. She sounded half-mad and didn't much care. Finishing this, sticking with him to the bitter end, might just cost her her sanity. "Then we'd be closer to making the scorecard even. I called that reporter for—"

"Hell, no," he interrupted, his blue eyes flashing. "You made that call for yourself."

She hadn't stooped to such nasty fight tactics for more than a decade. Her molars would crack any second now if she didn't find a better way to maintain her self-control. "I made that call for Frankie," she finished stubbornly.

She wanted to give a victory shout when his shoulders drooped in defeat. "That's right," she continued. "I called that reporter, strung him along so you had a better chance of living long enough to reconcile with your daughter."

He stared at her, his jaw slack.

Mad as hell at herself as much as at him, she held up the car keys and aimed toward the driver's door. "Get in and do this my way or find another way out of this mayhem you created."

"I won't let you do this."

She turned, the heel of her tennis shoe grinding into the sandy soil, and stared him down. "Try to stop me, Frank. Just try."

Apparently the man's wisdom triumphed over his pride as Frank hopped into the passenger seat. His seat belt clicked as she merged with traffic on the two-lane road. With the voice app on her phone, she searched and found a regional airport a few hours away with more than one motel nearby. Even if Halloran caught their scent again when she ordered another flight from the charter service Leo Solutions used, he'd be hard-pressed to find them in time to do anything about it tonight.

Which was fine with her. She had her own agenda for the evening, and it revolved around getting even with the bastard and his cronies. She'd keep her promise about staying within legal lines, but there were ways to get her point across. Ways even Halloran couldn't misunderstand.

FRANK DIDN'T SPEAK again until they were in a room on the first floor of a family-owned motel. What could he say? She was right about all of it, and, though he and

Torres had made progress, without Sophia he wouldn't be able to topple Halloran's operation.

He pulled the curtains closed and took note of the few amenities while she booted up her computer. He wanted to apologize for everything he'd done wrong in recent years. There had to be something he could say to crack that wall of ice she was hiding behind now. She was his wife, damn it. At one time he'd known her better than he'd known himself. In light of his recent choices, he still knew her better. On the other hand, he hardly recognized the man he saw in the mirror anymore.

"You and Frankie were always the most important pieces of my life."

She lifted her gaze, taking his measure over the rim of her reading glasses, her brown eyes clear and emotionless. "I know."

"Everything I did, every choice good or bad…" He didn't bother finishing when her attention returned to her laptop. "Sophia," he said, not above begging at this point. He desperately needed to clear the air.

"I'm listening."

She wasn't—her eyes were skimming through whatever she'd found on the display. A rosy glow lit her cheeks, and her lips parted with excitement. "Good Lord."

"What now?"

"Farrell and Paul." She glanced up at him again, her eyes lit with excitement. "I've been thinking about his quip about clients and the cybersecurity program."

"He pretty much confirmed Farrell is part of the import-export team."

"Right." She pursed her lips for a second. "He said Farrell once worked at World Bridge Shipping."

"I assumed he just mixed up the name."

"He did." She leaned back in the chair, pointing at the screen. "Look."

Frank squinted, didn't see what had her so excited. "Help me out. What am I looking for?"

"It's been right under my nose, to quote Paul again," she muttered. "He had a private client list and kept World Crossing, Incorporated, listed under a different name. The phone numbers and website addresses match."

"Holy crap." He stood. "This is good news, right?"

"This puts us in the driver's seat." She opened another window and started typing again. "Frank, how had you been tracking incoming shipments?"

"I followed a hunch. Halloran spent some time with a transportation unit early in his career. Torres had started digging through the shipping reports on military gear coming back to the States. Some of the weights didn't add up." As he spoke, she made notes, and he knew she was locked on to every word. "After the verdict, I started staking out East Coast ports according to a pattern Torres suspected. I never thought about the import-export broker, but I noticed the same freight line at every destination and went from there."

"Makes sense," she said.

"You remember the next shipment is due any day."

"And we can be sure Halloran is there to meet it," she announced.

The brilliant smile she aimed at him might as well have been a hot dagger through his heart. The idea of his enemy within his grasp was almost too much good news. "What do you mean?"

"I think I can access the World Crossing computers in Seattle."

"Remotely?" he asked, praying she'd say yes.

"No." She bit her lip. "Once we're on-site, it shouldn't be a problem. We can download files and give CID the info they need to move on Halloran and Hellfire."

"Besides the fact that it's illegal, it could get you killed trying. We don't know where Engle and Farrell are." He felt miserable watching how his response—his logical response—dulled the happiness on her face.

"If we can link Halloran to this company, if we can show abuse of the contract or find evidence of drugs on-site, CID can take it from there." She frowned at him. "You've wanted to intercept that shipment from the start."

"I want to force him to do something incriminating, yes," Frank hedged. He didn't want her there when things got ugly. He pulled up a chair. "Teach me what to do and I'll go in."

She shook her head. "I'll probably have to finesse things a bit." Her smile was back in an instant. "I've booked us a plane to Seattle early in the morning so we'll be ahead of the shipment. We can fine-tune how to get into the office at the port once we see what we're dealing with."

"I've been on shipping piers and docks, Sophie." He'd met their enemy firsthand and hated the danger he'd be escorting her into. "There are so many risk factors. Are you sure remote access isn't an option?"

She removed her glasses and pressed the heels of her hands to her eyes. "All right. Let me see if I can find another path."

He waited while her fingers moved swiftly and quietly over her keyboard. Whatever she was doing, she muttered and grumbled here and there as she poked at the system software. It was his last respite. When she was done with this attempt, he had to come clean about the rest of it. He had to unburden himself and give her a chance to forgive him, just in case the worst happened when they finally caught up with Halloran.

"Oh, good," she said without much enthusiasm. "My laptop is connected with the Leo Solutions network. I can fiddle with a few things." Her teeth nibbled on her lower lip as she continued. "We'll see if that causes a stir. I want to make them sweat."

"What next?"

"Not much until we're on-site." She closed her laptop and set it aside. "Then I suggest we kick ass."

He nodded, knowing what he had to do now. It could very well be his last night alone with her. "Sophia?" he began, dredging up the courage to continue.

"Yes?"

This would be so much easier if he'd never left her out of his professional decisions. Better to just spit it out and let her start hating him now. "You mentioned how things changed before our last move." The abrupt wariness in her eyes didn't make this easier. His heart pounded. "Things changed because that's when I first met Torres," he confessed. "CID wanted help with a soldier in my command who'd flipped out and joined the local resistance."

He could practically see the wheels turning behind her eyes as she rewound reports and news footage to that time.

"The Penderson case?" She sat back in the chair, pulling her knees up to her chest.

He wasn't surprised she'd figured it out immediately.

While situations such as the Penderson case were rare, very few people had access to the full facts and circumstances. Sophia would've been one of a handful of analysts cleared for the details and, still, she didn't know the worst of it.

"Why you? What could you possibly have known about some morally conflicted private?"

He sank onto the edge of the bed. Her reaction to this could break him, but he couldn't be a coward any longer. "I didn't know the soldier as well as I knew the family he killed."

That warm brown gaze turned chilly. "Knew them how?"

He could see she was already willing to believe the worst—that he'd turned into one of those men with no self-control who took up with women to scratch an itch during deployments. "I was trying to grease the wheels to get one of their sons to the States. I called a few friends in DC looking for a favor."

"You didn't call me."

"No."

She took a deep breath, studying him. "What really happened, Frank? It's not unprecedented to help locals who go above and beyond while we're working in their country. Nothing like that was worth hiding."

And yet he had hidden things from her and all his reasons seemed flawed as he tried to explain. "Penderson shot up a village. He went after that particular family because of me. I'd sought them out to thank them for their service and to grieve with them. The father and son lost their lives in an action that saved my men. It was a gruesome act. I'll never understand why Penderson murdered the rest of them."

"Oh, Frank." She moved to sit beside him on the bed, tucking her feet under her. She rubbed slow circles over his back. "Why didn't you tell me?"

For a moment, he reveled in the miracle of having her close. "The army needed me out there to keep things from falling apart while they investigated Penderson's motives and influences."

"You had the authority to be respected by both sides," she said with a comprehending nod.

"We found Penderson's body about ten days later." The butchered remains of the errant soldier had been laid out on the side of a hill, in full view of the main road into the base. The army cleaned it up swiftly, managing to smother all pictures, but Frank had been carrying that grisly image and the guilt ever since.

She took one of his hands in both of hers, smoothing the flesh over and over until his fist relaxed. "I remember. None of that was your fault."

"Maybe not directly. Penderson wasn't the only soldier on that base who'd become a sympathizer. Rooting them out was like kicking a nest of rattlesnakes."

"I didn't hear anything about that."

"The army prosecution focused on other charges. Sex trafficking in particular," he said pointedly. "Halloran's son was among those arrested."

"Mike? No way."

"Yes. He dodged the worst of it, thanks to his dad. Torres and I always suspected he was actually the ringleader."

"Things get very strange out there."

"They do," he agreed. Her touch soothed him as nothing had in years. He was ready to beg, borrow or steal more than the basic comfort she was offering.

"Sophia, you have to know I wasn't one of those guys out there."

Her palm soft on his cheek, she turned his face toward hers, blessed him with a sweet kiss. "I know. I know you, Frank." Her lips were delicate as rose petals against his. "I trusted you implicitly."

"Until I shut you out."

"Even then I trusted you," she countered in a voice as gentle as her touch. "It hurt me when you pulled away, but I trusted you to come around."

"And I let you down." He shouldn't let her close, couldn't force himself to be honorable and pull away. "It wasn't supposed to go that way. The sex operation sting, connecting with the drug lord, Hellfire was supposed to welcome me with open arms, not pin me down with treason charges."

"It's okay," she crooned. "We'll get out of this. Together."

He scooted away from her warm body, and those few inches felt like miles. "Torres and I were sure Halloran would have me killed. Coming clean at that point would've given Hellfire room to escape with their money and no consequences. I wouldn't have left you if we'd thought there was a better option. I swear it. They'd already made one attempt during a transport to see if I'd flip on him."

"You passed."

"Of course." He leaned forward, elbows on his knees as he rubbed his temples. "It was weak and obvious, but it was enough to convince me Halloran had spies everywhere."

"Still does, apparently," Sophia agreed. "Is that everything?"

"Yes." He felt clean, almost weightless now that she knew. "I'm so sorry, *dolcezza*."

"You did what you had to do."

"You have my word," he promised, "I will never let you and Frankie down again and, if you will allow me in your lives, I will spend the rest of my life being there for you and proving in everything I do how very much you both mean to me."

"You are all I've ever wanted, my love."

The phrase caught his full attention. "You…" He was afraid to ask her to repeat the sentiment.

"I've never stopped loving you, despite how infuriating you've been recently."

"But—"

"Hush. Don't ruin the moment," she warned, pressing a finger to his lips. "Just accept it and count your blessings."

"You. You are my blessing."

"Promise to remember that from this day forward?"

"Yes." He stole a kiss from her smiling mouth. "Promise not to take it back?"

She laughed. "I promise."

He kissed her soundly, letting all his hope and passion and need pour out, pour into her. He felt whole at last as she accepted him, her heart pounding against his. The sun could rise tomorrow or fall into the ocean—he had the most important element in his world in his arms at last.

SOPHIA GAVE HERSELF up to the irresistible desire Frank's touch invariably ignited. His reticence and distance were at last well and truly gone. Under her hands her husband felt like himself again. There was tension, a by-product of their mutual excitement, but the secrets and guilt that had been lurking beneath the surface had disappeared.

Here was the man she'd loved with her whole heart and spirit. Her body trembled with the need to love him again.

"Frank," she whispered over and over, kissing every part of him within reach. The rough whiskers at his jaw, his ear, his corded neck. He mirrored her movements, teasing her and reacquainting himself with all the places that elicited her passionate reactions. That tender place behind her ear, the ticklish spot at the base of her throat.

One of his big hands cruised over her hip, holding her tight to him, while the other cupped her breast, teasing her nipple through the fabric of her tank and bra.

She'd known his body since they were young twenty-somethings, before he'd filled out and she'd gone softer with motherhood. Fit and able, they'd been blessed with good health and a hefty dose of humor as they'd matured. She didn't want to be anywhere but here in this precious place they created, just the two of them.

Her hands worked the buttons of his shirt until the panels fell open and she could devour his muscled chest with her hands, eyes and mouth. Amid gasps of anticipation and breathless kisses, they rediscovered and reclaimed all that they'd missed.

Impatient, she tugged off her tank top and bra while he dealt with his boots. When he'd stripped away his pants and her jeans, they fell on the bed together, giddy as teenagers, eager and awkward and in a desperate hurry to make up for lost time.

He settled her with long, sensual strokes and touches, kisses across her collarbone and lower to her breasts.

She breathed in his scent, rising to his tantalizing mouth as he suckled on one nipple and then the other. She sifted her fingers through his salt-and-pepper hair, the texture so familiar despite the longer length.

He feathered kisses over her quivering belly to the juncture at her thighs. As he parted her legs with his broad shoulders, she knew he was settling in for a long siege. At the first flick of his tongue on her sensitive flesh, she bucked and tried to squirm away. His heavy hand held her in place and she had to plead with him.

"I need you inside." She wanted that intimate unity above anything else. "Please, Frank. Now."

It didn't take much coaxing. Rising over her, he nudged at her entrance. She was so ready for him. He plunged deep, hard and hot inside her. Joined completely with him, she knew he felt that priceless sense of connection as keenly as she did. Tears of joy blurred her vision and she smiled up at him, savoring the homecoming they'd been denied for so long.

"I missed you, *dolcezza*." Braced over her, he rolled his hips, stroking her body inside and out.

He felt amazing in her arms. The laughter bubbled out of her in simple, pure delight of being together, body and soul. Her whole body clutched around him as she ran her hands over every part of him. His powerful arms and shoulders, his wide back, down to his hips.

He knew precisely how to move to heighten and extend their pleasure. It seemed a lifetime of practice hadn't been lost or forgotten while they were apart. She knew him, too. She kissed his throat, raked her nails gently down his sides while her legs cradled his hips.

When at last he drove her up and over that sensual peak, the climax hit her full force, leaving her gasping for air as stars flashed behind her eyelids. He found his release a moment later, his body shuddering before he collapsed over her in sheer bliss.

A minute or an hour might have passed in that beautiful, euphoric state until at last he rolled away, pulling her back tight to his chest. He snuggled her close and wrapped her in his arms. She'd fallen asleep this way almost every night they'd been together during the course of their marriage. When his breathing eased, becoming the rusty snore she'd missed so desperately, she let the tears fall once more.

They weren't done or safe, but she felt confident that together they could conquer any new obstacle Halloran or anyone else placed in their path.

Chapter Eleven

Frank woke before the sun, content and refreshed, with Sophia's warm, generous curves tucked beside him. It had been over a year since he'd slept so well and she'd been beside him then, too. He pressed a kiss to her silky sable hair, determined to make this the first day of the rest of their lives together.

He was indulging in a daydream of life after Hellfire when her cell phone hummed with an incoming message. It shouldn't have been enough of a sound to wake her, but her eyes popped open. Her gaze tangled with his and her smile bloomed.

"Good morning." He kissed her softly, before she could roll away and be distracted by their problems. "I'll shower while you check on that."

"Okay." She seemed almost shy today. "It's the pilot. The plane is ready when we are."

He grinned and kissed her again. His body was primed for the upcoming confrontation and he finally felt as though he had his head on straight. They'd get to Seattle and put an end to Halloran's operation once and for all.

A few minutes later, with a towel wrapped around his hips, he opened the door to let the steam from his shower dissipate and caught her pacing. She wore only his blue button-down shirt from yesterday and he took a moment to admire the excellent view of her shapely legs.

Then she turned and he saw trouble stamped on her face. "What happened?"

"There was a cyber attack on Leo Solutions last night," she said, brushing by him to take her turn in the bathroom. "You can read the email while I shower. I'll be ready in ten minutes."

He dressed quickly, lacing up his boots by touch as he read the email outlining the situation. According to his future son-in-law, someone had tried to hack into the cloud servers, using administrative codes previously assigned to Paul Sterling.

Frank wanted to punch something. "I need a target," he muttered. Hearing the water shut off in the bathroom, he read the entire report once more.

Aidan relayed assurances that no data had been lost and all client information and systems were in order. He said the closest thing to a breach had been in the financials. The attacker had been focused on battering down the firewalls with no success.

Naturally, Frank thought. This had Hellfire and Farrell written all over it. On a whim, he checked his offshore account and found the balance had doubled overnight. Hellfire planned to pin everything about the drug operation on him.

"Did you read it?" Sophia asked as she came into the room, toweling her wet hair.

"Yeah. Not the ideal way to meet my future son-in-law."

Her eyes widened, and then her smile seemed to set

her whole face aglow. "At least you know he's competent." Sophia explained a few of the more technical details of the attack while she dressed, and they were out the door within ten minutes, as promised.

On the way to the airport, he told her about the money and his theory that they were framing him up tight.

"We won't let them," she said. "I'll have a team make sure nothing managed to get added to our servers or accounts that would put us or our clients in a compromising position."

He thought it through, reading the email on her phone one more time while the private pilot waited for clearance to take off.

"Sterling claimed Farrell didn't care about money," he said once they were in the air.

"Right." Sophia arched an eyebrow, then both eyebrows, as his meaning dawned on her. "Power and respect are his priorities. The money is disposable." She tapped her fingernails against the arm of the seat. "I am sure he's using that bank somehow. I just need to find a transaction."

He knew what she was trying not to ask. "Go ahead and have your team pick apart the offshore account." From what he knew about his daughter, that wasn't her area of expertise. Hopefully, giving in on this would be a compromise to the request he knew she'd make as soon as they landed.

He let her work while he considered the best way to breach the import-export brokerage offices.

When the pilot started the descent, Frank felt the pressure dragging at him again. It was all he could do to stand tall and hide the stress beating at him as they collected their bags and picked up a rental car, another Leo Solutions company perk.

"Well, they'll know we arrived," he said, following the signs toward the waterfront.

"I don't want it to be a secret," she said. "After last night, I'm done hiding."

"Have you found any record of Halloran or Farrell in the area?"

"Not yet. I have feelers out. You know she'd love to see you," she suggested quietly.

Naturally, she'd seen straight through him to the root of the problem. He never should've opened up last night. The relief of her forgiveness only intensified his desperate need to be sure she remained safe.

"Ask anything else," he said, ignoring the desperation in his voice. "I can't see her until I know this is over."

"You walked into a prison for me," she said, trying to lighten his mood. "This is your daughter."

"It's different." The guilt and shame were like grains of sand chafing at his skin. "Let's finish this first."

Despite how he and Sophia had reconnected last night, he wouldn't presume he could stay in her life or Frankie's in the same capacity as before. Forgiveness was more than he'd expected. If only they allowed him to be a small part of their lives, it would be enough. It would take time for them to trust him after all the lies and deceptions.

"All right," Sophia said, reaching across the console to rub his shoulder through his jacket. "Halloran probably has someone keeping tabs on her anyway."

He hated that it was true. "He'll expect you to ditch me in favor of protecting her."

"She's capable of protecting herself and the company," Sophia said. "And she has her own kind of backup."

"You like him a lot, don't you?"

"More than that. I adore Aidan. You'll see when you meet him and see them together. Victoria recruited him away from Interpol."

"She has an eye for investigative talent," he said, keeping to the safer portion of this topic.

"Yes, she does. We're very fortunate as a company and as a family to have friends like Victoria and Lucas."

He did his best not to get his hopes up at the way she automatically included him in their future. From the moment he'd had to start lying to her, his secret hope had been that one day they could manage a genuine reconciliation. Now he wasn't sure he could get them all through this nightmare alive.

Halloran had had years to perfect his team, to increase his reach and influence. What chance did he and Sophia really have at stopping him at this late hour? "You're sure the data at Leo Solutions is secure?"

"Yes. With every update from the team, we're all more convinced it was primarily a distraction."

"So we wouldn't notice what?"

"That's the big question," she said. "The computers and servers have been scrubbed for viruses, malware and data tampering. We can even show our customers how secure everything is if this gets out."

"It won't." He wouldn't let it. One way or another, Halloran's threat to his family ended here.

Down near the waterfront, he chose a decent independent hotel with a vacancy sign. "Will this work?"

Sophia grinned. "Like a charm. Ready to make some heads roll?"

Her expression was contagious. When had he allowed himself to forget her inherent fighting spirit? Probably while he was in exile berating himself for not trusting her with the truth from the beginning.

They checked in, a valet whisked away the car and a bellman carried their bags up to the room. "It's better service than our honeymoon," she murmured when they were in the elevator.

The memories put another kind of contagious smile on her face. He wanted to talk about what came after, but he was afraid of getting ahead of himself.

She seemed to understand, declaring the signal was fantastic when they reached the hotel room of the day and her computer was up and running.

"One more positive sign," he said, shrugging out of his jacket. "How can I help?"

"First, we have to confirm Halloran and Farrell are here." She pointed him to the phone in the room. "I'll let you do the honors."

He entered the numbers she gave him and listened to the phone ring several times. He was about to give up when a rough voice answered, "World Crossing."

"This is Halloran. I need a status report," Frank demanded.

"No sign of trespassers. Container is off-loaded and heading this way now."

"Good." Frank replaced the receiver and grinned at Sophia. "Worked like a charm. The guy who answered said the container is there and trespassers are not." The hired help had no reason to question the identity of anyone who had the right number to call.

"Then let's go." She pulled her hair back into a ponytail. "This is the perfect time for me to try to break into their computer."

"You promised to try it remotely," he said.

"And I failed." Tucking her phone and a flash drive into her pocket, she started for the door.

He knew it was a losing argument and they were wasting time. "On one condition."

She paused, sending him an expectant look over her shoulder. "Which is?"

"I'm in charge." He stowed a camera, binoculars and his notebook in his various pockets. Then he added his gun and handed her the knife they'd taken from Halloran's son.

"All right, General." She stepped aside. "Lead the way."

He didn't expect the cooperation to last, but it gave his heart a moment to catch up with the idea of leading her into danger.

SOPHIA WAS CERTAIN she could draw Halloran out with the right incentive and she was certain that incentive was on the World Crossing computers. Money wouldn't be enough. By now he and the rest of his crew had their wealth hidden away and protected.

It helped that Eddie was archiving her reports and her new reporter pal Bradley Roth had already run a follow-up based on the few pieces of Frank's puzzle she'd felt safe sending him. Still, after the cyber attack and the windfall deposit into Frank's offshore account, she knew nothing short of a confession would pull the noose tight around Halloran's neck.

"Got him," she said as Frank approached the pier that was home to the shady import-export brokerage.

"Say again?"

She laughed at Frank's slide into a more military lingo. "I just got confirmation Halloran is in Seattle." She showed him a grainy surveillance picture from a camera at the airport. "He arrived last night."

"You can't honestly believe he'll personally oversee the arrival of a drug shipment. He considers himself the deal maker, not the labor."

"He didn't come to Seattle just for the golf."

"It is a tourist destination, Sophie."

She loved it when he sweetened her name that way. Only him. "Then score another point for us. We're not here for tourism—we're focused on bringing Kelly Halloran to justice."

"Retired General Drug Lord." Frank swore. "It still pisses me off."

For just a moment, she let herself envision immediate success and what might come next. With Frankie and Aidan capable of running Leo Solutions, would Frank want to modify their original plans and travel more? One minute she thought she knew the answer; the next a flood of different questions rolled through her mind. The only thing she knew beyond any doubt was how much it would break her heart if he got hurt or couldn't see them as a couple the way they used to be.

"We'll walk from here." Frank parked in a space close to the main street and came around to open her door. "We'll stick together." He tipped her chin his way, holding her gaze. "I mean it. If I say we're done, I don't want any argument."

She gave him her most cooperative smile along with the verbal reassurance. He rolled his eyes, knowing her far too well. In the past she might've added a salute, but today the gesture would be more exasperating than humorous. It was becoming clear that however they cleared his name, his career was over. She wondered if he was already lamenting the loss of that lifestyle or if he was struggling with what to do with retirement now that the business they'd planned was up and running and in capable hands.

They walked together down the docks as if they were looking for one of the several import-export businesses scattered among the warehouses. This was a working terminal rather than one converted to retail, and the scents of fuel, oil and heavy machinery mingled with the cleaner aromas on the sea air. It was a strange combination that put Sophia in mind of healthy industry and thriving business. It angered her that Hellfire tainted that with their illegal activities.

"There's the office," she said, pausing to peer into the window.

"Easy, tiger."

In the past, she would've bristled at the admonition. Now she just stifled a smile, knowing he was right. Impatience here could get one or both of them killed. "There are times when your cool-and-collected routine drives me up a wall," she teased.

"More fun for me," he said.

She glanced up at his face and caught the smirk. "Think Hellfire will agree with our definition of fun?"

The smirk turned edgy. "Absolutely not." He lifted his chin a fraction. "We've got company."

"Took longer than I thought it would."

"They can afford to hang back now," Frank said. "They know if we had the evidence it would be over already. The only way to get stronger evidence is to get closer."

"They *think* they know," she corrected. The piece about the adjusted weights on official contracted shipments might be Hellfire's downfall. "Why don't we just go right in?"

"Because they would capture you as soon as you crossed the threshold." He shoved his hands into the pockets of his jacket. "Not a chance I'm willing to take."

He had to know taking chances would be required to wrap this up quickly. Like him, she couldn't imagine losing him to that kind of aggressive maneuver. Not without the right backup. Backup Frankie and Aidan could provide if Frank would stop being stubborn.

They were nearing the end of the pier, coming as close as visitors were allowed to the unloading area. Cranes slid and scraped back and forth, groaning with the load of some containers. Diesel engines rumbled, the sound broken only by the call of gulls wheeling in the sky.

"He can't possibly have a full container of drugs," she muttered, unable to imagine a bust that big.

"Drugs, money, military equipment. It's likely combined."

Knowing he was right didn't make it easier to stomach. If she blurted out all the violent thoughts in her head, expressed every dire, vengeful idea, he'd never let her help. She recognized the recklessness and reined it in, unwilling to let her emotions jeopardize the ultimate goal of restoring her family.

When Frank turned to walk back up the pier, she followed, her mind turning over more options. Halloran had put all the right pieces in place, recruiting the people with the power to make things run smoothly. How could they dismantle that definitively? There were chinks such as Lowry in the armor, but Halloran would replace those people, shore up the weaknesses and keep right on banking the profits. Frank couldn't have his life back and none of them could rest until they cut the head off this long-tailed snake.

"What are you thinking?"

"Pretty much the same thing I've been thinking," she replied. "Aside from racking my brain for a contact within the port authority, I'm trying to decide how we can get Halloran into the open where some decent, honest person with the right sort of badge can arrest him. If he slips away, he'll start over. Even if your name is cleared in the process, someone else will be vilified. Much as I hate to admit it, the cyber attack and the money transfer worry me."

"I know."

The grim, resigned tone caught her attention. "What are *you* thinking?" It better not be another self-sacrificing idea.

"I want a bird's-eye view," he said, nodding toward the high-rise buildings on the other side of the access roadways running between the dock and the city.

They left the car parked and walked away from the pier, knowing Hellfire spies watched every step. It was all she could do to ignore them. She wanted to taunt them, to dare them to make a move. Again, too reckless. She was better than those self-destructive urges.

"He destroyed our family," she said when they found a place that gave Frank an effective overview of the pier. "I want him to pay for that."

"Does Eddie handle civil suits now?"

"Stop." She bumped his shoulder with hers. "You know what I mean."

"Uh-huh," he said, preoccupied with whatever he saw through the binoculars.

He had always known what her heart needed—frequently before she did. That intuition of his was probably why they were out here in broad daylight when he'd rather be safely ensconced in another motel room.

While Frank studied the pier, Sophia's gaze shifted north, toward her house on Queen Anne. She hadn't been gone a full week, but she missed it. Temptation rode her at every turn. Her house, a home she'd never shared with Frank, felt as if it were within walking distance. She wanted to dump the suitcase and sleep in her own bed beside her sexy husband.

But it was her husband, larger than life, that presented her biggest temptation. Her palms itched to touch him, to reassure her body and heart that he wouldn't disappear again. Would anything ever convince her?

Now that they'd been blessed with a second chance, she wanted him back in her life like before. Forever. She needed to reclaim the dreams they'd shared, and unless she was wishfully misreading his signals, he wanted that, too. The sooner they had Halloran trapped, the better. There was a wedding to plan.

"I need some air," she said suddenly. "Didn't we pass a vending machine?"

His eyes met hers and her feet froze in place. "You aren't going alone."

"I am." Making love had turned her overprotective husband into a nearly obsessive guardian. She rolled her shoulders back. "I thought I'd go for a walk."

His laughter cracked like a whip through the small

room. "Not alone. You're not going out there as bait, Sophie."

"We have to do something. What do you suggest?"

"Carpet bombing comes to mind," he said. "Take a look." He handed her the binoculars.

She adjusted the view in time to see a forklift heading up the pier to Hellfire's warehouse. It carried a sand-colored container labeled with an army code. "No way." She dropped the binoculars to stare at Frank. "You think this is another tweaked contract shipment?"

"Yeah." The camera whirred as he took burst shots. "That number is for armored vehicle parts."

"Parts that must be padded with contraband." She watched a bit longer, awestruck by the audacity. "We need to get our hands on the computer records." Lowering the binoculars, she turned to her husband. "They're so damned sure of what we will and won't dare do. Why don't we throw them a curveball?"

Anything to go on the offensive. It wasn't in her nature to sit back indefinitely, hoping the right things would happen. "We have a family to reunite and wedding plans to adjust accordingly," she reminded him.

He looked away. She told herself it wasn't personal, that he was focused on fixing the bigger threat of Halloran—and rightly so—before he could focus on renewing their personal life.

And hadn't she told him those decisions could wait? She'd told herself she wouldn't pressure him into doing what *she* wanted. He'd been exiled from everything he'd known and loved. That experience had to have an effect. She needed to give him the time and space to adjust.

Except she didn't see anything so different from the man she'd fallen for, married and built a life with. He was the same in all the ways that mattered. Focused, strong, determined. Protective and honorable. His choices, though difficult on all of them, proved it. Why couldn't he see himself through her eyes?

"Hang on." His jaw clenched, the muscle in his profile jumping.

"Frank?"

"We're staying put," he said in that ironclad tone no argument would overcome. "Farrell is here." He dropped the binoculars and raised the camera once more.

A ripple of excitement coursed through her body. She wanted to get down there immediately. "Mr. Accounts Receivable. Can we intercept him?"

"And what would we do with him?"

She arched an eyebrow, her silence speaking volumes.

"Aside from tear him limb from limb," Frank said. "Or demand statements that won't hold up in court."

She jerked her thumb toward the pier. "He's diverting at least one container labeled for military use," she said. "That will get someone high on the food chain involved, right?"

"If the someone offering up the tip isn't wanted for treason, fraud and now murder."

She swore against his logic. "Mitigating circumstances. I'm calling the police unless you have a better suggestion."

He sighed as he put his camera back in his pocket. "I'll create a distraction and you do what you can."

"Just you and me?" Did he think she wouldn't notice his avoidance of Leo Solutions' resources?

"I'll need a two-minute head start," he said as they

crossed the street once more. "When all hell breaks loose, you can go in and do what you can."

She caught his shirtfront before he could dash off and planted a kiss on his lips. It was quick, but it sizzled right through her. "Be careful."

He nodded, a smile slowly spreading across his face. "You, too. We'll meet back here."

During her two-minute delay, Sophia sent a text to Frankie: Don't worry, sweetie. We're all going to be okay. Her time up, she strolled down the pier, walking with purpose but not fast enough to draw attention. It didn't really matter. Halloran's men knew who she was, and though she couldn't see them, she knew they had to be watching.

FRANK STUCK TO the shadows of equipment waiting to be put back in use, clearing every corner and roofline. The spies were gone or had found better perches. No one was watching the pier at all right now. Frank counted his blessings and pressed on.

Getting in and out would be easier at night, but if they waited, any product or evidence might be gone. As he searched for the right distraction, he thought an explosion would be ideal. He'd love to plant it in the heart of World Crossing and call the mission complete. Except that left Halloran out there free to start over with a different crew.

One thing he'd learned since going undercover for CID was how many people could be manipulated for the smallest stakes. It made him wonder what kind of world he'd been safeguarding throughout his career.

His jaw set, Frank paused to listen at the open bay door. Hinges squeaked and voices rose and fell with excitement. An engine whined and he peered around the corner as a forklift with yet another sand-colored container moved up along the pier.

He had to come up with something fast. Sophia wouldn't wait forever and Halloran's crew probably wouldn't stick around admiring the haul much longer. Frank jogged ahead and waited for the forklift operator to drive by on his way back to the ship.

The machine moved at a good clip, but Frank caught it, hauled himself up and pushed the surprised driver out of the seat. Turning the machine around, he drove straight to Hellfire's warehouse.

Farrell and the men with him saw Frank coming and scattered. A few bullets sparked off the forklift. He kept the machine moving, driving right through the door as they tried to lower it. Metal screeched and groaned. Gunfire erupted, echoing through the warehouse as more bullets ricocheted around the space.

He did as much damage as he could with the forklift, hoping like hell the chaos gave Sophia enough time to pull something useful from the computers. He picked his targets carefully, systematically clearing a path to return to the car. He had to keep them engaged, but if they took him down, Sophia would be trapped. Any second now they'd have men on the roofs with a better firing angle. He had to get her clear before that happened.

A high-pitched scream carried over the cacophony and froze him in place just outside the warehouse.

The gunfire ceased and a deep voice taunted him, "Give up the fight, Leone."

Frank peeked at the man shouting, saw it was Farrell and quickly decided that was the only good news.

Halloran's crew had Sophia surrounded. Farrell had pushed her to her knees, holding her by her hair. Four men fanned out around them, all of them focused on the trashed bay door and the forklift idling noisily.

"Give up," Farrell called out again, "and I'll let her go."

"Don't do it!" Sophia's shout ended in a sputter. Frank's vision hazed red—someone had struck her. He moved silently to a better vantage point, forcing himself to think as a tactician rather than an enraged lover.

She didn't need to worry that he'd believe any promises from Farrell. The man was scum. Taking in the situation, he continued his assessment. Halloran and Hellfire hadn't succeeded because they were sloppy or lazy or left a flank uncovered. They were a brutal team, led by a smart man.

At last Frank spotted the man guarding the path to the front office, and another perched in a makeshift snipers nest in the shelving, covering the men below.

Damn. Even if he had the ammunition, one against seven was long odds. "Way to go, Leone," he muttered under his breath. What had possessed him to let her come along for this one-way ride?

Obviously, he couldn't go straight at them. Farrell or any one of the others—likely all of the others—would riddle him with bullets in an instant, leaving Sophia unprotected. Surrendering was out of the question. Farrell would be sure he and Sophia were sinking to the bottom of the sound within the hour.

While Farrell shouted impotently, Frank crept around, looking for something more effective than his pistol. An airstrike or mortars would be helpful about now. Too bad those were out of his reach. With a start, Frank recognized more numbers and crates. Halloran must be diverting weapons shipments along with the drugs.

Frank quickly found the part numbers he wanted. Quietly, he raised the lid on an open crate and found grenades and a launcher. A bit more firepower than absolutely necessary, but he couldn't help smiling at the potential.

Knowing the guy on the shelves would have the advantage and the best view, Frank took what he needed and shifted to a better strike point. A plan developed as he went along. Take out the guy up top, scatter the others and pick off only enough to ensure Sophia's safe escape.

Much as he wanted to roll a grenade to Farrell's feet, he couldn't risk hitting her or giving them room to take her beyond his reach.

He hefted two types of grenades, his decision made. Making a big enough move to be noticed by the guy nesting in the shelves, he lobbed a smoke grenade in the direction of the office.

The shout from above, along with the pop and smoke, confused Farrell and his men. Frank used those precious seconds to toss an explosive grenade into the steel shelving just under the sniper's perch. Rifle reports sounded and the bullets flew wide when the shooter realized what Frank had done.

The grenade exploded and that end of the warehouse erupted in dust, fire and bits of whatever product might've been stored there. The scream that followed was male this time.

Frank raised his pistol and kneecapped the man

closest to the crumpled door. The men flanking Farrell fired, coming closer to hitting Frank's position.

Above the noise of combat, Frank thought he heard Sophia shouting again. He checked, a murderous urge beating in his blood, only to find her armed and Farrell doubled over.

"This way!" he called to her, pinning down Farrell's men with covering fire as she ran to join him. Once she was clear, he pushed her behind him and took the pistol she'd taken from Farrell.

He hefted another smoke grenade and rolled it into the space between them and Farrell's men. They moved closer to the egress, and once Sophia was clear, he pulled the pin and threw another grenade deep into the warehouse. The explosion pushed at the walls as they ran for the safety of the rental car.

Farrell and his men in the warehouse were too busy trying to survive the explosion to give chase. Frank cranked the engine and put the car into Reverse, hurrying away from the compounding destruction as fast as he dared. He wanted to make sure their car wouldn't be caught inside a taped-off crime scene, but he also wanted to be sure the men didn't escape the authorities.

Sirens wailed up and down the pier as police cruisers rolled in and a fireboat churned up the water as it rushed into position.

Frank kept the car running, watching it all unfold from the corner of the parking lot. In the passenger seat, Sophia shivered. Her hands were fisted tight enough to turn the knuckles white.

"We're almost clear." It was the best reassurance he could offer. Everyone was focused on the warehouse. No one cared about a dark blue sedan.

"You did great," she said. "Look, the cops have him now."

Farrell was in cuffs, several of his men behind him. It was a beautiful sight. He turned to kiss Sophia, and his priorities changed when he took a hard look at her. "You're pale. Are you sure you're okay?" Her hands were clamped between her legs and he didn't know what to make of that strange, not-quite-neutral expression on her face.

"I'm fine."

She didn't sound fine. "What happened in the office?" He thought about the scream, the way Farrell had cut her off when she shouted. "Are you hurt?"

"It's not serious."

He put the car in gear and drove away from the pier, aiming for the nearest hospital. "You need an emergency room."

"No, it's not bad, I swear." Her breath hitched. "A rib. That's all. We can't risk an emergency room right now. You're still wanted for murder."

"Who cares? I'm not taking any chances with your health."

"Look at me," she said when he stopped for a traffic light.

He obliged. There were signs of pain in the set of her mouth, the squint of her eyes. "Sophie."

"I'd tell you if I needed a doctor."

"Promise?"

"You can look me over when we get back to the room."

"I'll hold you to that." If he decided she needed medical attention, he wouldn't let her argue.

"Good." She raised a hand and flicked it, indicating

he should move along. "I saw an email on the system," she said, her breath catching. "Halloran ordered the warehouse cleaned."

"Guess we helped him out with that explosion." Anything that ultimately helped Halloran maddened Frank, but there hadn't been a choice.

"I don't think we'll get a thank-you note."

His short laugh made her mouth twitch in a semblance of a smile. "Is that all you found?"

"Not even close." She reached under the collar of her shirt and pulled out the flash drive. "Your distraction gave me just enough time. We'll see what we have when we get back to the room."

And after he checked her ribs. "How did you get out of Farrell's grasp?"

She chuckled and then sucked in a breath at the pain. "He should know better than to put a woman on her knees. His crotch was a prime target. Great job with those grenades."

"Thanks."

"One more thing. I changed the passwords, locking them out of the system and preventing them from wiping any more data."

"Nice."

"I couldn't let you have all the fun," she said.

"Of course not." In all their years, he'd never seen Sophia do anything other than lead by example. Though he'd prefer to spare her any amount of pain and suffering.

He didn't let down his guard until they were back in the hotel room with every available lock engaged.

It worried him a little when she didn't mount much of a protest as he checked her injuries. Her ribs were bruised on the right side, but nothing felt broken. The red welts were already rising and she'd be black-and-blue in the days to come. As she'd said, it wasn't serious, though she needed rest.

He knew better than to suggest it. "We need supplies to tape your ribs…and something for pain."

"I'll be fine." She gave him a wobbly smile. "Bring me the laptop. You're going to want to see this right away."

The familiar gleam in her eye relaxed him more than anything else. Although she was battered and unhappy about it, her focus hadn't wavered. He helped her get comfortable on the bed, then settled beside her.

Silently, he prayed the risks were about to pay off. He didn't know what he'd do if they couldn't get a net over Halloran and put an end to Hellfire.

Chapter Twelve

Sophia inserted the flash drive into her computer, eager for the relief she knew would flood Frank's face when it all came together. "Getting past the security was easy. They never updated their software and they were too arrogant or neglectful to change the basic admin access codes."

"Was it too easy?"

She turned her face up to look at him, her gaze dropping to his lips for a moment. Kisses should probably wait. "Are you asking if it was a decoy?"

He nodded.

"I don't think so. Take a look." When the files came up, she angled the laptop a bit more for Frank.

He placed his cheaters on his nose and started reading. Those half-glasses shouldn't be a turn-on. He was so sexy, his serious blue eyes taking it all in. In a silly burst of curiosity she wondered if her cheaters had the same effect on him. The man made her want to sigh, though her aching ribs prevented such a response.

He whistled as she pointed out the files she'd managed to grab. Halloran and Farrell had communicated openly with Engle and the crew through emails they considered secure. "Arrogant bastards," Frank muttered.

"As I said, he's ordered inventory cleared out and hard drives wiped. Unfortunately, he can't finish without the new passwords. He can call in someone to help him get back in, but that will take time."

"If we'd waited another day, it would've been too late."

She nodded as he continued to read, his eyes narrowing and his lips flat-lining as the scope of Halloran's treacherous operation started to click. "We have files with monthly reports showing the product and transports. It will take some digging to learn how they diverted the containers."

Frank grunted. "Special Agent Torres suspected Hellfire was behind some of the lost gear."

"The proof is here," she said quietly. "Farrell and Lowry must have won the contract as part of the wink-and-nod system. The contract violations are the least of it." She adjusted the pillow at her back, giving herself a moment as she opened another window. "There was an archived file on Torres, and another on you."

"Kill orders."

She nodded, though it hadn't been a question. "I can't believe Halloran communicated so candidly about the diverted shipments and tweaked manifests, but the murder?"

Frank tugged off his glasses and gave her a weary smile. "Expecting code words and secret handshakes?"

"A girl has her standards," she said, trying to follow his attempt to lighten the mood. They'd survived to this point and, bruised ribs or not, she wasn't giving up yet. "Halloran must already know we were there. When he hears where I was found, he's bound to panic."

"I've been thinking about his exit strategy and options," Frank said, tapping his glasses against his thigh. "He knows his options. He's made a plan."

It took some effort to keep her mind on the data rather than the man beside her while she waited for him to explain.

"How do you suggest we use this?" he asked.

"I'd prefer to send pieces to various places. CID, the reporters and Eddie, too." She hesitated, a little concerned about his reaction. "Because I wasn't sure how much time I had in there, I already forwarded a string of emails to Leo Solutions."

He shifted, dropping his head with a soft thud against the headboard and rubbing his eyes. "Are you using this as leverage against Halloran or me?"

"Oh, stop it." She would not force him into a reunion he wasn't ready for, no matter how eager she was to become a whole family again. "You know me better than that. No one at the office even knows to look for the emails." *Yet.* "I want to contact Halloran and offer to trade this proof of his crimes for our lives." That wouldn't quite restore Frank's reputation, but it was a step in the right direction. "With CID's help we can sort out how he railroaded you."

"Halloran won't go for it." Frank stood and started pacing the room. "He knows I have to throw him under the bus to clear my name."

"We know he's prepared an escape route. The details might be in here."

"If they are, he's moving on to plan B right this minute. At this point, his only chance is to skip the country."

She concentrated on taking slow, careful breaths. "No statute of limitations on murder," she said. "Arranging an exchange for this particular material, evidence he could never shake, is the key. We'll still have plenty to use against him to clear your name. Ideally, we can get a confession out of him."

"Sophie." Frank sighed. "The man isn't a fool."

"No, but we've made him desperate."

"Desperate men do crazy things," he warned. "Let CID take it from here."

"We can do that," she admitted. "Or we can make sure he doesn't slip past them. If we get Leo Solutions involved…" She stopped short at the dark look in her husband's eyes.

"I will not put Frankie in the line of fire," he stated.

She flashed him a look that had made people from several government agencies stop and reconsider. "Find a better argument. Halloran has been using every weapon at his disposal against us, including the press. We have to counter with everything we've got and prove we are the stronger force." The uncertainty in his blue eyes told her he was reconsidering. "If we leave it, that half-baked attempt on the company could be an all-out assault next time," she persisted. "Now is the time to make a stand, and to bring in the heavy artillery."

That earned her a choked laugh. She counted it as progress.

Frank raked his hand through his hair and tugged at the roots. She sympathized with his frustration. Halloran had played a nasty game and they were so close to stealing a win.

"I won't allow you to push us away again."

"Sophia." He sighed, his eyes so sad. "They nearly killed you a few hours ago."

She pulled the clip out of her hair, shaking it loose, an effective distraction for him. When his gaze warmed, it melted the last of the persistent chill in her veins from the near miss. "They didn't succeed. All thanks to you."

He turned his back to her and she realized how close she was to losing everything. Again. How many times could a woman pick herself up from a pit of despair? If he went after Halloran alone, thinking to protect her and Frankie, the odds of restoring his reputation and life were slim to none. If he walked away in some misplaced gesture of honor, it would break her. She refused to give him the option.

She ignored the discomfort and slid out of the bed. The short carpet was rough under her bare feet. She moved up behind him. His muscles felt warm and strong beneath her palms when she pressed her hands to his shoulders. She dug her thumbs into the tension at his neck. "You know that bringing in Frankie, Aidan and whoever else we need at the company is the right tactic," she murmured quietly, letting the words drift over him.

"She's…" His voice trailed off.

"She's not a child," Sophia reminded him. "She *is* a warrior, Frank—you know that." She swallowed back the urgency, the desperation. She couldn't give Frank any reason to dismiss her idea too quickly. "We have to look at our daughter as a peer in this case, not as our baby." She kept up her massage as she shared her idea. "There is one man left."

"One man with who knows how much support."

She ignored that for the moment. "We have Frankie, Aidan and the assets of our company."

"Your company."

She ignored that, too. When this was over, they could argue ownership versus partnership. "The point is we have backup. Let's use it, throw everything we've got at him. Halloran and Hellfire will crumble under the barrage."

He reached up and trapped one of her hands at his shoulder. "You won't take no for an answer, will you?"

"Would you, in my place?"

"No." He took a deep breath, let it out slowly. "I've never stopped loving you," he said quietly.

"I know." While she hadn't appreciated his distance or extreme methods, in his shoes she would have done whatever seemed necessary to protect the family. That was what she was doing right now, in fact. The challenges and pressures of his career and hers had reinforced their independence even as they'd been forged into a team. Through different means and skills, both of them had a deep, intrinsic need to protect and defend. Had there ever been two people better suited?

"I love you, too." She hoped the depth of love rekindled through this crisis would make them stronger— strong enough to stick together through the rest of their lives. First they had to survive this. If even one of the bastards slipped free, they'd forever be leery of another attack. She wouldn't allow that kind of trouble to hover over her family's horizon.

He turned around, cradling her face and kissing her with devastating tenderness. Relief and hope washed over her in a sweet wave. Her lips moved against his, giving back every precious touch and affirmation that they would get through this together.

Frank eased back, his hands gentle on her arms. "I don't want to see Frankie until Halloran's in custody. Not until it's all over."

"Why not?" She thought she knew, but better to hear it from him, to make him state his reasons aloud.

He took a sudden interest in the ceiling. "I can't," he whispered. "I don't want her to see me when there's a cloud hanging over my head."

She felt for her husband. Frank had shouldered the weight of a bad situation and blamed himself for the actions of a few bad men. "She never stopped believing you were a hero," she reminded him, though it wouldn't change his mind.

He said nothing.

"Let's work out the details of tempting Halloran," she offered, "and then we can decide who else we'll need from the company." Getting him back into analysis mode was essential to wrap this up.

He nodded, his mind working on the tactical problem again. "The money isn't enough of a lure. The password lockout might not be enough." He sighed. "How do we convince him we haven't already passed the murder evidence up the line?"

She loved watching her husband think. Or pace, or simply sleep, she admitted, yanking her mind back on point. "What if we make it personal?"

"It's never been anything but personal. These are proud men, Sophia."

"I know the type," she muttered.

"The stakes in Hellfire were clear from the start," he continued. "Failure carries the death penalty. Everyone involved created places to hide in countries that don't cooperate with United States extradition orders. Much as we can't stop until we catch them, they can't leave anyone alive who knows their secrets."

She'd suspected this from the beginning, watching the ax swing ever closer to Frank's head. Hearing the brutal facts stated so simply in his resounding baritone threw her heart rate into high gear. "We need a confession," she insisted. "We'll be the bait. You and me. We can offer him the evidence if he lets us be. We'll choose the place and Leo Solutions can watch our backs." It was the only option left, Frank had to know that.

"They'll anticipate the move," he argued.

"I know. We'll give them what they expect to see."

"Which is?"

She swallowed the ball of nerves lodged in her throat. "A scared wife and mother begging for mercy."

Frank snorted. "He'll never buy into that. He knows you, remember?"

She'd preen over that compliment later. "Well, maybe a variation on that theme." She returned to the bed and her laptop to draft the email that would hopefully bring Halloran close enough to catch.

They worked and debated every word until Frank was sure they had the hook in deep. They set the meet for tomorrow on the first ferry from Seattle to Victoria, British Columbia.

"What next?" Frank asked as she booked the ferry tickets online.

"As connected as Halloran's spies have been all along, I think it's only fair we let him think he's got us. I'll ask for what I need from Leo Solutions in a way that looks benign to Hellfire in case that hack left them some access the company hasn't spotted yet." She started typing her email, fine-tuning that as well before she filled in the recipient address. She glanced at Frank. "Thoughts?"

His eyes widened, his salt-and-pepper eyebrows arching as the scope of her suggestion took shape. "A spin on the classic headache ploy."

"Yes." When Frankie had started going out on her own to parties and on dates, they'd taught her she only had to call home, claim she had a headache and Sophia or Frank would come get her, no questions asked.

"You're sure Frankie will understand what amounts to a coded message?"

"Absolutely." A few months ago her daughter had been avoiding every attempt at contact or reconciliation. Now Sophia enjoyed a close relationship with Frankie again as if no time had passed. It would help that she'd kept Aidan updated through a private channel since she'd left the hotel in Chicago. She didn't see the wisdom in revealing that to Frank just yet. The plan gave him enough to chew on as it was. If everything worked, he'd be reunited with his daughter before the three-hour ferry trip was over.

As long as no one died.

Chapter Thirteen

Saturday, April 23, 7:00 a.m.

"I don't like it."

Frank looked out over the water as they waited in line to board the ferry. His wife would be bait. He could practically see the blood staining his hands. His daughter and her fiancé were supposedly close, though he hadn't spotted her. "Three hours on a boat with Halloran and his men." He wanted to cover Sophia in body armor and send her far from here. This was a bad idea. "Too much can go wrong."

Sophia linked her arm through his as their boarding group time was called. "We need the confession to wrap this up," she reminded him gently.

His wife wore a wire a tech from Leo Solutions had dropped off at the hotel last night. She had a script memorized so she could chat up the monster trying to flee the country. It wasn't right. To his eternal frustration, Frank knew he'd only lose the argument again if he advocated for tossing Halloran overboard.

"You're entitled to reclaim your life," she added. "More than that."

What did that mean? He focused on the current crisis

rather than the questions about their future. "It will be at least three against two with all these civilians caught in between."

"You're right," she said. "He doesn't stand a chance." She tipped up her face and gave him a razor-sharp smile.

That look, that sheer determination and faith in what they were about to do, anchored him, reestablishing his focus. Thankfully, he didn't have more time to question the plan. All around them people boarded the ferry, several families chattering with excitement about the trip ahead and the whales they might see along the way. It was painfully normal.

Frank bent his lips to her ear. "I won't let him hurt you." Never again.

"Same goes," she whispered, her smile softening. "Let's finish this."

His stomach twisted a little tighter. Failure wasn't an option. His daughter needed her mother. If only one of them could get back to Seattle, Frank was determined it would be Sophia. His daughter had learned to live without her father once. He wouldn't let Halloran rob Frankie of her mother, too.

Frank and Sophia walked together along the ferry, pausing periodically at the rails as though they were tourists heading off for a weekend getaway. Neither of them had spotted Halloran yet, though Frank recognized one man from yesterday's attack on the warehouse and assumed the grim-looking man with him was also a Hellfire spy. The men were sticking a little too close to the stairs to the upper deck.

"They've made us."

"Naturally." Sophia was so cool it unnerved him.

"Relax. I doubt he'll even approach me until we're under way."

"You can't go to him," Frank insisted. "I won't let you be alone with him."

"Frank." Her voice was stone-cold, in direct contrast to the soft smile on her face. How did she do that? "I'm a general's wife—your wife. He'll come to me."

Frank glanced around the deck. It was a beautiful day with soft morning sunlight filling a blue sky and glazing the water. If they got the confession, he might just enjoy the trip back. "Something's not right."

"That's enough," Sophia scolded. "I'll toss *you* overboard and handle this myself if you don't pull yourself together."

The image of his wife doing just that made him laugh. "God, you're incredible."

"I know it." Her smile was sincere and warm this time. "He'll come to me, Frank, because we have what he needs to get away cleanly."

He knew she was right. Taking a deep breath, he draped his arm across her shoulder and resigned himself to letting the operation play out. "Remember our first time on this ferry?" They'd come to Seattle to check out the quarters in anticipation of their move to his last duty station. It had been a whirlwind trip of sightseeing, exploring the area and talking about what they might do with retirement.

Her cheeks turned rosy. "I was recalling our second water excursion."

"If I spend any time thinking about that, I might not care if Halloran gets away." That had been a private, guided cruise around the nearby islands. After a stunning sunset, they'd retreated to the cabin and made love the whole way back to Seattle.

As the ferry eased away from the Seattle terminal, she leaned back into the rail, pulling her sunglasses down so he could see her eyes. "Want to know a secret?"

"Always." No matter how much time together or apart, he loved discovering and rediscovering every nuance and detail about his wife.

"I'm hoping one day soon you and I will resume our exploration of the many islands and waterways around here."

His heart hammered at the hot, blatant invitation in her eyes. There was no mistaking her intent. She wanted him to stay if they managed to succeed. He had opened his mouth to say the words, to leave no room for her to doubt how much he wanted to spend every remaining day of his life with her, when he spotted their target.

"Halloran."

She reached up and laid her warm palm on his cheek. "Here we go."

He inhaled her words, willed them to be true. At least three against two and she obviously *believed* they held the advantage.

What did he know? She'd been right about everything else and planned for every contingency. Thanks to Leo Solutions, they had the best recording device available. They knew what Halloran could and couldn't do to disable it. With a bit of luck, this long nightmare would be over soon. Frank had spent enough of his life apart from the people who mattered most. It was high time the right man faced justice.

Sophia squeezed his fingers and moved toward the

stern, the place Halloran had designated for the exchange in his confirmation email. When the bastard accepted that flash drive, it would be over.

Provided his men didn't kill Frank and Sophia in the process. As Sophia walked toward the meet with Halloran, Frank strolled aft to intercept the man he'd recognized earlier. With a cluster of tourists between them, Frank knelt to tie his shoe. When he stood, his ball cap was a different color and he'd pulled off his dark windbreaker, tying it around his waist.

It gave him room to work and he used those few seconds to his advantage. Getting behind Halloran's man, Frank heard him admit he'd lost visual. Almost immediately his counterpart changed direction and hurried to the upper level.

He waited until a family with excited children hurried down the stairs, using them as a distraction. Cautiously, he moved along the upper deck, searching for Halloran's other spy. He caught sight of him near the crates of checked baggage. Knowing Halloran was planning to escape the country, what had he brought along that warranted two guards?

Ducking out of sight, he slipped his jacket back on, one more layer of defense if this turned into a fight. He assessed his potential opponent. Young and tall, the spy would surely have been warned about Frank's skills.

Frank boldly approached. "Nice view up here. Too bad your boss is missing it."

"He probably prefers sharing the scenery with your wife." The spy stood loose and light on his feet, clearly eager for a physical conflict. It was a good thing Sophia had refused to let Frank carry any weapons today, he thought. He'd happily kneecap this guy and consider it a public service.

Frank raised his chin to the locked baggage crates. "What does he think you can successfully protect?"

"Everything." It had to be drugs or cash for a bribe at the border.

"Let's test that theory." Frank stepped in close and stomped his boot hard on the spy's foot. The man groaned and Frank drove his knee up into his belly. Amid gasps and curses, Frank swiftly struck and retreated until the younger man crumpled. No weapon required.

As he patted down the stunned spy, he found a belt wallet with a bit of heft and a small revolver in an ankle holster. Frank pocketed both for later analysis and took the spy's earpiece, as well.

One down, one to go.

As the ferry churned along, Frank found a vacated seat in the center section, waiting for the second spy to come up the stairs any minute. It was a struggle not to break the plan and go check on his wife. He forced himself to stay put. His task was to keep Halloran's thugs busy and the playing field even. He drummed his fingers on the belt wallet, listening and waiting.

The second spy didn't come upstairs and he didn't check in. The lack of communication alarmed Frank. Taking a minute, he unzipped the wallet and found a small fortune in uncut rubies. He felt like an idiot for not anticipating another wrinkle. Halloran had his hands deep into every possible pie.

Untraceable, gemstones were easier to hide and to liquidate than laundering vast amounts of US currency. For a man on the run, rubies could very well get Halloran out of the country. "Not today," Frank murmured to himself.

Plan or not, with no concern from the second spy, Frank couldn't waste another minute. Even with Leo Solutions' support and technology, Sophia needed him watching her back personally.

NEAR THE STERN with the wake of the high-speed ferry streaming white behind them, Sophia watched Seattle drift farther into the distance. She'd lost sight of Frank, which didn't worry her, because Halloran and one of his men were with her. Frank could hold his own one-on-one with anyone.

She had yet to get Halloran to admit or agree to anything. She worried it wouldn't happen at all. The retired general would rightly assume she was wired and would be trying to jam that signal. He couldn't know about the video feed Aidan and Frankie had managed to get installed on the ferry last night—unless he'd bribed someone else to keep watch. As confident as she'd been for her husband, she was starting to have doubts about success.

"Just tell me why," she suggested, not for the first time. "We were friends once. You owe me that much at least."

"It was business," Halloran said, his voice cold. "You and Frank were merely casualties of an operational success."

"Cut the crap." Throwing him overboard was sounding better. "You railroaded my husband for what? A few thousand dollars."

He laughed. "I know you've looked into the accounts."

She shrugged. "I didn't find anything that would stick. I'll hand over everything, Kelly. Just tell me why you chose Frank as the patsy."

"Hellfire had a stiff admission price," Halloran said. "You'll notice the price for betrayal was higher still." He held out his hand. "Give me the drive."

She didn't take her eyes off his weathered face. It made her sick to think how he was touted as a hero, yet he'd sacrificed innocent lives for the sake of lining his pockets with gold. "You haven't given me any assurance that my family will be safe."

Another humorless laugh made her cringe. "You were one of the rare gems," he said. "Frank was lucky to have you."

Her eyes darted around the deck at the use of the past tense. "He *is* lucky to have me," she corrected. "Give me some sign of good faith that if I hand this over you'll leave us alone," she repeated.

"What's better than my word?" he asked. "You can't expect me to put it in writing."

She affected a sigh, as if he'd outmaneuvered her. "You know I'm wired."

"Of course I know," he said with a slimy smile. "You're no fool. How else would you prove you haven't been cooperating with me all along?"

Halloran's smug expression made her queasy. She supposed, if she let that sick feeling show on her face, he'd think he had her. "Lawyers and investigators picked through my life when Frank was on trial. They know I wasn't complicit."

She had to get Halloran to admit to something, preferably the treason or the murder. She pulled the mic and wire from beneath the collar of her sweater, showing him it was disconnected, and dropped it into his open palm. "Why, Kelly? Between you and me and the disabled wire, tell me why."

"Calling a stalemate, huh?"

She nodded. "You'll disappear, Frank will be haunted by false charges and I'll forever be waiting for you to strike again." She held up her hands in surrender, though she was doing nothing of the kind. "You win."

"Give me the drive." For the first time, his voice resembled the man who'd been her friend.

She handed it over, praying the closed-circuit system and the secondary mic running on a different frequency were working properly.

He signaled his spy to come closer. The man inserted the flash drive into a tablet. After a moment he gave his boss a nod that the contents were genuine and moved out of earshot again. "Thank you." Halloran's face twisted into a sneer; evidently he believed he had the only remaining evidence she'd gathered against him, along with the new passwords giving him access to his system again. "It was business," he repeated. "With a little personal," he said slowly. "I couldn't believe he turned on me. He saw the numbers, the potential. Through Hellfire, he could've given you a limitless future."

"With blood money."

"The whole world runs on blood money," Halloran said, flinging out a hand. "We made this bed we're stuck in, manipulating this leader for that resource. I did terrible things in the name of your freedom. My pet project wasn't anything different than what the government has done. What made me a criminal was doing it for personal gain."

"You actually believe that." She kept an eye out for Frank, eager to give him the takedown signal.

"I've lived it," Halloran was saying. "Frank's lived it. That's what made him such a great fit."

"Kelly, you can't really believe that."

"Don't take that tone with me." He snatched her elbow in a hard grip and forced her to look out to sea, away from any passengers. "A report doesn't convey with any accuracy the things we've seen and done in the field. I did plenty of good out there and then I took control. Made things even better. Only God will tell me if I went too far."

Sophia felt more than qualified to tell him he'd gone too far, but it would fall on deaf ears and an empty conscience.

"You have what you need. Take your hands off my wife."

At the sound of Frank's voice, Sophia nearly cheered.

"I'll do whatever I please," Halloran said, twisting around and using Sophia as a shield.

"Keep that up," Frank said to him. "Give me a reason to do what I so desperately want to do. Right now. Right here."

Furious at Halloran's pointless actions, Sophia didn't bother to struggle. There wasn't much he could do here on a crowded ferry. Had he overlooked the two hundred witnesses milling around?

"Let my wife go." Frank took a menacing step closer. "Or you can take a swim right now."

"Your hands are as tied as mine, General Leone!"

Halloran shouted the name. Faces turned their way with varying degrees of concern and irritation. "I control all of it now." He shoved Sophia hard, the deck railing biting into her bruised ribs. Frank took a step, and Halloran whipped out a knife and pressed it to her throat.

"Stay back," Halloran yelled.

People around them gasped and moved back. Some pulled out phones and started recording, while others urged children to a safer distance. Sophia wanted to laugh. Knives were a respected weapon but hardly a challenge to the Leone family. Frank had given countless young soldiers classes on knife combat and defense.

"This is ridiculous, Kelly," she said. The man was coming unhinged. "You have everything you demanded."

The ferry's minimal security team was already approaching. There was nowhere for Halloran to run.

She exchanged a look with Frank, hoping he understood and trusted her judgment. "What was the plan, Kelly? Take the evidence and bribe your way across the border?"

Frank nodded his support of her tactic. "Uncut rubies," Frank answered, holding up the belt wallet.

"Give that to me!" Halloran couldn't hold her and take the rubies. Something had to give.

Taking advantage of his indecision, Sophia plowed an elbow into his ribs as she pushed away the knife with her free hand. The second she was clear, Frank lunged, slamming Halloran hard on the deck. Security closed around them. Focused on Halloran, the security team didn't see Halloran's spy draw his gun and take aim at Frank.

Sophia shoved Frank, knocking him into one of the security guards. As the men stumbled and scrambled, the spy fired. The bullet missed Frank and hit Halloran in the chest. Sophia rushed to the man who'd put them all through hell, determined to keep him alive long enough to clear Frank's name.

Time blurred as paramedics arrived, nudging her into Frank's solid embrace. The ferry reached the island and slowly the passengers were cleared one by one to disembark. Halloran and his last two loyal spies were taken into custody and ushered back to Seattle by a hydrofoil.

Through the combined support of Sophia's connections, the Colby Agency and Aidan's international contacts, she and Frank were transported by helicopter to Joint Base Lewis-McChord, where an army CID special agent took their statements. When the formalities were completed, the special agent confirmed Engle, Lowry and Farrell would all remain in federal custody, along with their associates.

By nightfall, Frank was declared officially alive and cleared to go home, no longer a murder suspect. In the coming days, his service record would be set straight and he would be absolved of any and all crimes. Though they were asked to remain in the country until the paperwork was complete, the special agent addressed him by his proper rank and ordered an official car to take them home.

"Home," he mused, his voice full of wonder, as they stood side by side waiting for the car. "I'd almost given up on the idea."

It had started to rain and Sophia wanted nothing

more than to be at peace with her husband watching that rain from the little bistro table on her front porch. "Come home with me," she said. "At least for tonight."

"Sophie…"

"What is it?"

"Did you hear from Frankie? Was she there today? Too ashamed to speak to me?"

Sophia smiled up at him. "She wasn't there. Knowing your wishes, Aidan and I had other people onboard for any needed backup."

He rubbed his eyes and swallowed hard. "Thank you."

Her heart ached for everything he'd endured. "Come home with me, Frank. We've had enough hotels for a while. I think you'll like what I did with the house." She'd asked Frankie and Aidan to wait for them there. "There's a perfectly tidy guest room if—"

He moved so swiftly she lost her breath as he kissed her soundly. "I won't sleep if I'm apart from you."

The earnestness in his blue eyes melted her heart.

The car arrived and she took his hand when he seemed frozen by uncertainty. "Then come home, Frank. It's past time."

FRANK KNEW SHE was up to something. She had that look in her eye, the same look he'd seen on his fortieth birthday when she'd surprised him with a party at the office. He didn't deserve a party tonight. Not after he'd shut out the two people who meant the most to him in this world. He wasn't sure he deserved to stick around, to maintain any sort of contact.

His choices had hurt all three of them. Would they truly be able to overcome it?

"I should stay at a hotel," he murmured, terrified he knew exactly what Sophia was up to. The idea of seeing his daughter again scared him more than Halloran's potential escape. How could he face Frankie? How could he ask for her forgiveness for all he'd put her through? "I wouldn't know where to start explaining to her."

He watched the rain-soaked streets flash by under the streetlamps.

Sophia's hand slipped into his. "You knew well enough where to start with me."

"That was different."

"Why?"

He couldn't articulate it, couldn't push the words past the lump in his throat. "Maybe after the wedding. I shouldn't intrude."

"Oh, what a ridiculous thing to say." Her fingers dug into his a little too hard. "And selfish."

He turned away from the gloomy view. "Selfish? I'm trying to do the right thing here." He attempted to tug his hand free, but she wouldn't let go.

"Then do the right thing."

He was surprised to see no judgment in her deep brown eyes, only peace, affection and an underlying understanding.

"She loves you," Sophia said. "Planning the wedding has been a delicate balancing act because she's so happy with Aidan and so sad you're not around."

"She can't possibly still need me. You've told me repeatedly how capable and independent she is."

The car turned into Queen Anne, and he felt his

heart rate speed up, knowing the moment of truth was nearly upon him.

"Frank," she urged gently, "no matter how independent or capable, a girl always needs her father." She raised his hand to her face and rubbed it against her soft cheek. "If you bail now, you'll do irrevocable damage."

His wife's assessment scared him. Was it selfish to want to put this off another day?

"She understands mission and classified information," Sophia continued. "Trust her. Trust me."

"I do." He trusted her more than he'd ever trusted anyone. Loved his girls. "I love you. Both of you."

"We know."

"The idea of hurting you, of adding to the damage I've already done…" He ran out of words again.

Sophia shifted closer, her thigh rubbing along his. "You did what was necessary. Do you honestly think we'd fault you for it?"

"*Dolcezza*, you're too good for me." The car stopped on a neighborhood street and he looked around. "Queen Anne?"

"Just as we planned," she said, her eyes bright.

"I was convicted of treason," he said, stunned. "Why hang on to our dream?"

"I suppose it was my way of hanging on to you, my love. Come inside and let's be a family again."

Before he could protest or beg for more time, the front door flew open and Frankie raced down the steps, heedless of the wet weather. She nearly careened into the sedan in her haste to wrench open the door.

"Daddy!"

Frank climbed out and found himself tugged into his daughter's embrace as the soft night rain washed away the last of his guilt and trepidation. He held her tight in his arms and Sophia joined them in a group hug.

The nightmare was truly over. He was home and nothing would tear him away again.

Chapter Fourteen

Saturday, September 27, 6:30 p.m.

Frank's heart pounded as he waited for his daughter
to join him at the back door of the lovely estate where
she would exchange vows with Aidan in the garden in
mere minutes. He'd thought this day out of his reach.
To be reunited with his family, to feel whole inside and
out—well, the reality of it was still sinking in.

He'd never been happier, except on the day he'd exchanged vows with his remarkable wife, Sophia.

Frankie peeked around the corner, then rushed forward, a glowing vision in her mother's redesigned
wedding gown. She lifted her veil to kiss his cheek,
bouncing a little on her toes. "You're radiant," he whispered, kissing her cheek in turn. A stronger voice was
out of his reach. "Aidan will be speechless."

"Not too speechless, I hope," Frankie said, her eyes
sparkling with absolute joy. "He has some important
words to say." Her gaze dropped to the bouquet in her
hands before she raised those warm brown eyes, so
like her mother's, to his once more. "I'm so thankful
you're here, Daddy. This day wouldn't have been the
same without you."

He placed her hand on his arm when the music changed for her entrance. They heard the rustle of movement as guests got to their feet. "Thanks for your faith in me, sunshine."

She took a deep breath and gave his arm a little squeeze. "Let's go before they send out a search party."

They started down the aisle, as stately as they'd rehearsed, each step taking him closer to the moment when he would give away his daughter, his only child, to the man of her dreams. He knew his first look should've been to double-check the groom's reaction, to be sure the young man was up to the task to love, honor and cherish Frank's baby. Instead, his gaze landed on his wife, the woman who had embodied all his dreams from the first moment he'd laid eyes on her over three decades ago.

Somehow he managed to give his daughter to her groom and take his seat beside Sophia without tripping over his lines or his feet. He had to assume the ceremony was perfect, as the moment overwhelmed him and he didn't hear much of it. Thank goodness, there would be video. In what felt like a matter of seconds, the minister pronounced Frankie and Aidan married.

As the guests were ushered toward the reception, Frank couldn't stop smiling as the families were posed this way and that for official pictures. At last they were done and heading back up the lawns to join the reception in the estate ballroom.

Sophia slipped her hand into his. "Congratulations, darling. We did it."

He wasn't sure if she referred to the dangers they'd survived or reaching this milestone as parents. Not that it mattered. They were together and they'd get to enjoy the next stage of their lives together. Just as they had planned.

Still, he felt as if the moment needed a bigger gesture, some way to symbolize his return to the man she trusted with her heart and her future.

Sophia stroked her free hand over their joined hands. "Will you walk with me a minute?"

He smiled. "You should know by now that I'd walk with you anywhere."

She smiled back. "To hell and back maybe?" she queried. "Yes, I noticed."

To Frank's surprise, Sophia led him to a quiet, meditation garden. At the far end a waterfall trickled merrily down over a clever tumble of rocks. Flowers spilled over the edges of big planters, and benches flanked a reflecting pool in the center.

As if on cue, the minister stepped in front of the waterfall, Victoria and Lucas in his wake.

"I'd marry you all over again, Franklin Leone. I thought it would be a nice gesture if we renewed our vows."

Nice? He thought it would be perfect. "I'd be honored, *dolcezza.*"

She twisted off the wedding rings she'd just started wearing again and put them in his palm. He gave his ring to her and they stepped forward.

Frank's voice was strong as he spoke his vows, as strong as the spirit of the woman who'd loved him through thirty years of better and worse already. When she gave him her vows and slid that band of gold back into place on his finger, his heart soared.

"I love you," he said, his hands at her waist. "You're stuck with me forever now."

"For at least thirty more years," she said, wrapping her arms around his neck. "I love you."

The kiss was interrupted by a happy cheer and the pop of a champagne cork as Frankie and Aidan surprised them. Frank planted another kiss on Sophia's sweet lips. Then, amid delighted laughter, he opened his arms wide for a family hug and a private toast to the most important people in his life.

VICTORIA DABBED AT her eyes with the handkerchief Lucas had given her. Her husband wrapped her arm around his. "How lucky we are to have witnessed a miracle," Lucas said gently.

She smiled up at him. "We've witnessed a few in our time."

Lucas stopped a waiter and claimed two glasses of champagne. He offered one to her and then tapped his glass to hers. "To many more, my dear."

Victoria savored the bubbly taste and smiled. "Many more, indeed."

* * * * *

MILLS & BOON®

Why shop at millsandboon.co.uk?

Each year, thousands of romance readers find their perfect read at millsandboon.co.uk. That's because we're passionate about bringing you the very best romantic fiction. Here are some of the advantages of shopping at www.millsandboon.co.uk:

* **Get new books first**—you'll be able to buy your favourite books one month before they hit the shops

* **Get exclusive discounts**—you'll also be able to buy our specially created monthly collections, with up to 50% off the RRP

* **Find your favourite authors**—latest news, interviews and new releases for all your favourite authors and series on our website, plus ideas for what to try next

* **Join in**—once you've bought your favourite books, don't forget to register with us to rate, review and join in the discussions

Visit **www.millsandboon.co.uk**
for all this and more today!

MILLS & BOON®

Why not subscribe?
Never miss a title and save money too!

Here's what's available to you if you join the exclusive **Mills & Boon® Book Club** today:

✦ *Titles up to a month ahead of the shops*
✦ *Amazing discounts*
✦ *Free P&P*
✦ *Earn Bonus Book points that can be redeemed against other titles and gifts*
✦ *Choose from monthly or pre-paid plans*

Still want more?
Well, if you join today, we'll even give you
50% OFF your first parcel!

So visit **www.millsandboon.co.uk/subs**
to be a part of this exclusive Book Club!

MILLS & BOON®

INTRIGUE
Romantic Suspense

A SEDUCTIVE COMBINATION OF DANGER AND DESIRE

Available at WHSmith, Tesco, Asda, Eason, Amazon and Apple

Just can't wait?
Buy our books online a month before they hit the shops!
visit www.millsandboon.co.uk

These books are also available in eBook format!

46